Deep Cover

By Leslie Jones

Deep Cover

Bait

Night Hush

Deep Cover

Duty & Honor Book Three

LESLIE JONES

WITNESS
IMPULSE
An Imprint of HarperCollins*Publishers*

EPub Edition JANUARY 2016 ISBN: 9780062363183
Print Edition ISBN: 9780062363206

10 9 8 7 6 5 4 3 2

I dedicate this book to Ulysses H. Jones,
who gave me unconditional love,
unwavering support,
and unflagging pride to his last breath.

Acknowledgments

I WOULD LIKE to express my gratitude to the people who helped me with this book. First and foremost, my thanks to Kim Jones and Scott Jones for their patience, support, and the many meals that magically appeared in front of me. Thank you to my wonderful editor, Nicole Fischer, for her insight and ability to make my books better, stronger, faster—she has the technology. Megathanks to my (insert many wonderful superlatives here) agent, Sarah E. Younger, for taking a chance on a debut author three years ago. I'm proud to be part of Team Sarah.

Thank you to my critique partners, Kim Jones and Shannon Orso, for patiently reading the third and fourth iterations of the same scene. Many thanks to my beta reader, Bill Moroney, who is just so darned good for my ego.

I'd also like to thank Bob Bartlett for educating me on Carroll Shelby and the 1968 Shelby Mustang GT. You know your cars, sir!

Last but certainly not least, thank you to my readers, for taking a chance on me.

Acknowledgments

I would like to express my gratitude to the people who helped me with this book. First and foremost my thanks to [illegible] and Scott Jones for their patience, support, and the many meals that magically appeared in front of me. Thank you to my wonderful editor, Nicole Fischer, for her insight and ability to make my books better, stronger, faster—she has the technology. Mega thanks to my (insert many wonderful superlatives here) agent, Sarah E. Younger, for taking a chance on a debut author three years ago. I'm proud to be part of Team Sarah.

Thank you to my critique partners, Kim Jones and Shannon Curtis, for patiently reading the third and fourth iterations of the same scene. Many thanks to my beta reader, Bill Moreno, who is just so darned good for my ego.

I'd also like to thank Rob Bartlett for educating me on Carroll Shelby and the 1968 Shelby Mustang GT. You know your cars, sir.

Last but certainly not least, thank you to my readers for taking a chance on me.

Chapter One

June 10. 11:58 p.m.
Canary Wharf, London

"You're asking for trouble."

Trevor Carswell ignored the uneasy voice. He watched the long black limousine creep into the construction site near the north dock of Canary Wharf, in the shadow of the tall HSBC building. The huge cranes at the dock sat as silent sentinels this time of night. He moved out of the shadows so the limousine's driver could see him. Eric Koller followed him. The limo changed direction and eased to a stop forty feet away. The driver killed the engine and flipped off the headlights.

Trevor stayed put. He could feel Eric's anxiety pulsing behind him. The construction site seemed eerie and a fitting place for this meeting. A jaw crusher sat perpendicular to two ten-foot stacks of gravel; an equally tall pile of long pipes hemmed him in on the other side. Nothing moved. Even the hum of the few cars still out at midnight seemed far away.

After an endless minute, a man emerged from the front passenger seat and walked toward them.

Eric tensed up, muttering something.

"... dangerous...."

Of course it was dangerous. This whole mission was dangerous; but insisting on meeting the brains behind the anarchists who called themselves the Philosophy of Bedlam was doubly so. A calculated risk. It was a good sign that the man had agreed to meet, but that didn't lessen the pucker factor one whit.

Nor did the fact that he had the cell's leader at his back.

The man from the car stopped a few feet away. "All right, Eric?"

Eric nodded, but didn't come forward. "No one followed us, Mr. Smith. It's all gravy. This is Trevor Willoughby. Like I told you, we fought together in Northern Ireland back in the day. He's sound."

The man frowned. His short, compact body looked soft to Trevor. Neat hair stopped well above the collar of his starched white shirt. The creased wrinkles in the shirt told Trevor he'd worn a suit jacket today. "So what's the purpose of this meeting, Willoughby?"

"I meet the man I'm risking my life for. I take his measure, or I walk." As he had when he'd been undercover as a new officer with the Special Air Service, he dropped his voice into a growl. Rough. Threatening.

Mr. Smith continued to scowl. Trevor supposed he was trying to look threatening, but his attempts were laughable.

"Very well," the man said finally. "Our focus is the ridiculous trappings of a corrupt society. People need to wake up and realize how much government money is spent on useless pastimes like making movies instead of feeding the poor."

Trevor feigned outrage. "On that we agree. It's bollocks that faux celebrities warp public opinion. They're not the gods they pretend to be. They're just stupid, self-centered fools. But it's been proven time and again that socialism doesn't work."

Mr. Smith's lip curled. "Socialism is just another form of bondage. A privileged few ruling sheep. We're for Great Britain shaking off the blinders, so our people realize government does not have their best interests at heart. Skewed policies keep Britons as little more than slaves."

"We don't need a government to control us," Eric said. "It's long past time the English butt out of our business and let us live as we want. In Ireland and everywhere else."

"I hear you." Trevor nodded to show he understood. "Now, how about the meeting I asked for? I talk to your boss. I thought I made it clear. I don't deal with flunkies."

Mr. Smith widened his arms, turning his palms up as if to say, "Here I am."

Eric frowned. "Jaysus, Trev. You're gone in the head. Stop messing about."

Trevor's lip curled. "Not bloody likely. He's just a kiss-ass. I want to talk to the real Mr. Smith."

Both the man and Eric shot Trevor startled looks.

"What makes you think—"

"He *is* the—"

Trevor cut a hand through the air, effectively stopping both men. "No. You're not. I want to talk to the man in the back of the limousine, not the lackey in the front."

The man stilled. Trevor read the indecision on his face.

"Now. Or stop wasting my fucking time," he snapped. His mission hinged on finding the brains behind the brawn. If Eric's cell fell, another would simply rise to take its place.

Finally, the man shrugged and walked back over to the limousine. The back window rolled down, and the man bent over to speak to whoever was inside. When he returned, he jerked his head at Trevor.

"He'll talk to you."

Trevor stalked past him, Eric and the man following. The driver exited the vehicle on an intercept course. Massive shoulders and bulging biceps declared him the muscle. He put out an arm, halting them.

"Just him," he said, pointing a sausage-sized finger at Trevor.

Annoyance flashed across Eric's face, but he obediently wandered to the bonnet of the limousine and lingered there, lighting up as he waited. The flunky returned to his seat in the front of the limousine.

"Arms out," the driver said, voice and face expressionless.

Trevor raised his arms and suffered the man to pat him down. He found Trevor's .380 and stuffed it into his belt. Jerking his head, he led the way to the back and opened the door. Trevor ducked inside, settling into the seat directly opposite a man sitting in the deepest shadows.

Trevor could barely make out the graying blond hair and lines on the fifty-ish face. The unwelcoming stare. The real Mr. Smith had a slender build and wore an unbuttoned suit coat.

"Always a pleasure to meet Eric's friends." The cultured voice rolling out of the darkness contained an undertone that wasn't British English. Trevor strained to identify it.

"So who's the suit? He looks like a bloody bureaucrat. Come to think of it, so do you."

The man's dry chuckle held little humor. "He's no one of consequence. My accountant. And I assure you that I am no bureaucrat. Just a man who sees a problem that needs repairing. Now. To what do I owe the honor?"

Trevor leaned forward, looking directly into the man's eyes. He seemed vaguely familiar, but Trevor couldn't put a name to the face. "I make it a habit to know exactly who I'm working with before I risk my life. No exceptions."

"An understandable precaution." His tone suggested he did the same.

"So precisely who are you? Why would a suit want to dismantle our government?"

The man's voice grew icy. "As far as you're concerned, I'm Mr. Smith. Consider me the money. As for as anything else, my reasons are mine alone."

Trevor sat back, dropping his voice even lower. "Well, that bloody well explains nothing."

Mr. Smith tapped his fingers on his leg. "I'm meeting you as a courtesy to Eric. Don't overstep your place. You're easily replaceable."

"Untrue. Each person in your cell brings his own expertise to the table. Safecracker, arsonist, hacker. I'm the only explosives expert. Your last bloke blew himself to bits, I believe?"

The head of the joint MI-5/SAS task force, Brigadier Lord Patrick Danby, had informed Trevor that the dead man was the only clue to finding the anarchists. They identified him through dental records as Jing-sheng Qiū. He had been a textile mill worker in

Leeds before moving to London and joining the Philosophy of Bedlam.

Mr. Smith slashed a hand through the air. "An unfortunate turn of events."

Unfortunate? A man had died. A terrorist, to be sure, but Smith's callous disregard for Qiū's life vibrated in the quiet of the limousine.

"The man knew shite," Trevor said, burying his disgust.

"I trust you will not make the same mistake?"

He forced himself to laugh. "Not bloody likely. Pipe bombs are some of the most dangerous to use. Even something as small as static electricity can set them off. As Eric tells me, Qiū was fifty feet away when it exploded, and the shrapnel still killed him. I prefer plastic explosives. PE-4. Stable until detonated."

"And you can acquire this?"

"Already have. My question is, why should I waste it on you?" Trevor had to walk a razor wire to learn who the head of the snake was, and to be accepted as an anarchist.

Mr. Smith nodded. "A fair question. Let's just say I have certain interests in the weapons arena. Government agencies scrambling to stop terrorist bombings won't be searching for me."

He was an illegal arms dealer? Maybe that's where Trevor had seen him—on a wanted poster. He sat back in the soft leather. "So this isn't about ideology for you. Just money."

Mr. Smith laughed. "There's no such thing as 'just' money, Mr. Willoughby. Now. I've answered your questions. You answer mine. Do you support the anarchist philosophy of my Bedlamites?"

The cover MI-5 had given him was rock solid. No one here knew he was Trevor Carswell, British SAS. Trevor had known what lies he would tell before he insisted Eric introduce him to

Mr. Smith. "I don't give a shit what your anarchist philosophy is. I want to bring the government to its knees. Starting with the bloody National Health Service all the way up to Her Fucking Majesty and Parliament. If you're the real deal, I'm in."

"Why?"

"That's none of your business. Just be assured I'll do what needs doing."

The man stared at Trevor for a moment, then picked up a file folder from the seat next to him. "But it is my business. I, too, make a point to know with whom I'm dealing."

He opened the folder and flipped up the top page. "Trevor Willoughby, born April 23, 1980, to blue-collar parents. The oldest of five children, which kept your parents poor. Spent your teenage years getting into fights. Vocally critical of the disparity between the social classes. Joined the Provisional IRA in 2004, left in 2005 to join those trying to reestablish the Saor Éire, which failed. Was there not enough action for you, Mr. Willoughby?"

Trevor didn't answer. So far, his cover was holding.

Mr. Smith shrugged, and flipped to a new page. "Married in 2011, divorced in 2012, when you caught your wife cheating. You beat the man half to death and spent eighteen months in prison for it. Daughter diagnosed with a rare form of leukemia while you were being detained at Her Majesty's pleasure at Gartree. National Health Service wouldn't cover the cost and you couldn't. Daughter died last year."

"All right," Trevor gritted out. "Enough."

Mr. Smith put the folder back on the seat. "You'll get your chance with the NHS, Mr. Willoughby. But I have something else in mind, first. Are you interested?"

"Bloody hell. Yes."

Chapter Two

June 13. 5:15 p.m.
August Museum of Modern Art

SHELBY GIBSON FOLLOWED Floyd Panderson as he led her into the Suffolk Gallery of the August Museum of Modern Art. The fifteen-by-nine meter exhibition hall held artwork borrowed from other museums for this special exhibit. Paintings adorned the alabaster walls, crowned by Edward Shamblet's *Memories of the Gods.* The centerpiece of the exhibit measured an impressive one hundred forty by ninety-two inches. Various gods and demi-gods fell from Mount Olympus, chased from their home by demons and monsters.

Normally, she loved visiting art galleries and museums. Bad luck had been plaguing her all day, though, starting with a dead car battery, following her onto the Tube, where her briefcase had been stolen, to the blisters developing on the balls of her feet from walking too far and too long in her strappy high-heeled sandals.

Pedestals supporting sculptures in various shapes and sizes dotted the room. Both visitors and artists with sketch pads perched on leather-topped benches placed at convenient intervals down the center. Others wandered from painting to painting, reading the plaques on the wall near each one. This close to closing time, a docent moved from person to person, letting them know they had a mere fifteen minutes left to gather their things and leave. The artists began to pack up their sketching materials.

Floyd steered her toward the left wall, to a twenty-four-by-thirty-six-inch painting. As the curator, closing times were meaningless to him. The docent nodded respectfully to him as he herded the last few visitors back out into the lobby.

Floyd brushed a hand over his neat hair, then smoothed it down his tie before continuing his lecture. "In the early twentieth century, Fauvism gave way to the cubism of Picasso, Georges Braque, Juan Gris, and others. They all came at it from different directions, of course. This painting is *Still Life with Acorns and Apples*."

The small, square brushstrokes and bold colors reminded her more of Cézanne's later works than anything by Juan Gris, but she kept her peace and let him talk.

"I have a particular fondness for the cubists. In fact, I have something in the works to possibly acquire a Picasso."

Shelby's brows shot up. "Really? That would be a major coup for such a small museum. It could triple your annual visitorship."

"I know." Floyd sounded smug as he slid an arm around her shoulders. "Do you know what my favorite Picasso quote is? 'It is your work in life that is the ultimate seduction.' The passion in these paintings, and your love of art, makes me realize life is too short not to go after what I want."

She knew what he wanted. He'd made no secret of his desire. She tilted her head away and stepped free as he nuzzled her ear. He reluctantly let his arm slide away as she approached the painting for a closer look. They'd only been dating a few weeks, and despite his efforts to talk her into a more intimate relationship, she just wasn't ready to take that step. They had so much in common. A love of art. Similar tastes in literature and music. Floyd—attentive, sophisticated, and urbane—had a handsome face and trim body that should have appealed to her. Why was she hesitating?

"My favorite painting from the early modern period is *The Kiss* by Gustav Klimt. I have a reproduction in my office downstairs. Would you like to see it?" Somehow, Floyd had moved closer again.

"I thought your office was in the lobby? Who painted this still life?" she asked, to distract him. She bent forward to read the plaque.

But Floyd had straightened with a frown, turning back toward the entrance to the gallery.

"What is it?"

"Shh! Do you hear that?"

Shelby caught the shouting a moment later.

"Blast it! Some patrons are beastly. It's probably someone whining we're closing. I'll get it sorted in short order." Floyd strode to the gallery's exit, Shelby following close behind. As he stepped into the lobby, he stopped so abruptly that she ran into him.

The ripping sound of automatic gunfire, ear-splitting in the confines of the lobby, had her ducking and throwing her hands over her head, heart slamming into her throat. Adrenaline spiked through her system as she heard screaming and more angry shouting. Floyd cringed, backing up so rapidly he collided with her as he whirled again. Before she could formulate a sentence, he shoved past her and ran.

Finally, hands clapped over her mouth in horror, she saw what was happening.

Five men, dressed in a motley assortment of military clothing, shouted and pointed wicked-looking assault rifles as they shoved and chivvied the remaining visitors into a cluster. No, wait. There were four men and one woman, who dropped the horizontal metal bar across the front door with an intimidating clang. Chunks of plaster and cork chips rained down from the acoustic tiles, now full of bullet holes.

The first police car screeched into the car park, blue and red lights flashing. The small hatchback with its trademark yellow stripe and blue checkers drove almost onto the front steps before slamming to a stop. Two more followed; not the standard police vehicles, but the far more intimidating armed response vehicles.

One of the gunmen caught sight of Shelby and leveled his weapon at her, shouting something she couldn't hear through the roaring in her ears. He stamped toward her, lifting the muzzle of the rifle and firing several rounds into the air. She shrank back, hands slamming over her ears. He reached her and grabbed her arm, yanking her around. As he made to shove her toward the frightened group, he jerked her to a stop instead.

"Oy!" he shouted. "Bring 'em in here. No windows. Police snipers can't get to us."

The other gunmen herded the hostages in her direction. Several were crying or clinging to one another. A woman, nearly hysterical, tripped and fell to her hands and knees. One of the gunmen stopped to help her back up. His back was to Shelby, but something familiar about the shape of his head and the breadth of his shoulders started a tingling in the back of her head. Then he turned, and she stopped breathing.

Trevor.

He looked feral in his two-day growth of beard and long hair, well-worn black cargo pants and black T-shirt. Despite that, she recognized him immediately. The cotton molded to his torso. His shoulders were wider than she remembered, his biceps thicker, his chest deeper. And the rifle balanced across his shoulders enormous.

Their eyes met across the room, and they both froze.

Chapter Three

10 months earlier
Ma'ar ye zhad, Azakistan

TREVOR HID A yawn behind his hand. Despite his best efforts, Ambassador Stanton had persuaded him to attend this gala, a celebration marking the culmination of the week-long Music and Art Foundation's Ma'ar ye zhad Festival. Dignitaries crowded the Prince Kashif Hashmi Hotel. Trevor found it tedious.

He'd agreed to come for one reason, and she had yet to put in an appearance. The US ambassador to Azakistan, whom he had not fooled one whit with his subtle queries, had assured him that Deputy Political Counselor Shelby Gibson would attend. So far, she had not. Disappointed, he tossed back the rest of his bourbon, grimacing as it burned its way down his throat. Had he stayed long enough to be polite?

He gently disengaged himself from the chic, leggy blonde

who'd attached herself to him about ten minutes ago. She leaned against him as she spoke, rubbing against him, and couldn't have been any more clear if she used semaphore flags. He felt nothing but a vague distaste. Murmuring apologies, he meandered toward the lobby. The blonde followed, sliding her hand around his arm again and walking next to him. He resisted the urge to yank his arm free and bolt from her cloying perfume. "Look . . ." he started to say. "I beg your pardon, but—"

A movement in his periphery had him glancing toward it out of habit, and he halted in his tracks. A vision of loveliness drifted across his path. Shelby Gibson's appearance stunned him; gone was the severe buttoned-down professional he'd met last week, who'd briefed an advanced Secret Service team on the political climate in Azakistan. This woman dazzled. The red dress she wore had straps that gathered to become a draped semicircle of fabric brushing across the tops of her breasts. The skirt clung to her hips and drifted down to the floor, pooling slightly and making him wonder how she could walk without tripping. As she moved, the thigh-high slit showed provocative flashes of leg. She stopped to chat with Admiral Leighton, turning away from Trevor, and he stopped breathing.

The dress had no back.

A richness of silky, perfect skin led his eyes inevitably downward, past the small of her back, to where more material clung just a little to the cleft in her derrière, but stopped short of revealing the sweet curve.

Suddenly, he wanted nothing more than to see those smooth, lovely globes.

The dress tantalized him, but so did her bare arms; the tousled, curly hair brushing the nape of her neck; the slope of her spine.

Her sultry laugh. He reached her before he even realized he'd moved. "Good evening, Admiral Leighton. Ms. Gibson."

She tensed, her gaze bouncing off of him before returning to the admiral. A pink flush rose in her cheeks. "Good evening, Major."

"Major Carswell," the admiral said. "I'm so pleased you could join us this evening. You are acquainted with our lovely Shelby, I see. Your timing is perfect. Perhaps you could keep her company while I make the rounds?"

Amusement glittered in the older man's eyes. Trevor grimaced. Obviously, the admiral had noted Trevor's laser focus on Shelby.

"I'm quite all right, Admiral. There are a few people I need to chat with as well." Her gaze focused over Trevor's shoulder, and he winced as he felt the unwelcome touch of the blonde on his arm. Shelby swallowed a healthy mouthful of champagne. "Hello, Babette."

So that was her name.

Babette curled her fingers around his bicep. "Shelley. How are you?"

Trevor eased away from her, and she immediately glued herself to his side again. He sent the admiral a helpless look.

"It's Shelby. Why don't you three chat, and I'll get you a plate from the buffet, Admiral." Shelby tried to withdraw, but stopped when the admiral touched her arm. He moved his hand to her wrist, gently guiding her forward so she could not extricate herself without jerking her arm free.

"I've already eaten more than my fair share. Besides, you should enjoy yourself. Instead of talking to me, you should be dancing." His face lit as though he'd just had a brilliant idea, and he beamed at Shelby and then Trevor. "In fact, the orchestra is lovely. Why don't you young people dance together?"

Babette slid her hand up Trevor's arm. "This dance is mine."

Trevor took hold of her wrist, peeling it off his shoulder. "I believe you are mistaken, madam."

Shelby allowed Admiral Leighton to take her champagne flute and pull her to Trevor's side. He wasted no time slipping an arm around Shelby's waist.

Admiral Leighton turned to Babette, who shot him a dirty look. "Mrs. Jowat, why don't I escort you to the dining area? I believe I saw your husband there just a few minutes ago." The admiral placed his hand in the small of Babette's back, guiding her away. She scowled, but mercifully went.

Trevor remembered Colonel Louis Jowat only too well. He'd patronized Shelby during her briefing to the Secret Service in preparation for President Cooper's visit to al-Zadr Air Force Base. Had verbally patted her on the head and told her to let the grown-ups talk. Trevor disliked him for that alone. Apparently, his wife found him tiresome as well.

As they made their way through the crowd, Shelby shifted closer to him to avoid bumping into anyone. He enjoyed the brush of her arm against his, the soft bump of her hip.

Hell, who was he kidding? The simple truth was that he burned to hold this woman in his arms.

She stopped just short of the dance floor and turned to him. "We're out of the admiral's sight, Major Carswell. Please don't feel obligated, if you need to be elsewhere."

Instead of answering, he moved closer. Oh, no. He was getting his dance. Touching her upper arm, much as Admiral Leighton had, he skimmed his fingers down her silky skin to her wrist, curling his fingers around the delicate bones there. He guided her hand to his shoulder, holding his over it for several beats. He snaked his other arm around her waist and tightened his grasp.

"Not at all," he said, swinging her onto the floor in a fluid move. "The admiral just wants you to have a bit of fun."

Her face softened with affection. "He's a sweetheart."

A foreign sensation lurched in his innards. What would it take for her to look at him that way? "He's clearly fond of you."

"We've worked together for quite a while now. He's a brilliant diplomat."

Trevor had no use for diplomats. In his experience, they mucked things up more often than they solved problems. Admiral Leighton, however, was also a military man, and understood the SpecOps community better than most.

His feet moved of their own accord, obliging her to sway with him, taking the opportunity to ease her closer. His fingers slid across skin like brushed silk, splaying as they reached her lower back. She said something else, but he couldn't hear it through the roar in his ears.

"I said, perhaps you should have eaten more at dinner. You look hungry." Her tone was light, amused.

He looked into her face, not trying to hide his desire. Answering attraction flared in hers, causing his pulse to leap.

"I'm starving," he admitted, voice low. His head spun just from her nearness, clouding his senses. "But not for cocktail shrimp. That dress looks amazing on you. You're incredibly striking."

Her face closed down. Somehow, he'd said the wrong thing.

"Beauty is a trick of genetics, nothing more."

For a moment, he lost himself in her brown eyes, unable to look away. What had she just said? "That's not the kind of beauty I'm talking about. Yes, you are beautiful. But I'm talking about your confidence, your intelligence, the way you carry yourself and interact with people. You are as lovely as Babette Jowat is, erm, not."

Her eyes rounded as she stared at him, mouth agape. "You don't think Babette is beautiful? That would put you in the minority."

He laughed. "Sharks have their own allure as well. It certainly doesn't mean I want to swim with one."

She searched his face. Trying to judge his sincerity, he thought. He took the opportunity to gather her closer. She fit perfectly against him. Just the right height, slender but with curves in all the right places. And her scent intoxicated him. Was it grapefruit? On her it smelled exotic. He fought to focus.

"Most people don't see that about her."

"Most people don't see that about you," he replied. "Not the shark bit. Seeing beyond your pretty face. Seeing how capable you are."

She'd stopped moving, so he did as well. Her brows were pulled down. "Usually, I just wear a simple black dress. I'm practically invisible."

"You never could be. Not to me."

"It's better that way, though. More professional. I end up at a lot of these events." She dropped her gaze.

Trevor opened his mouth to speak, but she lifted her lashes and met his eyes, and he promptly forgot what he'd been about to say.

"The same people I work with attend these functions. I don't want there to be any confusion," she elaborated.

They were doing little more than swaying to the music, which was fine by Trevor, as Shelby had nudged closer and the tips of her breasts shifted back and forth across his chest. The last thing he wanted was for her to draw back. His body had taken up an insistent throbbing. Gritting his teeth, he eased his pelvis away so she wouldn't feel his erection. Unfortunately, that stopped the sweet agony of her subtle brushes against his chest as well.

"And the people you don't work with?"

Humor lit her eyes. "Has it been awhile, soldier?"

A dull flush stained his cheeks. "I was impressed with the briefing you gave to the Secret Service," he said doggedly. "You have a solid grasp of Azakistani politics. The shift toward fundamentalism has our Ministry of Defense concerned. When you listed out which members of the Azakistani government were pro-Western, that helped not only the American Secret Service planning President Cooper's visit, but my government as well."

A smile tipped the corners of her lips. "I'm glad it was useful. And your take on what sorts of weapons these terrorists are acquiring was useful to me. I hadn't thought of it in those terms."

"We approach the same problem from different perspectives."

She made a wry face. "It became brutally obvious you've visited Azakistan far more often than you let on."

"Perhaps I dissembled a bit," he said. "Goes with the job, I'm afraid. But you ran a high-power, national-level briefing with confidence and authority. You had the respect of everyone in that room. Me included."

Shelby wrinkled her nose, as though she'd encountered a bad smell. "Not all. Colonel Jowat is a constant thorn in my side."

He smiled at her. "He's a gnat's ass. He just made himself look foolish."

"Gnats buzz around being annoying. It fits." She laughed. "May I ask you a personal question? You seem so dedicated to your job. Very much the take-charge type. Do you have a life outside the military?"

No. He'd never wanted one. He enjoyed his dalliances, but the women he slept with didn't want a relationship any more than he did. Lately, though, he thought maybe there might be more to life than soldiering. Shelby presented a complicated, fascinating puzzle, and he found he wanted very much to know her better.

"Maybe now's the time to start having one. Maybe I'd like to give up control for once." He threw her his jauntiest grin. "Come on, then. Take charge. What would you have of me?" He'd meant to sound flippant, but his voice came out low and hoarse. "Command me."

She shivered against him. Her head turned so that her nose brushed the collar of his military jacket. He felt her soft exhale burn across his skin. "That's a lot of power for one woman to have."

The music started again, the rich, lilting strains of a Strauss waltz. He forced himself to swing into the long lines of the dance, startled and delighted when Shelby matched him step for step. "You must attend a lot of these," he said, "to have learned the Viennese waltz."

Her eyes sparked amusement. "Classes. The Kettering Center for Dance, when I lived in D.C."

Trevor firmed his hold on the small of her back as he drifted them out of the way of another couple. He found himself grinning foolishly down at her. "Just a fascination, or were you preparing to dance with me tonight?" he said, keeping his tone light and teasing. To his shock, her face shuttered, though her body still moved sinuously with his. "What did I say?"

Shelby shook her head. "Nothing. My fiancé wanted me to learn the waltz for one of the White House Correspondents' Association dinners."

"Fiancé? You're engaged?" Trevor nearly stumbled over his

feet during a turn, barely correcting and almost losing his grip on Shelby. After a moment, his brain unfroze. Stupid man, to leave a woman like Shelby unescorted. "Where is he tonight?"

"In hell, I hope." She sounded tired, and a little defeated. "Ex-fiancé."

Trevor exhaled with more relief than he liked to admit. The waltz ended, and he turned her into a careful dip. She arched back, neck elongated, all grace and allure. As he righted her, he pressed her entire length against his and inclined his head until their mouths were a whisper apart. Locking eyes with her, he said, "Clearly, he did not deserve you."

Her gaze swam with remembered hurt and pain. She dropped her hands and he released her, questions hard in his head. Before he could say anything more, she took a step back. "It doesn't matter. You've had your dance, Major. I'm sure you have more important things to do, and so do I."

Chapter Four

SHELBY FELT THE burn of tears behind her eyes as she walked away, mildly surprised when Trevor didn't try to stop her. Well, that's how it went. Men married to their careers, ambitious men, took what they wanted and then left, careless and unconcerned about the havoc they left in their wake.

Lord, he looked incredible in his formal military wear. The short scarlet jacket with its black lapels hugged his frame and flecked his eyes with rubies. The black waistcoat and bow tie, the red stripe down his trousers, even his shoes, shined to a high gloss, seemed exotic to her.

"Shelby." He followed her from the dance floor.

"No," she said, not even sure to what she referred. She just knew she needed to put distance between them. To her relief, he stopped, though she could feel the weight of his gaze. It didn't seem to matter how far away from him she moved, though. Her awareness of him vibrated through her. It had been that way with Bruce, too.

At first, anyway. Later, she'd been more like a dog awaiting notice by her master.

Shelby blinked rapidly, horrified. What if someone noticed her tears? What if Trevor had?

Of course he'd noticed. Like Bruce, like her father, he noted everything about her. Unlike them, he seemed to approve.

He'd made his interest clear. He tempted her; she forced herself to acknowledge her own desire. Before she did something foolish like act on it, though, she remembered the arrogance tilting his head and widening his stance. The unflappable surety of hands maneuvering her through the crowded dance floor. She even disdained his nose, which had dropped to her ear and nuzzled there as though he couldn't resist her scent.

Her firm grasp of politics caused her quick rise through diplomatic circles. She still fought, though, for her male and female colleagues to see past a pretty face to her sharp mind. She wanted Trevor's respect. The realization didn't surprise her.

She'd been pretty certain he'd be at this gala tonight. And she'd chosen to wear this dress.

The daring design outdid anything in her closet. Her roommate had taken one look at it in the shop window, and dragged her inside to try it on. And had practically clapped her hands in glee when it fit as though it had been made for her. It had been outrageously pricey, but she'd let Deirdre talk her into it, and into the slim, sexy heels she now wore. Even then, she'd nearly chickened out; her roommate, sensing her impending cowardice, bullied and shoved her into the dress, the shoes, and then the cab.

"I won't be home," Deirdre had reminded her for the fourth time, before slamming the cab door shut. "I'll be in Mosul all week. So . . ."

Yeah, right. Like she would bring someone home with her.

"Ah, Miss Gibson. And how did you find the young major?"

Shelby turned to Admiral Leighton, who had walked up to the buffet with an empty plate. "An excellent dance partner. I see your appetite has returned."

He grinned, unrepentant. "He's handsome, too."

Shelby suppressed a grin. A diehard sentimentalist, Admiral Leighton saw romance blossoming everywhere.

"He was a bit too full of himself," she told the older man. Told herself, too. "Not my type at all."

The admiral chuckled. "Well, he couldn't keep his eyes off you, my dear."

"Let me freshen your drink, Admiral," she said diplomatically. She found one of the floating servers and motioned him over. Exchanging his nearly empty flute for a fresh one, she took a glass of champagne for herself as well. Several members of the admiral's staff joined them, and Shelby smiled and chatted and tried to ignore Trevor Carswell.

It proved impossible.

No matter where she was in the ballroom, she sensed his presence. Each time she glanced in his direction, his gaze tracked her. He didn't approach her, though. Was he as rattled by their dance as she had been?

Not likely.

She snagged another drink. Her third, or her fourth? It hardly mattered. Practiced in the art of appearances, in reality she was doing little more than taking a sip or two of each.

Usually virtually invisible at these events, her dress brought men flocking around her, flirting outrageously as they tried to move in for the kill. She could hear Bruce's voice whispering into her ear. "Be a good girl for me, hon. Be nice to my friends." A commodity. That's all she'd ever been to him. And her father, before that. "Find a man to take care of you, Shel. You won't have your looks forever."

She drew the line at Louis Jowat, however. Couldn't believe he'd even had the gall to ask her to dance. She muttered a quick apology and all but ran for the ladies' room.

She saw Trevor sitting at one of the tables, deep in conversation with an Azakistani staffer she knew by face only. He looked up, right at her, as attuned to her as she was to him. The sharp concern in his eyes startled her.

Shelby made it to the ladies' lounge and sank into one of the chairs.

What the hell was it about the SAS major that drew her in so thoroughly? She'd worked with plenty of attractive men; he was far more than just a handsome face. His gentle strength, his impeccable manners, his sharp intelligence all appealed to her.

Well, she couldn't hide in here forever. And she needed to know what she would do when she exited the room.

Maybe he wouldn't be there. Maybe he'd lost interest.

Leaning against the hallway wall, Trevor straightened when he saw her, and zeroed in on an intercept path. "Are you all right?"

She forced an airy laugh. "Of course. Why wouldn't I be?"

He just looked at her.

"I'm fine. Really. Just tired."

He frowned. He had a sensuous mouth. A thin upper lip, and a full lower one. He was probably a very good kisser. "Something I said earlier upset you. I'm sorry."

She didn't know what he saw in her face, but the concern in his didn't lessen. "It really had nothing to do with you, Major. Just old memories."

"Trevor."

She gave a wan smile. "Trevor, then."

"I didn't intend to upset you. It was mention of your fiancé, wasn't it."

It was a statement, but she answered anyway. "I'm silly to let it upset me. Because you're right. I deserve much better."

His eyes crinkled at the corners, though he didn't smile. "How long ago was this?"

She shook her head. "I don't want to talk about him. Tell me about yourself instead."

This time he did smile. "I'm pretty uncomplicated. What you see is what you get."

She laughed, thoughts of Bruce fading from her mind as she relaxed. "Far from it. Don't forget, I read people for a living. You're about as far from uncomplicated as it's possible to get."

"Then get to know me."

The heat in his eyes nearly scalded her. A man passed them in the short hallway, heading for the restroom. Trevor moved closer to her to let him pass. She put a hand on his chest and he halted. Before she could stop herself, her hand smoothed over his chest to his shoulder. His hand came up to cover hers, pressing it more firmly against him. His other arm snaked around her waist, snugging them together. He looked like he wanted nothing more than to unwrap her like a present,

Back away. Don't stare into those deep brown eyes. Don't—

She found herself hypnotized. For long moments, they just stood there, staring at one another. His scent, clean and masculine, teased her nostrils, as it had during their too-brief dance. She leaned in, reaching for his lips.

If she'd thought they were close together before, he now enveloped her, the hand at her waist coming up to cup the back of her head as he crowded her into the wall. His lips found hers and he devoured her, licking into her mouth. She tasted the champagne on his breath as it mixed with hers. Heat shot through her core as their tongues dueled.

All too soon, he lifted his head, his fingers brushing the nape of her neck as he withdrew. His gaze traveled from her hair to her lips, parting as she watched him, and to her breasts with their sensitized nipples straining at the fabric. The hunger lingered in his eyes, in his body.

"Let's get out of here," he said. "Go somewhere quieter, with fewer prying eyes."

She found herself nodding, but immediately shook her head. The dead-last thing she should do was give this man any encouragement. He would be all over her. And then he would trample all over her, and leave her mangled.

"I've done my duty," she said. "I think it's time for me to call it a night."

"I'll escort you out."

"All right." The truth was, she wasn't ready for the evening to end. A few more minutes with him before he put her into a cab would be all right, wouldn't it?

They walked together through the lobby and out into the hot night. A taxicab immediately pulled up, and Trevor held the door for her as she slid inside.

"May I share the taxi with you?" he asked.

"Where do you live? Oh, never mind. Get in."

She scooted over, and he folded more than six feet of muscle and sinew in next to her.

"Where to, guv'nor?"

She gave the cabbie her address, then sat back. Their shoulders brushed. The woman in her purred as his arm came around her, pulled her to his chest. She deepened the contact.

All too soon, the taxi pulled up to the curb in front of her apartment building. Reluctantly, she sat up, reaching into her clutch for some crumpled bills. "Thank you for the escort home."

He put a hand over hers as he handed the driver money, then slid out and held the door for her. "I'll walk you up."

"That's not . . ." She was going to say *necessary*, but one look into his face shut her up. The gentleman in him would see her to the door, end of discussion. She slid over the seat to the door and swung her legs to the pavement, holding the sides of her skirt together at the slit. Trevor's gaze followed her hand. She edged out of the taxi and swallowed her protest when he took her arm.

Suddenly nervous, she led the way to the elevators. Trevor pressed the up arrow, guiding her inside when the doors swished open.

"They're pretty reliable," she said. "A lot of embassy personnel live here, so they keep things running pretty well for us. One of the mail room guys got stuck a few weeks ago, though. He was in there for hours. We took turns sitting on the ground and shouting to him." She was babbling. Great. Shelby clamped her mouth shut and pressed the button for the fifth floor.

The doors slid open and he put his hand at the small of her back to guide her out. Her skin became instantly sensitized.

"Which flat?"

She pointed left. "Five-twelve."

At the door, she opened her evening bag and rooted around inside. Lipstick, compact, comb. Rats. Where was her key?

He pulled the bag from her and plunged a hand inside. And

voila! Her key appeared. He inserted it and twisted. Her door opened and she stepped inside.

"Okay, we're here. I'm safe."

He loomed large in the doorway, but made no move to enter. "Good night, then, Shelby."

As he started to turn, she reached out a hand. "Would . . . would you like some coffee?"

He smiled, and her heart beat faster.

"A coffee would be brilliant."

Closing and locking the door behind him, she led the way to the kitchen. "Truthfully, I usually just stop at Starbucks on the way to work."

She pulled down a bag of their winter blend, which always amused her here in Azakistan, where the temperature hovered at a balmy hundred-and-two. Setting the bag of coffee on the counter, she chewed her lip as she turned back to him, and found his gaze traveling from her hair to her lips, parting as she saw his perusal, to her breasts, down her legs to her feet in the very high heels. The hunger lingered in his eyes, in his body—but tightly controlled.

She gazed at him, shocked at her body's reaction. Heat pooled low, her nipples straining at the fabric. Well, she allowed, it had been awhile. A long while. An extremely long while, now that she thought about it. When was the last time she'd liked a man enough to invite him into her bed?

"I'm out of filters." She flushed a deep red when his glance flickered to the counter, where the pack of filters sat beside the coffeemaker.

"Some wine, then?"

She forced herself to hold his gaze. "I was thinking . . . dessert."

His slow smile, sensual and knowing, caused her heart to pound in her chest. Without another word, she took him by the hand and led him down the hall and into her bedroom.

SHELBY STIRRED TO the soft chirr of a phone. The mattress shifted, and the solid warmth at her back disappeared. She made a muted sound of protest and opened her eyes just far enough to see Trevor pad, naked, across the floor. She took the time to admire his firm, yummy butt as he bent to slide a phone from his pants pocket. Damn, the man was fine. Hard muscles, tight ass, strong legs. She stretched like a luxuriating cat, full bodied and contented, feeling a delicious soreness and a smile.

"Carswell."

He kept his voice low, his back turned so as not to disturb her. Where had the hard military man gone? The Trevor she'd experienced last night had been warm and caring. Sweet and attentive.

It had surprised her. Despite devouring her with his hot gaze at the gala and the fire that had ignited when he'd kissed her, if she had said no—if she had so much as shaken her head—he would have walked right out of her apartment.

Last night had been a revelation. Her fingers trailed down her neck to her breasts, eyelids drooping in pleasurable memory. He'd been more concerned with her gratification than his own, bringing her to heights she'd never experienced. So that's what great sex felt like, she mused. Her other encounters paled in comparison. She hoped he finished the call quickly and returned to bed. Maybe she could seduce him into a repeat performance?

"Jesus! Where are you?"

The sudden tension in Trevor's voice roused her.

"Right. All right. It'll . . . yes. Me. I can. I'm in Ma'ar ye zhad, not more than an hour from you." After a pause, Trevor exhaled a soft laugh. His voice dropped, became softer. "I remember, princess. We do seem to be making a habit of it. Do you need me to bring anything?" Trevor chuckled at whatever he heard on the other end, a low, masculine sound men only used with women. "Hang tight. I'll be along shortly." He disconnected.

That men only used with women they had slept with, or wanted to sleep with.

Shelby's heart fragmented. The disappointment crushed her, more so because it surprised her. She knew better than to fall for a man like him. She'd warned herself to steer clear of him. Career soldiers did not commit. They were faithful to the military. Everyone else took on the role of a mission—get in, get out. Pun intended.

They had one-night stands, sure. The affair might even last a few weeks, but, in the end, he would pack up and go and never look back.

He pulled his pants on with a contained urgency, tucking in his shirt before buckling his pants. Draping his jacket over one arm, he picked up his shoes. Shelby closed her eyes.

She felt more than heard him cross to the bed. He hesitated there for what seemed like forever, then bent and brushed his lips across her cheek. Shelby kept her eyes shut and her breathing even. *Go away. Just go away.*

Apparently he heard her mental command, because he crossed to the bedroom door and eased it open. She didn't hear him tiptoe through the rest of the apartment; didn't even hear her front door open and close. But she knew as soon as she was alone.

Shelby rolled onto her back, arm up and over her eyes. The man she had spent an incredible night with, with whom she had shared amazing sex, had just left her bed to go to another woman.

Guess the amazing part had just been on her end.

Looking at the bedside clock, she saw it was barely three in the morning. Maybe it had been a work emergency? She exhaled a disgusted laugh. Yeah, sure. And pigs would fly to the moon. A hot tear slid from the corner of her eye and down into her hair.

Well, what had she expected? One night with her would make him fall in love? Who was she kidding? Men—real men, decent men—didn't fall in love with her. And the rat bastards—like him, like the hometown boys of her youth, like her ex-fiancé—got what they wanted and vanished into the night. At three in the morning.

She turned onto her side, hugging her pillow to her. This time the tear slid across her nose and down the opposite cheek. Shelby didn't bother to brush it away. She knew the numbness and disbelief would eventually dissipate, to be replaced by a hot wash of anger. She even welcomed it. Anything was better than the shards of hurt impaling her.

Maybe his departure had come earlier than she had expected, but at least sneaking out in the middle of the night had allowed them to skip the awkward next-morning bit. The embarrassed stammering as they realized they each knew next to nothing about the other one. The question of whether she'd cook him breakfast. The humiliation of seeing him dart glances at the front door, wishing he were elsewhere.

Yes, better to accept the night for what it had been. Scratching an itch; nothing more, nothing less. A pleasant interlude that meant absolutely nothing. She sat up abruptly, squaring her shoulders. She would face the day as she always did, with a brave face, no matter how she felt inside. And no one would know.

No one ever knew.

Chapter Five

June 13. 6:15 p.m.
August Museum of Modern Art

WHAT IN BLOODY hell was Shelby doing here?

Trevor tried to unclench his jaw. This whole bastarding situation had spiraled out of control. Eric's plan to set off a bomb in the museum—which he still hadn't figured out how to stop—had now turned into a hostage standoff with police. Eric was strung tight as a bow; anything could tip him over the edge into violence. His team was worse.

A telephone began to ring in the lobby. A bullhorn screeched feedback from the front doors. "Inside the building. Pick up the telephone."

"Should we pick up, Eric?" Fay Star probably wasn't any older than twenty-four, but her thin face decorated with prison tattoos made her look older. The pentagram on her forehead and blue dots running along her cheekbones could have meant anything or nothing. Her hair twisted messily around her head, held up by a careless rubber band.

"Bugger 'em. They can kiss my arse."

Trevor glanced in Shelby's direction. She must be scared out of her wits. She crouched behind one of the pedestals with a wild-eyed girl and a man in a suit. Her eyes tracked him, lips parted as she sucked in short, sharp breaths. There was no way to reassure her. He forced himself to turn away.

"We're going to have to talk to the police, Eric," he said. "Sooner's better."

Nathan Scopes joined them near the front of the gallery, peeking around the corner into the lobby. His bright red hair was buzzed close to his head, but his usual cocky grin was missing. He scratched two fingers through his scruffy beard. "Must be two dozen coppers out there. What, they got nothing better to do?"

"I think we have their full attention," Trevor said drily.

"Someone need to shut that fekking blower off," Crawley grumbled. As though on cue, the telephone stopped ringing.

"Jukes," Eric called. "Get us on their network."

Jukes whipped his laptop out from under his unbuttoned camouflaged jacket. He cleared space on a pedestal by shoving the sculpture off it. The bronze abstract of a couple twined together hit the floor with a bang. Several of the hostages let out cries or screams. Shelby winced.

Incongruously enough, there was a knock on the front doors. "We've placed a mobile outside the door," the man on the bullhorn said. "Please answer it so we can talk."

"Ha. What the fuck makes them think we want a chin-wag?" Crawley's mean eyes glittered with dark humor.

Eric's hand tightened on the butt of his rifle. "First things first. Crawley, you and Fay search the rest of the museum. Make sure there're no surprises waiting for us."

"I'll go, too," Trevor said. Maybe he could find a way to communicate with the outside.

"No, I need you here with me," Eric said.

"I'm in," Jukes called. "Plugged into their security. Video, no audio."

Trevor walked with Eric to peer at the laptop screen.

"Coppers," Jukes said. "Lots of them all over the car park, and Armed Response Vehicles. They can't get too close 'cause the fountain and stairs are between us and them."

Eric swore under his breath. "What the hell happened? How did they know where to find us?"

Because he'd told them, that's why. Trevor narrowed his eyes. "What's your play, Eric? We can't get out."

"We'll make our own way out," Eric insisted. He turned meaningfully toward the hostages. "Through them."

"Not a good idea. If we have hostages, they'll want to take us out."

Eric snorted. "Shoot a couple of them, the coppers will back off quick enough."

"We're not going to start murdering people."

"We've been in tight spots before," Eric snapped. "We've killed before. What's your problem?"

Trevor pulled Eric around so they were nose to nose. "We're anarchists, not murderers. These people are innocent."

Eric shoved himself free. "We're whatever I say we are."

"Bloody brilliant. So we kill them. Then what?"

Eric glared. "You've gone soft, Trev."

Shite. He needed to be defusing the situation, not spinning Eric up until he felt he had no choice but to start shooting. Trevor forced himself to back off a step or two. "Maybe. But in Northern Ireland, we were at war. Here, we're what, exactly? What's the point of bombing museums?"

Eric looked around the gallery. "I have my instructions. I tell you what, after this, I'll catch you up."

He knew he needed to stop pushing. "Right. It'll do. We need to make contact."

Eric looked around. "Jukes!"

"Yeah?"

He jerked his head. The teenager left his laptop and went to him.

"Go get that fekking phone."

Jukes blanched. "Me?"

Eric grabbed him by the shoulder and pushed him forcibly toward the lobby. "Do it!"

Jukes looked around, clearly uneasy, and lunged for a woman in her early twenties, who shrank from him. He grabbed her by the arm and hauled her to her feet. Shelby could see the whites of her eyes. Her body shook with fear as Jukes pulled her in front of him, exiting the exhibition hall into the lobby. Using her as a human shield. Every person in the gallery strained to hear. There was the screech of the metal bar lifting and the lock turning.

"Back away!" Jukes shouted. Then, "Bend down and get it."

The hostage squeaked. "Help us," she croaked.

"Shut up, you moose."

The lock turned, the bar crashed down. In moments, they were back. Jukes released the woman, whose face regained some color as she scurried back to her spot on one of the benches.

"Give it to me," Eric ordered.

"Sure, Eric. Whatever you say." Jukes handed over a large-screened smartphone. It began to ring.

Eric pressed a button. "Clear off, or we start killing hostages... I don't care what you need... No. Get us a helicopter with a pilot. You have one hour."

He tossed the phone onto a wide pedestal holding a male bust. It slid across the surface and nearly fell.

"I can't see what they're doing from here," Jukes complained. "This only gives me the front of the museum and the interior. A view of a loading door, maybe. I can't tell what it is. They could come in, and we wouldn't know till too late."

"Outer door?" Eric asked. "What's going on there?"

Jukes rolled his eyes. "I just told you I can't see what's back there. All I can see is a metal door that looks like it rolls up."

Eric turned his attention to the hostages. "Who works here? Who knows the back way out?"

The hostages moaned or uttered little cries, but no one said a word.

"Look, you lot," Eric shouted. "We came in at closing time. Some of you work here. Speak up."

The cell phone began ringing again. With a curse, Eric picked it up. "Jukes, tie into the traffic cameras. We'll be able to see better where the coppers are." He pushed the button to answer the phone. "Why haven't you cleared off yet?"

He'd evidently turned on the speaker phone, because a soothing voice sounded from it. "Good morning. My name is Chief Inspector Tapley of Scotland Yard. What's your name?"

"You don't need to know our names. We're members of the Philosophy of Bedlam, that's all you need to remember. You can call me E, though, if it makes you feel better."

"Well, E, you know that Great Britain does not negotiate with terrorists, right? So we have a bit of a pickle."

"We're not terrorists. Bugger off."

"You know we can't do that as long as you're holding hostages. I need to know they're all right."

"The government has become complacent and corrupt," Eric said, ignoring him. "The only way to regain balance is through anarchy. Bring the government to its knees."

"You've attacked three other museums over the past six months. Might I inquire why?"

Eric tightened his grip on the phone. "They're symbols of the ridiculous path our society has taken. We can't feed our hungry, but we can pay millions of pounds for some paint slapped on a canvas? Where are your priorities?"

"I understand your position. And I know you don't want to hurt those people. We can talk more about it after you let them walk out."

Eric laughed. "And my arse smells like rainbows. You're part of the problem. You and the other coppers. Big yaps full of teeth and ignorance."

"I think we're getting a little off track, here. I'd like to get this sorted as quickly as possible, obviously. Why don't you release the hostages, and we can sit down and talk about your philosophy?"

"Not going to happen."

"Can you at least tell me about the people in there with you? Are they well?"

"They're fine. Where's our helicopter?"

"We need more time for that. It's not as easy as—"

"It's as easy as you make it," Eric said. "Things might get rough if you dick about. We'll let the hostages go when we're safe."

"That's going to be har—"

"Dumb shite." Eric pressed the button to end the call. He shrugged out of his jacket and tossed it against a wall. "We do what we came to do."

"And what is that, precisely?" Trevor asked. "They could storm the place at any time. We need to find that back door."

"In my own bloody time, damn it."

A chill crawled down Trevor's spine.

"JAM YOUR HYPE, mate. Calm the fuck down." Trevor balanced his assault rifle across his shoulders.

Shelby shivered. In place of his normal cultured voice, harsh tones ripped from his throat. What the hell was going on?

She'd easily identified the leader. Probably late twenties or early thirties, dark hair brushing his collar, tanned skin, the shadow of a beard darkening his jaw. Once he'd taken off his leather jacket, the scar running from below his ear and down his neck became visible. Good-looking in a rough way. He swept the museum with eyes burning with some sort of fervor. She pressed her hands together. In her experience, zealots were the most dangerous human beings.

"I don't want to die." The girl next to Shelby started to cry again.

"We're not going to die," she said, wishing she believed her own words. She clamped her mouth closed as the tattooed woman glared in her direction, unable to control her body's trembling or the slight quaver in her voice.

She never thought she'd see Trevor again. She'd visited him once after their single night of passion, when he'd been wounded while stopping a group of terrorists from detonating a deadly cocktail of poisonous gases and killing hundreds of people. The visit had been short, and she'd left him, broken and bleeding, in the hospital on the airbase in Ma'ar ye zhad, Azakistan. Her requested transfer to London had nothing to do with the fact that he lived here. No, she'd fallen in love with London from the time she'd done a study abroad with the University of Alabama. When she'd come here, it was not with the hope of running into him. Absolutely not.

Although, if they had run into one another, it ought to have been under better circumstances than her cowering near a pedestal with Floyd Panderson and the sobbing girl.

Trevor seemed to tower over the hostages as he paced back and forth. Something was wrong with this picture. What the hell was Trevor doing with these terrorists? He served in Her Majesty's Armed Forces, for God's sake. In the Special Air Service. What had happened?

Get a grip. You're an analyst. Analyze.

Special operations forces around the world worked clandestine operations. He hadn't gone rogue. He'd gone undercover.

The five terrorists and he made a rough-looking group. He glowered and shouted and waved an automatic rifle around without ever really pointing it at them.

He'd seen her. She knew that. But other than a slight tightening of his eyes, he'd betrayed no recognition. So neither did she. Until she learned his mission, the safest course for both of them was to pretend not to know one another.

But she couldn't stop her eyes from following him. Surely he would find a way to free them.

Time crawled by. The police phone remained silent. The skinny, jittery teenager with the low Mohawk and big ears worked on his laptop, but she couldn't see what he was doing. Eric, rifle slung over his shoulder, popped the magazine on his pistol and slammed it home again, over and over. Trevor paced. Fay leaned against a wall cradling her assault rifle in her arms, looking like she would relish shooting a hostage or two.

The redhead and Crawley returned, pushing an elderly woman in front of them.

"No one here but this old bat," Nathan said. "Found her in the bleeding loo pulling up her knickers."

"Put her with the others."

Crawley shoved the woman toward the other hostages. Shelby leapt to her feet, catching the woman as she stumbled, and helped her to the ground.

"Who are they?" the woman whispered. "What do they want?"

"Shh!" Floyd motioned for her to be quiet.

"Maybe we can reason with them. Get them to let us go." The elderly woman squeezed the young girl's hand, giving her a reassuring smile. Floyd remained silent, crouched behind her.

"Somehow I don't think they're open to reason at the moment," Shelby said. She swallowed several times. Floyd was the curator of the museum. He knew his stuff when it came to art, but Shelby found him less and less charismatic the longer he hid behind her. She shifted on her knees, wishing she'd worn something more practical than the close-fitting red-lace dress that hit her mid-thigh and the matching strappy platform heels.

"Trev, you and Fay collect the wallets and mobiles. You lot!" Eric shouted. "Anyone who doesn't hand over a wallet and a mobile will be shot. Get me?"

Trevor made a beeline for her. Their eyes met. He gave an almost infinitesimal shake of his head. She dipped hers once in response, but both remained silent as Shelby handed over her wallet and cell phone. Eyes narrowed, he glanced around before flipping open the wallet and slipping her United Nations identification from its plastic sleeve. As he made to pocket it, Fay joined him.

"What's that?" She snatched it from his hand. "UN? What are you, some sort of ambassador?"

Trevor closed his eyes briefly.

"No, nothing like that." Shelby shook her head for emphasis. "I mostly just read things."

Fay snorted. "Read things? What kind of job is that? What do you read?"

"Just . . . just reports, mostly."

The leader came over. "What's the problem?"

Fay gave him a look akin to hero worship. "We have a celebrity, Eric. This bitch works for the UN. She *reads* things."

Trevor snorted. "She's nothing. A cog in a wheel. We have more important things to worry about."

Eric ignored Trevor and took Shelby's ID, looking it over carefully. "What do you read?"

"Reports on sweatshop conditions in third-world countries. Substandard materials in clothing manufacturing. Child labor."

Eric took her wallet from Trevor, who looked like he wanted to protest, and looked through it. "Driving license, travel card for the Tube, credit cards. Starbucks gold card? You must drink a lot of coffee."

"She's nothing," Trevor said again. "A nobody."

The police cell phone began to ring again. With a grunt of irritation, Eric shoved her wallet into his pocket.

"Check her phone," he ordered Trevor. "Her contacts. See who she's called. Fay, check the rest of them. See if we got an ambassador in here."

Trevor spent a few seconds pretending to look through her phone, glancing at her once or twice. Finally, he dropped the phone into the leg pocket of his cargo pants. Eric shut off the police phone without answering it. Fay went around the room, covered by the redhead, who wore an insolent half-smile.

"We still have the bomb. All I do is bung it, an' Bob's yer uncle," Crawley said with a giggle. His high-pitched, almost feminine voice froze Shelby's innards. She'd never heard insanity before, but she knew she was hearing it now. The man's bald head gleamed in the careful museum lighting, but the hair around the rest of his head bristled in all directions. Low brows pulled down over a round face highlighted small piggish eyes, made more so by the glasses he wore. Several days' growth of beard marred his scruffy goatee. Of them all, he looked the most dangerous. His statement caused more cries and moans.

"Shut your yaps!" growled Eric, running two fingers along his scar. "Crawley, do it."

Crawley stabbed his fingers inside the knuckled hilt of the knife at his waist and drew it from its sheath. The blade had a drop point and gatorback ridges, and showed signs of hard use. He started toward *Memories of the Gods*. Floyd sucked in a breath.

"This one?"

Eric slung his rifle over one shoulder and pulled a notebook from his pants pocket. He flipped through it, then pointed. "Yeah. And the one over there, too."

Crawley padded over to Shamblet's *Autumn in Madrid*. The trees in the painting swirled with vibrant colors and shapes, leading the eye downward to a sea ablaze with fire, earth covered with water, and clouds frozen in place, icicles dripping. The painting was a masterpiece of surrealism, painted in 1932 by one of the geniuses of the period. Crawley didn't pause to admire the brush-strokes, though, as he stabbed at the edges of the canvas with the point of his knife and sawed downward.

"Stop it!" Shelby rose on shaking legs. "What are you doing?"

"Shelby, get down!" Floyd reached up a hand and pulled at her wrist. The girl beside them whimpered and threw her arms over her head.

Trevor whipped around to glare at her, warning clear in his eyes. "Shut up," he growled, his voice deep and rough.

Don't put yourself in their path, he meant. Don't let them notice you above any other hostage. The knowledge that he was trying to protect her warmed her.

She had not treated him well during their last encounter. He'd been lying in a hospital bed, shot, with broken wrist and ribs. Hurt and disillusioned that he'd deserted her bed in the middle of the night to go to another woman, she'd ruthlessly squashed her budding feelings. Blurting out the first self-preserving thing she could think of, she'd told him to forget about their unforgettable night, to pretend that magic had never happened, and to forget about her as well. She'd walked out of his hospital room, and had gone on a date with a Marine embassy guard.

It had been a shitty thing to do. She lived with the shame of her actions every day. But she hadn't been able to face the strength of her growing feelings in the face of his betrayal. She'd thought she'd put it all into perspective—had almost convinced herself it hadn't meant a thing—until she caught sight of him. Right now, he acted like a growling, snapping dog. That didn't change her memories one whit.

Eric broke the frame of *Autumn in Madrid* and searched through the wreckage as Crawley grasped the much larger frame of *Memories of the Gods* and lifted it off its hanging hooks. An alarm immediately began to shriek.

Fay put her hands over her ears. "Shut it off!"

Jukes began tapping commands into his laptop. In about fifteen seconds, the high-pitched noise cut off.

"What do you intend to do after you mutilate that painting?" Shelby heard herself ask. At least her voice had stopped shaking. Although she was a political analyst, not a politician, she had acquired enough knowledge over the years to speak in a soothing yet authoritative voice. Establish a human connection. She'd used the technique often in her job to diffuse tension in a difficult situation. "If you go out the loading bay door, you can escape, right?"

Museums always had discreet entrances where pieces of art were delivered or shipped elsewhere for special exhibits. Shelby chanced a sideways glance at Floyd. He would know. He remained silent, staring at the floor.

"You stupid cow," snarled the bald man. "We're going to make every last one of you motherfuckers worm food, unless those bleeding wankers out there clear off."

"Do you think they will?" she asked, keeping her voice noncommittal. *Please, please let Scotland Yard pull back and let these men leave.*

"They will," Eric said, "unless they want fourteen dead bodies in this museum. Sit the fuck down."

She obeyed, kneeling next to Floyd. She mouthed, "Tell them where the loading bay is."

He shook his head frantically, motioning her to be quiet. "Shh. They'll hear you."

She understood his desire to escape the attention of the gunmen. Still, if it got them to leave . . .

Eric came to loom over Shelby's terrified little group and pinned Shelby with a glare. "I change my mind. You seem to have the biggest mouth around here. Do you know where the back door is?"

Shelby shook her head, not daring to look at Floyd. "I don't know."

Trevor strode over. "I'll get it out of her, if she knows anything."

"Why you?" asked Crawley. He pulled his knife and let it dangle from one finger, then twirled it in a lazy circle. "I bet I could get it faster."

Both craziness and malevolence burned in his eyes. Shelby sent a wide-eyed plea in Trevor's direction.

His lip curled as he watched Crawley. "We want answers. We don't want her catatonic."

Crawley bared his teeth in what was supposed to be a smile, she thought. "Ain it don't hurt she's a looker. Is your John Thomas aching for a bit of rumpy pumpy?"

Chapter Six

TREVOR GRITTED HIS teeth hard. He tightened his hand on the grip of his Heckler & Koch short-barreled carbine until his knuckles turned white. He wanted to kill Crawley. The man was a serial killer. A sadist, pure and simple.

And he'd seen Shelby. In no universe was that acceptable. Once Crawley set his sights on something—or someone—nothing swayed him.

The dislike was mutual. The man was as mean as a rabid wolverine, but he had good survival instincts. Crawley didn't trust Trevor. And nor should he, despite Eric Koller's endorsement.

"Eric, leash your pet," he snapped. He ended the argument by reaching down and grabbing Shelby's upper arm, hauling her to her feet.

Eric's brows snapped down. "Crawley, get the hostages together. We're moving out into the lobby."

There was an office behind the ticket counter; Trevor dragged Shelby into the lobby, staying well back from the windows, and crossed behind the counter to the office. He might have been too forceful in opening the door, because Shelby flinched as it banged back against the wall. He shoved her inside and kicked the door shut with a foot.

Free of his grasp, she took several steps before turning to face him.

"What the hell are you doing here?" he rasped.

"I came to see the surrealist exhibit—"

"No. What are you doing in London?" He balled his fists in frustration. "Why aren't you still in Azakistan?"

Instead of answering, she shook her head, puzzlement in her eyes. "Trevor, what's going on here? Who are these men?"

"They're dangerous. I need to get you out of here." Even as he spoke, he sorted through his limited options. He could simply unlock the doors and push the hostages out—but he'd lose Eric's trust, and that was the only thing keeping him in the group. And the probability was high that Fay or Crawley might simply shoot him in the back.

Never in a century could he have envisioned putting Shelby in harm's way, however unintentionally. Conflict and frustration roiled inside him. He had a mission to complete, and that required him to keep Eric believing he was one of them. But he'd be damned if he'd let any of the anarchists lay a finger on any of the hostages.

Especially Shelby.

Was it simply because he knew her, while the others were strangers? Or because they'd once been lovers. His pleasurable memories of that night were tainted by the clock in the face she'd given him less than a week later while he lay in a hospital bed. Still, life often buggered up one's emotions. As a career soldier, he needed to put his feelings aside and accomplish what he'd been sent to do.

"All of us, Trevor. There are fourteen of us." Stubbornness flashed in her eyes. "Not just me."

He raked a hand through his shaggy hair. "I know."

"What's your mission?"

She sounded remarkably calm. He couldn't help the smile tugging at his mouth. "You mean you don't believe I've become an anarchist?"

She shot him a *don't be stupid* look. "We don't have a lot of time."

He sobered. No, they didn't. "Tell me what you know about the hostages. The museum. Anything."

She didn't hesitate. "The curator is the man who was next to me. Floyd Panderson. He'll know where the other exits are. Museums have protected access points to load and unload artwork. Three of the hostages are docents. I don't know anyone else. They were just here to enjoy the exhibit."

"Will we be able to exit that way? The protected area? Do you know?"

"I only know about my experiences as docent at the Huntsville Museum of Art. Huntsville was small, so we were also trained to move and pack objects. In a museum this size, there will be a dedicated packing room. Special exhibits like this one require a lot of coordination and care. The transportation area will be close; art pieces need to be moved as little as possible. Probably a double door for larger pieces, and it will be below ground if possible, to keep the artwork at as stable a temperature as possible. Also, for insurance purposes, there will be cameras both in the packing room and in the loading area."

"Okay, good. What's Panderson like?"

Shelby snorted her disgust. "Well, he was hiding behind me. That should tell you something."

"Are you . . . close?" The question stuck in his craw. He had no claim over Shelby. She'd made that crystal clear when she visited him in the hospital. The memory still churned in his gut.

She wouldn't meet his eyes. "We've been dating."

Are you sleeping together? He clamped his mouth closed over the question.

Both heard the sounds from the lobby at the same time. Eric was moving the hostages. They had mere moments before he would send someone to check on them. Shelby evidently came to the same conclusion.

"Hurry," she whispered. She backed herself up against the desk. "Come here."

He came close, frowning down at her. "What are you—"

"Undo your pants." She reached for his web belt, jerking him close and tearing at the button fly, then tugged his shirt from the waistband.

What the devil was she doing? Before he could say anything, she reached up, tearing the lace sleeve of her dress at the shoulder. "Put your hands in my hair. Mess it up."

"What the hell?"

She wrapped her legs around his waist and yanked him in. He ended up leaning over her, eye to eye, his hands braced on either side of her head, his pelvis snugged tight against her heat. For half a second, he lost himself in her amber eyes, which had haunted his dreams for almost a year. Then reality snapped him back. Shelby had both hands in her hair, messing the neat waves.

"Shelby, this is dangerous—"

"It's what they expect. You know it as well as I do."

The door opened, and suddenly Shelby was pushing at his shoulders, crying and struggling to get away. Trevor stood so abruptly his watch snagged in the lace at her shoulder, further tearing it. He glared at Crawley.

"Get out."

Crawley leered at Shelby, who swung her legs off the desk and put it between herself and the two men. Trevor stepped in front of Crawley, blocking his view of her. "I said scram."

Crawley's laugh was nasty. His hand dropped to the hilt of his knife. "You don't order me, Willoughby. If that's even your proper name. You being with Eric in Northern Ireland doesn't mean shit to me."

Trevor shrugged, boredom in his face. "You're a gnat's ass in my world, Crawley. Now get the hell out of here before I squash you."

Crawley sneered. "Eric wants you out front. Bring your bit of fluff out with the others." He turned and left.

Shelby and Trevor looked at one another.

"I'm sorry." Shelby tried to arrange her dress so that it didn't look quite so torn, and rubbed her eyes, effectively smearing her makeup.

"I am, too," Trevor said. "I'll get you all out of this, Shel. You have my word."

She gave him a tired smile. "What can I do to help?"

Her courage awed him. She'd deliberately made it look as though he'd attacked her, knowing it would explain away their alone time. Knowing that it would bring her to the anarchist's attention, but she hadn't hesitated. He felt a swell of pride for her.

"Keep out of Crawley's way," he said. "He likes to use that knife of his, and not to slit open box tops."

"All right. Let's get back out there." She settled the matter by turning and walking toward the door.

"Shelby, wait." In seconds, he was around the desk and heading her off. "Come out behind me. Look cowed."

"Not a hard stretch," she mumbled.

He grabbed her hand, pulling her with him until he cleared the office doorway, then gave a sharp yank. She stumbled after him. He shoved her. It hadn't been rough, but she played it up, staggering away from him. "Get back with the others."

In the time they'd been talking, Eric had moved the hostages into the main lobby. They now stood, shoulder to shoulder, across the front panes of glass. The asshole was using them as human shields.

The anarchists stood toward the back of the room, near the ticket desk.

"Well?" Eric turned to him expectantly. "Did she know anything?"

"Yeah. She says there will be a loading area of some sort, underground or under cover in some way for when they ship paintings and stuff back and forth."

"Shit, I already knew that." Jukes showed the fine-tuned contempt of a teenager. He swiveled his laptop around to show Trevor a series of cameras. "It's here. I just don't know where *here* is."

Trevor shook his head. "She doesn't know anything else."

That would satisfy Jukes. No way was he bringing another hostage, Panderson, to Eric's attention unless it was absolutely necessary. "Send Nathan and Crawley to search. This is a small museum."

At least it would get the odious little man out of his sight.

SHELBY TOOK HER place in line next to Floyd. He wouldn't meet her gaze. It was obvious what he thought. What they all thought, because that's what she'd intended them to think. Their glances were pitying, skittering away before meeting her eyes. It was no more or less than she'd expected, but she'd needed to talk to Trevor, to try to figure out what was going on.

As soon as she'd been alone with him in the office, her fear had evaporated.

"Have they said anything about what they want?" she asked softly.

Floyd shook his head. "They mutilated *Memories of the Gods*. Tore it to shreds. Bastards."

"Are they looking for something?"

He gave her an impatient sideways look. "I don't know."

Shelby looked out the window, at the confusion of police cars and uniforms swarming the parking lot. "Tell them where the loading bay is. They'll leave."

"Not necessarily. They might just shoot us. Or me, for trying to help them." Floyd hesitated. "That man. The one who . . . you know. He's taken an interest in you. Maybe you could, you know, be nicer to him. Use your influence to get us out of here."

Shelby gaped at him. Had he just suggested . . . "Are you insane?" she hissed. Memories swamped her. Instead of Floyd by her side, it was Bruce. "Make them want you, Shel. Use what you got to get us where we want to be." Where he'd wanted to be. His not-so-subtle hints to seduce important politicians had ended their relationship, such as it had been. What Floyd now suggested was equally monstrous.

"I'm not insane," he said, turning to look at her. "If it can get us out alive? Why would you even hesitate?"

That she had ever considered him charming burned like bile in her gut. They'd only been dating a few weeks, but this was the first time she'd seen the real Floyd Panderson.

"Why don't you tell them where the loading bay is?" she hissed, anger leaking through so that her voice came out louder than she intended. "That will get them out of here just as quick."

His face whitened, the coward. She barely suppressed a snort of disgust.

Behind them, Eric shouted, "Who works here? First person to tell me where the back door is goes free."

At that, Floyd half turned, looking over his shoulder.

"You," Eric shouted, advancing on him. "You work here?"

"I do." Floyd finished the turn, chin lifting. "Look, I agree with your philosophy. The government is corrupt and ineffectual. We need to free ourselves through a major societal shake-up. We're on the same side here."

Eric laughed. "You think we're even in the same hemisphere? You look like a politician, you in your fancy suit. Gobshite."

"But I can tell you where the back door is—"

"Won't help," Jukes interrupted him. "Cops are already back there. We can't get out that way."

Eric swore.

Floyd wiped his palms on his trousers. "I'm the curator of this museum. There's . . . another way out. A private door that's not on the blueprints. I had it installed last year."

Eric came over to him, eyes narrowed in suspicion. "Where is it, then?"

Floyd squared his shoulders. "I'll take you to it, if you keep your word you'll release me."

Shelby jerked around to stare at him. Release him? Not all of them? The rat bastard!

Eric grinned, the odd light in his eyes making her nervous. Like Crawley, there was something wrong in his eyes. "Done. You take us there, you go free."

"We should leave the rest of 'em behind," Trevor said, voice carrying clearly. "Slow us way down. We don't need that kind of baggage."

"Sure, Trev. As long as we can get out without the coppers knowing." Eric gave Floyd a hard look. "But if you're jerking my cock, I'll put a bullet in your brain."

"It's there, I promise you," Floyd said. "It's in the basement, at the end of the hall just before you—"

"Save yer breath. You're going to show me, aren't you?"

Floyd stepped toward him. "Follow me, then."

The five anarchists and Trevor walked with him across the floor. Before they exited the lobby, Fay swung around. "What if it's a trap? We can't leave these people here. We need to keep them between us and the coppers."

Eric stopped and thought about it for a long moment. "You're right. We don't know what we're heading into. All right, you lot! Line up in front of us. Leave your damned purses."

The hostages were slow to obey until Fay swung her rifle in their direction. "Move, you godless dogs!" she screamed.

Thirteen scurried to obey. The fourteenth, the elderly woman whom they'd found in the bathroom, lagged behind as she took slow, painful steps.

"Move, it, grandma," Fay snarled.

"Leave her," Trevor said. "She can't keep up."

Eric waved an irritated hand. "Fine. The old biddy can stay. Tie her up."

Fay swung her firearm around. "Why don't I just shoot her?"

The woman straightened her spine and lifted her chin, looking Eric full in the face. His gaze faltered. He swung around to glare at Fay instead. "She's just an old woman. No threat. Tie her up and leave her. The rest of you, move it!"

The unlikely group trailed Floyd as he took them to the very back of the museum, to a double-wide door set discreetly into the wall. He took out a key ring and unlocked it. Eric shoved him through first, then Shelby and the rest of the hostages.

This private area of the museum consisted of a wide landing, a freight elevator in front of them, and a set of stairs off to the left. Several doors to the right were evenly spaced along a hall. The walls were plain cement, with no adornments of any kind.

"Now where to?" Eric asked.

"Turn left and go down the stairs."

Pushing and prodding, Eric got the whole group down the stairs, which ended in a huge room filled with crates, padding, and long tables.

"This is the packing room," Floyd said. "When artwork is brought in or sent out, this is where we handle it. It's all very carefully orchestrated. The delivery door is there." He pointed to the other end, where a rolling metal door stood closed and padlocked.

Eric glanced around with zero interest. "Where's this magical door, then?"

Floyd pointed to the right. "My private office is along that wall. Around the corner is an access door that leads into the service tunnels. I had a door installed at the end. It comes out on Chipper Lane."

Nathan's brows wrinkled. "Why the hell would you put a door in access tunnels?"

Floyd's face reddened. He half glanced at Shelby without quite meeting her eyes. "There are times I prefer a discreet means of entry and egress."

Crawley barked out a laugh and went to the office door, pushing it open and peering inside. "That's one hell of a couch in there, divvy. Does your wife know you got this posh shag-room down here? That her picture on the desk?"

Shelby stared at Floyd in shock. "You're married?" she blurted out.

Floyd didn't answer, which was answer enough for her.

"You motherfucker!"

Several of the anarchists laughed. Trevor glared death at the man.

Nathan, covering the rest of the hostages with his semiautomatic rifle, barked impatiently. "The longer we wait, the more likely the coppers are to find a way in. Let's move."

"Enough of this bullshit. Is the door locked?" Eric asked.

Floyd nodded.

"Give me the key."

Floyd made to slip a key from the ring he carried, but Eric snatched the entire thing from him. "Which one?"

Floyd pointed to an all-black key. "The deal was I go free once I showed you."

Crawley swaggered over to the curator, getting nose to nose with him. "That's right, you arsehole."

Floyd's face registered shock, then slackened. Slowly, he slid to the floor, clutching his gut, blooding spilling over his fingers. Shelby screamed, echoed by several other hostages. She'd never even seen the knife come out of the sheath.

She ran to him, throwing herself to her knees and pressing

her hands over the wound. Glaring up at Crawley, she said, "You didn't have to stab him."

Crawley ran his tongue up the side of his knife. Floyd's blood dripped onto his lips. He licked them clean and gave the peculiar cackle she'd come to hate in the past hour. "He's free, right? I gave him what he wanted."

Trevor came to crouch on the other side of the body. He checked Floyd's eyes by lifting his lids and pressed his fingers to the carotid artery. "He's still alive. We need to call the London Ambulance Service."

"Why?" Crawley shrugged. "He'll be dead soon enough."

Eric looked down at Trevor, rifle balanced against one shoulder. His face was pale, and he seemed to be having trouble swallowing. "Have the years thinned your blood, Trev?"

Trevor stood abruptly, pinning the other man with a stone-cold look that would have most men shitting their pants. Eric stepped back, a defensive look on his face.

"There's a difference between casualties of war when we were with the IRA, and this." His hand swept out, encompassing all of them. "This was completely unnecessary. Cold-blooded, just for the sheer pleasure of it. That's not who we are. We're anarchists, not killers."

Eric rubbed a shaking hand across his hair. "Crawley, keep that knife sheathed. Got me?"

Crawley's grin lacked even the smallest hint of regret. "Sure, boss. Whatever you say."

Shelby stood, hands shaking so badly she pressed them together to stop. "He needs a doctor."

Eric ignored her, gesturing to the rest of his crew. "Get everyone together. Into the tunnels we go."

"Are you joking? Leave them here," Trevor said.

Eric got a stubborn look on his face. "Until we're clear, they go where we go. Now, move out."

He opened the access door and peered inside. "No lights." Glancing from side to side, he found and flipped a lever. Small yellow emergency lights winked on, giving faint illumination.

Eric grabbed Shelby's upper arm, pushing her into the tunnel first. Trevor placed himself beside her. Nathan and Fay shouted and threatened, and soon the small access tunnel was crowded with sweating bodies. The scent of fear hung heavy in the small space. They moved slowly down the hall, past pipes and spigots and God knew what else. Visibility was poor.

Shelby had a bad feeling about what would happen when they reached the end. If Crawley had stabbed Floyd with so little provocation, what would happen when the hostages were no longer needed? Would they all be gunned down? She didn't dare look at Trevor. Did he have a plan?

Placing a hand on the bare cement, she used it to help her maneuver in the dim light. She got too close to the wall, though, and her knee collided with something solid. The pain was excruciating. Crying out, she stopped, hands going to her knee.

Jukes pushed her from behind. "Keep walking," he said, trying to sound tough. But he wasn't as hardened as the others, and it came out as more of a plea.

She twisted her head to look at him. "I can't. My knee."

He hesitated.

"I'll watch her," Trevor said. "Bugger off."

Jukes sneered, but moved on.

Shelby leaned against the wall, tears welling in her eyes as she waited for the pain to subside. It seemed to take forever. Trevor squatted on his haunches, hands circling her knee as he felt carefully. The other hostages and Bedlamites passed them one by one, until Fay pulled even with them.

"What's the problem?" she snarled. "Bitch don't wanna get her pretty dress dirty?"

"She cracked her knee pretty hard. I don't think she can walk."

Fay swung the muzzle of her assault rifle toward Shelby, bringing it up to her shoulder. "Then she stays here. With a bullet in her brain."

Shelby straightened. The pain levels were slowly coming down. "No," she said hastily. "I can walk."

She never saw Trevor move. One minute he crouched beside her. In the next, he had wrenched the rifle from Fay and clocked her in the temple with it. Fay stumbled, banged into the wall, and slumped to the concrete.

Shelby gaped at the prone figure. Shaking, she bent and pressed two fingers to the tattooed woman's neck. "She's alive."

Trevor grunted. "Turn around and leg it back the way we came."

Shelby rose, eyes widening as fear coursed through her. "I can't leave the others."

Trevor bit off a curse. "You can't help them. Neither can I, any more. Run!"

He gave her a hard push back the way they'd come. Still she hesitated. "What about you?" she whispered.

His gaze softened. "I'll be right behind you."

Chapter Seven

AFTER ANOTHER AGONIZING moment, she nodded, turned, and sprinted back the way they'd come. After a few seconds, Trevor shouted.

"She's making a run for it. I'll go get her."

Crawley pushed and shoved his way through the mass of bodies until he reached Trevor and Fay, lying on the ground.

"What the fuck happened?"

"She found a rock," Trevor said. "Pretended to hurt her knee."

Crawley started back down the access tunnel. "She won't get far. I'll drag her back by her fucking cunt hair."

Trevor put a hand out, effectively stopping the other man. "No one goes but me."

Crawley let out a raucous laugh. "Thinking with your John Thomas again, Willoughby? Just make sure you catch back up. Hate to leave you behind for the coppers to snatch."

Without replying, Trevor turned and sprinted after Shelby. They reached the packing room at the same time.

"Now what?" she gasped. She knelt next to Floyd, who rolled his head to look at her.

"I don't want to die," he said.

Trevor ran to the rolling door. "It's padlocked."

"Wait!" Shelby called. "They're out there. The police. Jukes said they were at the back door. What if . . . what if they shoot you?"

Trevor gave her a grim look, but hesitated. "I'll surrender."

Shelby gazed up at him, wide-eyed. "That will blow your cover, won't it. Your mission will be a bust."

Trevor sighed, looking up at the ceiling. "I'll figure something out."

"No." Shelby couldn't believe what she was saying. "Use me as a hostage."

A surprised laugh burst from Trevor. "No."

"Then . . . then . . . isn't there another way out of here?"

Trevor looked down at her. "Don't you know?"

She narrowed her eyes. "I've never been down here."

"I saw another door, just as we went into the access corridor," Trevor said.

"Where do you suppose it goes? Floyd, do you know?"

"Get me out of here."

"Floyd," she said. "Unless we find a way out of here, we can't get a paramedic in here to save you. So do you know where that door leads, or not?"

"Old . . . steam tunnels, I think. Don't . . . leave me here to die."

She patted his shoulder. "Sooner I get out, sooner you get medical help. Just hold on, all right?"

He shivered, going into shock.

Trevor pulled a small leather packet out of his back pocket, and went to work on the lock, which gave way only grudgingly. It took some muscle to get the door to swing open. It creaked loudly.

"We need to move. Fay'll be awake and telling them I knocked her out."

"Oh, no! I didn't think of that. Won't that compromise your mission, too?"

"Let's worry about one problem at a time." He felt around inside until he found a switch and flipped it. Eerie blue lights flickered on. "Let's go."

Floyd groaned behind them, but Trevor spared only one look at him before pushing Shelby into the dimness. He pulled the door shut after them and turned the lock. "That'll hold them for a while." He moved swiftly down this new tunnel, ducking his head to keep from banging it against the ceiling, eyeing the pipes all around them. "Steam pipes. That's how they used to warm buildings, back before central air. There's going to be some sort of an exit."

They moved as fast as they could, given the poor lighting. Dust and cobwebs hung in the air, which was thin and musty smelling. In about a hundred yards, the tunnel curved around to the right. A few more yards down, and they both saw it at the same time.

"Manhole," Shelby whispered.

Trevor reached up to the wheel, pulling hard to get the old mechanism to work. At last, it clicked, and he tugged it open.

"No fresh air," he said, disappointed. "I wonder where this goes, then."

He gripped the edges of the hole and lifted himself up, then reached down a hand for Shelby. She gripped his palm tightly, and he lifted her through. He couldn't help a spark of pride flickering somewhere deep inside him. She was calm, strong, and capable.

He would protect her, whatever the cost.

Pulling a small penlight from his back pocket, he used it to chase back some of the shadows around them. This tunnel was even smaller than the last, and both ended up crouching as they made their way through. Unlike the others, this access path was littered with rubble. Rocks, chunks of wood, old pipe fittings. Footing was treacherous, and he kept a hand on Shelby's elbow to help guide her.

He stopped several times to let them rest. "You're doing great," he said.

Shelby rubbed her knee. "So what are you really doing with that group of lunatics?"

"An apt name," he said. "They call themselves the Philosophy of Bedlam. They consider themselves to be a force for change to bring down a corrupt and ineffectual government."

"So, what? Their goal is to create chaos? Just that? No ideology, no philosophical mandates?"

"That sums it up neatly. They purport to believe that undermining the foundation of our civilized exterior will allow our true chaotic selves to emerge. That if all humans were permitted to do exactly what they wanted to, with no societal restrictions, humanity would bloom into something greater than the sum of its parts."

Shelby sucked in a breath. "But that's insane. There'd be anarchy."

Trevor dipped his head. "Quite so."

She massaged her knee again. It had begun to swell, but there was nothing he could do about it right now.

"And your mission was to . . . disband them?" she guessed.

"Not exactly. My mission was to discover the names of the

members of the Bedlamites, but to find the brains behind the movement as well. Eric Koller is the cell leader, though truth be told I have nothing to support the idea that there's more than one cell. Eric is the one with the scar, which he got in Northern Ireland during the Troubles. He's smart, but the entire anarchist movement is being pushed from above him. I need to find out who and why." He held out a hand, which she took. "We need to keep moving."

She followed him as he moved. "What did you find out? And what happened upstairs? Why were you in the museum in the first place?"

Trevor sighed. "It's too long a story to get into now. For the moment, our priority has to be getting you somewhere safe. I'll check in with my superiors, and we'll reassess at that time."

"Do you have a cell phone?"

"A burner phone for this mission. Not a single bar, I'm afraid. We're too far below ground and the walls are too thick."

The tunnel curved again. This time, as they turned the corner, they saw a ladder bolted to the wall on their right. Trevor inspected it, and the cover above them. They heard faint sounds of water dripping. Trevor tested the ladder, then put his weight on it.

"Sturdy enough." He pushed against the barrier, which lifted with difficulty, and poked his head through. "Another tunnel. This one's a bit taller. We won't be crouching, at least."

Shelby followed him up the ladder, and he closed the cover behind them. Water dripped down the walls and pooled on the floor. At least, he hoped it was only water they were walking through. The smell suggested otherwise.

The light seemed brighter here as well, but that could just be because they'd gotten used to the dimness. As they walked, the gloom around them lightened. They reached another built-in ladder. This one ended in a manhole cover. Light and shadow chased across it.

"We're under a street," he said. He checked his phone. "Two bars."

"Call—"

"I am." Trevor dialed nine-nine-nine. "A man's been stabbed inside the August Museum and needs immediate medical aid. He's in the basement packing room."

She heard the voice on the other end start to say something, but Trevor disconnected and pocketed the phone.

"Let me go first and see where we are," he said.

He had to put some muscle into it to lift the heavy cover, shoving it back just far enough to risk a quick peek. Shelby radiated anxiety below him.

"The main traffic is just west of us," he reported. "I'll tell you when to go. When you're out, turn right immediately and go into the alley."

"Okay," she whispered. "Or . . . or we could just stay here."

He understood. The tunnels gave a false sense of security. Soon they would have to face the reality that would come when they crawled out of their dark hole.

He, at least, was a wanted fugitive. At best, the authorities would assume she was his hostage. At worst, they would brand her a terrorist, too.

Trevor pushed the cover halfway open and climbed out. He immediately turned and offered her a hand. She climbed out next to him and took it, letting him steady her for the last few steps. He squeezed her hand reassuringly.

"Go."

ONLY AS THE daylight hit them did Shelby notice that he still had the semiautomatic rifle slung over his shoulder, muzzle down.

"Get rid of it," she hissed.

"Agreed." He lowered it into the manhole and slung the strap over the edge of the ladder. Kneeling, he pushed at the cover, which barely moved. He shoved and strained until it covered most of the hole. "Damned thing must weight two hundred pounds. Staying here is riskier than leaving this thing ajar. We could be seen at any moment."

He took purposeful steps toward the alley, grabbing her hand and pulling them halfway down its fifty-foot length before slowing and looking around. It was narrow, dank, and putrid with the stench of human waste. One man, dog on his chest, sat inside a cardboard box. The dog woofed halfheartedly. Several other bodies lay wrapped in blankets or sleeping bags against the wall. The hopelessness and despair of these men and women—one with a child—was palpable.

Shelby instinctively reached for her purse, only to stop, momentarily confused as her hand encountered nothing but air. Trevor slid his wallet free and placed a few bills in the mother's hand.

"Your ID," Shelby said. "What if you'd been searched?"

Trevor smiled briefly. "They'd've found a driving license for Trevor Willoughby and a couple hundred quid. I've done this before."

Her face reddened. "Of course. Sorry."

They kept pushing through. About two-thirds of the way down, a figure, then two more, materialized from a doorway. In their late teens to early twenties, also homeless by the look of their clothes and the unpleasant aroma of body odor, these three were predators, pure and simple. Shelby made no protest when Trevor pushed her behind him.

"I don't know you." The one in the middle, dead-eyed and whip thin, spoke first. "I don't like strangers in my alleyway."

"We're just passing through, lads," Trevor said, holding his hands open and away from his body. "We don't want trouble."

"Too bad, mate. This place belongs to us. You can't be going through our home spot without paying the toll."

Trevor glanced over his shoulder. Shelby half turned, and sure enough a fourth young man was taking the money from the woman's hand. A fifth held a metal pipe.

"You have two choices, mate," the skinny one said. "There's five of us and two of you. Hand over your cash, and we're done. Or we take it, and you and your pretty bird here get hurt."

Trevor stiffened. "You only have one choice, *mate*. Leave now, and I'll let you live."

The other two men laughed, but the leader's eyes grew deadly. He drew a butterfly knife from his front pants pocket and flipped it open. To Shelby's untrained eyes, he seemed alarmingly comfortable with the weapon.

Don't panic. She swiveled her head, trying to watch all of them at the same time.

"Stay behind me." Trevor didn't stop walking. Shelby obeyed, heart racing. Why wasn't he backing away? Shouldn't they try to run?

When he was within ten feet of the gang, the one to Trevor's front left charged him, fist raised, swinging at Trevor's jaw. Trevor swiveled toward him, bringing both arms up and slamming them into the boy's forearm, effectively stopping the punch, then rammed his elbow into the boy's jaw. Grabbing the boy by the neck and bicep, he yanked him in close as he brought a knee up into his stomach, then punched him twice in the face before shoving him hard toward the leader. They collided; the boy sat down hard as the leader stumbled back.

Trevor grabbed Shelby's upper arm and pushed her with him so that they were both beyond the gang. "Go to the other end. Wait there."

Instead of running with her, he turned back to the pack. Shelby took several steps away, but then stopped. No way was she leaving him to face five attackers by himself.

In the short time they'd maneuvered around the first three, the other two reached the group. The one with the pipe in his right hand swung it overhand toward Trevor's head. Trevor threw his left arm up, blocking the attack by smacking his forearm against the man's wrist. He looped his right arm under Pipe's and seized his own left wrist as he stepped close and jerked his arms inward, forcing Pipe's elbow into Trevor's chest. Trevor yanked his arms down hard, hearing Pipe's shoulder ligaments pop, then punched his kidneys several times before letting him sag to the ground. Pipe clutched his shredded shoulder, screaming obscenities.

"You fucking son of a bitch!" The first boy got up, wiping blood from his nose with the sleeve of his shirt, and lunged for Shelby. He grabbed her upper arms, pulling her in front of him.

Her training as a Foreign Service Officer included an annual self-defense course for women. Mustering her courage, she raked her shoe's sharp heel down his leg, wrenching herself free as he cried out in pain. Curling her fingers back, she brought her palm up, striking him as hard as she could under his jaw, then grabbed his shirt at the neck and drove her knee up into his groin. And again and again, until he sagged to the ground, clutching himself and moaning. She backed up several steps.

The other boy hit Trevor from the side, fist slamming into Trevor's jaw and temple. Trevor ducked away. Before she realized what she was doing, she darted forward, hitting the man from the side and pummeling him with her fists. He turned and clocked her in the face. She fell hard, ears ringing.

With a roar of rage, Trevor seized her attacker and swung him around, fist cocked back, just as the leader's hand arced down. The knife bit deeply into the boy's shoulder. He screamed.

"Shelby!"

"I'm okay," she croaked, managing to get to her hands and knees.

The man on the right reached for something at the small of his back.

"Gun!" she gasped.

Trevor leapt past the first two to the third just as the man brought a revolver out from under his shirt. The man yelled something she couldn't make out. Moving almost too fast for her to see, Trevor drove his left palm into the man's right shoulder and smashed his fist into the man's face. The man ignored the blood spurting from his nose, managing to bring the revolver up to Trevor's midsection. Trevor knocked the gun aside, capturing the man's wrist and continuing to swivel his own body so he cradled the man's arm under his own. Scooping the man's wrist and turning, he brought the gun up and tore it from the man's hand, reversing it so it was now pointed at him. The man froze, gaping.

Trevor pressed forward half an inch so that the barrel of the revolver pressed into the man's eye. He leaned forward until his mouth nearly touched the other man's.

"Run."

The man held his shaking hands up in a gesture of surrender, taking several shaky steps back. "No trouble, mate, yeah? We're gone."

One of the boys put his arm around the bleeding leader's shoulder, lifting him to his feet and supporting him. The one who'd grabbed Shelby groaned as he struggled upright, clutching himself. All five backed away and shuffled to the mouth of the alley, disappearing around the corner.

The entire fight had taken less than a minute.

Trevor watched for a moment more, then came to squat next to her. She gave up trying to get to her feet. He gripped her chin lightly and turned her head, making a soft sound as he traced the puffy part of her face where she'd been hit.

"Bastard."

Shelby couldn't seem to drag enough air into her lungs. "Knife. Knife. He had a knife."

Trevor put both hands on her cheeks. "Shelby. It's over. They're gone. Breathe."

She was embarrassed at the tears clogging her vision. "Are you . . . hurt?"

Trevor grinned at that, the cocky grin she remembered so well from Azakistan. "From those juvenile delinquents? You don't think much of my training, if you think they posed any kind of a threat."

His *I can take on the world and win* attitude radiated from him. But anyone could fall to the stab of a knife. Shelby couldn't stop Floyd's face from swimming to the fore. "Do you think your friends left the museum? Do you think Floyd is still alive?"

Something shuttered in Trevor's face. He still thought she

and Floyd were together. Now wasn't the time for that particular conversation, though. "We need to get somewhere safe. Regroup. Wash."

They were both filthy, with blood and dirt and God knew what else stuck to their clothing. Walking to the opposite end of the alley, Shelby paused while Trevor peered out. "We're not far enough from the museum. It's about a block down, but all the focus is away from us." He batted ineffectually at the grime and sweat. "If we move naturally, we should be okay. There are a lot of gawkers."

Shelby gathered her nerve. "Okay. I'm ready."

They stepped into the street. She couldn't help the glance toward the museum and its mass of emergency vehicles. She couldn't see much. The street was clogged with people watching the drama unfold, and the news crews had arrived to add their chaos to the mix.

Trevor grabbed her hand, and they walked casually, hand in hand, down the street and away.

"Why don't you turn yourself in now? Get it all straightened out?"

Trevor pulled out his cell phone. "I'm putting you somewhere safe first. There's no telling what Eric or Crawley might do. I need to get an update."

They reached the end of the street and turned left. Trevor cursed. "Pardon my language. There are too many people ringing or taking videos. All phone circuits are busy. All right. Let's grab a taxi."

"And go where?"

"Your flat," he said at once. "We can get cleaned up and you can pack a hold-all. I'll take you to safety, and then go back to HQ."

The taxis passing took one look at their disheveled appearance and passed them by. Finally, a minicab slowed beside them. He looked almost as rumpled and dirty as they did. "Show me some cash."

Trevor pulled out his wallet and held up a few bills. The driver nodded, and they climbed into the back seat.

"We've had a load of building material dumped on us," Trevor said. "We're not sleeping rough, though I agree we look like tramps."

The driver grunted acknowledgment. "Where to, then?"

Shelby gave him her address, then settled back in the seat. Trevor remained tense beside her. It took almost thirty minutes of driving through the congested London traffic before they reached Shelby's flat. Trevor paid the man, adding a generous tip. The building housing her London flat, though much nicer than her apartment building in Azakistan had been, had no elevator. They walked up the three flights of stairs to her door.

"I don't have my key," she said, realization dawning. "No keys, no ID, no money."

"Not a problem," Trevor said. He pulled out a leather tool kit, and in a short time, her locks clicked open.

"If I knew it was that easy to pick a lock, I'd've gotten five or six deadbolts."

Trevor opened her door and gestured for her to enter first, ever the gentleman. She made a beeline for the kitchen, and grabbed two bottles of water. They both drank thirstily.

"Why don't you shower first," she suggested. "I'll pack a bag."

"Brilliant. After I check your knee."

"What? It's fine."

"It's not. Don't think I haven't noticed you limping, though I appreciate your willingness to soldier on."

She also wanted to see how bad the damage was. Pulling out a kitchen chair, she sat down, unbuckling her strappy platform heels and kicking them off. Her dress hit her mid-thigh, so it was simple for Trevor to crouch in front of her and probe her knee. She sucked in a breath.

"Hurts, does it?"

"A little."

"Well, the good news is I don't think you've done any damage. When you hit your knee just in the right place, it hurts like a moth . . . er, it hurts a lot. Your knee is swollen and you'll have one hell of a bruise, but you'll be fine."

"Thank you."

Before she could think too much about how good it felt to have his hands on her, if only to check her knee, she fetched some towels and put them on the back of the toilet. "You'll have to use my soap and shampoo," she said. "You're going to end up smelling like a grapefruit."

He smiled at her. "I don't mind. I remember your scent very well."

Her breath whooshed out. Had he really just brought that up? His face closed down, as though he, too, realized the poor timing. Without another word, he went into the bathroom and closed the door in her face. She waited until the water turned on and the shower curtain screeched back before she went into the living room and turned on the television. She flipped to BBC One. As expected, they were covering the hostage crisis.

"Specialist Firearms Officers stormed the museum after negotiations with the terrorists failed to yield results. The suspected terrorists, members of anarchist group Philosophy of Bedlam, fled on foot and evaded police blockades. Twelve of the fourteen hostages were released unharmed. One hostage was apparently shot; he was rushed to St. Baldwin's Hospital, where his condition remains closely guarded. Specialist Crime and Operations Chief Superintendent Stuart Anton reported that the fourteenth hostage, a woman whose name has not yet been released to the public, is believed to have been taken with the anarchists when they fled. It is unclear whether the woman is actually a hostage, or is herself a member of the Philosophy of Bedlam. We will, of course, keep you updated on this serious situation. Anthony, back to you."

They'd gotten the detail about Floyd's stabbing wrong, but it was possible he might still be alive. She breathed a silent prayer. He might be a rat bastard, a married man who'd pressured her for weeks to sleep with him, but he didn't deserve to die in the basement of his own museum, stabbed in the gut by a madman.

The shower stopped. Shelby couldn't stop the shiver of awareness that Trevor stood, naked and dripping wet, less than twenty feet from her. Memories of his amazing physique swamped her. For a moment, she couldn't breathe. Running her hands across soft skin over steel muscle had been a treasure. Feeling him holding her while they writhed together . . . her breathing deepened and moisture gathered at her core. The bathroom door opened and he stepped out.

He'd evidently used her razor to scrape the scruff from his jaw and had slicked back his long dark hair. Water droplets winked at her from his broad shoulders. One slid down past his ear. She traced the movement with her eyes, then dropped her gaze to his trim waist and narrow hips, hidden by the towel. His skin was bronzed by the sun, testament to his long hours of training and multiple missions.

His chest deepened, and she realized he'd inhaled, and jerked her gaze back up to his. His attention was laser-like, dark slashing brows over intense brown eyes centered on her lips. His own parted on a sigh. His eyes swam with remembered passion and heat and a craving she could see pouring from him.

He turned away abruptly, one big hand holding the towel. "It's your turn in the shower."

His curt tone made it clear he wasn't interested in a repeat performance. Shelby couldn't blame him. Did she want to make love to him under the stinging spray of hot water? Yes, if she were going to be honest. But it would be the worst idea to become involved with him again. He lived a dangerous, unpredictable life. And he'd left her bed to go to another woman. That still hurt, all these months later. Still, if her life thus far had instilled anything in her, it was the knowledge that men were rarely reliable.

"Thank you." She walked past him down the hallway, entered the bathroom, and closed the door in his face, much as he had to her earlier. She turned the water as hot as she could stand it, using her loofah to scrub herself clean. Of the dust and grime, the terror of being held hostage, the betrayal of finding out Floyd was married. Of his stabbing, of rekindled feelings toward Trevor she thought she'd crushed. When she finally finished, there was not a drop of hot water left, and her skin was red from scrubbing.

Wrapping a towel around her torso and another around her wet hair, she peeked out the door to make sure Trevor wasn't nearby, then darted across the hall to her bedroom. She changed quickly into fresh clothes, dried her hair, and reapplied her makeup. Finally ready, she went back out into the living room. Trevor wasn't there, but enticing smells wafted from the kitchen. She followed her nose.

Trevor stood at the stove, feet planted wide, clad in nothing but that stupid towel as he stirred something in a saucepan. Watching him, half naked and cooking, caused hot flashes to travel from her hair to her toes and back again. He looked like a wet dream.

As though sensing her presence, he half turned, looking over his shoulder. "I thought as long as we had a minute or two, I'd create sustenance."

It was such an odd way of saying he was cooking a meal that she laughed. She tried to ignore him, but all that golden skin made her ache for something she'd lost. Maybe never had.

"It's just an omelet," he said, turning back to the stove.

She couldn't help the way her eyes tracked down his spine to the white towel. To say the day had been stressful would be a major understatement. Taken hostage, finding out the man she'd been dating already had a wife and might even now be dying, then banging around in dark tunnels. Her knee ached, though the swelling had gone down. The last thing on her mind was sex. But intimacy? A warm, reassuring hug?

Well, she'd made her bed when she'd rejected him.

"You keep looking at me like that, and I'll have to do something about it."

She gasped. "Your back is turned. How did you know I was . . . um . . ."

"I feel your eyes on me. I like it that you look at me that way. Shelby—"

Suddenly, she did not want to hear what he had to say. All the reasons she should never have gotten involved with him were still there. Nothing had changed. It had been one night, and it couldn't happen again.

"I'm sorry," she said, "that I didn't think to put your clothes in the washer before I showered. I'll do it now."

He nodded, still without turning around. "I have a small pouch under the inner sole of my shoe with some cash in it. Would you get that while you're at it?"

"Sure."

As she tossed his clothes into the machine, she couldn't help but bring his shirt to her nose. Beneath the grime, it smelled of him. Delicious and sinful. There was no underwear. Did he go commando?

By the time she returned, he'd put two plates on the coffee table and was flipping through the channels.

"The news said earlier they escaped, but left the hostages behind," she offered. "They're all safe. There was no update on Floyd."

He didn't respond. She sat as far from him on the sofa as she could and dug into her omelet. It was delicious. "So you can cook, too?"

"Too?" He looked at her, his expression unreadable. "As well as what?"

Make love like a dream. She bit the words back. Trevor had proven to be the same as any other man. They liked to fuck. Sometimes they liked to fuck enough to marry. They didn't stay faithful for long, though. Inviting a physical relationship with Trevor would just lead to heartache and betrayal.

"Fight," she said instead. "Go undercover. Be an SAS officer."

"Hmm."

He looked like he was about to say more when adverts ended and the news came back on. The newscasters gave a recap of the hostage situation, now resolved but for the disappearance of one of the hostages. Her picture flashed up on the screen, and the commentator gave a few brief lines about her background and job with the State Department.

"One of the hostages, Floyd Panderson, curator of the August Gallery, where the standoff occurred earlier today, is in critical but stable condition at St. Baldwin's Hospital near Soho. He is expected to make a full recovery."

"Oh, I'm so glad he's not dead," she whispered.

"Not dead is different from still alive." Trevor's voice was soft and questioning.

She met his eyes. "Not that it's any of your business, but we'd only been dating for a few weeks. I didn't know he was married."

"Obviously. Did you"—he stopped to clear his throat—"visit his office?"

She pressed her lips together and released them; a nervous gesture. "No. He was pushing to become intimate. But I wasn't ready."

"Good." This time, his voice was even softer.

"Trevor, I'm not sleeping with you, either," she said baldly.

His eyes narrowed and his mouth flattened. "I didn't suggest you should. After last time, it's not worth it to me."

That stung. "Look, I owe you an apology. What I did in the hospital . . . it was a shitty thing to do, and I feel terrible about it. But you did, in point of fact, leave my side to go to another woman. I met her at the hospital. Christina Madison."

Trevor nodded slowly. "Who has just become engaged to Gabriel Morgan from the Combat Applications Group."

He meant Delta Force. "Are you . . . okay?"

"Natch. Why wouldn't I be?"

"I mean, with her, you know. Being with another man."

Trevor frowned. "I did not go to her for any romantic reason whatsoever. She'd been arrested by a local imam. She needed a male to pretend to be a family member to pay a fine and promise to beat her and lock her in her room. Does any of that sound romantic to you?"

"Only if you're into that." Shelby scratched the corner of her eye with her forefinger. "You and she were involved prior to that, though. I heard things."

"Speculation and innuendo. My team and I were able to give assistance during an operation gone wrong. There was never anything more to it than that."

So the rumors were inaccurate. That shouldn't surprise her. "You have the reputation as quite the womanizer, though," she said. "Is that gossip, too?"

Trevor simply looked at her, puzzled. "No. I'm a healthy man with healthy appetites. The issue is my profession. The life of a soldier is hard enough, with deployments and separations, missing birthdays and holidays. Multiply that by a hundred, and you come close to the life of an operator."

"What do you mean? Because it's dangerous?"

"Yes, but it's more than that. I deploy at a moment's notice. Often, I either don't have the time, or am not permitted, to call and let someone know I'm going. Not parents, not a wife and children, not a girlfriend. How would you feel if the man you're dating simply disappeared, for weeks or months at a time? My chosen career makes relationships challenging."

"But the right woman—"

"Is incredibly rare to find. I love what I do. I won't give it up. But it makes it damnably difficult to form a serious relationship. I'm not home often enough to build a solid foundation as a couple, nor to meet a woman strong enough to be a partner, to understand

and accept that part of my life. Divorce rates amongst special operations forces are extremely high, and there's a reason for it."

Her brows pulled down. "So you sleep around. It's easier that way?"

"The women I sleep with are looking for the same thing as I am. No strings, no commitments. Just healthy, recreational sex. Given those parameters, it's virtually impossible not to get a reputation. But it's equally difficult to find a woman who wants that."

He stood and took their dishes into the kitchen. She followed him in. He rinsed the plates and put them on the drying rack, then turned to her, hurt in his eyes.

"The irony of life is that the first woman I've had romantic feelings for in years dumped me while I was lying in a hospital bed."

Chapter Eight

BLAM. SO HE's said it. Put it out there for her to see, examine, pierce him with her indifference. He waited for her reply.

Her mouth opened and closed, but no sound came out. Finally, she croaked, "You have romantic feelings for me?"

"Had," he corrected, hardening his heart. "And yes. Why does that surprise you?"

She took a deep breath, then another. "You'd have to know how I was raised, and we don't have the time for that. I'm afraid we've stayed here too long as it is. Eric has my driver's license. They know where I live."

He knew that. He'd been mentally calculating how much time they had before Eric either called him or came after him. And he would. He didn't take betrayal lightly.

"He's got to get organized first. That probably means a visit to my mystery man in the limousine."

"Who?"

"You've sussed out my mission, I presume. Get tight with the Bedlamites and stop them from bombing any more museums.

The difficulty is they're not acting alone. I know Eric Koller from years ago. I did some undercover work in Northern Ireland when I first joined the SAS, during Operation Banner and beyond. Eric Koller was IRA, and we fought together, as far as he's concerned. Now, years later, MI-5 tells me he's the head of a home-grown anarchist group calling themselves the Philosophy of Bedlam, who have bombed three art galleries in and around London. MI-5 and the SAS have mounted a task force to find and arrest them. I'm the man on the inside."

Shelby gave a bitter laugh. "And I'm the one who screwed up your mission. Great."

"No," he said at once. "I made the choice. I take the blame."

"Huh." Clearly, she did not believe him.

"There's more to this than meets the eye, Shel. I'm posing as a sympathizer with my own reasons for wanting to hurt our government. I offered my services as an explosives expert. But for that incentive, I insisted on meeting the brains behind the group. We agreed to meet at Canary Wharf. Limo pulls up, man gets out of the front passenger seat. I know right off this isn't the brains. The man in charge rides in the back of the limo; the flunkies ride in front. So either Mr. Smith isn't there, or he's in the back, watching.

"The flunky talks to me about the anarchist movement, the whys and wherefores, the ideology. But this guy . . . there's something off about him. Expensive, tailored suit. Shined shoes. Nothing about him says he's a disaffected youth. Or that he has a grudge. Or that he's anything other than successful. So I told him flat out to stop wasting my time."

"What happened?"

"Turns out he's an accountant. I was invited into the back of the limo to meet Mr. Smith."

"Mr. Smith, huh?" Shelby said. "Clearly, this is no garden-variety terrorist."

"No. Definitely not. I convinced him I wanted in on the action. After I joined Eric's group, I barely managed to text the time of the attack to the task force. They tracked the GPS in my phone and called the police. We were supposed to go in after the museum closed, but the police very nearly beat us there. Hence the standoff."

Shelby blew out a breath. "Those paintings were priceless."

"Go pack a hold-all," Trevor ordered. "You're right; we need to leave. I'll just put my dirty clothes back on."

"It won't take them long to dry, and you're too conspicuous walking around with just a towel."

He laughed.

Following her as she headed down to her bedroom, he watched her pull out a hold-all. She threw in some clothing, toiletries, and her laptop. At the last minute, she went into her firebox and pulled out some cash and a Beretta.

"Here," she said, stretching her arm out to him. "For home protection. It's not much, but it's better than nothing."

"Bloody brilliant." He took it, automatically popping the magazine and locking the slide back. There was no round in the chamber. He corrected that, then flipped up the external safety and laid it on her bed.

"Oh, my God!" The horror in Shelby's voice had him whirling around. She'd stopped midway to putting the cash into her pocket and was staring, eyes glued to the telly, and he saw with dismay that his face filled the screen.

"This man is wanted for questioning in the hostage standoff that occurred this morning at the August Museum of Modern Art in Soho. He is a person of interest in the investigation, possibly even one of the terrorists himself. He should be considered armed and dangerous. If you see him, please do not approach him. Scotland Yard has set up a special hotline. If you see this man or know of his whereabouts, call . . ."

Trevor tuned out the commentator. The photo was slightly blurry, obviously taken with a cell phone, but there was no doubt it was him.

"How did they get your picture?"

"I don't know." His voice was tight. "Someone got a pic before the mobiles were confiscated; it's the only explanation. This changes things."

"Now you need to turn yourself in. Or contact your superiors."

"Yes. I'll do that, but first I have to put you somewhere safe. Do you have a friend you can stay with for a few days?"

Shelby met his gaze steadily. "I'm not leaving you to flounder through this alone. I can help."

Brows pulled down and confusion in his eyes, he asked, "Why would you want to help me?"

"Trevor, for God's sake. I don't hate you. I don't like what you did, but I understand now why you did it. So can we just move past that, please? I know I hurt you in Ma'ar ye zhad, but you said yourself you don't feel anything for me any more. Let me help."

He hesitated, but finally nodded. "Let's get moving, then. We'll go to a hotel."

His clothes were still damp when he pulled them on and shoved the Beretta into the waist of his cargo pants, leaving the T-shirt untucked to hide it. He took Shelby's hold-all.

"Last chance," he warned her.

"Come on." She ended the discussion by heading toward her front door. He beat her there before she could open it.

"Let me look first. Stay here."

She slowed, allowing him in front of her. He cracked the door and checked the hallway. Clear.

They moved down the hall to the stairwell that would lead them out of the building. Empty. They descended, but he placed an arm in front of her, tacitly warning her not to approach the door to the flats. He placed himself to one side, risking several looks through the glass panes to check outside.

A white Volkswagen Polo pulled in across the street.

"Bloody hell," he said. "We have visitors."

Shelby tried to peer around him, but he shifted so that his body blocked her view. "Who?"

"Nathan and Fay. Bedlamites. Is there a back way out?"

"Not really," she said. "There's a tiny patio and some grass. And a ten-foot privacy fence. Even then, all it gets you to is someone else's backyard."

"Shite. They'd head us off a long time before we made it out. Go back upstairs. Wait there, yeah?"

She trotted back up the stairs. He positioned himself to one side of the door, reaching out long fingers to click the lock open. In a few moments, he heard footsteps coming up the walkway. The doorknob began to move.

"It's open," Fay whispered. "Stupid bitch."

"Shut up and open it," Nathan said.

The door cracked open, then eased inward. Just as Fay made to enter, Trevor clamped a hand onto her arm, yanking her forward. She slammed into the door. He immediately let go, pushing her backward and into Nathan. Fay tumbled down the three steps, but Nathan leapt over her and barreled through the door. Trevor used his momentum, pushing the man past him and into the wall. Two short jabs to the kidneys. Nathan grunted, but turned and threw a punch that Trevor slipped. Nathan catapulted himself into Trevor. The table onto which residents dropped junk mail broke apart as two heavy male bodies fell onto it.

Trevor was back on his feet in an instant. He saw Nathan draw a Smith & Wesson small-frame revolver from his coat pocket.

"Gun!" Shelby shouted.

Trevor crossed his wrists, catching the short barrel in one palm and Nathan's fingers in the other. He twisted the revolver free while yanking the fingers up. Nathan screamed as two of them broke. Trevor reversed his arm's trajectory, nailing Nathan on the temple with the grip. Nathan slid to the floor, unconscious.

"Come on."

Shelby ran down the stairs.

Trevor grabbed her hand and hustle her out the door. "Where's the Tube from here?"

"Finsbury Park. This way."

They ran down the street, bypassing curious stares until they reached the mouth of the London Underground. There, Trevor forced them to slow, fingers still entwined with hers. He paid for two day passes. They inserted their tickets into the turnstile. The paddles opened, and they went through.

Once they reached the platform, they faded to the back of the crush of people. Even late on a Saturday night, crowds swirled around them.

"Thank God they switched up the Victoria line to be twenty-four hours."

"The constancy of movement and the crush of people will help conceal us," Trevor said quietly. "But there's the danger of being tracked via camera or seen by local police. London is called the Most Surveilled City in the World for a reason."

"Let's head into Central London. This is how I go every day."

"Okay, good. Just follow my lead, okay?" Trevor turned to scrutinize her face. "Are you all right?"

Her laugh sounded forced. "I'm good. You?"

"Right as rain." Of course she wasn't all right. It had been a silly question. This type of situation was as foreign to her as it was normal for him. Still, she was being a trooper.

"I know where the cops patrol in the Underground," she said, and seemed gratified by his look of surprise.

"How?"

This time, her laugh was more genuine. "Training in counter surveillance is mandatory for all Foreign Service Officers. I took a refresher in Azakistan before I left, just for fun. The Tube ride is pretty long and can get boring, and I can't work because what I do is mostly classified. So I started playing a game with myself on the Tube, and in and around Central London. I know numerous ways from around the city to get to the United Nations' UK building, which stops and at what times the Tubes are the most crowded, and I even trained myself to notice cameras and patrols."

He stared at her, dumbfounded. She crossed her arms defensively.

"What?"

A slow smile spread across his face. "That's grand."

For the next hour, Shelby used her knowledge and Trevor's expertise on a surveillance-avoidance run. They switched cars in the Tube frequently, avoiding security, hopping from line to line until Trevor announced himself satisfied.

"Even if Jukes picked us up at your townhouse, I doubt he was able to follow us. He's a good hacker, one of the best I've seen. He'll find us eventually, no doubt, but we've bought ourselves some time."

He felt the pull of fatigue. The museum already seemed a lifetime ago, and it was barely after midnight. If he felt it, Shelby must also feel drained of all energy. Adrenal letdown.

"Now what?" she asked.

"For now, let's find a hotel. I could use a coffee. We'll figure out our next step from there."

Chapter Nine

TREVOR TOOK THEM to a rundown hotel in Tower Hamlets. The place was beastly. The last time it had been painted was, no doubt, circa never. The window in the front door was cracked. The name of the horror was tacked to the office roof, listing to one side. An equally foul tavern had attached itself along one wall. He made a pained sound.

"It's okay," Shelby whispered. "I know why we're here. We have very little money, and you're a wanted fugitive. We don't have much choice."

He gave a sharp nod. Under normal circumstances, he'd never let her come within a hundred kilometers of a dump like this. Him, sure. He'd been in worse places. But Shelby deserved roses and champagne, silk sheets and soft towels. Now, though—He mentally hitched up his trousers and pushed through the front door.

The tiny reception area wasn't any better than the exterior. A couple of yellow plastic chairs rested on a suspiciously brown carpet. The scent of mildew hit him hard. Behind him, Shelby coughed.

"Help ya, mate?" The balding man with the horrendous comb-over let his chair rock back onto all four legs and folded his newspaper.

"A room. A clean one, if you have it."

The man hawked out something that was probably supposed to be a laugh, showing his chipped front tooth. He fished an old-fashioned metal key out from under the counter and held it up.

"A pony an hour, mate."

Trevor narrowed his eyes. "Twenty-five pounds? That's outrageous. I'll give you seventy-five for the night, and be damned lucky for it."

The man shrugged, turning his attention to Shelby. He leered at her, licking his lips. "If ye like. Looks like she'll ride you ragged. Aya, come on down here when you're finished with this blighter. I could use a roll meself."

Shelby made a choked sound; but then, to his astonishment, she snugged herself into his side, reaching up to caress his hair. "Like you said, luv, I intend to ride him ragged."

The man guffawed. "Room two-oh-four, then, ducks."

They walked up the flight of stairs, which creaked and groaned. When they reached their door, Trevor unlocked it and pushed it open, peering in uneasily. Shelby walked in, so he followed.

To say the room was outdated would be kind. At least the mildew smell was absent, but the bedspread had clearly seen better days and had several cigarette burns on one side. The telly was ancient, an old tube model. Despite the June warmth, heat wafted from the wall unit. Shelby made a beeline for it and turned the heater off.

Trevor dropped Shelby's hold-all onto the floor and pulled back the comforter and bedding to check the mattress for bedbugs, which were mercifully absent.

"I guess it could be more godawful," Shelby said, looking around with her hands on her hips. "Don't know how, but things can always get worse."

He grimaced. He'd slept in trenches half filled with mud that looked better than this rubbish heap. He switched on the telly and changed the channel to BBC News. The commentator gravely updated viewers on the state of emergency declared in an Asian country after a devastating earthquake.

"Those poor people," she murmured. "It's heartbreaking."

"Yes."

"So what now?"

Instead of answering, he sat in one of the two Naugahyde chairs. Shelby perched on the edge of the second.

"Not even a desk. This really is a hotel where prostitutes take their tricks." Trevor felt a grin tugging at his lips. "You were great downstairs."

"Thanks. Apparently I can do skank if I need to. Seriously, though. What's the next step, Trevor?"

He scratched his chin. "We lay low for the next day or so. I need you to think where you could go to be safe. If possible, I rejoin the Bedlamites."

"Is that even an option?"

"Could be. Depends on a lot of factors." The odds were slim, but best keep that to himself. She already blamed herself for his mission going balls up.

Shelby's shoulders hunched as she ducked her head. "I'm really sorry."

"Don't be. Things were going to get cocked up either way."

"Because of the hostages?"

"Because of me." His grin flashed and vanished. "I threw a

spanner in the works, but someone jumped the gun. The police showed early. The plan was for us to arrive after the museum closed and all the visitors had gone."

Shelby's shoulders relaxed. "But what about finding Mr. Smith?"

He shook his head. "No one in the Bedlamite cell knows his real name. I know what he looks like. As soon as we get you sorted, I'll do a police sketch and start combing Interpol's criminal databases until I find him. You should get some rest."

"I'm not tired."

"Doubtful. It's nearly one in the morning, and you've had quite the active evening."

Shelby stretched, rotating her neck to loosen the muscles. "What about you?"

"I'm good to go."

Shelby shrugged, a frown pulling her face. "Fine."

As expected, she fell asleep almost as soon as her head hit the pillow. Trevor watched the rise and fall of her chest. What would have happened if Christina hadn't called him the night of the gala in Ma'ar ye zhad? If he hadn't answered his mobile, or had sent someone in his stead? Might their delicious romp have blossomed into something more?

He shook himself like a dog shedding water. What was done was done. No use speculating about the could haves and might haves.

He allowed himself to doze, coming fully alert at the buzz of his mobile. Shelby bolted upright, alarm in her eyes.

Fishing it out from his front pocket, he checked the screen. "It's Eric. That took longer than I expected."

Shelby tensed. "You expected—"

He pressed the green button. "'Bout time you rang."

"What the fuck happened?" Eric sounded pissed.

Trevor didn't hesitate. "It took me a while to catch up with the girl. And I had to avoid the coppers, didn't I?"

"A nobody, huh, Trev? Seems like she's somebody to you. Do you have her?"

Trevor made a disgusted snort. "I did have, but Nathan and Fay bollixed that up. She ran off."

"Fay says you attacked them. What the fuck, Trev?"

His voice grew an edge that wasn't feigned. "What was their mission, Eric? Looked to me like they were there to kill the girl. Maybe both of us."

Eric didn't answer, which was answer enough.

"You fucking prick." Any chance of rejoining the Bedlamites evaporated. Eric no longer trusted him.

"See, here's the thing," Eric said. "I don't know if you're thinking with your pecker or if you're just a coward."

Trevor growled. "You know I'm no coward. Northern Ireland proved that."

Eric blew a breath down the phone line. "You've changed, Trev. Gone soft. I don't think you have the stones for it any more."

"What's really going on here, Eric? What does Mr. Smith want? Destroying a couple of paintings, even bombing a few museums. That'll change nothing. Fill me in on what you're really doing for him."

"I'd've done it once we were clear of the coppers," Eric said. "But now . . . ? Why did you really contact me in London, in the first place?"

Neither was going to answer the others' question over the phone. "Meet me, then. Let's talk it through."

Eric hesitated. "We used to be mates. We have history. Fought together. For that, I'll tell you. Mr. Smith doesn't trust you. Wants you dead."

"Who is he really, Eric? Do you even know?"

"Goodbye, Trev."

The line went dead. With a growl, Trevor flung the phone across the room. It shattered against the wall. "Fuck."

Shelby clasped her hands together. "What did he say?"

"Nothing good. We need to leave. Jukes will have traced the phone."

Shelby didn't say a word as she picked up her bag.

Trevor headed for the window, which overlooked the pub instead of the street. It opened with minor protest. He sat backward on the sill, tilting his body through so he could grasp the outside top of the window. He swung himself out butt first, lowered himself to the bottom of the sill, and dropped the eight feet to the roof of the pub.

Shelby leaned out the window. "It's too far."

"It's not. Turn onto your stomach and crawl through feet first."

"Okay." She looked doubtful as she stuck one leg then the other out the window, then wriggled around until her stomach pressed into the sill.

"You're doing great. Now let yourself down with your hands as far as you can and drop. I'll catch you."

"How can you?" Her voice sounded shrill. "I'll squash you."

"Shelby," Trevor said, "you need to trust me. I won't let you get hurt."

They couldn't stay here. The Bedlamites were coming for them. Finally, *finally*, Shelby nodded, took a deep breath, and wriggled backward until she hung outside the window.

"Good. Now let go."

Eyes scrunched closed, she released the windowsill.

He closed his arms around her before she could touch the ground. With a gasp, she clutched his shoulders, body sagging in relief. He set her down.

"I did it," she said in wonder.

"I knew you could."

They stood on the pub's roof. Trevor went to the side away from the street and looked over the edge. "I'm going to lower you down, okay? You won't have more than a few feet to drop."

She joined him. "That concrete looks awfully far away to me."

He wasn't going to lie to her. "A bit farther, yes. We'll do it same as before. Lie on your stomach and dangle your feet over."

She did as instructed. "I don't want to do this."

"You'll be fine." If he had another option, he'd have taken it. This was the best way for them to leave the hotel unnoticed. Laying down next to her, he pushed himself back. "Wriggle off. I'll let you down as far as I can."

"I *really* don't want to do this. Why couldn't we just go out the front door?"

"One, do you really want that weasel seeing us leave? Because two, if he doesn't see us leave, he'll assume we're still inside. In the time it takes Eric to threaten or bribe him, we can be well away from here."

"Okay." Her voice was small. Shifting backward, she gripped the edge as tightly as she could, lowering herself until she hung from the edge. She closed her eyes.

Trevor hung next to her, holding on with one hand as he offered her the other. "Give me your hand."

She cracked open an eye. "You can't be serious. I'll yank you right off the roof."

"You won't. But you can't hang here forever. Didn't you climb trees as a child?"

"I had a tire swing that we'd use to jump into the river. Concrete isn't as soft as water. And it was a lifetime ago."

Trevor grabbed her hand. "I promise I won't drop you."

She squeaked and let go.

The muscles in his arms bunched as he absorbed her weight, lowering her even farther. As he'd promised, she was mere feet from the ground.

"Ready?"

She risked a glance down. "I don't have much choice."

He opened his fingers. She fell the last few feet, landing on her heels and immediately falling backward onto her butt. Trevor dropped down beside her, offering her a hand up.

"Are you hurt?"

She shook her head.

"Let's go, then."

He took her two streets over to another dive. This time, she unbuttoned her shirt almost all the way, showing her bra and the tops of her breasts. Sauntering up to the counter, she leaned against it, prepared to play her role.

The proprietor had leaned back in his chair, head tilted back and mouth open. A tiny rivulet of drool trailed its way into his beard. He snored softly.

"Working off a bender, I'd say," Trevor said. He reached around the desk and snagged a room key. "He won't even notice."

This hotel at least had an elevator, which they took to the third floor. The room itself was marginally better than the last one, with two full-sized beds, a guest chair, and a desk. Shelby flopped into the chair. Trevor stood next to the window, drapes closed but for a small sliver through which he peered. He paced to the bathroom and back several times before finally sitting on one of the beds.

"Finally. You were making me dizzy."

He grunted. "You should sleep."

"What about you?"

"I'm fine."

She made a rude sound. "Big tough he-man never needs food or sleep?"

He frowned. "Of course I do. Just not as much as a civilian."

She rose abruptly and went to the bed, kicking off her shoes and crawling between the sheets without hesitation. "Fine."

"The truth is, I could use a kip as well." He took her Beretta from his waist and set it on the bedside table within easy reach. Unlacing his combat boots, he set them next to the bed, stripped off his T-shirt, and lay down. "For the moment, we're as safe as I can make us."

It seemed to take a long time for her to relax. In contrast, Trevor slept almost instantly. For a while, she simply watched him. Finally, her eyes fluttered closed.

SHELBY SHIFTED IN her sleep, caught in a nightmare where Crawley used his huge knife to gut Floyd, then turned the knife on Trevor. Blood ran in rivers, getting onto her hands, clothing, even into her hair. She began to thrash.

"Shh. It's just a dream. You're safe."

She came awake with a cry, fighting against the bonds holding her.

"Shel. Shelby. It's me. You're safe."

It took her several moments to realize the bonds were simply

Trevor's strong arms around her. He was sitting on the edge of the bed holding her. She collapsed against him with a weak cry.

"I dreamt you were dead," she whispered against his chest. His bare chest.

"Us big tough he-men are hard to put down." A soft laugh rumbled through his chest.

"Trevor, that man. Crawley. He's deranged. You know that, right?"

"Is that what you were dreaming about? That Crawley killed me?"

She nodded against him.

"I know how dangerous he is, believe me. I will not let him near you." He started to shift away from her.

"Don't let go. Not yet." She couldn't bear it if he moved away from her right now. In his arms, she felt stronger. Safer.

He gathered her close. "My pleasure."

She realized she was smoothing her palm across his pecs. As she made to remove her hand, he reached up and captured it, pressing it over his heart. She tilted her head up to look at him. He had a small scar on his left temple, near the hairline. Reaching up a trembling hand, she traced her fingers over it. Suddenly, being held wasn't enough. She wanted what they'd shared in Ma'ar ye zhad. In her apartment, in her bed. No one had ever set her aflame like that. Nor satisfied her as he had. Her mouth dried as she drank in the sheer presence of him. She bit her lip, uncertain.

Trevor zeroed in on that small movement. His body tensed, but he didn't move. Shelby didn't know whether to be disappointed or relieved.

For long moments, neither of them stirred. Then, with a groan, Trevor closed the distance between them and settled his mouth on hers. Electricity shot through her body. Her lips parted of their own accord, blindly seeking deeper contact. Their tongues met, stroking softly, tenderly, making her shiver. She went limp as he brushed his lips across hers, light-headed from the crisp, woodsy scent of him. At last, he pulled back, looking into her eyes, a question in his.

A question she couldn't answer.

She cleared her throat, sitting up. He let his arms drop into his lap.

"What time is it?" The heavy drapes shrouded the room in perpetual gloom.

"Around nine-thirty, I think. We needed the rest."

She stood and grabbed her gym bag. "I'm going to shower and change. I'm sorry you don't have any clean clothes, but you can use my toothpaste and deodorant, at least."

He grinned. "Are you politely telling me that I stink?"

"No!" She put a hand to her mouth to stop the giggle trying to break free. "Well, okay, maybe a little bit."

He made a production of raising each arm to sniff his pits. "I've smelled worse."

A laugh escaped. "I'm just messing with you. You smell . . . good."

He stood abruptly and closed the distance between them. "Not now, because the timing is all wrong. But soon. We need to talk."

Before she could think how to respond, music started playing from one of Trevor's cargo pockets.

"What the devil?"

Her heart sank as she recognized Avril Lavigne's song, "Complicated." Trevor reached for his cargo pants and pulled her cell phone from his pocket.

"I forgot you still had my cell phone."

His brows snapped down as he examined her phone. “Bruce Clinton?”

She held out a hand that visibly trembled. Why on earth was her ex-fiancé calling her? She didn’t want to answer the phone, but she knew him. He’d keep calling until she broke down and answered. “I’ll, uh, take this in the hall.”

His eyes narrowed, but he finally handed her the phone. “It’s not safe. Stay inside.”

“Then . . . will you go outside?”

The ringing stopped.

“I’m not leaving you alone until we get this mess sorted.” By now, suspicion simmered in his eyes, and Shelby knew with a sinking heart he’d figured out who was on the other end of the phone. It began ringing again. Reluctantly, she pressed the green button. “Hello?”

“Well, this is a hell of a mess you’ve gotten yourself into.”

“What are you talking about?”

“Haven’t you seen the news?” Bruce used the voice she hated the most. The slightly condescending tone that implied she was a complete moron. “Turn on CNN.”

She found the remote and pressed the power button. The tubes flickered and glowed, finally turning on. She sucked in a breath. On the screen, right next to Trevor’s photo, was her own picture.

“Oh, my God,” she breathed.

The female anchor looked grave. “Authorities now believe that the missing hostage, State Department employee Shelby Gibson, might be part of the group who took hostages yesterday at the August Museum of Modern Art. Gibson disappeared along with the Philosophy of Bedlam, and was originally believed to have been taken against her will. She is now believed to be traveling with this man, Trevor Willoughby, who has a long history of violence dating back to IRA attacks in Northern Ireland in the late nineties."

The news anchor droned on, but Shelby tuned her out. "I can't believe this is happening."

"What the hell's going on, Shelby? Are you with that Willoughby character?"

She turned her back to Trevor and walked to the window, as though that could give her any sort of privacy. "Why are you calling me, Bruce?"

"I care about you." His voice dropped, becoming cajoling. "If you're in trouble, I want to help you out. It's been a year. Aren't you done punishing me?"

"I'm not punishing you. I broke up with you."

"The truth is, I haven't been the same since you left."

"I'm sorry you feel that way." And she was. A Bruce who didn't want her was far easier to deal with than a Bruce who did.

"Don't you miss me, too? Even a little bit? I know I was hard on you at times. I've gotten help, though. I'm not the same man I was."

She didn't answer. While she believed absolutely that people could change, she just didn't believe that Bruce had.

"Shelby? Are you there?"

"I'm here. What about Bunny, or whatever her name was?"

"Bitsy. That was over a long time ago. Baby, I want you back."

Shelby gripped the phone tighter. "What's the real agenda here, Bruce?"

"I'm just worried about you. Are you with Willoughby? You need to go to the police and turn yourself in. I can help you get everything straightened out. Let me get you a good lawyer. We can beat this thing together."

She sighed, massaging her temple with one hand. Her head hurt. "So let me read this conversation back to you. The police contacted you in the States, and you said you'd help them bring me in. If you succeed and I'm innocent, you're on the news as a savior. If you succeed and I'm actually a terrorist, you're on the news as the hero who brought me to justice. That about sum it up?"

He was silent. When he spoke again, his voice was full of hurt. "Why would you think that? Baby, I love you."

"You love what I do. You love the exposure it gave you. You used me, Bruce."

"I know I made mistakes. I'm a changed man since you left. You're the best thing that ever happened to me. Let me make it up to you."

Her head dropped. She didn't believe him for an instant. He'd lied to her so often in the past.

"Just think about it, okay? I don't need an answer now. I'll wait for you, baby, for as long as it takes. Let me make it up to you."

She should have said, "You're a lying sack of shit." Or maybe, "You'll wait till hell freezes over." But she knew Bruce. He would take that as a challenge. The fastest way to get rid of him was what came out of her mouth. "I'll think about it."

"Think hard, Shel. You're in a lot of trouble, and I can help you."

She hung up without answering. It would hold him off for now. She leaned her forehead against the wall.

"You'll think about it, huh? Think about what, Shelby?"

Chapter Ten

SHELBY TOOK IN a breath, steeled herself, and turned to meet Trevor's flinty gaze. "Nothing."

He made a disbelieving sound. "That nothing sounded like a whole lot of something. Who the hell is Bruce Clinton?"

His tone made her hackles rise. "He's nobody. Stop interrogating me."

Trevor grabbed his combat boots and yanked them on with jerky movements, then snatched his T-shirt from the floor. "A nobody who said nothing. Brilliant."

She took a step toward him, hand outstretched. "It was my ex-fiancé, which you've already figured out. He's offered to get me a lawyer. And yes, he said he wants to get back together, which you've also already figured out, so I don't know why you're asking me. I just said that to get rid of him."

He stopped with his T-shirt over his arms, ready to pull it over his head. "Does he know that?"

She dropped her arm. "It doesn't matter. He doesn't matter."

He yanked the T-shirt into place. "And what about me? Do I matter?"

She had no answer for him. He mattered, but she just wasn't prepared to be let down by another man.

"I can see the answer on your face. Message received, loud and clear."

Anger surged to the fore. "I don't see why you're acting like this. You're the one who said I was worthless."

Bent over his boots, he stilled, laces seemingly forgotten. "I said no such thing. I never would."

Humiliation suffused her face with red. "You said it wasn't worth it to—"

He interrupted her, voice grating against her eardrums. "Sleep with you. That's a far cry from saying you aren't worth anything. For fuck's sake, who did a number on you? Was it Bruce?"

Her spine stiffened. She was so not talking to him about Bruce. "What about you? Was Christina more worthy?"

"Bloody hell! For the last time—"

"I know." She raised her voice. "You didn't go from my bed to hers. So you've said. But you didn't come back, either. Or call. Or so much as leave a note."

He stared at her, not speaking. His face might have been granite. "Why are you in London, Shel?"

The question caught her off guard.

"Well?"

"It's a posting, like any other posting. I did a study abroad here my senior year of college. I took the General Course at the London School of Economics and Political Science at the University of London. I fell in love with the city back then, and I'm determined to live here permanently someday. If I leave the State Department."

He remained silent.

"What, did you think I moved here hoping to get back with you?" It was cruel, and she immediately felt ashamed.

"That would imply a relationship. We had a forgettable one-night stand. At least, that's what you asked me to do in the hospital. Forget it ever happened."

Her shoulders hunched. "Saying it was a mistake while you were lying in a hospital bed was beyond a crappy thing to do. I should have been throwing you a party, not . . . walking out on you."

"Again," he said, voice hard. "You made it clear you weren't interested in any kind of a relationship with me when you left my hospital room and went on a *date*."

Oh, shit. Hugo hadn't come into the room. How did Trevor know . . . ?

"Yes, I know you started seeing Gunnery Sergeant Bisantz. You were dressed to go out, and I heard a male voice in the corridor, outside my room. I put two and two together. It wasn't that hard."

"I'm sorry," she said again, heart aching. "Hugo is just a friend."

"Did you sleep with him? Bloody hell. Forget I asked that. It's not my concern."

"Trevor . . ."

"No." He cut an arm through the air. "No more. You run hot, then cold. I don't know what tune you're playing, but I'm done dancing."

The ache in her heart increased. Yet how could she blame him? He didn't understand her. Maybe she didn't understand herself.

"No comment? Right, then. Have your shower, and then we get to work."

SHELBY DUG HER laptop out of her hold-all and made use of the desk to set it up. Trevor stood to the side of the window, peering through the heavy drapes at the street below.

"Don't log in to work," he said. "Scotland Yard will have put a trace on your UN login credentials and official email."

"I'm not stupid," she said. "I know that."

He turned and leveled a long look at her. "Then what are you doing?"

"I don't know, exactly. Research?"

He turned back to the window, not bothering to ask what sort of research. Obviously, like him, she hated inaction. Nor did he want to dwell on their earlier conversation. What was going on inside that busy brain of hers? How the hell could she even consider getting back with a man who'd just used her for his own gain?

Her stomach growled, loudly enough that he heard.

"I'll get takeaway," Trevor said. "There's a Pret a Manger a few streets over. Lock the door behind me."

"All right. Be careful." She walked with him to the door.

Traffic was light on a Sunday morning. A few joggers, a couple holding hands, some pedestrians. Parked cars lined one side of the road; small shops with flats above them lined the other. A few transients huddled in a doorway, sleeping bags wrapped around them even in June. Incongruously, a colorful striped umbrella sat to one side. Trevor eyed them. If he were scoping out the area, he would pretend to be sleeping rough. But they stayed on the other side of the street, barely raising their eyes.

A man in spandex jogged down the next street and disappeared. Trevor quickened his pace. The sooner he finished his errands, the sooner he could return to Shelby. The odds were with them, but he knew how fast things could go sour. And, even as upset as he was, no way was he leaving her alone and unprotected.

He contemplated their limited options. Linking back up with the Bedlamites was out. He could turn himself in and let the government sort it. First things first, though. He needed to find a telephone and call in to his superiors.

He'd cocked up this mission. No one was going to be happy with him for his decision to rescue Shelby over his mission to stop the Bedlamites. He'd be accused of poor judgment, and he couldn't argue it. If he was going to salvage anything about this operation, it would have to be from the other end. Investigation instead of infiltration.

Handily enough, he saw a convenience store down the street. He could pick up a burner phone and maybe a razor. He pivoted abruptly.

Something whizzed by his ear and bit deeply into the wooden door beside him. The crack of a rifle followed a second later. Purely on instinct, he hit the ground, rolling twice before taking refuge behind the engine block of a Renault.

Sniper.

He scanned the buildings around him. The shot had come from his right front. There! The steeple of the church would provide a three-hundred-sixty-degree visibility in this neighborhood. The glint of light reflecting off the scope was all the confirmation he needed.

How had the Bedlamites found him?

He bit off a curse. Shelby's mobile. With everything else that had gone on, he'd forgotten he had it. Jukes had her driving license. With it, he could look up her address and telephone numbers, including her mobile. He'd've had to hack into the cellular network to trace her to the nearest cell phone tower, which would take time. Even then, it wouldn't give them her precise location. Hence the observer with the sniper rifle.

Come to it, why hadn't the police busted down their door? They could get a warrant for a line trace far more easily.

First things first. He risked a peek over the bonnet of the car. Nothing happened.

Okay, Carswell, figure it out. If he were searching for someone and had a general idea of where he was, he would post an observer somewhere high up, like the church tower. He would also have at least one, preferably two, roving patrols.

As if on cue, a Land Rover Defender turned the corner two blocks away. He knew he'd been detected when it peeled rubber in his direction. He turned and sprinted across the street, leaping to grab the top of the fence surrounding the church grounds and flipping over it. As he zigzagged across the lawn, a second bullet plowed into the earth behind him. Reaching the tree line, he ran flat out for the back of the church, keeping the trees between himself and the shooter. The sniper fired several more rounds, missing badly, telling Trevor this was an amateur. He didn't have clear line of sight to Trevor, and the gunshots would bring the police.

It wouldn't take the Bedlamites in the Land Rover long to circle around to the front of the church. When Trevor reached the church's back door, he found an old, slightly rusty padlock. Shielding his face, he drew Shelby's Beretta and fired at the lock. It popped open.

He moved swiftly but silently through the hallway, passing several offices and a kitchen. A staircase appeared on his left; as he turned to start up, he saw the body of a priest sprawled several stairs above him. Blood pooled from under his body and dripped down the stairs. He paused to press his fingers to the man's carotid artery. No pulse.

It took a high degree of either professionalism or stupidity to kill a priest in his own church and fire a rifle without a noise suppressor. He could already hear sirens in the distance. Leaping up the stairs two at a time, he paused at the bend of the staircase. Someone was thundering down the stairs.

He put his back to the wall and waited. A few seconds later, a man carrying a sniper rifle barreled around the corner. Trevor simultaneously tripped him with his leg and shoved him hard. The man tumbled down the stairs, losing his grip on the rifle. Trevor followed him down, not giving the man time to react as he flipped him over and twisted his arm up behind his back, dropping his knee into the man's spine for good measure. The man grunted in pain.

"Who sent you?" He patted the man down one-handed, removing a Springfield semiautomatic from a hip holster. He also pocketed the man's cell phone and a snapshot of himself and Shelby, obviously taken from the news reports.

"Fuck you."

Trevor increased the pressure on the man's arm. "Let's try an easier question. Were you sent to kill or capture? Because you're a lousy shot."

"Fuck . . ."

Trevor gave his shoulder a hard twist, dislocated it. The man screamed.

"I don't have a lot of time. You, you're going to jail. But if you answer my questions, I'll let you live."

The man's chest heaved as he tried to breathe through the pain. "Stop. For feck's sake, stop."

Trevor leaned closer to the man's face. "Kill or capture?"

"Capture," the man gasped.

"Just me?" He would not mention Shelby by name.

"You and anyone with you. Wounded was okay, so I took the shot when Liam said to."

"Who's Liam? Who sent you?" Trevor snapped. The sirens grew louder.

"I don't k . . ."

Trevor yanked the man's arm straight. He screamed again.

"Liam sent me. He's the one I work for. But I don't know who the big boss is. No one knows."

"Where were you supposed to take me?"

The man all but buried his face in the wooden floor. "To a dock on the wharf."

Probably near the area Trevor had originally met Mr. Smith. He had time for one more question. "Do you know why you're setting bombs in the city?"

"No. I just do what I'm told, don't I?"

The sirens cut off as at least two police cars reached the church. Time to go.

Trevor rose. "You tell your boss that the next person who comes after me will end up in a body bag."

He headed back the way he'd come. Leaving the door wide open, he crouched, running through the trees, reaching the fence before any of the cops thought to check the back door. He tried to tamp down his anxiety. Shelby's phone led them here. It would lead them straight to her.

Levering himself over the fence, he took several precious minutes to scan the area around him. Nothing raised the hairs on the back of his neck.

He would be taking a chance by making a beeline for the hotel, but he did it anyway, settling into a jog that wouldn't alarm the passersby. Halfway down the block, he saw the Land Rover, illegally parked in front of the hotel.

Shit.

He'd miscalculated. They hadn't followed him to the church. They'd followed the mobile's signal to Shelby.

He ignored the elevator and surged up the stairs three at a time, trying to ignore the unfamiliar feeling of panic pushing against his chest. When he reached the third floor, he cracked the fire door, but heard nothing. He risked a quick look. No one stood guard in the hallway. Continuing on silent feet to their room, he saw with a sinking heart that the door was ajar. The room was silent. He placed himself to one side of the door, the sniper's Springfield out, his finger along the trigger guard.

"Shelby?" he called.

The slight pause felt as though it stretched on for years.

"Yes?" Her voice, at least, seemed calm. That probably meant they hadn't hurt her. They better not have hurt her.

"How many are in there with you?"

"Two—" He heard the crack of flesh hitting flesh. Her voice cut off with a cry of pain.

"Shut up, bitch."

He didn't recognize the voice. "You bastards have exactly one shot at walking out of here in one piece. Let the girl go. Now."

"You come in with your hands up, or we'll kill you both." A different voice this time; the second man.

"Not your orders. Liam said bring me in alive. Let her go, and I'll come with you." Would he? Yes, he decided. To protect Shelby.

"I am Liam, you arsehole. An' I'll decide who lives or dies."

A chill swept down his spine. The voices gave him a rough idea where the men were, but entering the room was risky, at best. Shelby could be caught in the crossfire.

Before he could think too much about it, he darted in, low and to the left. In a nanosecond, he registered the scene. One man stood between the beds, holding Shelby in front of him like a shield. The other stood by the window. Trevor shot that one twice in the chest, then turned to the other one.

"Shelby, drop!" he shouted.

She went completely limp. The man, unable to support her dead weight, lost his grip, and Trevor shot him once in the head.

Before the man even hit the ground, he ran to Shelby, kneeling next to her. "Are you hurt?"

The shots had been deafening in the confined space. He ignored the ringing in his ears. Shelby had her hands over hers, wide eyes trained on the dead man inches from her.

"Shelby, look at me. Are you injured?"

She let out a shaky breath and lowered her hands, gaze finally shifting to him. "No."

"Then we need to hoof it. More might be on their way." He helped her to her feet, visually checking her over for injuries. Blood smeared her lip where she'd been slapped. "Bastards."

"I'm okay," she said, voice stronger this time.

"Where's your phone?"

She handed it over, a question on her face. He popped the battery out and went into the bathroom, dropping both pieces into the toilet. Returning to the room, he searched the two men, scooping up their two handguns and wallets. Stupid of them to carry identification.

"Let's go." He grabbed her hold-all, shoved her laptop and the five confiscated handguns inside, and hustled them out the door. He still had the Beretta on him, and the rest he would figure out later.

They went down the stairs and through the fire door into the car park behind the hotel. Holding her hand tightly, Trevor set as fast a pace as he dared, taking her past several maisonettes until they hit a roadway. The parked cars gave him an idea. He started checking them one by one. Once she realized what he was doing, Shelby crossed the street to do the same thing.

"Here's one," she called, holding open the door to an older model Ford.

"Brilliant." He trotted to her side and slid into the driver's seat. Shelby took the other seat. Reaching under the steering column, he popped the case, exposing the key chamber. "Check the glove box for a screwdriver, would you?"

Shelby opened it and rummaged inside. "No screwdriver, but a box cutter. Will that do?"

"Perfectly." He took it from her, leaning down so he could see the cluster of wires. He used the box cutter to strip the insulation off the three he needed. Carefully, he connected the ignition wire to the battery, then added the starter. The Ford sputtered to life. Without hesitation, he pulled out onto the street.

"Where are we going?" Shelby asked.

"Anywhere away from here." Truthfully, he had no idea. He just knew he needed to put a lot of kilometers between themselves and Tower Hamlets. He maneuvered them onto the A12. At Devas Street, he took a left, winding his way through neighborhoods randomly. Eventually, he pointed the bonnet west, heading toward London.

"My phone caused this, didn't it?" Shelby said. "They found us because Bruce called me."

"My fault entirely. I forgot I even had the damned thing."

She nodded. "Thank you. For saving my life."

He glanced over at her. Though her face seemed pale, she sounded calm. "You did great back there."

She nodded again, then turned to look out the window.

"It's okay to be scared," he told her. "You'd have to be every kind of a fool not to be scared when a gun's pointed at your head."

"Have you?" she asked, voice small.

"Had a gun pointed at my head? A time or two, yeah."

She finally turned to look at him. "Were you scared?"

"Natch. Of course I was."

She let out a long, ragged exhale. "Okay."

He relaxed marginally when they hit London proper, with its crowds and anonymity. Spotting a Starbucks, he pulled to the side of the road.

"I think we could both use a coffee," he said. "It's as good a place as any to catch our breath."

He grabbed the hold-all and came around to open Shelby's door. She nodded her thanks. "Won't someone spot the car?"

"Statistically, probably not. But we'll leave it here when we go."

He ushered her inside and set the hold-all on a table in the far back. "I'll be right back."

He felt her anxious eyes on him as he went to the counter and ordered two coffees. When he brought them back to the table, he saw that she had opened her laptop.

"We won't get a second look. People work at Starbucks all the time." She sipped the too-hot coffee and pursed her lips, sucking in air as the liquid burned its way down her throat. "If we can't get this mess straightened out, you'll go to jail and I'll lose my job, at the very least."

"We'll figure it out." And he would. Somehow. He couldn't let his rash actions jeopardize her career. He again considered turning himself in.

Above all else, he needed to find Mr. Smith. The puppeteer.

"As soon as we find a place to land, I need to call in to my task force commander. Update him. Although I think he's already aware of our situation, to some extent."

"From the news?"

"I'd imagine so. I think he intercepted a Metropolitan Police request for a trace on your mobile. That's the only explanation I can think of why the Bedlamites found us and the police didn't."

"So that's a positive. Is it safe to log into my personal Gmail account?"

"Safe enough."

Shelby logged on and scanned through her messages. "I have dozens of emails. Friends, coworkers, and my boss. All asking where I am and if I'm all right."

"You can't answer any of them."

She leveled a look at him, eyes narrowed. "I know that."

"Sorry." He drank the coffee, glad for the kick of caffeine. Shelby started deleting the emails, one by one. He discreetly scanned the other patrons and the perimeter.

Shelby made a sound halfway between a laugh and an "Aha!"

"Let's have it," he ordered.

She pointed to her email queue. She'd highlighted an email from someone at Cerberus News International. "I have an idea."

He was already shaking his head. "Do you know what they do?

They tout themselves as an independent watchdog news source. They are relentless."

Shelby swiveled around to look at him. "No, but my friend Lark does background research for news stories at Cerberus. She might be able to help us find your mystery man. Cerberus isn't far from the UN building I work in. We have lunch occasionally."

He pointed to the email. "This person wants an exclusive interview? No."

"Listen to me. I know Lark. She—"

"Shel, my face is all over the news. I can't go into a newsroom. Particularly Cerberus. Particularly to talk to a reporter, for fuck's sake."

"Lark isn't like that. You'll see. Anyway, I wasn't suggesting you go in. Maybe I can invite her for coffee or lunch? You could join us."

Trevor thought about it for a moment. "Dangerous, but possible. Do you trust her?"

"I do. She and I have worked together on some news pieces. I've been her source, she's been mine. I'll go in on my own."

"You have the same problem. You're no longer a missing person. You're a person of interest in a domestic terrorism investigation."

"Do you have a better idea? I'm all ears."

He hesitated. He didn't want to put her in any danger, either from the Bedlamites or the cops. Still, they couldn't stay here for long. "A cafe, then. It's too risky for you to go inside."

"All right."

"Do you want to stay here while I find a shop that sells mobiles?"

Alarm filled her face. "No, I'd rather stay with you."

"Done. Let's go, then."

She packed her laptop and walked with him to the counter. The young woman behind the counter smiled. "More coffee, luv?"

"Thanks, but no," Shelby said. "Do you have any idea where I might find a phone store nearby?"

"American, are you? Yes, as it happens, there's a Sainsbury's a few blocks up. Go out the door to your left, that's Fleet Street. Head toward Peterborough Court, and it's right there."

Shelby thanked the woman, and they went out and turned as instructed. Trevor kept his head on a swivel as they walked, but nothing seemed out of the ordinary. The convenience store sat right where the woman had said. Trevor took Shelby's hand as they dashed across the street and pushed through the doors.

"It's a supermarket," Shelby said. "Are they going to have cell phones here?"

He chuckled. "They will, and anything else we need, besides."

In short order, they assembled toothbrushes and toothpaste, razor, soap, shampoo, and changes of clothing for them both. To that pile he added two pay-as-you-go mobiles.

"I think that'll do for now," he said. "I don't want to muck about with too much baggage."

"I'll call Lark."

Chapter Eleven

THE WATERY SUNLIGHT did little to brighten the gloom of the day. The scent of rain hung in the air. Shelby turned left, and they walked for several blocks in silence until they saw the Pret a Manger at the corner.

"Having the taxi drop us away from the coffee shop was a good idea."

He shared a brief smile with her. "I might have done this a time or two."

"Well, at least one of us knows what he's doing." Her shoulders hunched. "I wish I could see a way out of this mess."

He did, too.

"Tell me about Lark."

"Her real name is Hadley Larkspur, of the Nantucket Larkspurs. Off Cape Cod in Massachusetts? Old money. Her parents have no idea what to do with a genius daughter with ADHD. They sent her to the best schools, but she's brilliant and easily bored. Right now, she's doing a study abroad, but she's supplementing her studies by doing research at Cerberus. She says she wants to be in front of the camera, reporting from the front lines, as it were. But her producers won't even talk to her about it. Not until she becomes more conventional. And I doubt that will happen anytime soon."

"What do you mean? More conventional?"

She slanted him a sly smile. "You'll see."

He let it go. He'd know soon enough.

"We've met there in the past. It's very quiet."

"How close is it to the Cerberus offices?"

"About three blocks. I don't know why, but reporters don't come here."

Bringing a reporter into this mess seemed risky, but Shelby trusted this Lark. Worse came to worst, he could disable Lark and get himself and Shelby out of there.

Both had changed their appearances before hailing a black cab. Instead of looking like a career woman, Shelby wore an overlarge, shapeless gray T-shirt, with a sweatshirt tied around her waist. Her sweatpants were baggy and indistinct. She'd scraped her hair up into a cap. With her face scrubbed free of makeup, she looked far younger than her twenty-eight years.

To him, nothing could hide her innate beauty.

He'd chosen baggy wide-legged jeans that sagged around his waist. He then paired a rugby sweatshirt with Timberland work boots, and topped it with a random cap of the Los Angeles Lakers. The look was popular amongst London teens.

He was down to a hundred thirty-some-odd pounds in his wallet, and Shelby had maybe a few quid left from her emergency stash at home.

"I'll call you when I've made contact with Lark," she said. "Don't get into any trouble, okay?"

"I'll do my best. But trouble seems to be following me around of late."

She screwed up her face into a playful frown. "Well, don't kill anyone."

"Right, then. Off you go."

He faded into a doorway, watching her as she walked down the block carrying the hold-all. The Pret a Manger chain was as ubiquitous in London as Starbucks was in America.

He didn't like letting her out of his sight even for a moment. Too many things could happen. Left with little choice, though, when she entered the coffee shop, he turned and jogged up the street toward the Cerberus offices.

Let's see how trustworthy this woman is.

The Cerberus offices crouched within a modern office building sporting a clear glass façade and exposed support beams. Most of the other buildings were older, with shops on the ground floor and offices above. He scrunched into a doorway half a block down, hands in his pockets, trying to look harmless. From here, he had perfect line of sight to the office building's entrance. The longer he waited, the more likely it was that something would go wrong. Either Jukes would find him, or—

"You there. What are you doing?"

—or the police would.

Trevor looked sideways at the cop in front of him. "Just waiting, aren't I?" he said. "For my missus to come off work. So we can have a bite."

"I don't recognize you, do I, and I've been patrolling this patch for three years. Show me your identification."

None of the Bedlamites had carried ID in their wallets for the museum job. Even his fake ID, which Eric had hidden at the hideout, announced him to be Trevor Willoughby, a man now wanted countrywide. He didn't answer.

"Sir, your ID." The cop came a few steps closer.

"My wallet was pinched, wasn't it? I haven't gotten my driving license replaced yet."

The man considered him, hands on his hips, head cocked. "Come with me, then. We'll get you sorted at the station."

Trevor grimaced. "My missus will be bleedin' pissed orf," he said. "She only gets the half hour for tea break, doesn't she."

"I've orders to detain anyone suspicious. We're searching for the men who took hos—"

Trevor saw the exact moment the cop recognized him. A slight flaring of the eyes and nose as he simultaneously reached for his radio and Taser.

Trevor lunged at him, closing his fingers around the man's wrist so he couldn't deploy the Taser. One hit with that, and he'd be cuffed before his muscles stopped twitching.

"Forty-eight Charlie Papa. Officer in need of aid—"

A quick punch just under his jaw made the patrolman stagger back. Trevor snatched the radio speaker from his hand. "Belay that. Everything's fine."

The radio crackled to life. "Dispatch to all available units. Officer injured. Proceed to . . ."

Bollocks. Trevor tuned out the noise. He hadn't really expected his ruse to work, but he'd had to try.

The cop tried to deploy the Taser again. Quick as a cat, he spun the beat cop around until his back faced Trevor, twisting the speaker cord around his neck several times to control him. The man's fingers scrabbled against the wires, trying to clear his airway.

Trevor put him into a choke hold, cutting off oxygen to his brain. Seven seconds later, the man slid to the ground, unconscious.

Trevor crouched down to unwind the speaker cord. Fingers pressed to his neck, he verified that the officer's pulse beat strong and steady. He would wake up in about fifteen seconds; Trevor had to be long gone by then. He walked briskly away from the office building. What would Shelby think when she saw him gone? Probably the worst.

A patrol car, siren wailing, squealed around the corner behind him and slammed to a stop near the beat cop. A motorcycle marked with red and blue checks tore in from a different direction, the police decal prominent. In a matter of seconds, he would be spotted.

Sure enough, the motorcycle revved its engines, making a tight turn and gathering momentum as it sped toward him. He opened the nearest door, ducking inside, and found himself in a bootmaker's shop. Rows upon rows of brightly colored fashion pumps, ankle boots, and shoes passed in a blur as he headed toward the back of the shop.

"Hiya, lover. Can I help you find anything?" The rather portly woman's eyes crinkled at the corners as she smiled at him. "A tasty snack like you will want the Jeffery Wests, yeah? I'm thinking the Lundy brogues."

Trevor forced a chuckle, stopping to rotate in a slow circle. "Those shoes cost near about three hundred quid. What about this costume says I can afford those?"

She winked at him. "Breeding shows, love."

That gave him an idea. "Right, you caught me. Here's the thing. I'm trying to avoid my ex. She's . . . relentless."

"And yer needing a back way out, am I right?"

"I do."

The motorcycle jerked to a stop at the curb.

"What makes it worse is she's a response officer. Motorcycles." He turned and leveled a resigned look out the window, silently urging the saleswoman to make a decision. "She's got a grudge on, and reported me in for something or another."

She followed his look out the window. "Right, then. Straight back are the restocking rooms; don't go there. Go into the far right corner, where it says the toilets are. There's a broom closet with a door at the back of it. I share it with my old man's shop next door. Good luck to ya, lover."

She gave him a push in the right direction, and Trevor sprinted across the shop. He ducked into the short hall just as the cop jingled open the bootmaker's entryway. Sure enough, a metal door led him into a duplicate corridor of the next area, which turned out to be a barbershop. Only this hallway also had a rear egress. The security gate had been propped open; a few short steps took Trevor past a trash bin to a narrow lane.

Barely taking the time to look around, he took off. A siren grew strident as it neared. The lane held a hodgepodge of architectural designs from different periods; a typical London street. He hesitated at a brick-and-concrete archway, but the gate was closed and padlocked. The next arch had no fence and led into a short tunnel with—*oh, shit*—a dome-shaped security camera mounted on the upper left. He turned his head as he ran past it.

A response car rolled into view in the street ahead of him, blue lights flashing. Trevor ducked into a stairwell and slid the six steps down the handrail to the bottom. His hand grasped the solid metal fire door's handle even before he stopped. Locked. Fuck and double fuck. That meant he'd have to return to the street.

The response car had continued on. Trevor doubled back the way he'd come and raced at top speed across the roadway and into the next lane.

And then he heard the helicopter.

Chapter Twelve

SHELBY TOOK A seat in the back of the coffee shop, dropping her gym bag at her feet.

"Howya, luv?" the blond man behind the counter called. "What can I make you?"

"Just water for now, please. I'm waiting for a friend."

"Lovely. Give me a tick."

She'd thought it strange when she'd first come to London as an undergraduate that the English found everything to be lovely. Later she realized it was their equivalent to "Okay" or "Got it."

The blond man brought her a large glass of water. Customers ebbed and flowed. The blond man poured tea, coffee, made sandwiches, and served up pastries. Some sat and ate; most took their food to go. None gave her a second glance.

The wail of police sirens jerked her upright in alarm. She twisted in her seat, trying to determine how close they were. Blocks away, at least. She found herself hoping for a simple fender-bender or bank robbery. Nothing that involved Trevor.

The sounds faded.

Finally, she saw Lark—Hadley Nia Larkspur—power-walking down the sidewalk, clutching an enormous handbag. As usual, she radiated inexhaustible energy. Today, her hair was bright purple, cut into a short, messy pixie cut. Her hair matched her makeup—purple lipstick, a shade lighter than her hair, and purple eye shadow, making her already huge eyes even more dramatic.

Lark saw Shelby and dashed the final few feet, bursting through the door and causing every head to turn in her direction. Rushing over, she enveloped Shelby in a hug and the scent of an expensive perfume.

Shelby returned the younger woman's hug with genuine affection, hiding her sigh. Lark was anything but subtle.

"Shelby! Fantastic! I was thinking about you this morning. You got my email? How's tricks?"

Shelby took a deep breath. "Been better, Lark. I need some help."

Lark dragged a chair out from the table and plopped into it. "Fucking awesome. I was bored with the shit I was doing. So what if that douche wants to run for president? He's got an icicle's chance in hell. Tell me what you need."

A helicopter buzzed overhead and moved away. Shelby rearranged herself in the chair and crossed her legs. "You heard about the hostage crisis at the August Museum?"

"Duh. It's been all over the news. It's why I emailed you. I wanted to be the one to find out who this Trevor Willoughby is, but they assigned fucking Trisha to it. Like she can get access to what I can. Simpering little bitch. Got into Danny's pants. Can't even hack."

Shelby smothered a laugh. "Well, you also know I was one of the hostages."

Lark's eyes became huge. "You're going to give me the exclusive? That's freaking awesome! I mean, not for you. But you're here. Clearly unhurt. So what was it like? Can you describe the terrorists? Are you here to do the interview? 'Cause I'd totally rock the interview."

She reached into her handbag and yanked out a laptop. As she opened the lid, Shelby saw the custom cover of a three-headed dog with a serpent's tail wrapped around it. Under the logo, Cerberus's questioning motto—*Quis Custodiet Ipsos Custodes?*

"Who watches the watchmen?" she murmured.

"Technically, it's 'Who will guard the guards themselves?'" Lark said. "But whatevs. Okay, I'm ready. Spill!"

"I'm not here for an interview. Not yet, anyway. But I will give you the story when the time comes. Deal?"

Lark's eyes shimmered with intelligence. "I'll hold you to that."

"And I'll get with the police to do sketches soon. It's complicated at the moment. It's just—I can trust you, right?"

Lark sat back with a snort. "Duh."

Shelby dropped her voice, forcing Lark to lean forward to hear. "The man? Trevor? He's not one of the anarchists. He was undercover. That's all I can say, but he's one of the good guys. And he needs help."

Lark's eyes brightened with curiosity. "What kind of help?"

"Someone else is pulling the strings. A mystery man is funding the Philosophy of Bedlam. Find him, and we stop this madness."

Lark bounced in her chair. "Holy shit holy shit. This is awesome."

"We have to figure out who he is."

Lark's eyes became shrewd. "We?"

Shelby dropped her eyes. "For the moment, yes. We."

"So who is he? If he's not a terror—anarchist, who is he? Scotland Yard? Interpol?"

Shelby managed a weak smile. "Would you like to meet him?"

"Hells to the yeah! Get his ass in here."

Shelby pressed the speed dial that should have connected her to Trevor, but he didn't pick up. After the third time the call routed straight to an automated system, she dropped the phone onto the table and twined her fingers together, squeezing them to mask her anxiety. Maybe those police sirens she'd heard . . . No. A highly trained SAS soldier would be able to avoid the police. She had to believe that.

"What's wrong?" Lark asked.

"He's supposed to be standing by to come in when I say it's okay. But he's not answering his cell."

A small line creased between the younger woman's brows. "You didn't trust me?"

Shelby heard the faintly hurt note in her friend's voice. "Of course I did—did and do. Anyone could recognize me, though. Or him. I promise I'll give you an exclusive once we get all this figured out. You'd be helping the greater good, Lark."

"Fuck the greater good," Lark said, clapping her hands together and rubbing them. "I'll nail that mystery man's candy ass to the floor."

Shelby felt a wash of relief. She knew she could trust Lark. They'd had first a professional relationship, with Shelby providing information required for news stories; and, later, when they'd established a mutual trust, she'd leaked Shelby tidbits as required to advance American interests in her arena.

"Thank you."

"Ha. Don't mention it. This could be my big break. Get me in front of the cameras."

Shelby stretched. She felt sore in places she didn't even know could be sore. "You still want to be a television reporter?"

"Maybe. But the producer told me I'd have to tone down the look. Don't know about that part. Where can I contact you?"

Shelby took out her phone. "This is my temporary cell number. I'm not going home. It's not safe. The cell's the best way to reach me."

Lark's eyes narrowed in concern. "Where are you staying? Do you have a place to stay?"

"Another hotel, probably."

Lark hefted her handbag and rooted through it. Pulling out a set of keys, she selected one and removed it. "You're staying with me. I want to meet Hunky Guy."

Shelby laughed. "Hunky Guy?"

Lark tapped a few keys on her computer and swiveled it toward Shelby. "That's how his pic got out there. Girl named Chastity69 posted the pic on her Facebook page."

Shelby leaned forward for a better look. Sure enough, there was the photo she'd seen on TV news, along with the caption, "OMG, he can marry me now. I want to have his babies."

"Good grief. She must have uploaded it before they confiscated the cell phones."

"Yeah." Lark took a business card and scribbled an address on the back. "You go be safe. I'll spider-crawl through the Philosophy of Bedlam like a motherfucker. If it's there, I'll find it."

Shelby reached over and hugged Lark. "You're the best."

Lark grinned. "I know."

TREVOR WAITED UNTIL the helicopter banked away from him to leave the concealment of the single tree decorating an intersection. One side of the street had been closed off for some sort of road repair. He stayed with the clump of Londoners crossing the street, then peeled off and walked through the narrow opening between the green-covered fence surrounding a construction site. Someone had left a yellow-and-gray safety jacket draped over a pile of bricks; he snagged it as he went by, tossing his cap away as he did so. The trick to evasion was to blend in. He could do little to alter his appearance, but every little bit would help. He shrugged into the safety jacket, then squatted to examine the small backhoe as a red BMW with orange stripes down the sides passed. Even without the blue letters declaring it a police car, he'd recognized the sedan for what it was.

The Armed Response Unit. They'd broken out the big guns to find him. These officers would be armed. They normally participated when a situation required special weapons and tactics, but clearly he was now the subject of a larger manhunt. He felt the first tightening of concern. He'd left Shelby alone too long as it was.

Crossing behind a Salvation Army church, he headed into a residential neighborhood. A long line of unbroken architecture told him he'd made a mistake. One side was connected townhomes. The other was upper-end flats. He couldn't see any egress other than the far end of the road. Reversing directions, he reentered the construction zone.

The Armed Response Unit sedan revved its engines as it backed up. A blue Mazda swerved into the next lane to avoid it, horn blaring. The cop must have realized construction laborers didn't work on a Sunday.

Left with little choice, Trevor ran past the Mazda and down the one-way road. The ARU couldn't back up forever. Trevor turned right past a sandwich shop and a bus stop onto another one-way street. On the left was some sort of school, but the right held some older houses. The rear of the homes backed up to an alley. Trevor didn't hesitate as he leapt for the top of a slatted gate, slapping his palms on the top and lifting himself up and over.

The usual trash bins, broken crates, and other rubbish littered the alleyway. He stripped off the safety jacket. By now, the ARU would have called for backup. He eyed the end of the alley and rejected it. The odds of another police vehicle cutting him off, or at least spotting him, were high. The best choice was up.

The rain pipe two buildings down looked sturdy enough. He went up it hand over hand, digging in with his toes where possible. When he was close enough, he leapt for the ledge of the roof, threw a leg over, and rolled onto the flat portion near the chimney, keeping his head below the roof line.

He heard no shouts or engine roars that told him he'd been spotted. Good. Keeping a low profile, he maneuvered to the other side of the building, checking several times for police cars. Nothing.

The gap between this building and the next wasn't more than ten feet. Backing up to give himself some room, he sprinted to the edge, leaping at the last moment into the air. As he landed, he rolled twice, coming to his feet in a nanosecond. From there, it was child's play to hop from rooftop to rooftop along the blocks of flats. Flocks of pigeons and sparrows took flight in protest.

He cut as straight a path as he dared back toward the Pret a Manger where he'd left Shelby. The rooftops ended at the next street. Trevor entered the roof door and took the stairs to the ground floor. Exiting into the washed-out daylight, he prepared to jog back to Shelby's location.

"Freeze!"

Trevor jerked around. He didn't know who was more shocked, himself or the young beat cop staring at him with round eyes. Of all the confounded luck, to walk straight into what had to be the greenest cop on the force. Who had managed to clear his weapon from its holster and point it at him with shaking hands.

"Since when do beat cops carry firearms?" he asked, surprised.

The question threw the youngster off for half a beat. "Since you, I think. They just got issued this morning."

"Lucky me."

The cop took a deep breath. "Down on the ground. Hands behind your head."

"Look, Junior—"

His eyes got even bigger. "I will not hesitate to fire this weapon. Get down on the ground right now."

Trevor sighed, dropping to his knees and clasping his hands behind his head. He really didn't want to hurt the kid.

Who had the sense to keep his Glock 17 trained on him as he pulled handcuffs from his utility belt and cuffed him, one wrist at a time. He patted him down, finding the Beretta and tucking it into his own belt. Helping Trevor to his feet, he walked him the twenty yards or so to his patrol car. Trevor obediently climbed into the back.

The cop had his weapon, but hadn't done a thorough search. Even with his hands behind his back, Trevor was able to slide his pick tools free. Before the youngster finished calling the dispatcher, voice triumphant, to declare that he'd captured wanted terrorist Trevor Willoughby, he'd already unlocked the cuffs. Three sledgehammer kicks to the door and it popped open, unable to withstand the force of the blows.

The cop cursed, jumping out of the front seat. Trevor popped him twice in the face, then grabbed him, spun him around, and threw him up against the police car. He whipped the cuffs onto the cop's wrists, closing them tightly.

"Doubt you have my training, Junior, so don't feel bad about this. I'm going to put you in the back of your car. Your buddies will be here soon enough. I'm sorry, genuinely sorry, if this causes you embarrassment."

The cop glared at him with one eye. Trevor turned him around, and the cop kicked him. If Trevor hadn't seen it coming and moved his leg, his knee might have cracked.

"You're brave, I'll give you that. Look, believe it or not, I don't want any trouble. Just . . ." Trevor shook his head, frustrated. "Would it help if I punched you a couple more times, so you look like it was a fight to the death?"

The youngster hung his head. "Yeah, maybe. I've only been in the job two weeks."

"And they let you out on your own? This is their fault, then." Trevor walloped the kid's temple right where it would swell and bruise. "All right, into the car. I'm really sorry, mate."

He closed the vehicle's door, turned, and ran flat out toward the Pret a Manger. With any luck, Shelby would still be waiting for him.

Chapter Thirteen

He'd done it again. He'd abandoned her. Left her high and dry. He'd lied about waiting for her. He wasn't answering his cell phone. He must have decided he would do better on his own.

What was she supposed to do? She couldn't go home. She needed to talk to the police, but how would she explain her disappearance from the museum without implicating Trevor? Yet if she didn't, they would assume she was one of them, and her status would change from Person of Interest to Wanted Felon.

For now, she'd go to Lark's flat. It was only about seven blocks from here. Needing the fresh air and exercise, she hefted the gym bag to her shoulder and started walking.

So what had Trevor decided to do? Go after Eric and the other anarchists alone? As well as he'd been trained, even he couldn't take on five of them alone.

Walking along the sparsely populated roadways left Shelby feeling exposed. What if someone followed her? What if Crawley found her? Without Trevor to protect her, she didn't stand a chance against the insanity swimming behind Crawley's eyes. Wishing now that she'd kept her Beretta, she quickened her step.

Lark lived in a brown brick building fronted by flat faux columns. Vertical windows leading to a tiny balcony were inset between each column. From the sheer number of windows, Shelby guessed the flats were small. The sign over the front door announced the building to be Gorse House. She pushed through into a plain, functional white hallway. Communal postal boxes lined the right wall. The lift, doors already open, beckoned on the left. Shelby darted inside, almost bowling over an elderly lady using a walker.

"Sorry! I'm so sorry. Here, let me hold the door for you."

The lady nodded her thanks and made her creeping way to a letterbox. Shelby pressed the button for the eighth floor, not relaxing until she found Lark's front door and closed it behind her.

Lark had installed a deadbolt to supplement the simple lock on the door. Shelby shot it home, then set the gym bag onto the floor. It made an unusual clatter.

It hadn't been her computer making the noise. Curious, she knelt and zipped it open, moving her clothes aside. Two revolvers and three semiautomatic pistols gleamed up at her. Where had they come from?

She racked her brains. Okay, one of the thugs from the alley near the museum had threatened them with one of the revolvers. Trevor had taken it. The other revolver he'd lifted from Nathan outside of her flat. Liam had threatened her with a gun; Trevor must have taken it. But the others? Where had they come from? For now, she closed the bag and left it by the front door, turning to inspect her surroundings.

Much like the woman herself, Lark's flat was full of life and color. The door opened into the living room, full of overstuffed chairs with bright pillows, abstract art, and lots of knickknacks. Magazines and several books littered the coffee table. Shelby peeked into the single bedroom. Lark's bed was unmade, and clothes were strewn all over the bed and floor. The door on the other side of the hall turned out to be the bathroom. Makeup crowded every surface. Nylons hung from the shower rod. The curtain, pulled back, showed SpongeBob and Patrick frolicking underwater.

Hoping the kitchen wasn't as messy as the rest of the house, she went through the door. Dishes filled the sink, and foodstuffs littered the countertops. Apparently when Lark shopped, she didn't bother to put the groceries away. Shelby opened the refrigerator, afraid of what she might find. A jar of pickles, mayonnaise, and a plastic container full of grapes that had probably gone bad a month ago.

"Good grief," she muttered. Lark was a flamboyant character, but a terrible housekeeper.

She jerked as someone knocked on the door, heart thumping. Had the Bedlamites somehow found her? No, that was silly. It was probably a neighbor.

This time, whoever it was pounded on the door. "Shelby!"

She recognized his voice. She ran to the door and almost yanked it open. "Trevor!"

He came inside fast, closing and locking the door behind him. He looked her over from head to foot, then surprised her by pulling her into his arms and holding her tightly.

"All right?" he asked.

She nodded against his chest. "I'm fine."

His scent enveloped her. God, he smelled good. She'd missed

that. She'd missed a lot of things about him; but above all, she regretted having missed the opportunity to develop a real relationship with him. It was too late. He no longer had feelings for her. That meant it wouldn't have worked out between them anyway, didn't it?

If he felt nothing for her, why did he hold her like he'd been worried? As though he cared?

Don't read anything into it. She let herself just enjoy the feel of him, disappointed when he released her and stepped back.

"Nothing untoward happened in the Pret a Manger?" he asked.

She swallowed, also stepping back. "No. Lark's going to help us. How did you find me, anyway?"

He gave the shadow of his usual grin. "I followed you."

She raised her eyes to his. "You were there?"

"I got back as you were leaving. I wanted to be certain no one else paid you any mind."

"I told you I trusted Lark."

"That's not why I did it." His look was somber. "Your face is plastered all over the news broadcasts, right next to mine. The cops launched a manhunt for the Bedlamites, but they're particularly looking for you and me. I didn't want us to be seen together, not with the coppers so close."

"They didn't find you, though, right? You did your SAS ninja thing?"

He chuckled, though it sounded forced to her. "I might have run into one or two."

She sucked in a breath. "You . . . didn't hurt them?"

Trevor gave her a disappointed glance and walked into the living room. "You've got a high opinion of me, obviously. No, I didn't hurt them."

"I-I'm sorry I asked. Of course you wouldn't if you didn't have to."

He seemed to have already put the matter from his mind as he looked around. "Good god. Did a circus explode in here?"

Shelby laughed, a surprised burst of sound. "You'll understand when you meet her. Lark is . . . unique."

Trevor checked the rest of the flat, much like Shelby had done. "That's one way of putting it. Slob is another."

She followed him into the kitchen. "She's offered to let us stay here for a while."

"That's good of her. You still trust her after talking with her?" He looked around the kitchen, hands on his hips. "I'm speechless."

She nodded emphatically. "Yes. I've trusted her in the past with sensitive information, and she's never let me down."

He picked up a box of cereal and looked at the back. "Good."

She cleared her throat. "The refrigerator is empty. Are you hungry?"

He continued to pace, picking things up and setting them down again. "Not particularly, but you should eat."

"I'm not hungry, either." Truthfully, her stomach ached, and she couldn't remember the last time she'd eaten.

Trevor stopped and they looked at one another. The silence was awkward. Shelby solved the problem by walking into the living room and sitting in a rose-patterned plush chair, pushing aside a pair of rainbow throw pillows.

Trevor followed her and claimed another seat, stretching his long legs in front of him and lacing his hands behind his head. "Well, I owe her one."

"She'll collect, believe me. So what happens now?"

Trevor rolled his head toward her. "Now I call in to my superiors. In a minute."

He clearly had something he wanted to say. She gestured for him to keep going.

"I'm sorry I dragged you into this. You need to clear your name. You need to go to the police. Explain what happened. They'll put you into protective custody."

Shelby narrowed a glare at him. "And how am I supposed to explain my disappearance from the museum? No matter what, I'm now a suspect."

"You can say I took you against your will."

"Which will make it look even worse. How would I have escaped?"

"I let you go?"

Shelby shook her head. "They'll have questions I can't answer. And if I go into protective custody, I have no chance of getting those answers. Until we find the brains behind the brawn, you and I are joined at the hip, buster."

"Buster?" He quirked a small smile.

"Yeah. I can help, Trevor."

He gave a slow nod. "All right. Joined at the hip."

For now. She read it in his face.

Someone knocked at the door. Trevor transformed before her eyes in a single instant from relaxed man to SAS warrior. He drew the Beretta and stalked to the door, placing himself to one side of it and peering out the hole. He looked back at her with raised eyebrows, unlocked the door and opened it wide. Lark walked in.

"You can't be anyone other than Hadley Larkspur," he said. The Beretta vanished.

She looked him over, admiration in her eyes. "And you're Hunky Guy. Nice to meet you."

Trevor stuck out his hand, and they shook.

"But call me Hadley again, and we're going to have a problem."

Trevor grinned. "Yes, ma'am."

Lark groaned. "Jesus. That's even worse." She came over to Shelby, bent down, and gave her a hug. "You find the place okay?"

"Yeah, no problem. Thank you again for—"

"Shut up, or I'll dope-slap you." Lark set her laptop case on the coffee table, making room by shoving some books out of the way. A magazine slid to the floor. "You know I'm only doing this for the exclusive."

That wasn't true, but she let it slide. Lark marched to her own drummer and obeyed her own logic, but if there was one thing Shelby had learned, it was that she was fiercely loyal to her friends.

"And you'll get it," Trevor said. "Thank you for your help. And for your discretion."

Lark laughed, a musical flowery sound that had Trevor smiling at her. Shelby felt a clench in her gut. "Discretion is my middle name. Actually, it's Nia, but if you call me that, we're going to have a problem."

Trevor inclined his head solemnly. "Lark it is, then."

She took her computer to the kitchen table. Shelby followed her. "Are you sure we're not going to cramp your style?"

Lark booted up the laptop. "Nah. I'm between boyfriends. Hunky Guy, want to see the Facebook post that nailed you?"

Trevor came to peer over her shoulder. "Actually, if you could just call me Trevor . . . ?"

"Trevor it is, then." She grinned as she mimicked his own

words. Bringing up a web browser, she typed in a few commands. Trevor's picture popped up. He read the caption and winced.

"Lovely."

Lark's eyes twinkled. "Not flattered, huh? I don't know. She's kind of pretty."

"She's jailbait." His brows wrinkled as he examined Chastity69's photo. "I'm a Muppet if she's even sixteen."

"A . . . Muppet?"

"Gullible. A simpleton."

"That's a new one. I like it."

Shelby stomach rumbled, loud enough for the others to hear. "Sorry."

Lark slapped her forehead. "Duh. It's almost seven. Who's up for Chinese?"

"Definitely."

"Brilliant."

While Lark phoned in their order, Shelby sidled closer to Trevor. "You want to tell me what really happened out there this afternoon? You seem to have acquired several more guns. Did you take them from the police officers?"

"No. I merely disabled them temporarily. But"—he paused.—"The two Bedlamites who held you in the hotel room had an observer outside."

"What does that mean? A lookout?"

"A sniper."

Her jaw dropped as she stared at him, dumbfounded. "A sniper shot at you?"

He shrugged. "Strictly an amateur. But it did give us another semiautomatic."

How could he sound so calm about this? When the two Bedlamites had forced their way into her hotel room, she'd been so scared her knees literally knocked together. She'd never been happier to hear Trevor's voice. A second later, she'd been face-to-face with a bloody corpse, his eyes open and staring at nothing.

"So this is just another Sunday for you?" She tried to modulate her tone, but knew it came out strident.

Trevor put his hands on her shoulders. "Shelby, look at me. I'm a highly trained special operator. I've served in the SAS for twelve years. I know what I'm doing."

"Shh!" She flapped both hands downward. "She'll hear you!"

He sighed, running a hand across the back of his neck. "I need to check in. They'll be wondering why I haven't."

"Check in with who?" Lark appeared beside them, her bright bird-eyes curious.

Trevor peered down at her. "What happened to your clothes?"

Shelby did a double take. When she'd met Lark at the coffee shop, she'd been wearing a tank top layered with a purple plaid flannel shirt and cropped leather jacket over skinny jeans and ankle boots. Paired with a long necklace and bangles, Lark had looked like the poster child for hipster dress. Now, however, she wore low-riding frayed denim short shorts and a cropped top that showed off her midriff. Her feet were bare.

"Those were my work clothes. These are my home clothes. You don't like them?" she asked, with an impish grin.

"They look . . . comfortable."

"Comfortable, eh?" Lark laughed. "So what exactly is your story, Hunky Guy?"

"Just a man caught in the wrong place at the wrong time."

Lark paused to consider him. "Not ready to trust me. Okay, I get it. So I'll tell you about me. Fair's fair."

Shelby's brows shot into her hairline. The Lark she knew was unbelievably closemouthed about her background. Shelby had gleaned what she knew over months of interaction with her. She waited, breath held, to see what the other woman would say.

"I'm twenty-three. Born and raised in Massachusetts, the most liberal state in the Union, to two unbelievably narrow-minded parents." She shrugged. "Whatevs. When I finish this semester here in London, I go back to Duke for my last semester of grad school. I can make computers sing and dance. I can program in eight languages. But the most fun I've had in years is digging up dirt . . . I mean, doing background research on the exposés Cerberus does."

Trevor settled his hips back against the kitchen counter. "You want to be a reporter?"

"For a while, sure. Maybe. I just want to do it to say I've done it, you know? I guess once I've done something, I don't want to keep on doing it. What's the point?"

"What about your studies? What do you see yourself doing after university?"

Lark lifted her shoulders and turned her palms up. "Still figuring that part out."

A knock sounded at the door.

"That was fast," Trevor said.

"They're literally right next to this building," Lark said. "I order from them all the time."

Trevor went to the front door and looked through the peephole. "Delivery man. Shelby and I will wait in the kitchen." He drew his wallet and extended several bills to her.

Lark didn't protest, taking the money with a grin. "Felons pay all incidentals."

In moments, she returned with several large bags, which she took into the living room and set on the coffee table. "Dinner is served."

They loaded their plates. Lark took the seat next to Trevor on the sofa. They watched a news segment on the aftermath of the museum standoff. Several of the former hostages gave interviews. All sent their prayers that Shelby Gibson would also be released unharmed.

"I'm glad they let the hostages go," Shelby said.

Trevor agreed. "I know you think I made the wrong choice, saving you above the other hostages. But I know Eric, and believed he wouldn't take unneeded baggage any farther than he had to. It's bad enough now that they'll be able to do a police sketch of him. He wouldn't want anyone privy to his plans."

"Your superiors clearly know who they are, since they sent you in because you knew their leader. Why can't they just go arrest them?" Shelby knew better than to name the MI-5/SAS task force with Lark in earshot.

"First they have to find them. I gave them the hideout's location, but when they got there, the PoB had gone."

"Well, I sure don't want to ever see them again."

He smiled. "You handled yourself very well in the museum. I got the impression you were more annoyed than frightened."

"I guess so. I should have been scared, but you were there. I knew you would find a way to diffuse the situation. I'm sorry you blew your cover, though."

"Not entirely sure I have. I can always say I was carried away by lust. That's what you wanted them to think, right? When you tore your dress?"

Lark looked up from her lo mein. "You did what?"

"I felt there needed to be a reason Trevor took me into the office. It seemed like a good idea at the time." Shelby's face reddened. "I guess it was stupid."

"Not at all," Trevor corrected. "Better me than that lunatic Crawley."

Lark speared some chicken into her mouth, talking around the edges. "That took guts. So did trusting me. So thanks for that."

Trevor looked at her. "Thank you for not turning us in."

"And miss all this excitement? No fucking way."

Chapter Fourteen

SHELBY AND LARK picked up the plates and food containers and went into the kitchen to wash up. Trevor waited until he heard the sink running, then switched on the telly to mask his conversation. He fished the burner phone out of his pocket and dialed.

His contact answered on the second ring. "Danby."

"It's Carswell."

"'Bout damned time you checked it. Have you seen the news?"

"I have. There's been a wrinkle."

Danby laughed. "I've gathered that, my good man. Where are you?"

"Someplace safe." He didn't want anyone knowing about Lark. "With a friend."

"So what do you intend to do next, old boy? The mission's gone to bust."

Trevor grimaced. "I had to separate from the Bedlamites. It was unavoidable."

"Take me through it. What happened?"

In his overriding need to keep Shelby safe, he'd blown the mission. That would go over like a lead balloon. "Scotland Yard jumped the pull. I had no choice but to allow Eric Koller to barricade us inside. Fourteen patrons inside became hostages."

"And?"

"I didn't feel they were in imminent danger. Eric Koller, the cell leader, is highly idealistic and will fight in a war, declared or undeclared. But he's never participated in executions, to my knowledge. As time passed and tensions heightened, he started losing control over two cell members. Fay Star—what she calls herself, anyway—blames the establishment for every wrong she's ever suffered, and has the ability to kill in cold blood, but I stand by my assessment that she wouldn't pull the trigger without Eric's okay. The other, Calvin Crawley, is simply a psychopath. He stabbed one of the hostages for no reason whatever."

"Mr. Panderson. So you erred in your judgment."

Trevor pressed his lips together. "Yes."

"Why did you separate from the cell?"

"I believed that when Eric found a way out of the museum, he would leave the baggage—the hostages—behind." Trevor hesitated. "One hostage was in imminent danger, though. I felt I had no choice but to remove the threat to her."

"A woman, eh?" Danby sounded less than pleased. "I hope she's worth it. We've lost our chance at them."

"Not entirely. When I first went undercover, I met the man directing the Bedlamites from the shadows. The puppeteer. He calls himself Mr. Smith. My objective now is to find out who this man is. The Bedlamites aren't just trying to cause havoc. They seem to be searching for something. Once I discover what it is, we can take them all in one fell swoop."

Danby was quiet.

"It would help if I wasn't being hunted."

Danby laughed. "My good man, you're too hot to touch right now. I can't get you off the hook with Scotland Yard. I can't even take the heat off you with the Metropolitan Police. The most I can do is quash any rumors about SAS involvement."

"And intercept the warrant to track Shelby Gibson's mobile, I assume?"

"Quite. Although, if Ms. Gibson is not a Bedlamite, she should turn herself in to clear her name."

He tightened his fist around the phone. "Not until I'm sure Mr. Smith wouldn't be able to get to her."

"Here are the options as I see them," Danby said. "You hunt down the Bedlamites and we eliminate that threat. You continue to search for Mr. Smith. Or, you come in from the cold and we declare this mission a bust."

"It would help if I had MI-5's resources."

"I'll relay any information you need."

The slight emphasis on *information* told Trevor he could expect no ground support or equipment. He closed his eyes, keeping his breathing deep and steady. "You're hanging me out to dry, *my good man.*" He didn't try to disguise his sarcasm.

"Aren't you SAS boys masters of pulling results out of your arseholes? This should be right up your alley."

Trevor indulged himself for several moments, imagining slamming his fist into Danby's smug MI-5 face. More than once.

"Right, then. How do you want to proceed?"

"I'll get back to you, Danby." Trevor jabbed the button to end the call with more force than necessary. He felt more than heard a movement behind him, and turned to see Shelby and Lark in the doorway, obviously eavesdropping. He gripped the phone hard before pocketing it. "It looks like I'm on my own."

He turned away from the hurt in Shelby's eyes.

"What about us?" she asked.

"As long as Lark's willing, I think you should stay here where it's safe. If Lark digs up anything, I'll use it or bring it to my contact. Otherwise, I'm going after them myself."

"Yourself."

"Yes."

Shelby seemed to shrink in on herself. "Yeah, I guess we're just liabilities."

"That's not what I meant. But I'm trained. You're not."

Lark threw up her hands, causing her multiple bracelets to jangle. "Then I'd better get started, before you start a one-man war."

"Were you able to find out anything about the Bedlamites this afternoon?" Shelby asked.

"Fluff and stuff. It's going to take some time to get to the real meat. The open source stuff says the Philosophy of Bedlam are zealots. I can't tell from their website if they want an unrecognized government or no government. Hey, did you know that Bedlam was the name of a hospital for the insane in the mid-thirteenth century? It didn't help people. It was just a place to shove the nutjobs so they were out of the public eye. Either way, these crazies seem to feel that the absolute freedom of the individual can only come about through lawlessness. Stupid fucks."

While Lark tapped away on her keyboard, Trevor and Shelby sat side by side on the couch, not speaking as they waited for an update on the Bedlamites. He felt her frustration and disappointment. But he knew these men. They were dangerous, and he wanted her safe.

When the news segment finally came on, he was disappointed to find nothing new. Eric and the others had made good their escape.

Shelby picked up the remote to turn the television off as the news shifted to a segment on American presidential candidates. Just as she went to press the button, Trevor leapt to his feet.

"Holy hell!"

"What is it? What's wrong?" Shelby looked around, eyes wide.

"That's him!" Trevor practically roared. "The puppeteer. Mr. Smith." He pointed toward the screen. "We need to find out who that man is ASAP."

Shelby dropped the remote. "I know exactly who he is, and why he's on the news."

"Spill it," he ordered.

"His name is Max Whitcomb. He's the CEO of Ward Defense International. He's in the news because there are rumors that his company is in financial trouble. And I can tell you, based on what's come across my desk, the rumors are true. He's opened the company to hostile takeover from an American defense contractor. The ripples are spreading through Her Majesty's Treasury and beyond."

Lark's jaw dropped. "*That's* Mystery Man? Holy crap holy crap! Max is a philanthropist. A bleeding heart do-gooder. He donates to dozens of charities, he supports orphanages and battered women's shelters. He's a freaking god among men."

Shelby felt a grin tugging at her mouth. "But . . . ?"

Lark made a rude sound. "No one's that clean. I'll find it. You can take that to the bank."

"Start with his childhood. Where he grew up, broken home, whatever. Then I need known associates. Personal and professional affiliations," Trevor said. "Financial status. Art, money, whatever you can dig up. Most importantly, we need to prove a connection to the Philosophy of Bedlam."

"Ha! Teach your grandmother to suck eggs."

Trevor's brow knit. "I beg your pardon?"

Shelby smothered a laugh. "She means she knows how to dig up dirt."

"Ah."

"I can do my own digging, too," she said after a moment. "I have access to databases and official records."

"Unless you can log in to those databases anonymously, we'd best not take the chance."

"Okay." Shelby's voice was small.

"However, there's plenty of open source material available. Put those analyst instincts to work. See where it takes you. Everyone thinks about problems differently. You'll no doubt go in an entirely different direction than egg-sucking Lark."

Shelby giggled, clapping a hand over her mouth to stop the sound. He allowed himself a smile.

Still, waiting helplessly did not sit well with him. He got up and began to pace.

"You'll just have to be patient," Shelby said. "Take up knitting or something."

He gave her an incredulous stare. "Knit-ting?" he said, drawing it out into two words.

"What, there's nothing in your commando training that prepares you for knitting?"

"Hell, no. I could make a bomb out of what's in Lark's kitchen, though."

"Fuckin' awesome! That might even be better than harboring two fugitives." She let her gaze run over Trevor. "About the hottest fugitive I've ever seen." She quirked a brow at him, eyes dancing. "You can take me hostage any day."

AN HOUR LATER, Lark looked up from her screen. "All right. I've got the basics."

"Shoot," Trevor said.

She brought up an image. "Here's his photo. Slim, graying hair. Good-looking, in a Tony Blair sort of way. He's fifty-three, but he looks older to me. Max is old money, dating back to the Great Depression. Or the Great Slump, as you call it here."

She clicked over to another page. "His paternal great-grandfather was in auto manufacturing and real estate, which didn't experience the same slump as, say, mining or steel. In fact, he made quite a bit of money."

She was looking at him as though she expected him to comment. When he didn't, Shelby said, "So what happened then?"

"Well, his paternal grandfather was a barrister. Again, very prominent, very successful. That's the good news. The bad news is that after World War Two ended, England was flooded with refugees. He helped the effort to settle them, many into the homes his father built. And before you think he was some kind of philanthropist, those homes went to those who could pay for them. A year later, he moved to South Africa."

"That's an awfully long way to go," Trevor said. "Do you know why?"

"Hmm. Did I forget to mention he sent his wife and son to Cape Town during World War Two?"

"Yes, you did," Shelby said. "As I recall, several million people were evacuated because of German bombings. I thought they were sent to other parts of Great Britain, though."

"Yeah, but also to other places. Australia, New Zealand. Seems the grandfather saw the writing on the wall and jumped early. Got his family to safety. Then, after the war, he joined them.

"Now here's the worse news. Two years after he moved to Cape Town, apartheid started. And guess whose lily-white butt helped draft some of the anti-black legislation?"

Shelby couldn't help a shudder of revulsion. "Seriously?"

"As a heart attack. Really gross."

"As awful as that history is, I'm more interested in Max. Do people call him that?" asked Trevor.

"Mostly they call him sir," Lark said. "Fine, then. But you're missing some interesting stuff. So, fast forward to Max the Paragon."

Shelby looked through the data she'd compiled. "Max was born in Cape Town and grew up during apartheid. His parents were killed during some sort of uprising when he was fifteen, so he came back to England to live with his father's brother. He currently lives in Havering, which is an affluent community in East London."

"Married and divorced twice," Lark added. "His current wife is thirty years younger than he is, the dog."

Trevor leaned his head against the back of the sofa, hands laced behind his head. "Is his uncle alive?"

"No. His uncle died in 1985."

"What about children? Relatives might provide leverage."

Shelby checked again. "One daughter from his first marriage, two children from his second. Whoops! Looks like wife number two got pregnant before he divorced number one. The trophy wife hasn't given him any children."

"He's probably already cheating on the trophy wife." Lark

jotted herself a note. "I'll follow up with that. Might be some dirt there we can exploit."

She swiped her touchpad, moving to a new screen. "CEO of Ward Defense International, a defense contractor that supplies the Royal Marines with something called an Advanced Illuminated Antitank Weapon. Also a mind-boggling array of different kinds of munitions. And some other stuff."

"The AdIAW's a night barrage system. It's used across all Her Majesty's Armed Forces. Nothing else stood out to you?" Trevor sounded disappointed.

He'd pronounced the weapon *addy-aww.* Shelby had never heard of it, but Trevor sounded quite familiar with it.

"Hey, I know zip-all about the military. Can you see me in a uniform? All like 'yes, sir' and 'no, sir'?"

The notion was so absurd that Shelby laughed.

"Some of the crazy fringe groups have theories, like always. You know how some missiles can curve and follow a target till it blows it up? One of the crazies thinks Ward Defense International is developing ammunition that can do that. Like bullets that curve. Did you see that movie with Angelina Jolie where they curved bullets? Bullets don't curve. They go straight."

Trevor stirred. "So why fund a group of anarchists?"

"That's the question of the hour. One I will discover, but not right now. I've been staring at computer screens all day and I'm tired."

Trevor looked at her, concern and apology in his eyes. "We can easily go to a hotel, if we're imposing."

"Don't you dare. This is the most fun I've had all semester. Listen," she said. "I only have the one bedroom, and no guest room. I have blankets and pillows, though. One of you can take the sofa, but the floor's the only other option."

Trevor stood. "I'll take the floor."

Lark left the room and came back with arms piled high with linens. "Okay. Here ya go. I can tell you're about done in, Shel."

Trevor gave her a sharp look, as though he expected her to drop unconscious any minute. "I'm sorry. I didn't realize."

"It's fine." Fatigue clouded her mind.

"You've been in a stressful place for the past few days."

She yawned. "I guess. Lark, thanks for everything." She gave the other woman a hug, which she returned with enthusiasm.

The news channel was still on in the background as Lark left the room. The hostage standoff had dropped from lead story to an after-mention.

"How quickly they move on to other prey," Trevor murmured.

"It's only because they escaped. Now it's just a manhunt, instead of a standoff between police and people who bomb buildings." She left the room without another word and went into the bathroom. Doing what she could to brush her teeth, she used her finger and Lark's toothpaste. When she was as ready as she was going to be, she exited the bathroom and ran straight into Lark.

"Here. It's just a sleep shirt, but it beats sleeping in your clothes."

Shelby took the pink shirt with an adorably scowling Tweety Bird on the front with the words *Don't talk to me* printed on the bottom.

"Thanks." She took it into the bathroom and changed quickly.

Trevor looked up as she came back into the living room, then did a double take. The shirt hit her halfway down her thighs, but she might as well have been naked the way he was looking at her. He cleared his throat and looked away. So he wasn't ready to forgive her. She couldn't really blame him.

She made up the sofa with sheet, blanket, and pillow. He did the same, bedding down nearby, between herself and the front door.

"Are you expecting trouble?"

"Hope for the best, prepare for the worst. Why take any chances?"

She lay down on her makeshift bed. "Well . . . good night."

"Night."

Even after she closed her eyes, sleep refused to come. Her entire life had been turned upside down today. How should she feel? What reaction would be considered normal under these circumstances? Trevor had been right when he noted she'd been more annoyed than scared in the museum. Why? The answer came easily. She didn't want to die, but nor did she particularly have anything to live for.

"You can't sleep either, huh?"

She rolled over so she could see him. Instead of lying down, he sat propped against the end of the sofa.

"No. I'm trying to process everything, I guess."

Even in the dimness, she could see his faint nod. "Is there anyone you want to call? Family? Friends?"

"I could, but what would I tell them?" She sat up, wrapping the blanket around her shoulders. "Oh, by the way, I was taken hostage the other day by a bunch of maniacs who bomb buildings and stab people in the stomach for no reason, but I knew one of the terrorists and he helped me out and I'm now on the run with him? Besides, I can't let on who you really are."

"No," he agreed. "Thank you for understanding that."

"Do you think she'll find anything?"

He shrugged. "Depends on how good her resources are, and how well Whitcomb covered his trail. We'll have to wait and see." He sounded disgruntled.

"We can still take up knitting."

He exhaled a soft, unamused laugh. "I hate sitting around feeling useless."

"I know. Is this your first mission since Azakistan?"

"No."

"And you can't tell me anything about where you've been or what's you've done?"

"That's right. I can't even share much with my wife, if I ever marry."

The thought of him married to someone else made her chest tighten. Did she care about Trevor? Yes. He was an honest, honorable man. The thing with Christina had been a misunderstanding. Did she dare open her heart to the possibility of a relationship, knowing her heart might be pulverized?

No.

Maybe.

She saw her life stretching out before her. She loved her work. But work wouldn't keep her warm on a cold night. Trevor could.

Would Trevor want to change her, as Bruce had? He seemed to like her well enough as she was, but they all started out like that. Bruce had been neither honest nor honorable, though it had taken her a long time to realize it. If she took a chance with Trevor, would he try to take her independence? No way she would let him, of course. She'd grown far beyond that.

It was all moot, though. Trevor no longer cared for her.

"I think I'll try to sleep again." This time when she closed her eyes, her thoughts drifted to the woman down the hall. Whatever else happened, they needed to protect Lark. What would Shelby have done if Lark had a live-in boyfriend? Husband? Child? She envisioned Lark, with a baby girl in her arms, sporting hot pink hair. It made her laugh.

"Share the joke."

"I was just thinking, that if Lark ever settled down, how many tattoos and piercings her children would have."

He chuckled. "She is quite the character, isn't she?

"She's a nice person."

"The two are not mutually exclusive. Is she properly a rave girl?"

"From the stories she tells, she really is a wild child."

"I'd hazard a guess she gave her parents a right bit of trouble. At least on this side of the pond, upper-crust families dress the same, sound the same, pursue the same white-collar careers."

Shelby propped her head on her hand. "She's authentically herself. She doesn't kowtow to anyone."

Trevor chuckled. "Nor do you."

"Thank you. It's been a fight at times. Small-town kids in the South have the same problems as your aristocrats do here. Anyone who doesn't like tractor pulls and moonshine is a misfit."

Trevor rolled his head toward her. "You had a difficult childhood?"

"In some ways." She didn't want to talk about her childhood right now. "But it's late and I'm tired."

"Good night, then." Did he sound disappointed?

This time when she closed her eyes, sleep came.

Chapter Fifteen

TREVOR POURED HIMSELF a bowl of cereal before realizing the refrigerator held no milk. Sighing, he mentally composed a list of groceries as he made do with leftover chicken with snow peas. To his relief, Lark at least had proper coffee beans and a grinder.

He'd eaten, showered, and put back on yesterday's clothes before either of the ladies stirred. Lark stumbled into the kitchen while Shelby used the bathroom.

"Coffee," she croaked.

Trevor nodded toward the pot. "It's rather strong."

"Thank Christ."

She poured herself a cup, adding a lot of sugar and half-and-half.

"Maybe I can persuade you to make a run to the market? I'll pay, of course, but it would be better if Shelby and I stay out of sight."

"Sure, I can do that. Make me up a list or something. I don't cook much."

She brought him a pad of paper, and he thought about what he might need. He jotted notes. When he was done, Lark took the list and scanned it, eyebrows raised.

"Pledge? Tea, eggs, et cetera. But Pledge? Fire extinguisher? What, are you saying something about my housekeeping abilities?"

Trevor glanced around the kitchen pointedly, then let his gaze encompass the rest of the flat. Turning back to her, he arched one eyebrow.

She blew out an annoyed breath. "Whatevs."

"Actually," he said, relenting, "they have nothing to do with cleanliness. I need aerosol for a makeshift flamethrower."

"Seriously? Wicked awesome." She looked over the rest of the list. "Lighter. Maglite flashlight. Screwdriver. Hair spray?"

"Good morning."

Trevor turned to Shelby. She wore a spaghetti-strap sundress, the purple on top fading to a white skirt with purple swirls at the hem. It hit her a few inches above her knees. She looked cool and elegant.

"Good morning. There's coffee."

"Pretty dress," Lark said. "I wish we were the same size so I could borrow it."

Shelby stood next to Lark and eyed her up and down. "You're what? Five-five? I'm only two inches taller than you."

"Still." Lark blew on her coffee and took a sip. "Perfection."

Shelby poured herself a cup. "Do you work today?"

"I have a class at noon, technically. I usually skip it, though. The prof's a moron. Anyway, staying here is way more interesting."

"Your tattoo is beautiful. How come I've never seen it before?" Shelby touched Lark's shoulder, tracing the outline of a beautiful woman with feathers instead of hair.

"They make me cover it up at work," she groused. She tipped

her head out of the way to allow Shelby an unobstructed view, then turned her left wrist over to show the symbol there. "Nothing they can do about my Ohm, though. You got any?"

"No—"

"Not you, Shel. You're too conservative to have a tattoo. I was asking Hunky Guy."

Conservative? Yes, Shelby would seem that way to a free spirit like Lark. But clearly the other woman didn't see the molten lava hidden just under the surface. The passionate woman he knew was there.

"Yeah." He pulled up the rugby sweatshirt to reveal an intricately detailed tank across his ribs.

Lark traced her fingers over it. "Nice. You were a tanker?"

"My Uncle Alfie. He retired as a Brigadier from the Royal Tank Regiment."

Lark pulled in her brows, tilting her head to look at him from an angle. "That's good?"

Trevor grinned. "Very prestigious. He influenced my boyhood more, I think, than even my own parents."

Shelby disappeared for a moment and came back with her laptop, setting it up on the kitchen table. Trevor couldn't see what she was looking up, but a moment later she pulled her mobile from her dress pocket and dialed.

"Yes, I'm calling to check the status of one of your patients? Floyd Panderson. Yes, I'll hold." She wouldn't meet his eyes. Perhaps he should have thought to call. "Yes, I'm here . . . I understand. Thank you."

She set her phone down. "He's in critical but stable condition. That's all she'd tell me, since I'm not family."

"The one who was stabbed? Did you know him? Other than him being one of the hostages, I mean."

"They were dating," Trevor said. He kept his tone bland.

Shelby's chin notched up. "Only for a couple of weeks, and I didn't know he was married."

Lark whooped with laughter. "Oh, that's precious. But you're still checking up on him?"

Shelby lifted her shoulders and let them drop. "He might be a jerk, but that doesn't mean I want him to die."

As though she couldn't keep still, she pushed her chair back and roamed into the living room, peering out the window. He followed her.

"I'd prefer you stay away from the windows," he said. "It's better if we stay out of sight."

Shelby moved to an armchair without argument.

Lark joined them, curling up in the rose-patterned chair. "So what's your story, Hunky Guy? Cop? Scotland Yard? MI-5? MI-6?"

He groaned inwardly. Truthfully, Lark had shown amazing restraint waiting this long to grill him.

"Just a patriot. And I thought we agreed on Trevor."

"Yeah, but you have a military background, right? Special Forces? SEALs?"

"That's the American military," he pointed out.

"Yeah, whatever. So what were you?"

Trevor slanted a grin at her. "I was a juvenile delinquent."

"No way! Join the Army or go to jail?"

He tilted his head. "I beg your pardon?"

Shelby kicked off her shoes and curled her legs under her. "That hasn't been the case in decades. The military raised their standards years ago. Now it's mostly college-educated kids, or kids looking to get an education."

"Oh. So you're rich and have a secret identity, like Bruce Wayne or Oliver Queen? You party all day and fight crime at night?"

Trevor sent Shelby a bemused look.

"Quite the character, as I said. I warned you. Lark, leave him be. He's had a tough couple of days."

Lark stuck out her lower lip, looking all of twelve. "All right, if you won't tell me about your military training, and you're not a masked vigilante, tell me something personal. I bet you started young with the girls. How old, and who was your first?"

"Lark!"

Trevor rubbed a hand over his face. Shelby sounded like she didn't know whether to be outraged or amused by the other woman's temerity.

"I started at sixteen," he said. Shelby's face creased in surprise. Why was he answering such a personal question from the inquisitive little sprite? Damned if he knew. "Rosemary Dane. She was seventeen and very experienced by then. I was a year away from my A-levels at Eton. She studied at Windsor Girls' School across the Thames. We were together nearly every weekend. When she went on to university, we said we'd stay together. I rang her up one weekend, and a man answered. She was having a bit on the side, but she gave me the cold shoulder, as though *I'd* done something wrong. That was the end of it."

"That blows. But it doesn't make you a juvenile delinquent. That takes wrecking a Beamer, at the very least."

Shelby groaned. "Lark, for the love of—"

"It was a Jaguar, but yes."

"No way! Freaking awesome! Unless you were hurt. Were you hurt?"

Trevor sighed, pushing his legs out in front of him. "No. But the lady I was with ended up in hospital. That was the end of my drinking."

Shelby's eyes were huge in her face. The very neutrality in his voice had probably told her there was more to the story. He met her eyes.

"Are you sure you want to hear this?"

"Fuck, yeah!"

But he hadn't been speaking to Lark. His attention remained focused on her. She slowly nodded.

"My father expected me to go into politics or law, as he did. Had no interest in either. I rebelled, as a lot of young men do. The usual—getting tanked up, fights, motorcycles. I was home on holiday from Eton. Went to a bar. Got laggered. Met a woman. Got behind the wheel." He stopped and cleared his throat. "She, uh, she was, um . . . kissing me. I crashed into a utility pole."

Lark started to laugh. "No fucking way! You wrapped your car around a pole getting a BJ?"

Trevor wouldn't meet Shelby's eyes. "My father had enough influence to get the DUI charge dismissed. But it snapped me out of it. My self-indulgent behavior could have had very serious consequences."

"Was she all right?" Shelby asked quietly.

"She had a broken arm and was concussed. She also turned out to be married."

"I'm sorry."

"I'm sorry she was hurt because of me. I paid her medical costs against my father's advice. He was more concerned with inviting a lawsuit, I think."

"Then you realized the errors of your ways," Lark said. "And became Batman."

Trevor snorted. "Hardly. Then I went to law school at Yale."

Lark pulled her feet in and turned sideways on the sofa. Her toes almost brushed his thigh. "So what's a freaking lawyer doing with a bunch of mangy terrorists?"

He laid his head against the back of the sofa. "I quit after two semesters. Now, leave off. I need a nap."

He folded his arms across his chest and closed his eyes. He wasn't really tired. He just didn't want to see condemnation in Shelby's eyes.

Lark tapped away on her computer. Shelby flipped though the channels on the telly and eventually settled on an action film. He tried to focus on it, but his mind kept drifting to Shelby. He knew she'd pictured his childhood as privileged, pampered, and perfect. What would she do with the truth?

"That's stupid," he said abruptly. Both women looked at him in surprise. His eyes were half lidded as he watched an action scene. "No one would do that in a proper fight."

Lark bounced on the cushion and clapped her hands together. "Oh! Show me, show me. Teach me how to kick ass."

That pulled a grin from him. "In one afternoon?"

"Why not? I've got my search engines running. There's not much else to do until they spit out something useful. What else we got to do?"

He stood and stretched. "God forbid everything go pear shaped, but in a dangerous situation, knowing one or two moves might save your life. Let's do it."

Shelby settled in to watch.

"Nope. You participate, too." Trevor crooked a finger at her.

Radiating reluctance, she joined them in moving the furniture back so they had space.

"I teach self-defense courses for military wives on foreign postings," Trevor said. "When I'm in garrison. Believe it or not, the most important thing isn't how to throw a punch or kick." He tapped the side of his head. "The battle is won or lost here first."

"Like, if you believe it, you can do it?" Lark asked.

"Not precisely. Women are nurturers. Mothers. Wives. A woman's instinct isn't to fight; it's to protect."

Lark puffed up. "Are you saying women are weaker than men? 'Cause if you are, we're going to have a problem."

"Not at all." Without warning, he transformed into warrior mode, stalking toward Lark with his fist raised. He made hostile intent radiate from every pore. As expected, Lark squeaked and threw her arms over her head, cringing away from him. He stopped, dropped his arm, and relaxed. Both Shelby and Lark's eyes were huge in their faces.

"I've found over and over again that women don't value themselves as highly as they do others," he continued, as though nothing had happened. "What they'll do for a loved one, for example, they won't necessarily do for themselves. Women can be more fierce and deadly than any man when you rouse their protective instincts. For example, think of the one thing, the one person whom you hold most dear. The one person you love more than any other in the world. The one person you would die for."

"My baby sister." Lark's eyes softened. "I'd do anything for her."

"Good. Now imagine that you are the only thing—the very last thing—standing between her and the rapist in front of you trying to get at her." Once again, he morphed into a deadly warrior.

This time, Lark's eyes narrowed and became ferocious as she raised her fists, clearly prepared to fight. "No way you get past me."

Trevor nodded and stopped. "That's what I mean."

Lark's jaw dropped and she stared at Trevor in amazement. "I did it! I stood my ground."

"Well done. It's that feeling, that instinct I want you to focus on as I teach you some basics. Shelby, your turn."

Her brows pulled down, she took her place in front of Trevor.

"Same thing. Place the one person you love the most in the world in the forefront of your mind." He came at her. Her breath left her lungs in a rush and she backed away fast, hands held out in front of her as though to ward him off. He stopped.

"Okay, we'll go a bit slower. Picture someone important to you. Sister, friend, lover? Pet?"

Her hands started to shake and she shook her head back and forth. She didn't seem to be able to pull enough air into her lungs. Alarmed, Trevor took her by the arm and pulled her to the sofa, pushing her onto it and bending her head forward between her knees. What the hell had just happened here?

"Easy, Shel," he said. "Take your time. Catch your breath." Without warning, she jumped from the sofa and ran from the room.

Chapter Sixteen

LARK ORDERED IN pizza for lunch, which Shelby ate mostly in silence. Trevor and Lark chatted, which was to say, Trevor listened as Lark chattered. Shelby couldn't even pretend to care.

Her entire world had just tilted on its axis.

Picture the one person you would die for.

Which of her family or friends did she care the most about? Trevor's question had seemed so simple, but it was one for which she had no answer.

There was no one.

She'd tried to pay attention while Trevor taught them something called a palm strike. Hold an imaginary pie by her hip, then smash the pie into the bad guy's face. Aim for under the chin or into the nose. He also taught them how to knee someone in the groin for maximum effect. Grab their shoulders and yank them forward as she drove her knee in and up. Do it until the attacker dropped. Her focus had been fractured. Trevor had noticed, but had mercifully given her space.

Picture the one person you would die for.

She was not close to her family. She'd left the insular world of Coon Bluff behind long ago. The poverty she could have handled. But the small-town hypocrisy had sickened her to the point of fleeing as soon as she was able. The gossiping, rampant intolerance, and holier-than-thou attitudes, while those same good folk cheated on their spouses and beat their children. Singing hymns on Sunday and gay-bashing on Wednesday. Everyone in everyone else's business, with dirty little secrets passed down from generation to inescapable generation.

Her family hadn't understood or supported her desire to leave home, go to college, build a career. Her rare visits were awkward and uncomfortable, punctured by crude attempts to set her up with some local boy so she'd come home, get married, and have babies. She had nothing in common with them. Eventually, it had been easier to stay away.

Her friends were also her coworkers. She had no husband, no lover. She'd allowed her career to consume her. And until now, she'd been happy with her decision.

After lunch, Lark resumed her computer research. Too keyed up to sit still, Shelby wandered from kitchen to living room and back again. Trevor lined up all six handguns on the coffee table and inspected them one by one, breaking them down and examining each piece. With nothing better to do, she curled up in one of the armchairs and watched him. The absolute expertise of his motions reassured her.

"This lot is filthy," he said, gesturing to the weapons he'd confiscated from the Bedlamites. "And the firing pin on the Springfield is worn. Doesn't look like Eric ever made them maintain their equipment. We'll have to pick up some cleaning supplies to make sure these don't jam up when we need them."

When. Not if. A chill slithered down her back.

"Have you ever fired this thing? It looks brand new." He held up her Beretta, grip loose as he pointed it toward the ceiling.

Shelby flushed. "Er, uh, I took a class when I bought it."

"Not good," he said. "If you're going to have a handgun, you need to know how to use it. You need to practice regularly at a firing range. If not, you'll likely freeze at the worst possible time, and have it taken from you and used against you."

"Okay. I understand." Maybe she'd get rid of the thing. It had seemed like a good idea when she'd broken things off last year with Bruce. For a while he'd virtually stalked her, demanding that she resume their engagement. Verbally abusing her until she was afraid he would physically attack her as well. Now, though, she couldn't imagine herself shooting anyone.

"All right, kiddies. News update time."

Shelby leapt to her feet and hustled into the kitchen, Trevor right behind her. "What did you find?"

Lark beamed at them. "Good stuff. So Max garners sympathy votes as an apartheid orphan. In fact, he's been vocal about the black violence in South Africa that killed a lot of whites—innocent victims, according to him. Contrary to popular belief and his official biography, Max's mother did not die in South Africa. Turns out she's alive and well and living in a nursing home in Kent."

Trevor tipped his head to the side. "Are you certain it's his mother? Could it be another relation?"

Lark puffed up indignantly. "No, it's his mother. I found a passenger manifest from 1977—and believe me, it was not easy to find—for a Nandi and Maxwell Whitcomb, traveling from South Africa to London on a cargo ship called the Cape Queen. The ship was German-owned, registered in Angola, and had an all-

Portuguese crew. No one to know or care about just two more apartheid refugees."

"Maybe a sister? Aunt?"

Lark blew out an annoyed breath. "Max is an only child. I found nothing whatsoever to suggest any other family in South Africa. His father had a brother here in England, but that's it. I could be wrong, but I'm not."

"All wonderful information," Shelby said. "Anything else?"

"Yeah. There are no records of Nandi after she and Max docked in London. Nandi must be short for something fancy. Amanda? Anastasia? I couldn't find her birth records because her last name doesn't seem to be mentioned anywhere, so I'm wondering if she went back to using her maiden name for some reason. But I did find a birth certificate for Max. Born in Cape Town in 1962. He went to live with his paternal uncle in 1977 at fifteen years old. From there on out, every reference to his parents shows them killed in a black uprising in 1976."

Shelby frowned, disappointed. "Well, it proves he lied to the public. But having a mother who's alive isn't a crime."

Lark flashed a smile. "It's a start, though. I'm combing through a lot of data. There's a reason Max wanted his mother out of the public eye, and I'm gonna find out what it is. Here, I found an old photo, though. It's Max's grandfather with Winston Churchill. How cool is that?"

She handed Trevor the picture centered on photo paper. It was a grainy black-and-white, but the man standing next to the former prime minister was a dead ringer for Max Whitcomb.

"Maybe it's really him. Maybe he's one of the immortals from Highlander. 'There can be only one.' Maybe he's the one."

Shelby laughed. "You watch too many movies."

"Not possible," Lark replied promptly.

Shelby studied the photo over his shoulder. The two men stood in front of a courthouse. The former prime minister wore a suit with his trademark polka-dot bowtie. The elder Whitcomb wore a plain black gown and barrister's wig.

"Is he still living?" he asked.

"Nope. He croaked about ten years ago."

Trevor clicked his tongue against the roof of his mouth as he contemplated the woman in front of him. "Hmm. Given what you just discovered about his mother, how can you be certain his grandfather is really dead? Or his father, for that matter?"

"I anticipated that question," Lark said. "The grandfather is dead because otherwise he'd be a billion years old now. A hundred and seventeen, actually. Still. As for Max's dear old dad, I traced his death record through Ancestry dot com. While there's no actual death record for Nandi/Amanda/Anastasia, Nicholas is recycled worm food. Definitely."

"It might have proved useful to talk to him. I want to talk to the mother, certainly."

"Certainly," Lark mocked. "We can do that after I make a store run. I guess you guys need to eat and all that. And Trevor here wants to Pledge the shit out of my place. I'll be back in about an hour. Make that two."

Shelby sighed heavily as she shut the door behind Lark. "I could really use some fresh air. Couldn't we go for a walk?"

Trevor pursed his lips together. "I appreciate your patience with this, Shel. I know this must be difficult for you. You've been a real trooper."

She glanced toward the window. "I take that as a no."

"I'm truly sorry. I don't want Jukes finding Lark. It would put her in danger."

"No, I understand. I don't want that, either." She flopped inelegantly onto the sofa. "I just . . . I need to *do* something."

"Believe me, I understand." He exhaled a soft laugh. "One of the hardest parts of training for me was learning to be still."

She curled her legs under her. "Tell me."

He joined her on the sofa. "Part of the training for Selection takes place in Borneo. Jungle training, as I'm sure you can imagine. We did survival exercises, a good deal of patrolling, that sort of thing. We also learned observation techniques. I remember one exercise that lasted three days. The objective was to monitor and report on movements inside an 'enemy' camp. We worked our way in close enough to get a good field of vision, each of us in a different area around the camp. Once we were in position, we literally did not move a muscle, for fear of being detected. We were that close."

Shelby raised her eyebrows. "You didn't move a muscle for three days? How is that even possible?"

"A matter of determination and discipline. A lesson I needed to learn."

Curiosity piqued, she leaned back against the armrest, resting her head on a fist. "Camp, as in a campfire with people sitting around roasting marshmallows? I mean, I know that's not what it was, but I don't really know the specifics of military training."

"This particular camp housed roughly a hundred and twenty men." Trevor stretched his legs out in front of him, lacing his hands behind his head. "It simulated a Soviet mechanized infantry unit. Armored personnel carriers, infantry fighting vehicles, anti-tank missiles. Our task was to identify their capabilities and their chain of command. Record the comings and goings, not only in and out of the camp, but also internally. Measure morale, identify dissenters who might be exploited. That sort of thing."

Shelby chuckled. "That sounds like exactly what I do in political circles. Minus the anti-tank missiles, of course."

Trevor laughed, as she'd hoped he would. "I think you walk a minefield every day you go to work. Politicians can be more lethal than any commando."

"Public image is so very important to the folks I work with," she agreed. "Sometimes I feel as though some of them would kill, just to maintain their reputations. But the truth is politics is mostly about bluster and bluffing and deal making. That's nothing like what you're trained to do. Jungle survival training, eating bugs, and sleeping in the mud. Doing that thing where you have to endure capture and torture?"

The contrast between gentleman and tough military man fascinated her. He appeared open and relaxed as he shared his stories with her.

"SERE. Survival, Evasion, Resistance, and Escape. A lot of candidates fail during that portion of training."

She shuddered. "I couldn't do it."

"Selection is all about self-discovery, learned at the very brink of human endurance," he said. "You're tested in training so you won't fail in the real world. Every man on a team is an expert. Anyone not up to scratch is a liability to the team and could get someone killed."

He spoke so matter-of-factly that it dimmed the finality of his words. She reminded herself that this man had been trained to do far more than eat bugs. "Can I ask you a personal question?"

"Of course." He gave her a warm smile. Was there something more flickering in his eyes? Hope? But it wasn't that kind of personal question.

"You've killed." She made it a statement, not a question. "Does it ever bother you? Some veterans never get over their war experiences."

He sat up abruptly. "No. Never."

"I'm sorry. I—" *Shouldn't have asked.* Had she crossed some sort of line?

Resting his elbows on his knees, he clasped his hands loosely between them. "It's tough for an outsider to understand the SpecOps mindset. I do what's necessary for the operation. If I have to take out a target, it's not a person. It's a terrorist or a criminal or an anarchist. It's not an enjoyment of killing; it's accomplishing the mission. Nothing more, nothing less."

"I'm sorry," she said again. "I didn't mean to upset you."

"You didn't. It's just not easy to explain to a civilian." He gave a tired smile. "Who Dares Wins."

"The SAS motto."

He nodded. "When you said you wanted to ask me a personal question, I was expecting something else."

There it was again. The bright question, the hope in his eyes. She didn't know what it meant. But she could finally tell him what she'd wanted to since their argument in the hotel room. Her shoulders tensed as she steeled herself to say it.

"I only went out with Hugo—Gunnery Sergeant Bisantz—three times. The last night, at dinner, he told me he was happy to play second fiddle if I just wanted to talk, uh, talk about . . . you, but that we should just plan on being friends, because I . . . I was obviously still hung up on you." She couldn't look at him. His silence made it so much worse. She drew a ragged breath and forced herself to continue.

"I never slept with him. I couldn't, not after what you and I shared. I lied to you. In the hospital. When I told you it meant nothing. You were lucky to be alive after being shot, and I—" She stopped, unable to push any more words through her clogged throat.

Trevor reached for her, tugging her toward him across the cushions so she ended up sprawled across his chest. For a moment, they simply stared at one another, hers fearful and his full of yearning. He slid a hand into her hair and guided her mouth to his, kissing her so softly she barely felt it. Without volition, her lips parted, inviting him in. He angled her head and fused their mouths together, but still so slowly, so tenderly she wanted to cry.

When he broke the kiss, he rested his forehead on hers. "I get that you were scared. Can you tell me why?"

She pulled away and sat up, every cell in her body screaming for her to remain exactly where she was. In his arms. He deserved an answer, though.

"I'd just broken things off with Bruce two months before I met you. We were together for two years." She risked a quick glance at him. "Having feelings for another man so soon, and so strongly . . . and having that man abandon me at the drop of a hat . . . I'm sorry. I do understand. But you did, and it hurt. You never came back. Anyway, having a man in my life would put all sorts of chains on me. So I'd sworn off relationships."

"Chains? That's an odd word."

"Expectations, then."

He settled his shoulders against the back of the sofa. "Can you give me an example? I'm not quite following you."

She thought about it for a minute. "Oh, say for instance I've been invited to a friend's baby shower, and my boyfriend has a fundraising dinner at the same time. I'm expected to drop my plans to accommodate his. Like that."

He didn't say a word. When she finally lifted her head, she found him examining her, eyes narrowed and frowning.

"Tell me about Bruce."

And reveal her stupidity in trusting a man like him? No.

"Shelby. Please."

The soft entreaty dissolved her resistance. "Oh, fine, then. I interned with the Public Affairs Office within the Bureau of Political-Military Affairs at the State Department. He met with the director a couple of times, and finally told me he kept making up excuses to come into our office so he could see me. At first, he was charming. Charismatic. Knew how to treat a lady. His words, actually.

"After we'd been dating a while, he started to change. Instead of letting me order in a restaurant, he'd order for both of us. When I told him I preferred to make my own choice, he told me to stop being difficult. That he couldn't treat me like a lady if I didn't act like one." Now that she'd started, she couldn't seem to stop the flow of words. "He'd be sweet one minute and sarcastic the next. Made fun of me in public. One time he disappeared for five weeks with no explanation, and when he came back, he just expected us to start up where we'd left off. I guess I'm a really slow learner."

"Or he's a horse's ass."

"Or that." She forced a chuckle. "He was furious when I accepted the posting to Ma'ar ye zhad. Azakistan is on the other side of the world. How come I can't be like a normal woman? Didn't I love him?"

"Yes, definitely a horse's ass."

This time, her laugh was more genuine.

"One hundred percent, grade-A asshole."

Chapter Seventeen

A KNOCK ON the door heralded Lark's arrival. Trevor jerked awake. When had he dozed off? He'd convinced Shelby to put her head in his lap and close her eyes. Apparently, he'd also closed his.

Shelby sat up slowly, rubbing her eyes. "What time is it?"

He glanced at the DVD player. The time flashed twelve o'clock. Naturally, Lark would be one of those people who never set the clock. "Not sure."

Lark came in loaded down with multiple bags, including a garment bag over her shoulder. Trevor took the bulk of it, setting them down on the kitchen counter.

"What is all this?" Shelby asked. She pointed to the garment bag.

"Disguises. I was thinking while I was food shopping that you're going to need to go out at some point. You can't prove your innocence hiding in my flat."

Trevor unzipped the garment bag and whistled as he pulled out a dark blue suit. "Burberry. Expensive."

Lark grinned, clearly pleased with herself. "I guessed your size, but I'm usually pretty good about these things. I also bought stuff for you, Shel."

Shelby opened one of the bags, pulling out a red silk dress. It had a low neckline with beading around it, tiny sleeves, and would end about mid-thigh. "Holy cow."

"Right. Wearing that and changing your hair, no one will be looking at your face, I guarantee it."

"Changing my hair?"

Lark opened another bag, pulling out several boxes of hair-coloring treatments. "Blonde," she said decisively.

Shelby twisted her fingers together. "I can't use my ATM card. I won't be able to pay you back until—"

"Pfft. Have you forgotten my über-wealthy family? Trust me. I can afford it."

Trevor nodded his thanks. "Nevertheless, I won't abuse your generosity. I will repay you."

"You can," she shot back. "News says you're Trevor Willoughby. As my reward for the disguises and for finding the not-dead momma, you can tell me your real name."

"That is my proper name," he said. Technically, it wasn't a lie. His middle name *was* Willoughby.

Shelby shot him a startled look. She didn't say anything, but Lark's shrewd gaze flicked to her and away again. He had to remember the younger woman was brilliant.

"Fine. Be that way." Lark grabbed Shelby's arm. "Come on."

Shelby followed her into the bathroom. Trevor took the opportunity to check in again with MI-5, but the situation hadn't changed. There were no clues as to where the Bedlamites were hiding. The Camden Lock headquarters had been abandoned.

"I've sussed out the identity of the man behind the mask. It's

Max Whitcomb. I didn't recognize him; I spend too much time out of the country, and not enough watching the news, obviously. Plus his face was in shadow. Can you authorize surveillance on him?" he asked.

"Naturally," Danby answered, a bit stiffly. "But if you're right, simple surveillance isn't going to get us enough to prosecute."

"I'm right," Trevor said. "I'm going to talk to his mother, who, contrary to popular opinion, didn't die in an apartheid uprising. She's in a nursing home in Maidstone, Kent. I'll be discreet."

"Stay under the radar, Trev."

"The only way I can do that is if there's an egress strategy. Is there?" he asked bluntly.

"Nothing's changed," Danby admitted. "We still have the same three options."

"Then what you're really saying is don't get caught and embarrass MI-5 as I walk a swaying tightrope without a net." He disconnected.

When the ladies finally emerged from the loo, he glanced up, then did a double take. He barely recognized Shelby. Her dark brown hair was now so blonde it looked almost white, and had been clipped into a pixie cut similar to Lark's. Her makeup was dramatic. Her eyes had been large before, but now glowed amber and huge with the addition of shadow and mascara. Her lipstick was a deep pink. And the dress . . . It hugged her slender curves, and the neckline plunged to reveal enough cleavage to make his mouth water.

"Amazing," he murmured. "You hardly look like the same person."

"That was the whole point, right?" said Lark. "Your turn, Hunky Guy. Come into my lair."

Trevor obediently went to sit on the toilet seat while Lark fussed over his shaggy hair, running her fingers through it and pulling it this way and that. "Hmm. This all has to go. You need short, neat hair to go with that expensive suit."

"Do you actually know what you're doing?"

"Look at Shel again and tell me I don't. Do you think I get this look by accident?" She gestured to her own style and makeup.

"I place myself in your hands, then."

Twenty minutes later, Lark allowed him to look into the mirror. The cut wasn't as military-short as he was used to, but it was neat and would complement the suit nicely.

"Here, use my razor," she said. "Shave off that scruff. As much as I like it, it's too biker-bad for your new look."

She left him alone, so he soaped up his jaw and shaved. He felt much more like himself after. He put on the suit and the shoes Lark had purchased. They pinched his toes, but the suit fit as though it had been tailored for him.

Both women stared when he walked into the living room.

"Holy shit!" Lark said. "You could'a just stepped out of *GQ* magazine!"

Shelby looked him over from head to foot, and he had to physically stop himself from asking if she liked the look. Then she smiled, and he knew.

"You look so handsome," she said.

"And you could knock me over with a feather right now." He touched her earring, a red cascade of sparkly stuff that drew the eye from her face to her breasts. "But you've always been beautiful to me, no matter what you wear. Your beauty comes from the inside."

"You always say the right thing." She tilted her head up and kissed him. Softly at first, then with more confidence.

"Ugh. Get a room." Lark didn't even glance up from her laptop.

Shelby exhaled a shaky laugh and stepped back. "Shall we go?"

"Hang on," Lark said. "Let me start this program running first."

Trevor and Shelby both looked at her.

"You can't go," Shelby blurted.

"No," Trevor said at the same time.

Lark looked up, stubbornness flashing in her eyes. "Give me one good reason why not."

"I don't want you drawn into this, if we're discovered," Trevor said.

"Look at yourselves. You won't be. And how are you going to get there without my car?"

Obviously, he could simply take the keys from her. Still, he'd agreed they were a team. He couldn't exclude her.

Lark read his expression correctly. "Great! I'll grab my purse."

She came back with the largest handbag he'd ever seen. She stuffed her laptop into it. "Okay. I'm set."

"What on earth can you be carrying inside that carpetbag?" he asked.

"Everything plus the kitchen sink," she replied promptly. She'd obviously been asked the question before. "I could live for a week on what's in here."

LARK DROVE THE way she looked—fast and free. The rules of the road seemed to be only suggestions to her as she wove through traffic, heading to Maidstone in Kent. By the time they arrived, Trevor was in a cold sweat. Facing down a squad of al-Qaeda terrorists armed with only a knife didn't compete with driving with the girl maniac.

Maidstone was a picturesque town. They crossed St. Peter's Bridge and turned left to follow the meandering route of the river. At Waterside, they turned right. Most of the buildings were old brick or stone, giving the town a medieval feel. They passed several churches. The GPS took them almost to the other end of town. Eventually, Lark pulled up in front of a yellow brick house with several bay windows.

Resisting the urge to jump out and kiss the ground, he instead looked over the property. It seemed newer than the buildings around it. Subtle brick curlicues gave it a quaint and homey feel. The sign announcing this was the Queen Mary Home for the Elderly had a crack running up one side.

It was chillier here than in London. Shelby crossed her arms over her middle. Trevor wrapped an arm over her shoulder and tucked her into his side.

The tiny lobby area had two plastic chairs and a waist-high pottery urn with fake flowers. As they entered, a small, wrinkled old man greeted them from a desk to the right.

"Afternoon. How can I help you?"

"We're here to visit Max Whitcomb's mother," Trevor said.

"Who?"

The three looked at one another.

"Nandi?" Lark tried.

"Oh, yeah, Nandi," the man said. "Nandi Mkhize, though, not whatever you said. She'll be outside in the garden this time of day. Fact is, she spends most of her time there. Sign in, please."

A sturdy woman in nurse's scrubs came around the corner from the hallway perpendicular to the lobby.

"Daniel, for heaven's sakes. How many times do I have to tell you not to take over my chair?"

The old man jumped down. "You weren't here. And see? I greeted these fine people. They're here to visit Nandi."

The nurse turned suspicious eyes their way. "Nandi? Why?"

"We're friends of her son's," Shelby said. "He asked us to check in on her while we were in the area."

"Hmmph. Nandi doesn't have a son. No relatives at all, as far as I know. She talks like she does, but you're the first visitors she's had in years. Maybe ever."

Lark frowned. "That's so sad."

"Be that as it may, she'll probably enjoy the visit. I'll take you down to her."

They walked down a long corridor with doors every fifteen feet. Most were open. They were little more than hospital rooms. Two beds, two dressers, some personal items. The hallway was dim and smelled of dust and mildew. The few residents they passed, mostly on walkers, also smelled musty. Or worse.

From the hallway, they entered the dayroom. Shelby gagged.

"What the hell is that smell?" Lark asked, pinching her nose closed.

"Body odor," Trevor said grimly. "Urine. Residents who haven't been bathed in days. Antiseptic to cover it up."

What kind of man would put his own mother in a place like this?

The nurse took them out a back door into the garden, which turned out to be a small square abutting a major street. The noise of passing cars and the smell of exhaust hung in the air. The garden itself consisted of a small grove of overgrown trees and a tiny patch of grass. Several white benches ringed the area. A single wheelchair sat near the fence by the road, with the occupant's back toward them.

"Nandi."

The nurse had to repeat herself twice more before the woman stirred. "Is it dinnertime yet?"

Trevor detected a faint accent under the English. "Es it dinna-toime yet?"

"Dinner was an hour ago. You ate pasta and green beans."

"Oh, right." The woman looked disappointed. "Could I have a cuppa?"

She'd pronounced it *hrroight*. Trevor finally placed the accent as Afrikaans.

He knew what he was going to find when the woman turned around.

"These nice folks are here to visit you." The nurse ignored Nandi's request. "Have fun, kiddies."

Trevor was glad when the nurse left. There had been no real care or concern in her face or voice. Just a woman doing a job for a paycheck. These residents deserved better.

"Mrs. Whitcomb?" Shelby asked.

The woman slowly pulled the wheels to swivel the wheelchair toward them. She appeared tired and careworn. Her dark skin contrasted with her blue patterned dress and head scarf, neither of which had been laundered recently.

The woman looked up at her. "I haven't heard that name for many a year."

Trevor gestured for Shelby to sit beside Nandi. She did. "Mrs. Mkhize, then?"

"Mkhize was my maiden name. My son thought it best to go back to using it, since my husband has been dead for so many years. My married name was Whitcomb."

Lark reached forward as though to touch Nandi's cheek. "You're black."

The woman's brows shot to her hairline. "Am I, then? I had no idea."

Lark refused to blush or back down. "But Max is white."

Shelby flapped her hands at Lark to shush her. "Would it be all right if we talked with you a bit about your son?"

The old woman harrumphed. "Stuck me in this old folks' home these past twenty years. Never once came to visit. What is it you want to know? I'll tell you."

"Thank you, ma'am," Trevor said. "I understand he hasn't visited, but do you follow him in the news, by any chance? I'm hoping you can shed some insight into him as a person."

A faded curiosity lit her eyes. "Why are you asking about him?"

"I talked to him just recently," Trevor said. "He's involved with a group of radicals calling themselves the Philosophy of Bedlam."

"Bedlam, like the insane asylum. That's rich, considering where I am. Why would Max be involved with those terrorists? Destroying precious works of art. Who does that?"

"That's exactly what we're trying to figure out, ma'am," he said.

Nandi gestured around herself. "The world can be a horrible, dangerous place. This patch of nothing is no protection. I keep track of the rest of the world, though it's forgotten about me."

Lark made a soft sound of distress.

"Anyway, the Max I raised wouldn't be involved in anything like that. His reputation was always so important to him. Seems he's still that way, because he comes across as some sort of philanthropist in the news. Even though he's not one."

"Why do you say that?" Shelby tipped her head to one side.

"Oh, he gives money to charities, all right," Nandi said. "But I've done the research. The donations are always to tax-relief organizations. Tax free, do you understand? Or he gets public recognition for it. Max is all about Max. He's been a bit of a disappointment."

Lark sat down in the grass and crossed her legs. "So your husband died during apartheid protests? Just you and your son got on that ship?"

"We're very sorry for your loss," Shelby said hastily.

"Was that rude? I didn't mean to be rude. But like you said, that was twenty years ago, right? But I'm still sorry."

Nandi peered down at Lark. "I see you've also done your research, young lady."

Lark grinned. "I like knowing things. You're interesting."

Nandi harrumphed. "You might have noticed I'm an old woman."

Lark twinkled up at her. "But your mind is sharp as a tack, lady."

Nandi banged her hand against the wheelchair's arm. "You got that right, missy. I just pretend not to know what's going on so those idiots who run this place will leave me alone."

Trevor smiled. "You're very convincing."

"And you're black," Lark said again.

The old woman slanted a sour look down at her. "You're very observant."

"No, but that means Max is mixed race."

"Colored, they were called in South Africa. Accepted by neither race."

"But white enough to pass." Lark was like a dog with a bone.

Trevor just shook his head. "Ms. Mkhize, are you familiar with Max's public rhetoric about black uprisings during apartheid?"

The woman laughed, a sudden braying as though she hadn't laughed in a very long time. "Call me Nandi. And if you are obliquely trying to tell me my son resents black South Africans for the death of his beloved *white* father, you needn't bother. He made his opinion known when he sentenced me to this place. He didn't hold back, believe me."

"Does Max hate art? Can you think of any reason he would want to destroy paintings?" he asked. They needed to find a link between Max and the Bedlamites. Trevor forced himself to have patience. This was a conversation, not an interrogation.

Nandi shook her head. "Our home was always full of paintings, carvings, tapestries. Even a pair of Syrian daggers. We had an extensive collection."

"Your father-in-law was a barrister, as I understand it?" Shelby said. "Here in London?"

"One of the best in the country," Nandi said, puffing out her chest. "One of the most expensive, too. Until the war."

"He knew Winston Churchill personally," Lark said, resting her chin on a hand propped against her leg. "Did they work together?"

"Side by side. He was one of Churchill's advisers in the lead-up to the start of World War Two. Churchill trusted him implicitly, until the rumors started."

"Rumors?" Lark's eyes went wide.

Nandi frowned, folding her hands neatly in her lap. "Ugly rumors. Some refugees from the Axis countries brought or smuggled in coins, pieces of artwork, gold and silver. Anything valuable the Nazis hadn't already confiscated. Hitler was fanatical about his art collection, and the Nazis stole ruthlessly from Jewish families and others. There were rumors that some Englishmen were seizing these valuables and hoarding them. There were a lot of rumors at the time, because people were afraid, and they didn't know what was going to happen. There were even rumors that some Englishmen were sending their assets out of the country, in fear of the same thing happening when Germany invaded Great Britain. But of course that never happened."

"Was there ever any proof anyone sent their assets elsewhere?" Trevor felt a tenuous hope. It was a spark that might go nowhere, but so far it was the best they had.

"A lot of museums sent their collections to other parts of Great Britain. The Ministry of Health evacuated valuables and people, mainly children and government employees, from London and the coastal towns that might be invaded. But no, no proof those valuables were sent *out* of Great Britain, though they must have done. A lot of Englishmen who were afraid of Germany's invasion sent their families elsewhere, including to South Africa."

"Did your father-in-law go to South Africa?" Trevor asked. Hadn't Lark said something about that yesterday?

"Eventually. First he sent his wife and son, Nicholas, to Cape Town. He came later."

"Could he have smuggled his art collection there?"

"I think it's very possible, young man. While as far as I know there's no proof of that ever happening, my mother-in-law was quite wealthy. I visited Nicholas's home in Cape Town several times while we were courting. And, of course, after she passed on, Nicholas inherited everything, including the collection."

"How did you and Nicholas meet?" Lark appeared fascinated.

Nandi smiled. "Now that's a story, young lady. He was a doctor, doing his medical residency in Sharpeville, where I lived. I had joined the thousands and thousands of people protesting the discriminatory laws of the time. The police beat a number of us before opening fire. I ended up in hospital with a broken arm and a concussion. Nicholas treated me, and we fell in love. As you can imagine, a mixed-race couple was not well received in Sharpeville, or anywhere else in South Africa, for that matter. We married in secret and moved to Cape Town."

"What about apartheid?" Shelby asked.

"Our marriage was prohibited, of course. Sometimes when visitors came to the house, I pretended to be a domestic."

Shelby's brows snapped down. "That's awful!"

Nandi frowned. "That's the way it was under apartheid. And it ultimately led to Nicholas's death."

"What happened?" three voices asked in chorus.

"When Nicholas's parents found out about us, they first pressured him to leave me. When he refused, they had me arrested, and finally chose to disown him rather than accept me as a daughter-in-law. We lived in a black neighborhood because Nicholas refused to have me pretend to be a servant. Even though as a doctor he treated both black and white patients, there was a lot of resentment toward both of us. Him for representing white South Africa, even though he was vocally anti-apartheid. And me because I married outside my race. Things were always tense.

"Then someone discovered who Nicholas's father was. How he'd contributed to the repression of blacks. I'm sorry to say that he was one of the proponents for the Population Registration Act of 1950."

Trevor's lip curled. "That abomination was the foundation of apartheid. It all built from that Act."

"Yes," Nandi said. "On the night Nicholas died, we had gone out to dinner. A mob grew outside the restaurant. I never did know what started it all. Nicholas tried to calm things down, but they were too worked up. Too angry, throwing their anger somewhere, anywhere. Nicholas was beaten to death. I didn't die, but my spine was damaged, leaving me in this." She gestured to the wheelchair.

The three of them were silent. Trevor grieved for the woman whose only crime was to love another human being.

Lark leaned back on her elbows. "What an amazing and tragic story. Do you think I could interview you another day for an article? I'm with Cerberus."

Nandi chuckled. "Isn't that what this has been? Very well, young lady. You are the most colorful young thing I've ever seen."

She gave a modest smile. "I'm just authentically me."

Trevor cut in fast, before Lark could say anything outrageous. "So after that, you and Max came to London to live with Nicholas's brother?"

"Coventry, but yes. We packed our belongings and snuck out in the middle of the night. Caught a cargo ship heading here and made a deal with the captain to sail with them. A lot of our possessions never made it to England. Thieves and pirates, that lot." She banged the arm of her wheelchair in disgust.

"What went missing?" Trevor asked quickly.

Nandi's brows raised in surprise. "Why, a great deal of our collection, now that you mention it. A lot of art history, lost in the space of weeks."

A smile spread across Trevor's face. "So it's likely your collection started in London pre-war, moved to Cape Town, and only some of it made it back to London. Was there a ship's manifest, or did you have a record of your belongings? Your collection?"

"There might have been. Honestly, I was in shock. Distraught. My husband had just been murdered in front of me, and I was forced to leave the only country I'd ever known to come to some damp, dismal land to live with a total stranger."

They stood in silence.

"That blows." Lark cleared her throat. "Uh, what was Max like as a teenager?"

Nandi snorted. "He was an angry child. Always in a temper, always blaming. He went from one addiction to another. He was fifteen when his father was killed, so I made allowances. Nicholas's brother and I put him in rehab variously for alcohol and drugs. All those records are sealed, obviously. The world thinks he's always been some shining ideal. I'm the only one who knows the truth."

Trevor hesitated to ask the obvious question. If Max's reputation was so important to him, why had he hidden his mother away in a sub-standard facility and pretended she was dead? If Lark could find Nandi Mkhize, so could others, if they thought to look. He feared the answer would be that the woman lived in squalor *because* Max's reputation meant everything to him, and having a black mother seemed intolerable to him.

Instead, he asked, "Can you think of any reason why Max might be funding this group of terrorists? They call themselves anarchists, but they're nothing more than a pack of criminals."

Nandi shook her head. "I can't think of a thing."

"But you can't remember if Max hated any sort of art?" he asked.

"I suppose he could have. I don't really remember."

Shelby stood and offered her hand. "Thank you for your time, Nandi."

"Visit any time. Things get fairly boring around here."

They were quiet until they were in the car and on their way back to London.

"Well, we know there's no love lost between Max and his mother." Shelby shook the tension out of her wrists.

"He's an asshat." Lark accelerated as she merged onto the A2. "Other than knowing Max's family history, did we find anything that will help you?"

"Actually, we very well might have," Trevor said. "It's possible there's a connection between the Bedlamites and Max's parents' art collection. If, as I suspect, Max is searching for something, and he's using the Bedlamites to target art museums, he might be looking for some of his family's lost art."

"And then destroying it? That makes no sense."

"No, but it's the best theory we have at the moment. If a ship's manifest exists, it would be very helpful to find it." He cast a hopeful look at Lark.

"If it exists, I'll find the shit out of it," she promised.

Chapter Eighteen

"LET'S HEAD BACK to your place, Lark, and do some computer digging."

Lark's face brightened. "Yes! Hacking. I mean, of course I wouldn't do anything illegal like that. Why would you suggest such a thing?" She started humming happily.

"Trevor, do you think I should call the State Department? I do work for them, after all."

He thought about it. "You would be safe inside the embassy. That's the positive. The negative is they almost assuredly have suspended your access and flagged your accounts. They'd be stupid not to. You're a potential national security threat."

She sighed. "They could provide legal counsel, if nothing else."

"It's your choice, of course. My suggestion would be to hold that in your back pocket for now."

"All right."

He experienced a rush of relief. He had the oddest feeling that if he let her out of his sight even for a moment, he would lose her.

He wanted to build on the tenuous thread of trust budding between them.

Back at the flat, Lark tapped away at her keyboard, muttering under her breath. Trevor flipped through channels on the telly and felt like a useless lump. None of his SAS training would help here. He was an expert in explosives and biochemical weapons, not computers.

"Why don't you whip us up a gourmet meal?" Shelby suggested. "I can tell you're bored."

"Or you can do my homework," Lark chipped in. "It's on cybersecurity laws. Policies. Privacy. Boring as shit, but it's a required class."

Trevor got to his feet. "Cooking it is, then."

Over a dinner of seared chicken with mushrooms, peppers, and broccoli on a bed of pasta, Lark grilled Trevor.

"So, Hunky Guy. How do you and Shelby know each other?"

"I thought we agreed on Trevor, Hadley."

Lark very nearly growled. Trevor found himself impressed. The sprite had a ferocious side.

"Just answer the question."

Trevor chuckled. "Right, then. We worked together in Azakistan about ten months ago. Shelby was the State Department liaison for the Secret Service when President Cooper visited al-Zadr Air Force Base."

"And fell in love?" Lark batted her eyelashes.

Shelby choked on a piece of chicken. She coughed to clear her throat.

Lark's eyes narrowed shrewdly. "Hooked up, then. What were you working on, hotshot?"

The terrorist incident had been widely publicized, but neither his nor Jace Reed's involvement had even been hinted at, for good reason. The SpecOps community was a closed one. "I just helped on some minor stuff. Shelby did all the work."

Lark snorted. "Classified, then. So if we can't talk about that, tell me of your homeworld, Usul."

"Pardon?" Trevor's brow wrinkled. What the hell was she talking about?

Lark laughed. "*Dune*? Frank Herbert? Ah, never mind. Where were you born. Let's start there."

"I was born and raised in Banbury."

"Keep going." Lark snapped her fingers several times.

Trevor sighed. "Very well. I'm the oldest of five, with three brothers and two sisters. I come from old money, but without any titles to go along with it like my aunt's family. Not that I cared, then or now, about such things, but it rankled my father. He tried for years to be knighted, at the very least. As all children of privilege do, I was educated at Eton."

"Did you like school? Parts of it are boring as hell. Things are just now getting interesting."

"Some things never change," he said. "What about you? What are you studying?" Maybe he could turn this around, and get Lark to talk about herself instead.

"Cybersecurity and digital forensics. I did my undergrad in computer science. I could have taught half those classes. This study-abroad thing I'm doing is cool. After I finish the classes, I can do an internship at GCHQ, if I want. But it's pro forma. Kinda hard for a non-British national to intern and do anything meaningful. Clearances and all."

"GCHQ?" Shelby asked.

"Government Communications Headquarters," Trevor said. "The sister organization to your NSA."

"I figure I'll go to work for the NSA or FBI when I graduate, as a forensic examiner or something. That sounded interesting."

"There are jobs in this day and age for ethical hackers," Trevor said.

Shelby cocked her head. "What happened to wanting to be a reporter?"

"Kinda getting bored with that. Now, quit stalling. You went to Eton. Dropped out of law school."

So much for that. "Like you, I was bored. And contemptuous of the power-mad group of entitled brats with whom I would work as a barrister."

Shelby was listening, he saw. It was good that she was curious about him.

"No offense, but you seem pretty straightlaced to me. Except for your tattoo."

Shelby smiled very slightly. Was it wishful thinking to hope she was remembering tracing the same tattoo with her tongue all those months ago?

Trevor lifted a shoulder and let it drop. "The tattoo was the result of a drunken evening after I . . . was accepted into the job I now hold."

Lark blew a raspberry. "Which you won't tell me about."

"No."

Lark sat back and picked up her fork. "But I still want to know what a rich boy does to piss off his parents."

"You're not going to let this go, are you?" But Trevor kept talking, aiming his words at Shelby instead of Lark. "I racked up eight speeding tickets on my Ducati and three more in my Jaguar. I got into drunken brawls more often than I'm comfortable admitting to. Although, in my defense, it was several times to defend a woman's honor."

Shelby smiled at that. Whew.

"You're lucky you survived," she murmured.

She had no idea. Rising, he took their dirty plates to the sink.

"Felons wash all dishes," Lark said, scraping back her chair. "I'm going to do my freaking homework."

Shelby followed him into the kitchen.

"Do you still have the number to the hospital? I'd like to check on Floyd."

Her brows lifted in surprise, but she didn't say anything as she dialed. A few minutes later, she had an answer. "Floyd is off the critical care ward and expected to make a full recovery. I'm glad he's not dead, but he's still a louse."

"Yes. But he's a louse we need to talk to."

"Why, for heaven's sake? We know what happened. We know what the Bedlamites look like. We even know who's funneling them money."

"But we don't know why. Eric told me he'd fill me in after the job. Then everything went pear-shaped." He ran water into the sink and added dishwashing soap.

Shelby straightened abruptly. "I'd forgotten till just now. Eric said, 'Crawley, do it.' And Crawley asked which one. Eric looked in a notebook and then pointed out the two Shamblet works, and told Crawley to cut them. They specifically targeted the Shamblet paintings."

Trevor cocked his head. "I know nothing about art. Who is he?"

"He was a prominent artist in pre-war London. One of the great unrecognized surrealists, because he started to smuggle his art out of Great Britain when the Germans started their blitz attacks in 1940. Most of his works have since been recovered, though not necessarily returned to their owners. A number of pieces are in the hands of private collectors, and others have never been found at all."

"How do you know all this?"

She grabbed a tea towel and started drying the plates Trevor handed her. "I minored in art history in college. I'm not a particular fan of surrealism, but the history of that period is fascinating."

"Brilliant. So where did he smuggle them to?"

"He was afraid that Germany was going to invade England. He was trying to protect his legacy, but it backfired, because he was killed in an IRA bombing just before the war ended. Art historians spent decades hunting down stolen artworks after World War Two, most of which were stolen by Germans and Austrians. Shamblet sent his works to Switzerland, to a cousin, for safekeeping. The cousin realized how valuable the paintings were, and sold a number of them to museums."

Trevor grimaced. "Okay, so Shamblet's paintings ended up all over the world. Can I borrow your laptop? I want to see if his paintings in other countries have been defaced as well."

"I can do it more easily," Shelby said. "I was a docent at the Huntsville Museum of Art in college. I still have subscriptions to a number of art-related sites. Plus, I have contacts."

"I didn't know that about you."

She smiled. "There's a lot you don't know about me."

"Yet."

She seemed to stop breathing. "It's late. If we're going to go talk to Floyd in the morning, we should get some sleep."

He nodded, disappointed. They returned to the living room. Lark looked up, yawning, and closed her laptop with a snap.

"I beat the midnight deadline by almost forty-five minutes. Go, me."

"Well done."

"Yah, it's easy stuff. I have class in the morning. The prof insists I actually be in the classroom, like I can't understand the reading without him having to explain it all. I'll be back by eleven, though."

"Good. I'd like to visit Floyd Panderson in the hospital after, if you're up for it."

"Hells, yeah!"

"Thank you," Trevor said.

"Hey, partners, remember? Anyway, this is the most fun I've had since I found out that footballer was doping."

He didn't remember a story breaking on the subject, but he didn't press. He had no use for so-called athletes who wouldn't last a day in Army training.

"I'm beat. I'll see you two in the morning." Lark gave them a two-fingered salute and disappeared down the hall.

While Shelby used the bathroom, Trevor stripped off his suit and hung it up. He was down to his skivvies, unless he wanted to sleep in his jeans again. He took the pile of linens, folded and set into a corner, and laid them out.

Shelby came back in wearing the same sleep shirt from the night before. Her eyes widened when she saw him. "We should have stopped on the way home to get you some pajamas."

Her voice sounded husky as she stared at him. He liked her eyes on him.

"I'm good. I'll just duck into the loo."

Shelby had wrapped a blanket around herself by the time he

returned. He flipped off the lights and padded to his makeshift bed, wishing he could join her on the sofa instead.

"I'm sorry you have to sleep on the floor," she murmured, stretching out along the cushions.

He chuckled. "Believe me, I've slept on worse. It's carpeted and I have a blanket. Both pluses in my world."

"You love it, don't you. What you do. The SAS."

"Yes." He'd found a true brotherhood within the SpecOps community. "I couldn't imagine doing anything else."

She twisted her head around to peer at him. He sat with his knees drawn up to his chest, arms loosely clasping them, head resting on the side of the sofa. Her eyes traced along his nearly naked body, her mouth parting on a sigh.

"*Nothing* else?"

"You keep looking at me like that, I'm going to have to do something about it."

She jerked her gaze away. "I'm sorry."

"I'm not. Look as much as you like."

She didn't speak for a long moment. "I'm afraid to."

What could he say to reassure her? For him, it was about so much more than sex. Sex with Shelby had been beyond amazing, but he wanted more. Nothing about their relationship had been easy. And they did have a relationship. As fractured as it had been, they'd managed in the past few days to find a tenuous thread. Even if it took him another ten months, he intended to build on that.

"Look, Shel—" he started.

"Are you going to sit up all night?"

"I'll catch a nap later." He wouldn't be able to sleep with her so near. All he wanted to do was drag her off the couch and kiss her senseless. "Listen, Shel—"

"Then come sit by me," she whispered.

What? What was going through that head of hers? He shifted around so he could see her more clearly. Did she even realize the invitation her body language was throwing off? "As much as I'd love that, I'm not sure it's a good idea."

Her voice barely carried to him. "Why not?"

How could he explain it? Things had ended so poorly the last time they'd been intimate. He didn't want her to have regrets again. Run from him again.

"Because if I do, I'll want to touch you. Kiss you. I don't think you're ready for that."

She drew in a deep breath and sat up. "What if I am?"

"Are you?" he asked baldly.

She fell silent. Well, that answered that. He tried to ignore the disappointment clenching in his gut.

"I'm sorry I said what I did, about doing something if you kept looking at me. I won't."

She laughed, a surprised burst of sound. "No?"

He imagined her smooth thighs under the T-shirt she wore. "Not unless you're very sure it's what you want. And you're not. See, here's the thing."

He stopped. The silence grew thicker as he waged war with himself.

What the hell. If she shot him down again, he'd bleed. But he'd survived it before; he could again, no matter how excruciating the wound.

"I think you're used to men letting you down. And I can't promise I'll never let you down, because I'm human and fallible. But I need you to understand that I'm not just after a shag with you. I want us to really, truly, get to know one another."

She let the blanket drop as she scooted to the edge of the cushions. "Do you really think I don't know that? Why do you think I'm scared? If it was just a . . . a shag, that would be easy."

He blinked in surprise.

"Don't forget, I read people for a living."

He didn't know what to say, so he stayed quiet.

She rested her forearms on her knees as she leaned forward. "I don't know about men letting me down, but they've never done much for me, either."

"The ex-fiancé. Bruce."

"For one, yes. He could be demanding, but I thought . . . I thought he was a decent man. Then I found out he wasn't. And I walked away."

Should he ask? His gut said to leave it for now. Any moment, she was going to withdraw inside herself and shut him out.

Fuck his gut. "He was more concerned with himself than you, clearly."

As he had feared, she fell silent.

"Come here," he said.

Despite the words, it was an invitation, not an order. His heart leapt as Shelby slid from the sofa and crept over to him. He lifted the blanket. She settled her head on his bare chest and soughed out a sigh.

His arm tightened around her waist, snugging her in closer, feeling at peace for the first time in months.

"This is the first time I've felt whole since Azakistan."

It so closely mirrored what he'd been thinking that he lifted his head in surprise. "Me too."

"You don't have to say that."

"It's the truth." Her scent enveloped him. He dropped his nose to her neck and inhaled deeply. To distract himself, he said, "You were telling me about Bruce."

She sighed heavily. "Way to kill the mood. I guess I just didn't know any better with him. The way I was raised . . . you have to understand where I came from. I was a true-blue redneck from Coon Bluff, Alabama. Population sixteen thousand and change."

He cocked a curious head at her. "Never heard of it."

"No one has."

"Do you still have family there?"

"Yeah. My sister and brother."

"Are you close with them?" Then, "Are your parents still living?"

Shelby shook her head. "My mother died in childbirth when I was very young. My father raised the three of us on his own. But he passed away a few years ago."

"I'm sorry."

She shrugged. "We weren't close. Do you know how I got my name?"

"How?"

"He named me after his 1968 Shelby Mustang GT. My older sister is Carol, after Carroll Shelby."

He smothered a laugh. "And your brother?"

"Named after my father. Roy Macon Gibson Junior."

"I agree, that sounds very red neck."

She laughed at his precise diction.

"It sounds as though you didn't particularly enjoy your childhood." It was more of a statement than question, but she answered anyway.

"I was a smart-mouthed brunette in a town that worshipped dumb blondes. What does that tell you?"

"That you had a difficult time." His voice dropped, became soothing.

"Boys dated me just to get close to my best friend, Raeanne Swinney, the head cheerleader. She could twist men around her little finger."

Trevor said promptly, "You can do that, too."

She looked surprised. "I can?"

"Didn't I tell you so in Ma'ar ye zhad?"

"I thought you were just trying to get into my pants."

"That, too." He grinned at her. Then he sobered. "Have you . . . ?"

"No," she said softly. "There's been no one between you and you."

"Good," he said, pleased.

A THRILL SWEPT down her spine. His hand stroked along her hip, but she could feel his restraint. He meant it when he said he wanted more than sex from her.

"It took me a few years to put Coon Bluff behind me," she admitted. "But I did."

"That took courage. A lot of people never rise past their origins."

"Yeah, well, there wasn't much for me there. Anything was better, really."

She didn't wait to hear what he would say. She was done talking about her family, her childhood. It no longer mattered to her. She brushed her lips along his neck where her face nestled. His hand stilled on her hip.

"Shel—"

"Shh." She brought her hand up to cup his cheek, turning his head toward her. His lips found her unerringly in the dark, whispering across her mouth until she opened for him, joy rushing through her. She hadn't ruined things by talking about Bruce. He still wanted her. And she wanted him.

He licked into her mouth, angling his head to deepen the kiss. Both hands speared into her hair, fingers delving into the thick strands. It felt wonderful. She stroked the nape of his neck. He made an approving noise.

"So much better than talking," she whispered.

"Fuck, yeah."

His needy tone made her laugh. "I agree. Fuck, yeah."

She caught his lower lip between her teeth and tugged gently. He immediately captured her lips again, mouth open and hot as his tongue tangled with hers. His breathing grew ragged.

"I love your mouth. You have one hell of a sexy mouth."

Before she could formulate a response, he licked over her jaw to the shell of her ear. She shuddered at the explosion of sensation. Who knew ears could be such an erogenous zone? She ran her fingers lightly across his collarbone, reveling in the silky skin over hard muscle. He radiated heat. She pushed herself closer to his warmth.

"I guess we could both sleep on the floor," she said. "We won't both fit on the sofa. If it's okay, that is. Would you mind holding me tonight?"

"Well, it's quite the imposition," he murmured. "But I suppose I could force myself to endure it."

She laughed. "Thank you. I appreciate your sacrifice."

"Any time."

She cuddled back into his chest, throwing an arm across his body. Purely by accident, her hand slid down his ribs to rest on his hipbone, her wrist brushing against the erection straining against his shorts. It *had* been an accident, right?

"Ungh," he said. In an instant, he had her flat on her back beneath him, leg thrown across hers. She felt him, hard and heavy, against her hip.

"We can't," she whispered, clutching his arm. "Lark is in the next room."

"I don't care."

"I do!" She was slightly horrified at the thought of the younger woman overhearing them.

"We'll be quiet. Unless you don't want to . . . ?"

Of course she did. She'd thought of him often in the quiet moments of loneliness over the past ten months. And she was ready to open herself to him.

Boldly, she stroked a hand down his stomach to his shorts, running her fingers over the waistband, feeling him move and jerk. He moved back far enough to shuck off the underwear. She sat up.

"How can any man be so perfect?" she whispered, touching him.

He groaned.

She pushed him flat, surprised when he let her. She'd assumed he'd like being in control in the bedroom, like he had in Ma'ar ye zhad. She explored him, tracing her fingers along his throbbing cock, cupping his balls and gently squeezing them. He made a small sound. Emboldened, she kissed her way down his chest, stopping at his flat nipples to scrape them with her teeth. His breath hitched.

"You're perfect, too." She could barely make out the words.

How far could she drive him before he groaned aloud? She continued her downward path, smoothing her palms across his stomach and hips, until she was where she wanted to be.

His hips jerked as she closed her lips over his shaft. She sucked, drawing him deeper into her mouth, reveling in his hiss of pleasure. Licking leisurely along his length, she very gently scraped her teeth over him. He half lifted himself, fingers spearing into her hair, cupping her face.

"You don't have to—"

"I want to." Her voice felt foreign to her, its husky rasp mirroring the fine trembling that shook her limbs.

"You keep that up, we'll be done before we start," he said, voice barely above a growl.

"Let me please you." Slowly she found a rhythm, stroking him with her mouth, tasting the saltiness of him. She rolled his balls in her fingers, massaging gently. His hips jerked against her. She purred, a feline sound of satisfaction. The sound must have traveled along his shaft, because he jacked upright, gripped her under the arms, and had her under him before she knew what was happening. He entered her at once, a desperate seeking that caused another purr to escape.

His hands gripped the insides of her knees, pushing her legs apart, baring her to him. He stroked into her fast and rough, and she threw her head back, spine bowing as sensation washed through her.

"Yes," she muttered. "Fuck me hard, Trevor. Like you mean it."

It was harder than she'd thought possible to stop the screams wanting to rip from her throat. Her breath came in spurts. He, too, was panting. Their flesh slapping together seemed loud in the silence, but suddenly Shelby didn't care. She met him thrust for thrust, and all too soon felt the tide begin to sweep over her. She tried to keep it back, make it last longer, but Trevor reached between them and stroked her nub with a calloused thumb, and she closed her eyes and bit her lips to stop crying out as she exploded.

She collapsed against him as he rolled off her and pulled her into his arms. She knew this was something special. It wasn't just that she'd never known how mind-blowing sex could be. It was this man, and the magic he created on her body.

"You're amazing," she murmured sleepily.

His laugh rumbled under her ear. "You are, too."

They fell asleep holding one another, and Shelby knew she would never feel like this with any other man.

Chapter Nineteen

TREVOR AWOKE WITH the sun pouring through the windows. Shelby still snuggled against him, her head on his chest as her breath stirred against it. He hated to move. He wanted to stay like this forever, just reveling in her softness and the scent of him on her skin. He hadn't woken up with a hard-on in years. Instinct told him she would not be receptive to a repeat in the light of dawn, so he eased away from her and moved her head to the pillow.

Retrieving his shorts, he slipped them on and went into the kitchen. He started the coffee brewing before heading down the hall for a shower. Pulling his jeans and rugby shirt on, he returned to the kitchen and started laying out what he would need for omelets.

A sound from the doorway had him looking around to see Shelby, hair tousled and eyes drooping, the cute T-shirt hugging her slender curves. He gave her a lopsided smile, unable in that moment to form words. She returned the smile hesitantly.

"Good morning."

He grinned. "Yes, it definitely is."

Before he could cross the kitchen to reach her, Lark staggered into the room.

"I smell coffee."

Trevor poured a cup and handed it to her. She dumped in sweetener.

"You added more sugar than there is coffee," he said, bemused.

"Have to get rid of the nasty coffee taste," she said, blowing across the top of the mug and taking a huge sip. "Ahhh."

Trevor poured another cup for Shelby, who still hadn't moved more than two steps into the kitchen.

"By the way, kiddies," Lark said sourly. "I'm a heavy sleeper. I might wake up for a tornado, but that's about it. You should have told me you were together. You could have had the bed, and I've taken the—unused—sofa."

Shelby's cheeks pinked, her eyes troubled. "I didn't know if—"

"We are," Trevor interrupted firmly, "together."

Her face relaxed. "Okay."

Lark shook her head in disgust. "Imma go shower while you two idiots figure things out."

Trevor barely noticed when she left. He reached for Shelby, who melted into his arms. He held her tightly, throat choked with relief. She wasn't going to run from him this time.

"We can take things slowly," he said into her hair. "I know you've had some bad experiences."

He felt her nod. "Thank you."

"But I need you to promise me something."

She tensed in his arms.

"I need you to promise me that if you get scared, you talk to me. No running away. Deal?"

Her breath whooshed out. "That's . . . it? Talk to you?"

"Yes."

She was quiet for so long he was afraid she was going to withdraw from his arms at any moment. He held his breath.

"I can do that."

He exhaled hard in relief. "Good. That's good."

"Trevor . . . you have to know. I'm damaged goods."

He laughed. That's not at all what he'd expected her to say. "Honey, we're all damaged to some extent."

"No, but . . . you don't understand. I chose Bruce. Even agreed to marry him. Dated Floyd. I make poor choices." She sounded bitter.

"Those idiots are a gnat's ass in my world. They should be in yours, too."

She all but hid her face in his chest. "Bruce was incredibly ambitious."

She stopped, and he waited quietly for it to come. He was pretty sure he knew what he was going to hear.

"I should say shamelessly ambitious. He used every advantage in his arsenal to climb the political ladder. Including me. I was his entrée into the so-called privileged world of politics. I was a commodity, nothing more."

"He used you." He kept his tone neutral, tamping down the urge to hunt Bruce down and beat him senseless. "Did you never want, yourself, to run for election?"

"Not once. I went to Girl's State during high school. It's like a make-believe Washington, D.C. You campaign and run for office and make political alliances. I hated having to do any of that. I liked to watch the machinations, and predict where everyone would end up. I was right more often than not."

He continued to hold her, pleased beyond measure that she

seemed content to rest within the circle of his arms. "So you were training to be an analyst, even back then. But you couldn't see it with Bruce?"

"No. The first time he cheated on me, it was with the personal aide to a member of a subcommittee of the Committee on Banking, Housing, and Urban Affairs. Soon after that, he landed a lucrative contract. That sort of thing."

"The first time?" Try as he might, Trevor couldn't keep the tightness from his voice.

She tensed in his arms, hearing it as well. "Yes. I forgave him. Didn't mean a thing, never happen again, all sorts of bullshit. Lies. I'm pretty sure he cheated on me a couple of other times, always where it would benefit his ambitions."

"So you dumped him."

She swallowed so hard he heard it. "Not then, no. I was a naïve twenty-four. He was everything the men in Coon Bluff weren't. He wore suits, used expensive cologne. When we were together, he paid attention to me, not my friends. I thought he loved me for me, not just to get close to someone else. I was so wrong."

"Like the boys while you were growing up using you to get close to Raeanne Swinney, head cheerleader."

"You remembered." She looked up at him in wonder.

He smiled. "I do listen when you speak."

"I thought all men were like that, until I met Bruce. And then he turned out to be the same."

"He never deserved you," Trevor said fiercely. "He was unworthy."

He felt her smile against his skin. "Well, thanks for that, anyway."

He put her from him, holding her by the forearms so he could look into her eyes. "No, I'm very serious. I'm sorry you ever experienced that. For you to say that you thought all men were that way, well, I can assure you we're not."

"I hope that's true. So what happens now?"

He hugged her closer to him. "Now you remember you're a kind, intelligent, wonderful woman who deserves the very best in life. You forget those morons as completely irrelevant. And I do my damnedest to prove I'm worthy of you."

She looked at him, wide-eyed. After a moment, she took a breath. "Please don't turn out to be a jerk."

Trevor started to laugh, but abruptly realized that she was dead serious. He chose his words with care. "I will never deliberately hurt you, Shel. That doesn't mean we won't have disagreements or even arguments. But I can promise you that I'm an honorable man. I will never belittle you or cheat on you."

"Well . . . good."

"Have you idiots figured things out yet?" Lark said from the doorway. She leaned against the doorjamb. Today she wore a teal shirt over a shell and black leggings, her triple earlobe piercings winking in the kitchen light. Dramatic makeup and spiky hair made her look even younger than she had the previous night.

"We're getting there," Shelby said with a shaky sigh. She pulled out of Trevor's arms.

"Then let's go talk to that gnat's ass, Floyd."

"Do you always eavesdrop?"

"What about your class?" Shelby asked at the same time.

Lark looked from one to the other. "Fuck my class. And yes, I frequently eavesdrop. I learn stuff that way. Stuff you can't learn in boring schoolbooks."

Chapter Twenty

DESPITE HIS SUGGESTION that he take the wheel, Lark slid into the driver's seat.

"No way. My car, my rules."

Trevor just shook his head. Lark was a force of nature. Shelby climbed into the back, so he took the front passenger seat. They'd taken the time to change into their disguises. He had his suit jacket folded neatly across his lap.

"Do you know St. Baldwin's?" he asked,

"It's in Soho. Siri knows the address. Although, I think I'll rename her Danby. She gives you a little information, but when push comes to shove, she's less than helpful."

"You really must learn not to eavesdrop. That was a private conversation."

Lark grinned, unrepentant. "So who is he? Scotland Yard? GCHQ?"

"Just drive."

Lark left the A400 by darting across two busy lanes to get to the exit ramp. A driver leaned on his horn and shook a fist at her, which she either didn't see or ignored.

"We're not in a rush," Shelby said faintly. "You can slow down."

Lark glanced at her, eyes wide. "I am driving slowly."

"Good Lord," she muttered, closing her eyes.

Lark made her way to Frith Street and found parking. St. Baldwin's Hospital rose huge and modern, twelve stories of glass and steel surrounded by shops and offices. As they walked past a Pret a Manger and the long row of blue rental bicycles, Trevor scanned the narrow street and surrounding buildings from behind his sunglasses. Nothing raised the hairs on the back of his neck. Going to visit Floyd was a risk, but it would be worth it if the man could shed some light on the artwork that was being destroyed.

The revolving door led them into the sizable lobby area, pristine and open. Two nurses and a security guard manned the intake desk at the far end. They bypassed it and entered an area to the right, with its rows and rows of plastic seats filled with patients standing by. The scent of fear and anticipation hung in the air.

"The elevators are over there." Lark pointed.

They checked the sign beside the lifts. "Critical Care is on the third floor," he said.

They entered the lift with two grim and silent teenagers.

"Anthony is alive," one said finally. "That's good."

The other started snuffling. "Tanked up and drives into a lorry. How fucked up is that?"

They exited onto the third floor in front of Trevor's group. Trevor paused while the boys spoke to an older woman, gray-haired and fierce, guarding the entryway from behind a counter. The sign on the wall behind her announced that this was the reception area. The typical computer, fax machine, and filing cabinets decorated the area. Several portable medical apparatuses rested against the wall. The sign on a door behind the counter declared it was a staff-only area. To the left, a set of swinging metal doors remained closed.

The teenagers pushed through the swinging doors. Lark leaned against the counter. "My father was admitted yesterday. Can I see him?" Her voice wobbled a little bit.

"Certainly, miss. What's the name?"

Shelby supplied it. In moments, they were trekking down an antiseptic white corridor, lined on either side with handrails for those needing extra stability. The door to Ward 312 was closed. Lark turned the knob and swung it wide.

The ward seemed large for a private room. Besides the mobile bed and medical equipment, there was room for an armchair and two smaller visitor chairs in front of the double windows. The armchair had been pulled up next to the bed and was occupied.

"Hiya, Floyd," Lark said cheerily. "What's up?"

"Who are you? I'm not giving any more interviews. Talk to my barrister."

Lark turned the cheery dial up another notch. "Nothing like that. I brought someone to see you."

He stepped into the room. Floyd glanced at him without recognition. His disguise was holding, at any rate. Shelby came in after him. Floyd squinted at her, pulled his brows down, shook his head slightly, and stared hard at her. Trevor watched the lights flicker on inside the man's head.

"Shelby? Is that you?" As realization dawned, he grew white as a sheet, throwing furtive glances at the woman sitting at his bedside, a hand on his arm. She looked young and sweet—and very pregnant. She gave a watery smile as she rose to greet them.

"Hello. I'm Cindy Panderson. Are you friends of Floyd's?"

Shelby stepped forward to shake the offered hand. "We share a common love of art. In fact, there is something I'd like to talk to him about, about a collection he has on loan right now. Would that be all right?"

Cindy shot Floyd a lovingly exasperated look. "Oh, him and his art. He could go on for hours. While you talk, I'm going to go down and get a sandwich."

Trevor closed and locked the door behind her. Floyd's eyes rounded as recognition and fear darted through them. He squirmed back in the bed.

"You were working with them the whole time," Floyd rasped, pointing a finger at Shelby.

"Don't be absurd," she snapped. "You're the only liar here."

"Liar, liar, pants on fire," Lark sang in falsetto.

"What are you doing with him, then?"

Shelby pinned him with a glare. "I don't think you get to play the victim here, Floyd."

Floyd had the grace to flush, but then pointed to his heavily bandaged abdomen. "You seem to have fared well. I'm the one who was stabbed and almost died."

"You're the selfish bastard who bargained for your own freedom, leaving the rest of the hostages behind," Trevor said. The ass. "Not to mention dating another woman with a pregnant wife at home."

Shelby shook her head. "That's the least important detail right now. I'm glad to see you're recovering. The man who stabbed you? Crawley? He is genuinely insane."

He looked slightly mollified at that.

Trevor glanced at the door. They had precious little time. Any minute now, they were going to be interrupted by a nurse or doctor on their rounds, or by the young wife returning to her husband's bedside.

They had to move this along. Shelby was an expert at reading people, though, and finding common ground with which to establish trust and confidence. He needed to let her lead this conversation.

"Floyd, I need your help. The police think I was involved somehow with the Bedlamites. I need to prove my innocence, but to do that I need information."

He looked at her suspiciously, but finally judged her to be sincere. "What information?"

"The collection in the main exhibit hall. The surrealists. What do you know about them?"

Floyd wrinkled his brow at her. "About the collection? About the donors? What?"

It had been too broad a question. Shelby narrowed it down.

"What's so significant about the Edward Shamblet pieces? Why did the Bedlamites choose those to deface?"

Floyd pulled his mouth down, remembered hostility in his eyes. He pointed an accusing finger at Trevor. "Why don't you ask him? He's one of them. Millions of dollars destroyed in an instant. My insurance is going to go through the roof."

Trevor clenched his jaw to prevent any words spilling out. Even now, the man focused on the money. The value of the paintings, the cost of insurance.

"And a lot of art history," Shelby said. "So let's make sure we catch them so they can't do any more harm. I know the basics of

Shamblet and his work. But was there something special about those two paintings?"

Floyd thought about it. "They were post-World War Two finds. Shamblet had a studio and gallery in Southampton, but they were destroyed during the Blitz. He had other works, not just in galleries but in private homes as well. He had the artwork he kept in his own home, too. It's thought that he took all the rest and shipped them out of the country, because his paintings are rare today. That's why the destruction of the *Autumn in Madrid* and *Memories of the Gods* is such a tragedy."

Trevor stepped forward. "Any idea where he might have shipped his art? Or why? This was after the war ended?"

"No," Floyd corrected. "The rumors at the time were that he basically smuggled everything he could out of the country during the war, so that if Germany did invade Great Britain, he wouldn't lose his life's work. But there is no record where he sent them, as far as I know. The rumors centered around stolen artwork during World War Two were thoroughly catalogued and investigated by Olga Berkowicz in her book *Stolen Riches: European Art and the Third Reich*. You might want to talk to her. She teaches in Kingston, I think. What's this all about? How is this going to prove your innocence?"

"I don't know," Shelby admitted. "But you're going to cooperate fully, unless you want your young, pregnant wife to find out what you do on the side."

His face became pained. "You didn't have to say it. You see that I'm cooperating, right?" He nudged his chin toward Trevor. "So what are you, some sort of undercover cop?"

Trevor kept his face blank. "Something like that."

"Well, you didn't do dick to stop me getting stabbed, did you?"

Trevor felt his eyes go cold. The asshole was lucky Trevor didn't stab him a second time here and now. "Let's fast forward to the present."

"I don't know much else."

Shelby scratched her nose. "Well . . . what other museums have Shamblet paintings or sculptures? The two in London were also ruined."

"I know there's one sculpture privately owned that's on loan to a museum in Wales. There are several in America, and one or two in Europe. I'm not sure."

"Can you think of any reason the Bedlamites might have chosen his works in particular?" Trevor thought it best not to mention Whitcomb. "Someone hate him? Did he double-cross someone? Did he have an affair while married?" He couldn't control the hard edge that crept into his tone at the last.

"Like me, is what you're implying?" Floyd flushed red again. "Sorry. I'm not an expert."

"All right," Shelby said. "If you think of anything else, give me a call." She scribbled the number of her prepaid phone onto a paper napkin on his bedside table next to the remains of lunch.

"And, of course," Lark said, smiling brightly at Floyd, "if we think of any other way you can help us, we'll be back."

Chapter Twenty-One

SHELBY SIGHED HEAVILY as they piled back into Lark's car. "I don't think that was very useful."

"It feels like we're missing a vital piece of the puzzle here," Trevor agreed.

"I'm starving. Let's stop for lunch." Not waiting for a response, Lark pulled off the road and parked in front of an Italian restaurant. They piled out.

Though it was barely half past noon, several patrons sat at the bar, drinking and watching the television mounted between the rows and rows of wine bottles. Despite the white linens on the tables and the lights mounted under the lip of the bar, the place managed to look gloomy. Shelby skipped the tables and led the way to three bar seats close to the TV.

"I've never been away from CNN for this long," she said. "I'm going through withdrawals, not knowing what's going on in the world."

BBC One played an old episode of *EastEnders*. Lark leaned over the bar and called to the barman. "Oy. Do you carry CNN?"

"I can change it to BBC News if you like, luv. But that's all I've got."

"Yes, please," Shelby said.

The barman switched channels, ignoring the protest from a portly man at the far end. "Whatcha have, then?"

"Menus, please. I'm starving. And a Coke."

"I'll have a cuppa. Thanks, mate."

Shelby rested her elbows on the bar. "Just a club soda, please."

"Lovely. I'll be back straightaway with some menus."

After they'd perused the menus and ordered, Shelby settled back to catch up on the news. The United States had targeted an al-Qaeda leader with an airstrike in Libya. An Israeli army jeep had struck and killed a Palestinian in the West Bank. The Sudanese president had fled to avoid an arrest warrant for alleged war crimes.

"Oh, my God!" She straightened, gripping the edge of the bar with tight fingers. "There's been another bombing."

All three stared up at the television. The reporter had a suitably grim expression as he relayed the story. This time, the Jewish Heritage Museum had come under attack. One person had been killed in the blast, and four others had been injured. The Philosophy of Bedlam claimed responsibility.

"Now they've committed murder," Trevor said. "This ups the stakes dramatically."

"Crawley tried to kill Floyd," Shelby pointed out. "They've proven they're capable of murder."

"Yes. And I have to see if I can salvage this thing."

Both women stared at him.

"You can't go back," Shelby pointed out finally. "You attacked Nathan and Fay and then ran. They won't accept you as one of them."

"They might if I tell them we used to be lovers, and I wanted to get you to safety. It's the truth anyway."

"And if you're wrong? They'll kill you."

Trevor shrugged. "I've been in tighter spots."

Shelby resisted the urge to hit him. How could he talk about risking his life so easily?

As the cameras trained on the police and investigators at the museum, Trevor leaned forward, scrutinizing the pictures on the screen.

"There," he said, pointing. "Do you see that man? In the blue windbreaker?"

Shelby picked him out just as the picture changed, showing the scene from above as a helicopter hovered.

"I saw him, yes. Who is he?"

"He's an operator."

"A what?" Lark asked.

"SpecOps. Special Operations. Like the SAS or Special Boat Service. The American version are the SEALs."

"Yeah, I got it at SpecOps," Lark said drily. "I play Call of Duty."

That got a brief smile, but Trevor was so focused, Shelby wasn't sure he'd actually heard Lark.

"He's most likely Mossad. Israeli special operations."

"Do you know him?" Shelby didn't understand.

"No. But we need to talk to him."

"You think he's Mossad because it's a Jewish museum?" Lark asked.

"Yes."

"All right. But how can he help us?" Shelby knew she looked as clueless as she felt.

"The Philosophy of Bedlam might have left a clue. He might

have seen something that makes sense to him, but that law enforcement missed. Maybe there's nothing. But finding out nothing doing something is better than sitting on my arse doing nothing."

He dropped forty pounds onto the bar and got up, radiating impatience as Lark tried to gulp down the rest of her Coke. The barman approached, balancing three plates of food.

"Sorry, mate," Trevor said. "We have to run. Free lunch for you and your mates, yeah?"

The barman shrugged and pocketed the money. "Cheers."

Lark grumbled as they piled back into her car. "This is fun and all, but all I got to eat was some little pieces of bread. Got to keep my strength up."

"Tonight I'll treat you to a steak dinner," Trevor promised.

"Excellent." Lark pulled out her smartphone and handed it back to Shelby. "Danby, take us to the Jewish Heritage Museum."

Shelby couldn't help but laugh as she looked up the address and entered it into the maps feature. On a whim, she scrolled into the phone's settings and changed the default female voice to a male, British one.

"Ask him again." She pressed the button to activate the microphone.

"The Jewish Heritage Museum, please, Danby," Lark repeated obediently.

"Getting directions to Jewish Heritage Museum," the male voice replied.

Lark clapped her hands. "Total awesomeness!"

"Put your hands on the wheel!" Shelby all but shouted.

Trevor started to laugh. After a moment, she joined in, content despite their circumstances.

After a few moments, she sobered. "So far we've found nothing that's going to exonerate me."

"You?" asked Trevor. "Just you?"

Shelby shrugged. "All you have to do is go back to your unit. MI-5 will make you disappear."

Lark turned sideways in her seat to look at Trevor. "You're MI-5?"

"Watch the road!" Shelby squeaked. Lark swerved back into her lane just in time to miss an oncoming car.

Lunch hour traffic snarled the streets and Lark was forced to slow to a crawl, cursing the whole time. Shelby shared an amused glance with Trevor. Truthfully, she felt relieved. She found driving with Lark a terrifying experience.

Trevor kept flicking glances into the passenger-side mirror.

"What is it?" she finally asked.

"We're being followed," he said. "No, don't look. Lark, take the next right."

She did so. "Where? I don't see anything."

"It's a gray Fiat. Don't look for him. Trust me, he's back there."

The Fiat accelerated so abruptly that Shelby saw it. "Oh, my God! They're going to ram us!"

"Lark, step on the gas. Now!" Trevor drew the Beretta. Shelby put a hand to her throat. Lark squeaked, hands tight on the wheel.

The Fiat roared up beside them. Fay was driving, with Nathan in the passenger seat levering a shotgun out the window.

"Duck," Trevor bellowed.

They bent as far down as they could. The shotgun blast hit the side of the car. Without hesitation, Trevor climbed into the back seat, behind Lark. He pressed the button to lower the window. Nothing happened. "Open the goddamned window."

"It doesn't work," Lark wailed. "I've been meaning to get it fixed."

Trevor solved the problem by using the butt of the semiautomatic to smash the window, shielding his face against the glass.

An opening appeared in the crush of cars, and Lark stomped on the gas pedal, jumping into the spot and putting several cars between themselves and the Bedlamites.

"What do I do?" Lark shrieked. Cars around them were pulling off the road, wanting to be as far away from the running gun battle as they could.

"Turn left. Now!"

Lark obeyed, jumping through a red light and nearly getting broadsided. The Fiat followed them, Fay laying on the horn to make the cars slow enough for her to bull her way through. She came up on their bumper fast, ramming them hard. Shelby screamed as the impact threw her forward. The car slewed. Lark wrested it back under control.

Nathan drove into oncoming traffic and pulled the steering wheel hard to the left, slamming the Fiat into their car. Lark lost control, spinning into the sidewalk and slamming sideways into a parking meter. The car came to a shuddering stop. Shelby panted wildly, hand pressed to her chest.

"Out," Trevor commanded. "On the passenger side. Move!"

Shelby dove for the door and shoved it open, turning to help Lark over the console. "Where do we go?"

"We're close to Leicester Square. Head that way." Trevor pointed.

Shelby turned back to the Fiat. Fay was struggling to open her door, which had caved in during the crash.

Nathan had the shotgun up to his shoulder, pointed straight at her.

WITHOUT THINKING, TREVOR threw himself sideways, shoving both women to the ground, covering them with his body as the shotgun blast split the air. Pedestrians began to run, screaming, in all directions.

He leapt to his feet, ignoring the fire that burned in his thigh. His legs worked; that was all that mattered. He pulled Shelby up, still between the gunman and himself. "Go!"

She and Lark took off running, dodging around cars and pedestrians, heading toward Leicester Square. Fay finally got her door open, and she and Nathan pursued them. If Trevor could get them into the pedestrian-only area, into a store or office building, he could gain the upper hand. As it was, they had to move, and fast. He sprinted after the women, catching up in three strides.

They passed a Burger King, racing past a telephone box and a street artist showing off caricatures. To their front left was a grassy area. It would leave them out in the open, but lessen the risk of pedestrians being caught in the crossfire.

"Into the park. Zigzag as you run," he said. Both women were panting. "Straight past the statue. Head toward the theater."

He checked over his shoulder. Nathan and Fay had hidden their weapons, but were pursuing at a brisk pace.

Buildings rose on both sides of them. The one to the right was under renovations. If he could hide the women, he could use the building as high ground. Realizing that neither of the women would be able to scale the barrier, he jettisoned the idea.

They burst into the street and turned right, passing a line of parked motorcycles. Nathan and Fay had abandoned any attempt at caution and were in full pursuit.

"Turn left into the alley," he said.

They did as he instructed, but then stopped. Shelby held her side, and Lark gulped in great mouthfuls of air.

"Keep moving." He pushed them farther into the alley, turning to guard their backs while they trotted to the other end, then followed. He passed a rolling delivery door, closed and locked. Strings of lights decorated the upper walls. A trash bin, too small to hide behind. This wasn't going to work. Neither woman had any escape-and-evade skills. He needed to reevaluate.

Fay appeared at the front of the alley, saw them, and opened fire. Trevor grabbed Shelby's hand and pulled her behind him, facing the hail of bullets as they exited the alleyway. It was damnably difficult to hit a moving target while moving, but he wasn't taking any chances with Shelby's life.

Lark, already out on the street, looked around. "Where to now?" she panted.

"New strategy," he said. "Let's find a crowded spot. I don't think they'd fire into a crowd. Too many cameras. They've exposed themselves too much already."

There was a convention center a few blocks away, if he recalled correctly. He led them at a steady lope. It wouldn't be long before Nathan or Fay reached the end of the alley and saw them.

"Can you run any faster?" he asked, trotting backward as he swept the area with a steely gaze.

They tried, he had to give them credit. He took them across two streets and into another alley, but then, hallelujah, the convention center appeared before them. He led them straight into the crowds outside.

"Crowds equal invisibility," he said. "Just walk normally. Don't look back. Don't look around. Just blend."

He led them on a meandering path toward a concave building, under the front dome, and joined the queue waiting to enter. A large group in front of them stopped to argue with the person checking tickets; Trevor eased the women around them and into the building.

The lobby was as crowded as he'd hoped. Huge support columns would give them additional cover. The rows of vendor tables with vibrant displays would help conceal them. He led the women past a resting area with benches, where groups chatted as they relaxed. A food court had been set up off to the left. They joined the milling throngs waiting in various lines. The tables were packed. People had resorted to eating standing up.

"Queue up," he said. "Face away from the front doors."

He scanned the area. He didn't even dare hope they'd made it inside unobserved. Nothing so far. When he was satisfied, he herded Shelby and Lark to the equally clogged escalators. They reached the top. He had them stand back against the wall whilst he stood at the railing and watched.

From his vantage point, he could see just how congested the place was. He was taking a calculated risk that Fay and Nathan wouldn't open up and fire into the crowds. That would bring the police, and questions they wouldn't want to answer.

It seemed to be some sort of gamer's convention. Lots of flashing lights and colorful posters, and even people in costumes he couldn't begin to identify. All the better.

"Do you see them?" Shelby had crept to his side. At least she had the good sense to stand behind him, away from the rail.

"Not yet."

"Do you think they know where we went?"

He turned slightly to look at her. Her eyes were too wide and her breathing was uneven, but her gaze was steady. "No way to know, really. But there's virtually no way they could spot us. There must be thirty thousand people here."

"So we succeeded."

He wasn't willing to go that far, but she seemed to need reassurance, so he nodded. "We'll find a less obvious way out."

They faded back to the wall. With her purple hair, Lark fit in well here. Even Shelby with her blonde pixie cut and revealing dress looked normal in this crowd. It was Trevor, in his suit and tie, who stood out.

Lark came to the same conclusion, running a critical eye over him. "So much for your disguise. Get rid of the jacket."

He slipped out of the expensive Burberry coat.

"Are you wearing an undershirt?"

"Erm, yes, actually." Where was she going with this?

"Lose the shirt, too."

He stripped off his shirt and tie. Lark tugged at his undershirt. He gently removed her hands and pulled it free from his pants. She flipped the tie back over his head and arranged it into some sort of complicated knot. When she was done, she stood back, hands on her hips, looking him over critically.

"Well, you still look like a dweeb, but it's better than Uptight Suit was. What do we do now, Hunky Guy?"

The truth was, he didn't know. "We're in a bit of a pickle. None of us have valid identification, and I'm down to about twenty pounds in my wallet. It's not enough to disappear."

Lark frowned. "I didn't think to grab my purse when the car wrecked."

Shelby bit her lip. "We should go to the police. Get this whole mess straightened out."

"You should do that," he agreed immediately. "You and Lark both. Ask for protective custody."

Lark blew out an annoyed breath. "And miss this? No way. So what I'm hearing is that we need money? Is that right?"

"In a nutshell." Maybe Danby would front him some funds.

"'Kay. I can handle that part." She rubbed her hands together. "I'm sure I haven't lost my touch."

Trevor just looked at her. Surely, she was not suggesting pick-pocketing?

"Hey," she said airily, "you're not the only juvenile delinquent here."

"That's a brave proposal. But might we consider some other options?"

Lark snorted. "I've lived here long enough to know that what you're really saying is that I've got a screw loose and you hate my idea. Fine. Give me a better one."

Unfortunately, he couldn't. Their options were too limited. "The police—" he started lamely.

"Will arrest Shelby. And Max is a pretty powerful guy. Do you really think he doesn't have at least some of England's finest in his pocket?"

Shelby put the nail in it. "Pretend you're on a mission somewhere, and you don't have the resources you need. Are you really going to tell me you wouldn't do whatever it took? I'm not thrilled with the idea, either. But what choice do we have?"

Lark laced her hands together and reversed them, cracking her knuckles. "Excellent. I'll be back."

Before he could stop her, she'd vanished into the crowd. He

couldn't even follow her purple hair, because too many conference attendees also had colorfully dyed hair, both men and women. He sighed. "If she gets caught . . ."

"She seemed pretty confident." Now that it was done, Shelby sounded troubled. "What do we do in the meantime?"

"We wait."

"HOW DID THEY find us?" Shelby asked.

Trevor continued scanning the crowd. "Facial recognition, I'd guess. Jukes will have tied into the traffic camera system. He probably got a hit on me, since they have that double-damned Facebook pic."

"Even worse, now they know about Lark." Had she dragged her friend into danger?

"I'm sorry. I'll get you two out of this, I promise."

"We're not leaving you to fend by yourself," Shelby said, for what seemed like the thousandth time. "We can—"

What was staining his pants leg? And dripping onto the floor?

"Good God, Trevor. You're bleeding! Were you shot?"

"It's nothing."

"Nothing?" she practically shrieked. "How can it be nothing?"

He finally turned to look at her. "Keep your voice down. I'll tend to it in a bit."

Don't freak out, she told herself. Clearly, he could still function so maybe it wasn't that bad. On the other hand, he'd proven himself to be stubborn when he got an idea into his head, and his sole goal at the moment was to protect Lark and her.

"We need to find one of those family bathrooms, so I can see how bad it is."

Trevor's grip on the rail tightened. "I appreciate your concern, but I'm fine."

Shelby felt like screaming. "You are a stubborn, hardheaded . . . *stubborn* man! It won't help us if you pass out from blood loss."

Before she could say anything else, Lark materialized next to them. She slipped her hand into Trevor's. When she disengaged, Trevor turned his back to the balcony at large and counted the bills.

"Just under five hundred quid," he said. "You did great. Time to stop."

Lark hummed happily. "Nice to know I haven't lost my touch. I returned the wallets, just so you know. Now what?"

Trevor pocketed the money. "Now we take the fight to them. Now we stop running, and become the hunters. Max wants me dead. I've seen his face. I can connect him to the Philosophy of Bedlam. Be damned that I can't prove anything. He can't take the chance. If I publicize what I know, his reputation will suffer, and apparently that's everything to him."

Shelby knew Trevor's next words were going to be to put Lark and her someplace else until he resolved the matter. "He's trying to kill us, too. He's probably assuming you've told us about him."

He shook his head decisively. "You're not the targets here. You're just collateral damage."

"Terrific," Lark groused. "Most fun I've had all year, and someone's trying to kill me because of it. I guess I should be scared, huh?"

Shelby felt a smile tugging at her lips. Lark sounded anything but scared.

"We have to go. I need to make contact with that Mossad agent."

"So we need to find a back way out of here," Lark said. "Happens I might know of one."

Shelby smiled at the younger woman. "Why doesn't that surprise me?"

They followed Lark down the stairs and into another wing of the building. Long lines of patient people waited to get into a lecture hall. The line wrapped around the area twice. They eased their way through, ignoring the mutterings of those who thought they were trying to cut into the line. Shelby murmured apologies.

At the other end, Lark directed them into the back areas of the conference center. They entered a storage area packed with pallets of water and coffee, sodas and teas. A walk-in refrigerator stored who-knew-what. At the other end, a fire door warned that opening it would set off an alarm.

Trevor studied the door for a few minutes, then took a Leatherman multi-tool from his front pocket. He followed the line of the door and probed it carefully with what looked like a wire cutter. In moments, he pushed open the door. No alarm sounded. He stepped outside, looking around for long minutes before he allowed them out. They ended up in a delivery alley. Two men pushing dollies were unloading even more pallets of water from a truck. They didn't even spare so much as a glance at the three.

"I'll get us a car," Lark said. "Want a Jaguar? Oh, sorry, that was thoughtless of me. How about a Ford instead?"

Trevor just shook his head. "I'll get us a car. You two wait here."

As they waited, Shelby wrapped her arm over Lark's shoulders and hugged her. "I'm so sorry I dragged you into this."

"Ha! I jumped in with both feet, remember? You'd've sucked if you didn't go to my apartment. And brought Hunky Guy, too, so I could meet him. He's fairly awesome."

He was, wasn't he? Shelby's thoughts returned to her earlier epiphany. She led a lonely life. Sure, she had friends. She went to functions and the occasional party. But who did she really have in her life to share things with? Trevor had made it clear he wanted more with her. Wanted to see what developed between them. Maybe, just maybe, they could make it work.

A nondescript white Camry pulled into the alley. Trevor pushed open the passenger door.

"Get in."

He'd removed his tie and wrapped it around his thigh, above the blood soaking his pants. She cast him a worried look. They couldn't take him to a hospital. The doctors there would report a gunshot wound to the police. Did they have a choice, though?

"How bad is it?"

"It's fine for now."

She just shook her head. "Stubborn man."

It took them more than an hour to get to their destination. The Metropolitan Police had cordoned off the area using blue-and-white police tape and strategically placed vehicles. Even exiting the car and trying on foot, they couldn't get close. Worse, the Mossad agent was nowhere to be seen. Trevor bit off a curse.

"He'll be at the Israeli Embassy," Shelby said. "He's certain to work out of it in some sort of capacity. Whatever his cover is. Or maybe the Mossad are different and don't have covers."

"No, you're right," Trevor admitted. "I don't know where it is off the top of my head. We'll need to stop somewhere."

"Easy peasy." Lark sat up straighter in the back seat. She pulled out her smartphone and brought up a browser window. "It's at the western edge of London, beyond Hyde Park. On Exeter Street off the B217."

The stolen car was equipped with a GPS. Shelby tapped in the address while Trevor drove. He was careful to stay with traffic, she saw. Nothing to draw attention to them.

Trevor had to drive around the block three times before they found parking. The spot sat about half a block from the embassy. There was nothing to distinguish this building from any other, except for an Israeli flag and a small guardhouse by the front gate. A low fence surrounded the structure.

"Plenty of surveillance," Trevor said. "You can bet no one goes in without being vetted."

Shelby reached for the door handle. "Do we just go in?"

Trevor grabbed her hand. "No. We wait for him."

"Why, for heaven's sake? We could just go in and ask for him."

"Too much surveillance, as I said. One look at me and they'll call Scotland Yard, then it's game over. For you, too. Your face is up there right next to mine."

"Oh." She settled back into the seat.

"I'm hungry," Lark announced.

Chapter Twenty-Two

In the end, Trevor sent Lark down the street to a café to pick up sandwiches and coffee. Stakeouts could be long and boring. It was possible the man they sought had already gone home for the night. It was going on six o'clock, after all. Trevor's gut said he was still inside, though, dealing with the aftermath of the bombing.

"I should go with her. Help her carry bags."

"I'm not letting you out of my sight." The point wasn't open for debate.

Shelby's eyes narrowed and she pressed her lips together. "Oh, and it's fine to risk Lark's life? I don't think so."

His eyes slid her way. "It's a calculated risk. They may or may not have gotten a good look at Lark. On the other hand, they know good and well what you and I look like."

She looked like she wanted to argue, but in the end sat back in a huff.

Lark strolled up the street, juggling bags and a drink carrier. She didn't seem to be paying much attention to her surroundings, and she came straight to the car. It was his fault, of course, for not giving her instructions. He supposed she could be less discreet, but he couldn't fathom how. Letting his head thunk against the seat, he briefly closed his eyes.

She climbed into the back seat, distributing food and coffee. They dug in hungrily. Halfway through his corned beef and pickle, their quarry stepped out a side door. If they'd been at the other end of the street, they would have missed him entirely. Trevor set his food aside.

"There you are," Shelby whispered.

Lark laughed. "He can't hear you, Shel."

The agent walked across the street to the park. He strolled past grass and trees, head down as though he were deep in thought.

"Will you ladies stay put whilst I speak with him?" Trevor asked, resigned to the chorus of no's that followed.

Shelby and Lark jogged after him into the park. He might as well be pulling surveillance with two of the Three Stooges. The agent paused to watch a group of footballers just as one kicked a goal, then continued on. The path curved to the left up ahead. Trevor didn't hurry. A copse of trees on the right side of the path was where the man would "introduce" himself. For there was no doubt in Trevor's mind that the agent knew he was being followed.

There. Those two trees. That's where the attack would come from.

He came at Trevor fast, shoving him back against a tree, forearm up and across Trevor's throat. He let himself go limp so as not to have the wind knocked out of him, leaving his hands loose at his sides. "I need to . . ." Talk to you, he'd intended to say. He didn't get the chance.

The Mossad agent clocked Trevor hard in the jaw with a left hook. He increased the pressure against Trevor's esophagus. A few more ounces, and he could crush it. He landed several hard blows to Trevor's ribs, and kicked him in the leg very nearly on top of his bullet wound. It would have sent him to one knee but for the pressure on his throat.

His training kicked in. He slapped the elbow of the arm across his windpipe, pushing it across his body and away from his throat. The agent twisted his body for a cross hit to Trevor's jaw. He parried it, slipping to the inside of the man's guard and clocking him in the temple with his elbow. Trevor grabbed the man's other wrist, controlling it as he shot his left arm up and over the agent's, wrapping the arm and catching his own wrist to complete the rear hammerlock. Quick as a snake, he hooked his foot behind the other man's and let himself fall backward, still maintaining the hammerlock. The Mossad agent twisted his body and Trevor lost the ankle hook. As they fell, the Mossad agent rolled forward. Each ended up stretched flat, head to head in the grass.

Trevor slammed his left palm against the man's shoulder, spinning himself around and planting himself across the other man's chest, twisting his arm up behind him.

"I just want to talk," he said through gritted teeth.

The Mossad agent cracked Trevor across the face with a palm strike up under his jaw. It snapped Trevor's head back. In a lightning move, the agent threw his legs over Trevor's head, wrenching him sideways. He lost his hold. Both were on their feet in an instant. They faced one another, both lethal, both ready to fight.

"I need your hel . . ."

With a banshee cry, a figure threw itself at the agent. At the same moment that Trevor recognized Shelby, the agent turned, already braced to punch her.

"No!" he shouted.

At the last second, the Mossad agent checked his strike, instead moving aside as Shelby stabbed her fingers at his eyes. She grabbed him by the shoulders and drove her knee at his groin. He twisted, taking it on his hip. Lark launched herself at his back, an arm wrapped around his neck as she clung to him, yanking his hair and trying to bite his ear.

"Ow," the agent said, moving his head away. "Leave off."

Trevor rose, ready to tear the man to pieces with his bare hands if he harmed either woman. But the man simply stood, holding Shelby away with one hand on her shoulder and keeping his head away from Lark's teeth. He looked more puzzled than angry.

"You bite me again," he said to Lark, "and I'll bite back. Now, get down."

Lark slid down till her feet touched ground. The Mossad agent turned so that all three of them were in his line of sight. Shelby glared daggers at him, still trying without success to punch him. The agent began to laugh.

Keeping his arms out and open to show he had no weapons, Trevor moved to Shelby's side.

"Easy, tiger," he murmured. "You can stop now."

Shelby lowered her arms. He was shocked to see her eyes were brimming with tears. "He was hurting you," she choked out, hiccupping as she tried to catch her breath.

The Mossad agent let go of her shoulder before Trevor could order him to. He gathered her into his arms, pulling her head to his shoulder as she collected herself.

"This your backup?" the Mossad agent asked, humor glittering in the depths of his eyes.

"Apparently so." Trevor released Shelby, tucking her behind his back. "I need your help."

The agent assessed him with cool, intelligent eyes, the humor disappearing as fast as it arrived. "You're a wanted felon. Why would I possibly help you?"

Trevor turned to the ladies. "We need to talk alone. Please wait here."

Shelby nodded, still looking at the other man distrustfully. Lark pouted, but stayed put as the two men walked farther down the path.

"It's unlikely a common anarchist would have your skills," the Mossad agent admitted. "You're an operator. Who do you belong to?"

Someone had to trust the other first. And since it was his picture on the telly as a criminal. . . . "I'm part of a task force trying to stop these maniacs."

"Done a bang-up job so far."

He couldn't argue that.

"You're bleeding."

He looked down at Trevor's leg. The white-hot agony of the kick to his wound had faded, but he needed to get the bullet out, and soon. Red seeped over the older, dried blood above his knee. "Why were you at the site of the bombing? Mossad doesn't investigate crimes."

A small smile flashed and was gone. He was older than Trevor had first assumed, with a fair sprinkling of gray in his dark hair. An inch or two below Trevor's own six-foot-one, he had a slim build, but he was hardened. Honed. This man had seen his share of combat.

"They do when the target is a Jewish facility being visited by a member of the Israeli government. I need to determine if she was the target."

Trevor stopped walking, turning to look at the other man. "Unlikely. Wrong place at the wrong time. The Philosophy of Bedlam is mutilating works of art in London in support of their nihilist philosophy. I haven't figured out why yet."

The Mossad agent stopped as well. There was no one around them.

"Who do you work for?" he asked bluntly.

"The task force is a joint MI-5 and SAS venture. I'm Major Trevor Carswell, 22nd SAS. At your service."

The man nodded. "Simon Rosenfeld."

Neither man offered a hand.

"What did you find in the Heritage Museum?" Trevor asked. "Anything that stood out? A clue? Were there Shamblet paintings? At the last museum, they mutilated two Edward Shamblet paintings."

Simon pulled a notebook from his back pocket and consulted it. "No paintings. A ceramic sculpture was smashed, but the sculptor's name is Louise Kaplan. *African Grace*. Also, an illuminated manuscript is missing. It has religious significance to both Jews and Christians. It might have burned. Or it might have been stolen."

Trevor shook his head, frustrated. "I thought their focus was this particular artist. If it's not, I have no clues where they'll strike next."

They resumed walking, this time back toward Shelby and Lark.

"There's a connection here. I just haven't been able to find it. Shelby knows a bit about art. Maybe she can piece together a link between these artists or their work."

Simon glanced toward the women, who were now seated under the tree. "Is that the boxer or the biter?"

Trevor grinned. "The boxer. Thank you for breaking off your attack."

The man inclined his head. "For now, I'll classify this as unrelated to Israeli interests. Neither an assassination attempt nor a hate crime." He pulled a card from his wallet and scribbled something on the back. "There's an art historian living here who happens to be the world's foremost expert on Nazi art theft. While that might not help you at all, she might have resources that will. Meanwhile, if you find these sons of bitches, give me a call. The Israeli government would be interested in prosecuting them."

Trevor took the proffered card and read the back. "Dr. Berkowicz. This is the second time she's been recommended to us."

"She's proven useful many times to Nazi hunters. If anyone can help with art research of any sort, it'll be her. We've worked together a number of times. Tell her I sent you. She'll be forthcoming."

"What's the second name?"

"A discreet doctor. Since you can't go to a hospital, he'll be able to take care of that leg."

They stopped by the tree, and the women got up.

"Shelby, Lark, meet Simon."

Both women shook his hand, though Shelby didn't smile.

"So you're neither a hostage nor a Bedlamite," Simon observed.

Shelby shook her head. "I just got swept up in the chaos."

"Pleased to hear it. I'll let my superiors know. They shouldn't bother you."

"Thank you for your help," Trevor said.

Simon nodded and walked away.

"What did he tell you?" Lark asked. "After we subdued him, I mean."

Trevor just shook his head. "You were very brave back there. Foolish, but courageous. Thank you for coming to my defense."

"What's our next move, Hunky Guy? I'm thinking I need to train for cage fighting."

As the adrenaline faded from his body, he became acutely aware of the throbbing in his leg. "Now we go see a doctor."

He let Shelby drive. He knew he was suffering blood loss, and he doubted Shelby would survive another drive with Lark. He settled into the back seat with a sigh that sounded too much like a groan. Shelby gave him a sharp look from the driver's seat.

"I'll get us there as fast as I can," she said.

"You want to get there fast, let me drive."

"I want to get there alive," Shelby told Lark, who sat back with a huff.

The doctor was nearby, which was a mercy. Bullet wounds just plain hurt. This time, he didn't bother to suggest Shelby and Lark stay in the car. Besides, he wanted them close by. If the police happened to realize the car was stolen, the women would be arrested.

The clinic sat inside an older building. Brick, but grayed from the weather. A single story with a small sign tacked above the doorway. As Simon instructed, they went around to the service entrance and rang the bell. The woman who answered looked to be about fifty, comfortably overweight with kind eyes. She took one look at Trevor and motioned them inside. She took them down a short hallway and put them in a typical exam room.

"I'll get him for you," she said. "Get up on the table."

Dr. Lowenstein came in within ten minutes, followed by the woman pushing a mobile table full of instruments.

"What happened here?" he asked.

"I got hit by some flying glass," Trevor said. The world started graying around the edges. His cover story was stupid, but the doctor merely nodded. The woman took a pair of scissors and cut his trousers up past his knee.

"This is my wife, Davina. She's a registered nurse." He set some instruments in the order he wanted. "That piece of *glass* is going to have to come out. I can give you morphine for the pain."

"No," Trevor said. "No drugs."

"Gee, I've never heard that before," the doctor said sourly. "I see a fair number of cases of flying glass. At least let me do a local to numb the area. It'll have to be stitched after."

"No." He wanted nothing that would impair him. "I need full range of motion."

The doctor just shook his head. "Gird yourself, then. This is going to hurt."

Trevor put himself elsewhere while the doctor probed the wound. In his fantasy world, he and Shelby lounged on a white beach in Waikiki, sipping fruity drinks with little umbrellas. Laughing. Making love. He kept himself in that happy place while the doctor removed the bullet, cleaned, and stitched up the wound. By the end, sweat dripped down his temples and back.

"Done," the doctor announced. "I'll write you a prescription for painkillers, though I doubt you'll make use of it."

Trevor eased himself off the table. Shelby looked green around the gills. Lark looked like she might throw up.

"What," he said, trying for levity. "You've never seen a glass shard before?"

Shelby shook her head and turned away. Lark looked around at the mess of bloody gauze and the bullet in a stainless steel tray on the portable table.

"It must hurt like hell," she said soberly. "Why didn't you take the morphine?"

Trevor shrugged. "I've had worse. And I can't protect you if I'm not one hundred percent."

"You're not a hundred percent now," Shelby said, a bite in her tone. "You were shot protecting us. We need to find a safe place to rest for a while. Give you a chance to recover from your *glass shard*." She didn't try to hide the sarcasm in her voice.

"Doctor, what do I owe you?"

"A donation to the charity of your choice," the doctor said. "I'm happy to help any friend of Simon's. And if you need a place to rest, I have a small room in the back. You're welcome to it."

As much as Trevor wanted to go right back out and talk to the art historian, he recognized that his body needed the rest. He nodded and thanked the Lowensteins. Davina showed them to a makeshift bedroom. A small bed, an IV stand, and monitoring equipment.

"I'll bring you some food in a bit," she said cheerfully. "There are extra blankets in the closet."

Shelby took his arm and pulled him to the bed. "You're pale and sweating. I don't want to hear any bullshit about you taking the floor. Lie down."

She was beautiful when she was fierce. He couldn't help the smile spreading across his face. "Yes, ma'am."

He eased himself down on the bed, mentally told himself he was safe, and passed out.

Chapter Twenty-Three

TREVOR STIRRED, MOANING a little in his sleep.

"He's starting to wake up. Run and get the doctor," Shelby said. Lark left the room.

His eyes opened, fogged with sleep. His gaze unerringly found her. Something in his eyes relaxed. "What time is it?"

"Nine-thirty. You slept for thirteen straight hours."

"Bloody hell." He sat up and swung his legs over the side of the bed. Shelby watched for any telltale signs he was still in pain. Other than a slight hesitation before he put his weight on his leg, there was nothing.

Lark returned, Davina in tow. The nurse checked his bandages, took his temperature and pulse, and declared herself satisfied. "You can leave whenever you're ready—that's not a hint—but come back if you develop a fever or the wound starts to fester."

"I will," he said. "I know this is a terrible imposition, but do you have a car we might borrow? Someone might be looking for ours."

Dr. Lowenstein came in on the tail end of his question. "You're welcome to use my car, but only for today. I have a class I teach on Thursdays."

"Thank you," Trevor said, meaning it. "I owe you a huge debt."

"Pay it forward," the doctor said cheerfully.

The three of them were starting to look a bit ragged around the edges. They'd all slept in their clothes again, and, even using the clinic's shower, were starting to ripen.

The car was an older model Mercedes. It had been well cared for, though, and the engine purred steadily as they drove out to Kingston upon Thames. The drive took about forty minutes.

Kingston University was beautiful in the way only an old English campus could be. They parked in front of a modern nine-story structure with a glass-enclosed staircase.

"I called ahead this morning," Lark announced. "She's in class until noon, but will see us over her lunch hour."

They waited on a white stone bench under a grouping of trees. Students streamed in and out of the buildings, laughing and joking or grim and silent. Shelby sighed, allowing the peace of the place to seep into her bones. It felt like the first time in days she'd relaxed.

Trevor didn't say much, but Lark was a fount of information. "I borrowed Dr. Lowenstein's computer last night while you were out cold," she told Trevor cheerily. "I might have happened upon a back door into Max's computer."

Trevor looked at her. "Why didn't you mention this on the drive out?" he asked.

"I was sleeping."

Shelby chuckled. When Lark slept, only an earthquake would rouse her. "What did you find?"

Lark hummed happily. "Tons of emails and browser searches for smuggled Nazi art and gold hidden in Switzerland between 1943 and 1946. He's accessed databases and specialized search engines. He's sent emails and arranged visits to people all over the world. Whatever he's looking for, he'd dead serious about finding it."

"World War Two again," Shelby said. "We dismissed it earlier because it was ancient history. But put Max's financial troubles alongside all the information we've heard about art theft during World War II—and I think there has to be a connection. Eric specifically targeted Shamblet works. Why? There are a million better ways to make money than to steal or destroy art."

"Unfortunately, the book and the sculpture lost at the Jewish Heritage Museum weren't done by Shamblet. And the PoB took credit for the bombing."

"I have an idea," Lark piped up. "But I need a computer. I want to see if I can find that ship manifest Nandi talked about. Her art collection that was stolen. What if Max is trying to track those down?"

Trevor thought it over. "And he's mutilating them? Why, for heaven's sake? If he's the original owner, he can petition to have them returned to him. That would solve his financial problems. Sell them legally."

"But it's a process that can take years," Shelby pointed out. "That might be too late."

"Then we need to find his next target before he strikes again," Trevor said. "We're not going to run any more. This needs to end."

It was a brave speech, but Shelby had her doubts. "He's been searching for years. What makes you think we can find what he hasn't been able to?"

"We don't need to find it," Lark mused. "We just need to make him think we have."

"That's incredibly dangerous," Trevor said. "He's proven he'll kill for this, whatever it is."

A church bell rang somewhere off in the distance, heralding a rush of students pouring down the glass-enclosed stairwell and out the front doors. Classes had ended.

"Let's go talk to Dr. Berkowicz," Shelby said, getting up to lead the way.

Dr. Berkowicz's office was the stereotypical disaster. Piles of books, parchments, and stacks of papers littered every conceivable surface. More books rested on the carpeting. Three filing cabinets stood along one wall. Maps, charts, and photos were clipped to the walls, overlapping in a way that made her dizzy. She finally located Dr. Berkowicz, a tiny woman perched behind a large desk.

"Hello," she said, her voice light and musical. She sounded decades younger than her probable eighty-plus years. "You're the student who wants to know about stolen Nazi artwork?"

"Yes, I am." Lark stepped forward and offered her hand. "I'm Hadley Larkspur."

"Oh, my." The woman hopped off her chair. She barely came up to Shelby's shoulder. "You are a colorful one, aren't you? Are you doing a thesis?"

"Yes," Lark lied smoothly. "These are my friends, Shelby and Trevor. Simon Rosenfeld suggested you could help us."

Shelby watched her for any sign she recognized them from the news, but nothing registered as she greeted them.

"Please, sit."

Shelby sat in one of the visitor's chairs, and Lark took the other. Trevor leaned against one of the filing cabinets. How was he feeling? He'd slept for a long time, but his bullet wound still had to hurt, right?

"So what is your focus, young lady?" Dr. Berkowicz asked, reseating herself.

Lark pulled a notebook from her back pocket and opened it to a fresh page, clicking her pen. "I'm doing my thesis on stolen Nazi treasure, but I'm taking a different tack than other people have. I know a lot of Englishmen who smuggled their own art, and sometimes money, into other countries—South Africa, for example—to safeguard it against the Nazis. I'm interested in those people."

"That's still a broad topic," Dr. Berkowicz said. "A great many wealthy families did that. Are you researching anyone in particular?"

She couldn't have offered a better opening.

"Yes," Shelby said. "A family called Whitcomb."

Dr. Berkowicz sat back abruptly and crossed her arms across her chest. "There are far worthier subjects. People who also smuggled Jewish children to safety, for instance. May I ask why that family in particular?"

"I'm approaching things from the other end," Lark said. "I want to focus on the not-so-stellar families. You know the Whitcombs?"

The woman dropped her hands into her lap. "Humph. Then you chose a good one. Max hounded me for years about information on his grandfather. I must say he did not make it easy to help him."

Shelby mentally groaned. "Of course he's been in touch with you," she said. "I should have realized."

The woman sent Shelby a sharp glance. "Are you writing a thesis, too?"

Shelby's gut told her to go with the truth. "No, ma'am. You've heard about the museum bombings, I assume? The Philosophy of Bedlam? I have reason to believe Max is funding them. I'm trying to figure out why he is searching for particular pieces of art, and then mutilating them."

"Well, I can tell you that."

Shelby's heart leapt. Finally! Someone who could shed some light on things. "Please go on."

"I collect documents from all over the world," the historian said. "Strange things you wouldn't think would be connected. Journals, receipts, personal accounts. In this case, I acquired a ledger. It was detailed accounts of valuables, including art and gold, that were smuggled out of England and into Switzerland between 1938 and 1944."

"Did Max's grandfather do that?" Lark sat forward, her elfin face full of curiosity.

"Yes, he did. This particular boat captain documented everything he transported. According to his records, twelve prominent English families sent one huge consignment of art and gold bullion to a bank in Geneva. He turned out to be an honest man, which is probably why the twelve families chose him. A lesser man would simple have stolen the cargo for himself."

Shelby leaned forward, resting her forearms on her knees. "And you have the names of the twelve families?"

"Indeed I do. Max Whitcomb's grandfather was at the top of the list. The first of the twelve. He arranged for the other families to deliver their art collections and the gold to the cargo ship, and monitored that it was all stored properly to protect the artwork. He personally made the delivery and payment arrangements with the captain. He received confirmation from the captain that the cargo had been delivered, according to the ledger."

"Holy shi . . . smokes. What happened then?" Lark asked.

"The captain delivered his cargo to the Banque Privée de Genève on schedule. Further, I have a receipt proving that those same valuables reached a particular banker at that bank. That's where it all ends, though."

"Why's that?" Trevor asked.

"Because Swiss banks don't open their records for anyone. Not unless you're the name on the account. And none of the twelve families were on the account."

"Do you know whose name was?"

"No one does. That's the crux of the problem. Some suspect the banker put everything under his own name. We'll never know, because he was killed before the war ended." Dr. Berkowicz leaned forward, resting her clasped hands on the desk. "Without the account information—name, account number, and password—no one can claim that wealth. My theory is that Max's grandfather, as the coordinator for the twelve families, received instructions on how to access their collective property. For whatever reason, he never acted on that information, because the contents of that vault have never been touched. That's the one fact that the Banque Privée confirmed for me. Well, for one of my grad students."

Shelby turned a palm up. "That explains Max's interest in lost World War Two art. It doesn't connect him to the Bedlamites, or explain why he's funding the destruction of artwork."

Dr. Berkowicz shrugged. "By the time I'd puzzled out all this information about his grandfather, Max became convinced that he'd hidden the account information inside one of the pieces he sent to Cape Town with his family."

Shelby looked up, pulse racing. "Did Max give you some sort of list? Because we know that when Max and his mother fled Cape

Town in 1977, the art collection shipped with them as part of their household belongings. But only a portion of it made it to England with them."

"Mother? I had no idea. He claimed both his parents died during an uprising in Cape Town."

"A bit of an exaggeration on his part," Trevor said.

"Why would he lie about that?"

"We went to visit her. She's a black South African woman."

Understanding and disgust warred on the professor's face. "I see. No, he never gave me a list."

Shelby shifted around on the straight-backed chair, trying to get comfortable. "Do you think you might have documentation on works of art that came back to Great Britain after the war?"

"Yes, well, I might have some sort of ancillary data, but only if a claim was made against a piece as having been stolen. Max tried to pressure me to use my resources to search for some pieces, but I don't remember which ones. Either way, I couldn't help him. My focus is and always has been to find artwork stolen by the Nazis from Jewish families."

Shelby cleared her throat. "So that was the end of it?"

"Almost. My knowledge is free for the taking, or was."

Trevor straightened from the filing cabinet. "He threatened you?"

"Oh, he couched it in pleasant terms, of course. But he did mention how old this building was, how faulty the wiring. He mentioned that it would be discouraging if any of my records were lost. I have two interns scanning and collating, but I have over sixty years of research accumulated. The loss would be devastating. I gave him the names of some other art investigators who might be able to help him, but I still refused to stray from my primary mission. I'm only telling you any of this because Simon sent you."

Shelby grimaced. "I'm so sorry. Thank you for sharing with us, though."

Lark leaned around to look at Trevor. "If we can find out what's missing from the grandfather's collection, we could get ahead of Max and figure out what he's going after next."

Dr. Berkowicz frowned. "Unfortunately, I can think of only one way to find that out. But I'm assuming you can't simply ask Max?"

"Uh, that would be a resounding no," Lark said. "He's the villain in this piece."

"Yes, so I see."

Trevor asked, "If you know all of this, why isn't it in any of your books? Why isn't it published anywhere?"

"Young man, my reputation rests on my being able to prove what I know. I verify everything through at least three sources. The information I've given you about the twelve families was pieced together from various bits of data, including the boat captain's ledger, but I can't prove any of it."

"When the bombings started, why didn't you go to the police with your suspicions?"

She gave Trevor a quizzical look. "And tell them what? Until you told me, I had no idea the museum bombings weren't just the actions of raving lunatics. I stopped dealing with Max years ago."

Shelby propped her chin on her hand. "So, in your professional opinion, the valuables are lost?"

"The twelve families thought so. They went on with their lives. You have to understand that what they thought they were safeguarding was only a fraction of their worth. Anyway, it's pretty much all hearsay and innuendo."

"And without the account information, there's no way to know. So Max believes his grandfather hid that information in with his art collection, and is finding the lost pieces to search for it." Shelby sat back, discouraged. "And we don't know what he had or lost."

"I'm sorry I can't be of more help," Dr. Berkowicz said.

"Did you ever run across a set of numbers that didn't make sense to you?" asked Lark.

Dr. Berkowicz gave Lark a smile of condescension. "No, dear, that never occurred to me."

Lark pinkened. "Sorry," she muttered.

"You understand this hasn't been the focus of my work. I investigate theft claims from people victimized by the Nazi regime. This information has all been ancillary. I doubt I'd even have remembered it, if it weren't for Max's threats."

Trevor slouched back against the filing cabinet. "So we still have no way of proving Max is linked to the Bedlamites."

"Unfortunately, I can't help you there."

"Well, thanks for all the great info. I'm sure I'll get an A on my thesis."

Dr. Berkowicz smiled. "I might be an old lady, young one, but don't take me for a fool."

Lark grinned. "Never."

Shelby asked, "Can I leave my number with you, in case anything else occurs to you?"

"Certainly."

Chapter Twenty-Four

LARK CURSED.

The late afternoon sun slanted through Lark's kitchen window, throwing a glare onto Shelby's laptop screen. She didn't even glance up at the profanity. Lark had been swearing for the past hour.

After their visit to Olga Berkowicz, the three had eaten lunch in Kingston upon Thames before returning to London. They'd stopped to buy more clothes and gun-cleaning supplies for Trevor. Now the two women worked at the kitchen table while Trevor grumbled in the living room.

While Lark searched for the cargo ship manifest from Nandi and Max's return to England, she combed every news source she could think of to find records of robberies or mutilations of artwork in Europe, then expanded her search to include South Africa.

She could get the information so much faster, she mused, if she could use the resources she had at her fingertips as a political analyst. Interpol member countries fed their data into a global network to facilitate multinational investigations, and included a stolen arts database. Their enormous store of information might give them what they needed. She glanced into the living room at Trevor, who had broken down all six handguns and was cleaning them. He'd never approve.

Dare she risk it? She needed her State Department credentials to log in, which would flag her account. On the other hand, they couldn't go on this way for much longer. All three of them had lives to return to.

"Lark."

"Yeah." She didn't pause as her fingers raced across the keyboard. "I'm going to find the shit out of you, you mother—"

"Lark," she hissed.

Lark's head came up and she focused on Shelby, who scooted her kitchen chair close.

"I need your help," she whispered. "I need to use my ID to log into Interpol. Can you make it so no one can track me that way?"

"Easy peasy. I'll mask your IP and bounce you through proxy servers. They'll never know what hit them. Let's do it on my computer. I wrote an app to do just that."

While Lark started some programs running, Shelby stared blindly out the kitchen window. The Bedlamites would strike again and again until Max either found what he sought or gave up. They had the small advantage now of knowing the truth, but everything hinged on beating him to his next target. They had to be stopped. All of them.

And after they succeeded, she would invite Trevor to go away with her. Two weeks somewhere tropical, where they could laze away the days sipping piña coladas by the pool and making love on the beach after dark. She craved Trevor's sweet, drugging kisses.

His strong fingers caressing every inch of her. His hard body rocking against her as they . . .

She stopped cold as realization hit her. They hadn't used protection. She'd been so lost in his touch two days ago that the thought of a condom hadn't even entered her mind.

She'd had unprotected sex.

Mentally calculating her cycle, she felt a wash of relief. Mother Nature would visit soon. It was highly unlikely she'd conceived. Still, the chance always existed. Without conscious volition, she opened her laptop and did a quick search. There was a pharmacy only a few blocks down. She could go and be back in ten minutes.

Now too anxious to sit still, she pulled the remains of her emergency cash from her pocket and counted. Six pounds and some coins. Not enough.

"I have to run to the pharmacy," she said, voice low. "Can I borrow a little money?"

Lark nodded, eyes still glued to her screen. "There's fifty pounds in the pantry, under the canned tomatoes. I'm almost ready."

"I'd . . . like to do this without Trevor breathing down my neck."

That got Lark's full attention. "Why?"

"It's personal, that's all."

Lark rose from the table and ran water into the kettle. As it heated, she found a scrap of paper and handed it to Shelby.

"Give me your login ID and password. And what I should be searching for. I'll start that while you're gone."

Shelby scribbled down the information. "I need you to access Interpol's crime database, and cross reference robberies or mutilations with their stolen artwork database."

"If it's there, I'll find it," she promised. Walking over to the now-whistling kettle, she grabbed a mug, put her left hand over the top of it, and poured the boiling water onto her hand and into the cup. She cried out in pain, dropping the kettle.

"Lark, what the hell did you do?" Shelby leapt to her feet and rushed over. Trevor was by her side in an instant.

"What happened?"

"Lark burned her hand."

Trevor took Lark's wrist gently and examined the burns.

"I have burn ointment in the medicine cabinet, in the bathroom. Which is where we should go. Right now." She leveled a meaningful look at Shelby as she led Trevor from the room.

For long moments, Shelby wavered between the need to leave and worry for her friend. But Lark had burned herself deliberately to give her the chance to leave undetected. Best not to waste the opportunity.

Crazy woman.

She jogged nearly the whole way to the pharmacy. Inside, with shaking hands, she picked out a pregnancy test. Should she take it right away?

Now that she held the box in her hands, common sense reasserted itself and she halted in place. After only a couple of days, a test would tell her nothing. She had been silly to panic and run out of the apartment. And Trevor and Lark would be done in the bathroom by now and wondering where she was.

What if she were pregnant, though?

Trevor had told Lark they were a couple, but what did that mean in his world? And how on earth was she going to raise a child on her own if he let her down?

Teenage pregnancy had been almost a town tradition in Coon Bluff. Her sister had gotten knocked up her junior year of high school, married Zeke Skelly, and went to live with his parents. By the time Shelby left for college, she had two babies and a third on the way. She was miserable, depressed, and drinking heavily.

Raeanne's situation was even worse. Six months after she married her husband, she ended up with bruises so bad she lost her baby. She'd stayed with him because, in her mind, what choice did she have in that small town?

Babies meant lost opportunities and dead dreams.

She set the box back on the shelf. She wouldn't know for a couple of weeks one way or another. And she'd exposed them enough just by leaving the apartment.

When she walked back into the living room, Lark was curled up on the sofa with one hand in a bowl of water and her computer balanced on her lap.

"How's your hand?"

She closed the laptop and set it on the coffee table. Shelby sat next to her and looked into the bowl. Lark's skin had reddened where she'd burned herself, leaving three small blisters.

"That was a crazy thing to do, Lark."

"Did you get what you needed?" she asked, voice low.

"Yeah." Shelby squeezed her good hand and went toward the kitchen.

Trevor was stirring a pot of sauce that smelled so good her mouth watered. He stopped what he was doing as she paused in the doorway. "Is everything all right?"

"Yes, everything's fine."

"Where did you go?"

"Just for a walk. I needed to clear my head. Too much staring at computer screens."

"Please don't go out again without me," he said, obviously trying to sound calm. "We know Jukes is actively searching for us through the city's surveillance system. I worried when I saw you gone."

"I was gone ten minutes. He couldn't have found me in that time."

"I don't know that, and neither do you."

Looking more closely, she saw how upset he was, though he was trying to conceal it. He had been more than worried.

"I'm sorry," she said, meaning it. "I won't do it again."

He nodded and returned to the pot, but she saw how tense the muscles in his back were. It had taken a lot for him not to try to find her, she realized.

Lark moved into the kitchen with her computer. Shelby scooped up the bowl and followed her, setting it in her lap. She dropped her hand back into it with a sigh. Trevor measured out pasta and placed it in another pot. While he finished shaping homemade meatballs for the spaghetti, Shelby brought mismatched plates and an odd assortment of cutlery to the table, and thought how domestic this felt—and how right. Lark added a bottle of Chianti and three wineglasses. When the table was set, Lark grabbed Shelby's hand and dragged her out of the kitchen.

"I'm going to see if I can find some candles," she called over her shoulder. Shelby followed her to the tiny linen closet at the end of the short hall. Lark yanked it open, but instead of searching for candles, she looked Shelby over curiously.

"So what was so important for you to buy earlier?"

She was surprised it had taken Lark this long to ask. The woman's curiosity was insatiable. "Nothing. I'm sorry I brought you into this."

"It was condoms, I bet. Was it condoms? You two seem pretty hot and heavy."

Shelby gave an internal eye roll. "No, it wasn't condoms. Leave it, okay?"

"Sure." The silence lasted all of two seconds as she rummaged through a plastic bin on one shelf. "He's really into you."

"He might change his mind if . . ." She just shook her head, unable to continue.

Lark's face fell. "You won't tell me? You suck. Here's a candle."

They ate dinner under the flickering flame of a pear-scented Yankee Candle.

Lark raised her wineglass. "Here's to us. Three caped crusaders seeking justice while being hunted on all sides. As Fezzik said to Inigo, I hope we win."

She said the last bit in a fair imitation of André the Giant in *The Princess Bride.* Shelby laughed.

"Hell, I'll drink to that," Trevor muttered.

"Where did you learn to cook?" Shelby asked. "This is delicious."

He rested his elbows on the table, pushing his plate away with a contented sigh. "Boarding school. I lived there a good part of the year from thirteen on, until I took my A-levels at eighteen. Our house master taught us during mid-afternoon tea. I found I enjoyed it. It calms me."

Lark forked a huge mouthful of pasta and slurped the strands into her mouth. "I have no patience for it. Why bother?"

"Yes, I did notice the SpaghettiOs in the cupboard." Trevor's lip curled. "That slop isn't even fit for hogs."

"No, well, this is so much tastier," Lark hastened to assure him.

Shelby eased back in her chair, twirling the wineglass idly by the stem. As dire as their predicament seemed, she would miss this easy camaraderie when they each went back to their individual lives. She collected the used plates and washed up while Lark got back on her computer, typing and muttering and swearing. Joining Trevor on the sofa, she curled her legs under her as he watched *Top Gear* on BBC Three. When he put an arm around her, she relaxed into his chest as though it were the most natural thing in the world.

Two and a half hours later, Lark bounced into the room. "So, I'm brilliant."

"What's up?" Trevor sat up, dislodging Shelby. He put a hand on her knee in apology.

Lark winked at Shelby and said, "I had the clever idea to use Interpol's enormous databases to cross-check known pieces of stolen art from private-home or museum robberies slash mutilations."

Trevor gaped at her. "You hacked into Interpol? Are you off your rocker?"

Lark gave him wide doe eyes. "Heavens, no. That would be illegal. They were out there in public, just waiting for someone to happen along."

"Right. And pigs will fly and demons rise from hell to save mankind."

"Hey, it could happen. Anyway, do you want to know or not?"

"Definitely," Shelby said.

"All right, then." Lark seemed mollified. "So that didn't get me anywhere, so I built an algorithm instead. Max scanned the ship manifest from when his grandfather sent his family and valuables to Cape Town, so I swiped that off his computer. But we don't have the corresponding list of what made it back to the UK, so we don't know for certain which pieces are missing. So I sent this search algorithm out . . ."

"This what?" She was talking so fast Shelby had a hard time following her.

" . . . after anything that refers to Max's art over the past thirty years. A search algorithm. It's a linear series of data queries that utilizes a cross-referencing model to turn a multistep operation into a single, recursive function . . . Do you want a lesson in mathematical algorithm engineering, or do you want to know what I found?"

"What you found," she said faintly. Trevor nodded encouragement.

Lark put her hands on her hips. "I wrote a program kind of like it in high school. Anyway, it searched news articles, interviews, photographs. Art associations or groups who've done news pieces about Max's collection. New purchases. Other sorts of interviews inside his home, or any pic from inside his house. I cross-referenced that with a couple of art databases to identify pieces he currently owns. His grandfather sent two hundred and twelve objets d'art to South Africa. I've identified, to a reasonable, imperfect certainty, almost a hundred and ninety. Max is extremely proud of his art collections and his freaking huge mansion. Mansions. There have been a lot of photos taken in various parts of his houses over the years. Anywho, so I'm missing about twenty-two pieces. Then I wrote another algorithm to search half a dozen or so art databases, to see if any of those pieces currently resided in museums. That narrowed it down to a handful."

"A handful of . . . what?"

Lark stopped talking, looking Shelby over in surprise.

Shelby tried again. "So you're pretty sure twenty-two pieces were stolen from Max on his way from South Africa to England?"

"Well, leaving some wiggle room for artwork or whatever that

Max felt was too valuable to have on display. He probably has a vault somewhere."

Trevor stood. "And you have a probable list of the stolen art? Well done."

Lark huffed. "Haven't you been listening? Oh. Did I forget to mention that when I cross-referenced the twenty-two missing pieces against robberies slash mutilations, seventeen of them lit up like Christmas trees?"

"Erm, yes, you might have forgotten that small detail." Trevor motioned her over to the sofa. She plopped down next to Shelby.

"Oops. My bad. Okay, so Max has been busy. Of the seventeen, I found five in Portugal and Spain. And I remembered that the *Cape Queen*, the cargo ship Nandi and Max sailed on when they came back to England, had a Portuguese crew. So that makes sense. It also makes sense that Max wouldn't want to pee in his own pool."

"By . . . ?" Shelby decided it was just easier to let Lark run with it.

"By searching the pieces farthest away from him first. Less suspicion that way."

Trevor started to pace. "So five objets d'art have been either stolen or ripped to shreds?"

"No. Good grief." Lark sighed heavily and spoke in a melodramatically slow tone. "Sev-en-teen."

"Sorry," Shelby said. "Keep going."

" 'Kay. Five in Spain and Portugal. One each in Paris, Munich, Salzburg, and Saint Petersburg. Three in the United States, and five in Great Britain."

"You did all that in three hours?" Shelby felt suitably impressed.

Lark sniffed. "My Internet is slow, or it've been faster."

Trevor stopped pacing. "So of the twenty-two, we can account for seventeen. Were you able to locate the other five?"

"Does the pope wear a funny hat? Four are in really weird places where Max or his lily-white Bedlamites would be remembered. One's in Palau—I had to look it up—which is near the Philippines and has a population barely over twenty thousand. Strangers would stick out like a sore thumb. Anyway, ask me about number five."

Shelby felt a grin tugging at her mouth. "Where is number five?"

"Right here in England," Lark said triumphantly. "In Basingstoke, to be exact. See, the Bedlamites have struck now four times in the London metropolitan area, destroying five pieces of art because they mutilated two paintings at the August Museum. Where you two star-crossed lovers were reunited." Lark put her hands under her chin and batted her eyes.

She and Trevor shared a warm glance. Shelby cleared her throat. "So, uh . . . so Max has been targeting those seventeen works of art for probably years. Otherwise, a whole string of thefts or destruction of property would have been splashed across the news."

"Exactly." Lark beamed at Shelby. "But he uses the Bedlamites here in London to make it seem like a political statement, so no one gets suspicious."

"And you have a photo of the piece in Basingstoke?" Trevor asked.

Lark tapped a few keys. "I've sent it to the printer. Shel, if you wouldn't mind?"

Shelby hurried down the hall to Lark's bedroom and snagged the paper off the printer. She found herself looking at a white long-case clock. Curlicues at the apex flared into a wide cap set atop a narrower clockface, which had ornate corners and hands. Faux pillars stood to either side of the clock door. Gold bordered the edges and floral designs decorated the flat panels of the rest of the casing. It was lovely.

She handed it to Trevor, who turned it from side to side as he peered at it. "It's a grandfather clock. I don't see any identifying marks, though."

"It's actually a grand*mother* clock," Lark corrected. "Smaller than a grandfather clock. This one is six feet. Here, let me read you the description. 'This clock is finished in ivory with gold and hand-painted decorations. It features a swan-neck pediment with finial'—that's the little topper thingy in between the two swan-neck curlicue thingies. 'The crystal glass door showcases a deluxe dial with shifting moon phase above the clockface. Gold-plated weights and pendulum bob driven by . . . blah-blah-blah. The rest is the technical stuff. Oh, it was built in 1926. And it's pretty."

Chapter Twenty-Five

"Now we know where the Bedlamites are going to be. That's great! Isn't that great? Why aren't you smiling?"

Trevor rubbed a hand across the back of his neck, then dropped it back to his side. "The Bedlamites are nothing more than pawns. This has nothing to do with ideology, and everything to do with getting an influx of capital to save Max's business."

"What if they beat us to Basingstoke?" Lark asked. "Is that why you're not smiling?"

"Natch. If they get there before we do, we're back at square one. No proof of anything."

"We have to try, though," Shelby said.

"There's no longer any 'we'," he said. "From now on, it's just me. You two are going back to the doctor's place to hide until this is resolved."

Shelby slapped her forehead with one hand. "We're having this argument again? Say we do get there first. We can help you find it three times as fast—"

“I’m not risking your lives,” he said flatly.

Shelby sat back with an exasperated snort, turning to look out the window.

Stomach roiling, Trevor tightened his hands into fists. Why wouldn’t Shelby let him look after her, and Lark? “So say we never prove any of this. Maybe it’s time you turned yourselves in. Let the police protec—”

“We’ve already had this conversation,” Shelby interrupted. “Max is a defense contractor. He works with military and police all the time. Are you really going to tell me he couldn’t get to us?”

Fair enough. But would they stay with the doctor—?

“So, I’m looking up stuff,” Lark interrupted. Apparently, she couldn’t sit still even for a moment. “The Burwell Estates in Basingstoke, where the clock is? You’re not going to believe this, but the old manor house is now the Intercontinental Museum of Clocks and Watches. How cool is that?”

“Right,” Trevor said, forcing his hands to relax. “It stands to reason it’s their next target. They averaged about one hit a week, but I think Max must be getting desperate by this point. It’s only been four days since they hit the August Museum. I need to get ahead of this thing. End it.”

Shelby finally looked at him, though her body was still turned away. “Has it really only been four days? It feels like weeks. Anyway, say you get to the clock museum before the Bedlamites. What then? You confront Eric, maybe kill him and the others? What will that solve? Max will just find some other idiots to do his dirty work.”

“Not if we get Max to come to the museum himself,” said Lark.

Truthfully, Trevor hadn’t thought that far ahead. The idea had merit. “Maybe I find a way to bait the trap. Make him think I found something. Would he still stay away, if the Bedlamites are out of the picture and I have what he wants?"

"Probably not," Shelby said. "But how do we get the Bedlamites out of the picture? If we can get them to come after us somehow, let them find us on purpose, we could lead them straight to the police, who would be waiting to arrest them all."

"And me too, if I'm there. Probably all of us. I'm willing to take that chance, but I'm not willing to chance either of you."

"Short of tying us up," Lark said, "how are you going to keep us away?"

A muscle moved in Trevor's jaw. "I'll tie you up, if that's what it takes. Between the three of us, we have a couple of pistols, not nearly enough ammo, and exactly one person with any knowledge of what the hell they're doing."

"Me, right? 'Cause I subdued that Mossad agent?"

"Lark," he said, shaking his head. "No."

"*Trevor.* Yes," she shot back. "Trevor Willoughby Carswell, born April 23, 1980 in Banbury, England. Thirty-five years old. Accepted to the Royal Military Academy Sandhurst at twenty-four. Awarded the Sword of Honor at graduation, which seems to be a pretty big deal. Means the commandant thought you were the best Army Officer Cadet in your class. Shall I go on?"

"No."

"Yes," Shelby said.

He gave Lark an exasperated look. "I won't underestimate you again. But I'm still not taking you into battle."

Shelby turned to him. "What about the Mossad agent? Simon? Will he help you?"

"Very probably, and he's my first call after I get you two back to the doctor."

Shelby hung her head. "You think this is going to come down to a shootout, don't you? And even with all those guns, you expect to lose? Is that what this is about?"

"It might come to that," he agreed. "I'd prefer not, obviously."

"How do we lure Max in?" Lark said, as though he hadn't spoken. "We could go on air. I could interview you, or Shelby. Cerberus would jump on a story of World War Two gold hidden in a Swiss bank. I could write the shit out of that story. I could get in front of the camera and really sell it."

Trevor thunked his forehead with the heel of his hand. "For the last time—"

"We know, we know," Lark said. "You're going to stash us somewhere where we can't screw things up. But then we can't see the end of this, either. Enough talking. First thing in the morning, take me to the Cerberus office. That should be safe, right? I need my other laptop."

Trevor thought about it. While Lark went for her laptop, if he could also get Shelby inside the building, he could simply drive away. She and Lark would be safe amongst the reporters.

"A brief stop. Then I drop you two at the doctor's?"

"Yes!" Lark pumped her fist in the air.

He sighed heavily. The ladies would be furious with him. But better angry than dead.

"It's going on midnight," Shelby said. "I, for one, could use a good night's sleep."

Trevor found himself anxious to curl up with Shelby in their little nest. This tenuous thread they were developing needed to be strengthened. As though reading his thoughts, Lark said, "You two take the bed. I'll take the sofa."

"I won't put you out of your own bed," Trevor said firmly.

"And I won't put up with guests sleeping on the floor," she retorted. "Are we going to have a problem here?"

She stared him down, which was an impressive feat.

He gave in with a chuckle. "All right. Thank you."

"Now that we have a plan, I can barely keep my eyes open." Shelby shuffled down the hall to the bathroom.

Trevor's heart leapt. He felt as anxious as a schoolboy, just at the thought of holding her. Hearing her contented sigh as she relaxed against him. Falling asleep in each other's arms. But when he'd performed his ablutions and went across the hall to Lark's room, he found Shelby dead asleep, stretched out facedown on top of the comforter, still in her clothes.

He was an idiot. Of course she was exhausted. They'd been running flat out since Saturday, and the clock told him it was nearly Thursday. Adrenaline kept the body going in times of stress, but when it finally drained, it left one utterly fatigued. He was accustomed to it, but she wasn't. Carefully, he slid her shoes off, then her shirt and pants. She mumbled sleepily in protest, but never truly woke. Peeling back the blankets, he set her down on the sheets, then joined her, pulling her into his arms. She immediately threw her leg across his and cuddled into him.

It felt wonderful. He struggled to stay awake simply to enjoy the sensation of her skin against his, but he knew he, too, needed the rest. He fell asleep with a smile on his face.

PULLING IN TO the curb at the Cerberus office building, Trevor turned to the ladies.

"Now would be the time to visit the loo," he said. "Buy some crisps at the shop. Get a bottle of water. In fact, while Lark goes to her office to get her other laptop, would you mind grabbing a couple of bottles for us, Shelby?"

Shelby raised her eyebrows and crossed her arms over her chest. "I know you think you're being subtle, but you forget what I do for a living. Your lame attempt to abandon us will not get me out of this car."

He sighed heavily. "So much for that brilliant plan. You can read me like an open book." Pointing a finger at Lark, he said, "Two minutes. After that, I come in and drag you out by your hair."

"Oooh! Tough he-man stuff. If you weren't already taken, I'd totally be into that."

Lark bounced out of the car and was gone.

Shelby bit her lip. *Was* he taken, though? He seemed happy just to spend time with her, but what would happen the next time he shipped out? Would he want to see her again afterward? And what if she did, by some small chance, turn out to be pregnant? Trevor was an honorable man. He'd insist on marriage.

Trevor *was* an honorable man, she realized abruptly. She'd known it subconsciously for quite a while. Despite the inherent violence of the SpecOps lifestyle, he retained an unwavering code of honor. She contemplated what their life might be like together.

She found herself grinning down at her lap.

As soon as Lark climbed into the back clutching a computer bag, Trevor pulled out into traffic, one hand on the wheel and the other dialing his cell phone. "It's Carswell. Is your offer of an assist still good? I could use your help." He listened. "Agreed. I know where the Bedlamites are going to strike next." Pause. "All of the above, actually. I have a couple of ideas."

He ended the call without a goodbye. "Change of plans, ladies.

Instead of taking you back to Dr. Lowenstein, we're meeting Simon Rosenfeld at the Israeli Embassy. He's agreed to let you stay until this is resolved. You'll definitely be safe there."

This time when they pulled up, they found a parking space directly in front of the embassy. The three piled out. Shelby hefted her gym bag, which now held five pistols wrapped in her clothing, a can of Pledge, another of hairspray, and a lighter. The Israeli Embassy would not permit any of the items inside. Should she leave the weapons in the car, unguarded?

Catching her look, Trevor gestured for her to walk ahead of him. "They're not going to wrestle you to the ground and throw cuffs on you."

She had her doubts, but followed him to the fence, Lark hard on her heels. Simon Rosenfeld walked out of the embassy doors and met them at the gate. He wore a short-sleeved olive green uniform, with some sort of rank on his shoulders. Above his left breast pocket was presumably a name tag, in Hebrew. His shirt had been neatly tucked into the pants and secured with a web belt.

"Shalom. Come inside."

The usual metal detector sat just inside the door, manned by a security officer in uniform. Another stood beyond them, rifle slung over her shoulder.

"Um," she started.

Simon's gaze slid from her face to the bag. Understanding glimmered in his eyes. "Put it on the scanner, please."

She did so. Simon walked to the other side, looking over the security officer's shoulder. Other than lifted brows, he made no comment as he took the bag. She walked through the metal detector. Lark placed her computer bag on the scanner. After Simon examined it, he slung it over his own shoulder.

"I'll take that," she said. "No, really. I'm sure it's heavy, and you have the bag of guns and all. Give me back my laptop."

The Israeli stopped and looked down at her. "Under normal circumstances, no baggage of any sort is permitted inside. No handbags, no cases, no biters."

"We appreciate the exception you're making," Shelby said. "Obviously, we'll respect your protocols and cooperate in every way."

Trevor drew the Beretta, dropped the magazine, and locked back the slide, catching the ejected round in one hand as it popped free. He set the pieces inside a bin and walked through.

Simon took the weapon, put it back together, and tucked it into his pants as they walked into the lobby. "While you're here, okay?"

Trevor nodded. "It's what I would do."

The group stopped at a standing desk. The second security officer stepped behind it.

"She needs a photo ID from each of you," Simon explained.

"That's a problem," Trevor said. "None of us have any. Mine says I'm a former member of the Irish Republican Army. The Bedlamites have Shelby's purse, and Lark lost hers in the car crash."

The Mossad agent made a pained sound. "You're not making this easy. I had to petition the defense attaché himself to permit you inside the embassy."

"Thank you," Shelby said, laying a hand on his arm. "For trusting us. Going out of your way to help us."

He looked across at Trevor. Some sort of unspoken communication passed between them. "My pleasure. The Israel Defense Force has only the highest respect for the SAS."

While the security guard set up visitor badges for them, Shelby glanced around. Rich mahogany paneling surrounded the lobby. Lighter, patterned wooden floors gleamed with polish, with the emblem of Israel covering the center of the area. A non-working fireplace nestled beside the switchback staircase. Twin Israeli flags framed the double glass doorways into the consular services area.

Shelby draped the lanyard around her neck, fingering the green visitor badge. Given their circumstances, it said a lot about Simon's pull that they'd been permitted past the gate, much less with their equipment.

Simon took them to a conference room right off the lobby. Windows lined one wall; Shelby had no doubt the glass was bulletproof. A chair rail bisected the walls, with warm beige paint above and white paneling below. Twelve armless roll-top chairs ringed the long oval table. Pale blue crystal pitchers filled with ice and water sat at either end. Shelby collapsed into one of the chairs, feeling right at home. She spent a lot of time in rooms just like this one.

Lark explored the sideboard, which held a brass lamp beside a marble bowl filled with fruit and a platter with a fancy array of cheese, crackers, strawberries, and grapes. She looked at the paintings on the walls and up at the cascading crystal chandelier. "Impressive."

"It's meant to be." Simon gestured for her to have a seat.

She snagged an apple from the bowl and came to sit next to Shelby. If she was nervous at all in her surroundings, Shelby couldn't detect it.

"So," Simon said, all business. He sat at the head of the table. Trevor took the chair to his right. "Fill me in."

Trevor briefed him on everything they'd discovered about Max's art collection and the missing objets d'art, the fortunes the twelve English families had sent to Switzerland, and their theories about Max's failing business and his need for those funds. Simon listened attentively, occasionally asking a question. Finally, he sat back, thoughtful.

"The attack on the Jewish Heritage Museum killed a janitor, who'd stayed late because he'd had an argument with his wife."

Shelby frowned. "I'm so sorry."

Simon nodded his thanks.

"I think that was probably an accident," Trevor said. "In each other instance, the Philosophy of Bedlam came in after the museum closed for the night. They presumably searched for the piece of art Max told them to, then set the bomb to cover up their activities."

A small smile played around the edges of Simon's mouth. "And the August Museum last Saturday? Or can I guess?"

Trevor grinned. "I called the cops." His smile faded. "Which caused the PoB to enter the museum prematurely to avoid them. They took hostages, which ended with the curator injured and in hospital."

"But it also brought you and Shelby back together, though," Lark piped up, waving her half-eaten apple in the air. "And what's-his-name, Floyd the Married Jerk, will be fine. So it's one in the plus column, right?"

Trust Lark to see the positive in the situation.

Simon assessed Shelby with cool, appraising eyes. "In your opinion, is Max Whitcomb desperate enough to kill for the account information he thinks is hidden? Personally?"

"Yes." Shelby didn't hesitate. "He's hunting us because Trevor saw him with the Bedlamites, and he can't afford that association becoming public. When he finds us, he's not planning to invite us to high tea."

Simon's quicksilver smile appeared and vanished. "Probably not."

"If."

"What?" She looked at Trevor, confused.

"If he finds you. Not when. And I'm not going to let that happen, so you can relax."

He spoke with an absolute certainty Shelby wished she shared. Because he'd said "you" and "If he finds you." Trevor planned to lock Lark and her inside the embassy while he went after Max and the Bedlamites on his own. She tried to quell her trembling hands. He had the best training the world could offer. If anyone could succeed with those odds, it would be Trevor.

Simon put his elbows on the table and steepled his fingers. "All right, Carswell. What's your play?"

Trevor rested his fists on his thighs. "I need to draw Max out of the shadows. Get him to come to the Burwell Estates personally, instead of sending the Bedlamites. I'll contact the head of my task force, Brigadier Lord Patrick Danby. He can have men standing by. The problem is the endgame."

"Your mission objective," the Mossad officer clarified.

"Indeed. Even if Max shows at the estate museum, even if we catch him red-handed dismantling or otherwise damaging the grandmother clock, he can claim it was an accident, or curiosity, or an attempt to prove he's the legal owner, which he is. Ultimately, you can't prosecute someone for destroying his own property."

"But if he brings Eric and the others, for security or as lookouts? Then everyone will see Max in the same room as the Bedlamites," Shelby pointed out. "Surely that would tarnish his spotless reputation as a humanitarian."

"Also easily explained away as coincidence. Wrong place, wrong time. There might be questions or suspicions, but no proof.

He wants me dead because I know he controls the PoB. But he only knows me as Eric Koller's friend Willoughby, the Irish nationalist. A terrorist who killed English soldiers in Northern Ireland. He can never know I'm an SAS officer. He doesn't realize it, but his reputation is as safe with me as with the mother no one knows exists."

"But then what do we do?" Lark asked. She balled her fists, glaring daggers around the room. "No way that scumbag wins. No way."

"There's got to be a way," Shelby said. "There's always a way."

Trevor rapped a knuckle against the tabletop. All three turned their attention back to him.

"The only way we'll be able to prosecute is if we can prove he's funneled money to the anarchists," he said. "Directly link him to the bombings. That will require access to his financials and forensic accounting measures."

Disappointed, Shelby looked around the room. "So even if we win, we lose?"

"Not what I'm saying." Trevor sat back. "I'm suggesting a two-pronged approach. At the same time we draw Max out to the Burwell Estates, we simultaneously execute search warrants at his home and office for his financial records."

"So he doesn't have time to erase everything," Lark said, clapping her hands. "Oh, you devious man!"

Simon tapped his steepled fingers against his mouth. "Will your Brigadier—Danby, was it?—Will he arrange the warrants? As I told you two days ago, my government will also want to prosecute for the murder of an Israeli citizen and damage to a Jewish historical building. I'll speak with the Deputy Head of Mission."

Trevor nodded his thanks. "What I need from you, if you are able, is information and equipment."

"Specifically?"

"Let's start with the easy stuff. I need a map of the estate and blueprints of the manor house."

"I can do that," Lark piped up. "I can get you blueprints. And photos. Simon, I'll need access to a computer."

Simon assessed Lark. "Something tells me it would be safer not to let you into our network."

"But—"

"No."

Lark slouched back in the chair, crossing her arms. "Fine. Whatevs."

His mouth curled up at the corners, humor in his eyes. "Both of those things will be a matter of public record. I'll have someone search the National Archives. Next?"

"Weapons. An assault rifle. Ammunition. Some sort of camouflage, depending on the terrain. I'd have to see what the estate looks like to know anything more."

"Anything else?"

"A sniper?"

Simon chuckled. "I'm the only soldier here. You can put me wherever you want me, but I'm it as far as backup."

"Fair enough."

Simon rose, ending the meeting. "I'll get things rolling at my end."

"Ditto for me."

Chapter Twenty-Six

TREVOR DIALED HIS mobile one-handed. Shelby set her clasped hands on the table. He noticed the fine trembling. Moving over next to her, he covered her hands with his free one. She attempted a smile.

"Danby."

"It's Carswell."

"Give me an update."

He filled the brigadier in on everything that had happened since they'd last spoken. "I'll be going out to the Burwell Estate. I could use additional men. My men. My team."

"I'll send backup. Havanaugh and the rest of your boys are in Libya doing some mop-up work, so it'll be another SAS team, a couple of MI-5 blokes, and me."

"Very good, sir. I also need you to contact the Magistrates' Court. Push for the search warrants, as we discussed, but see if you can swing an arrest warrant for Whitcomb. I realize evidence is lacking at this point—"

"I'll do what I can," Danby interrupted. "I know what I'm

asking of you, Trevor. This operation has always been considered high risk. If you succeed, there will be a medal and a promotion for you."

Trevor chuffed out a laugh. "If I fail, I'll be dead, and you can pin your bloody medal on yourself."

Danby's voice grew stiff and disapproving. "You're a military officer, Major. Please remember to whom you are speaking."

Trevor rubbed his forehead with his thumb, breathing deeply. "My apologies, Brigadier. I'll brief you on my plan once it's solidified. Oh, and there will be a man on location called Simon Rosenfeld. He's with me."

"Very good."

He disconnected. Shelby had risen and paced around the room, arms crossed over her stomach. He pocketed the mobile.

"Come here," he murmured, walking toward her. "How are you holding up?"

She met him halfway, wrapping her arms around him. "I'm fine," she said, then shook her head. "You're headed right into danger. Of course I'm worried."

"What are you on about?" he teased gently. He nudged her chin up with a forefinger. "This is big, strong he-man stuff. I've got it handled."

She gave the ghost of a smile. Truthfully, more things could go wrong than right, and they both knew it.

"Are you two through with the mushy stuff?" Lark said, blowing a raspberry. "Jeez. You totally forgot I was in the room, didn't you?"

They broke apart, laughing a little.

"Sitting here with nothing to do is boring." She wandered to the door and cracked it open. A security guard straightened from his slouch against the opposite wall.

"Sorry, miss. Mr. Rosenfeld requested you stay inside until his return."

"But I have to go to the bathroom."

The guard didn't blink. "He'll be back shortly, miss." He reached for the knob and gently closed the door in Lark's face.

"We're prisoners."

Trevor frowned. "I don't think you realize just how much Simon's going out of his way to help us."

"You," Shelby said. "He's helping you. And don't think I'm not grateful, because I am. I can't believe he's going with you."

How could he explain it? "Operators recognize other operators. We're a specialized bunch. It's kind of a brotherhood. I'd do the same for him."

"Just like that?"

He smiled. "You can bet he's already thoroughly vetted me. He probably knows more about me than Lark does."

"Okay."

He took her hand, turning it over to examine her palm. His thumb rubbed gently over it. "After this is over, what do you say we go away? Maybe Hawaii? Sip mai tais on the beach. Snorkel. Or I can teach you to scuba dive."

"I'd really like that," she whispered.

He let out a breath, the tightness in his chest easing. "Good. That's . . . good. Let's do that."

Shelby squeezed his hand before pulling hers free. "I know how to get Max to the Burwell Estates."

It took him a second to switch gears. "How?"

The door opened and Simon walked in, a sheaf of papers and a roll of tape in his hands. "We'll have to do this the old-fashioned way," he said. We don't have a printer big enough for blueprints."

The four converged on the table.

"How?" Trevor asked Shelby again. It was the one part of the plan he hadn't been able to figure out.

"Olga Berkowicz said she and Max were in contact regularly for quite a while," Shelby explained. "She helped him with his research. What if she were to call him, tell him she found some critical piece of information? Tell him there's a hidden compartment in the grandmother clock. Tell him the data is on a microdot or something."

He felt a slow smile spread across his face. "You're bloody brilliant, Shel. Do you know that?"

Simon set the printed pages on the conference table. "I won't put her in any danger. But I'm willing to make the call. The decision will be hers. Okay?"

"Fair enough."

"Make yourself useful," Simon said to Lark. "This stack is an aerial map of the estate, and this one is the blueprints of the house. Do you think you can piece it together?"

Her chin lifted. "I can tape the shit out of this."

"Good." Simon stretched. "Trevor, come with me. I have a pair of pants that should fit you."

The Mossad agent took him to a small locker room. Two sets of combat uniforms hung neatly inside. Trevor accepted one of them, changing into olive-drab combat pants and brown boots. He swapped out his footballer's jersey for a plain brown T-shirt.

Shelby did a double-take when he walked back into the conference room, but didn't say a word. She and Lark had set the copy paper out in rows, taping each sheet with the next until they had covered a third of the table.

"I'll make the call to Dr. Berkowicz." Simon moved to the far corner, mobile up to his ear.

Trevor eyed the two sets of maps. "Nice work."

"If the most we can contribute is taping pieces of paper together, then that's what we'll do," Shelby said.

"That's my girl."

Her face flashed surprise, then doubt. She clearly thought he used the term generically, in place of a "well done." But that conversation would have to wait.

"She's willing," Simon said. "Once I give the signal, she'll make the call."

"Simon, can we call the clock museum and have it evacuated? I don't want anyone caught in the crossfire," Shelby said.

Trevor shook his head. "If we do that, Max will know it's a trap."

Shelby frowned, clearly unhappy. "All right."

"The Bedlamites so far have broken in after closing. The building will be empty." The whole plan hinged on everything appearing normal.

She took a breath. "Can we at least call the curator? Have him make sure no one stays late that night?"

"Odds are he'd ring the police straightaway."

She just shook her head.

For the half hour, the four of them studied the blueprints of the manor house. Trevor and Simon marked entry and egress points, discussed possible places for cover or concealment, and noted potential blind areas for security cameras. Both had years of experience; they quickly fell into a rhythm, talking in shorthand as they learned one another's style and mindset.

"It's like you're speaking another language," Shelby observed.

He grinned at her. "But one we both understand. All right. The plan is we get in, secure the premises, and detain Max when he arrives. Now let's talk contingencies."

Out of the corner of his eye, he saw Shelby pull Lark to the other end of the table. She probably didn't want to hear about all the things that could go wrong. He couldn't blame her for that.

Simon pointed to the centralized great hall, just beyond the entrance vestibule. "This is where he'll stage."

"Agreed. From there, he'll send his men in teams of two, if he's smart, out into the museum. He'll start downstairs."

"It would help if we knew what was in each room."

Trevor grinned. "Clocks."

Simon just shook his head. "Any idea how many he'll bring with him?"

"No. That's the biggest variable. I only know of five. But Eric hinted there were others, so let's assume twice that."

"Or more."

From the aerial photographs, Trevor learned that the terrain around the estate was mostly an open expanse of grass. A cluster of some sort of trees abutted the manor house, behind a wall that looked to be at least fifteen to twenty feet high.

"All right," he finally said, pushing away from the table. "That's about as much as we can do in the time we have."

"Time to assemble our toys."

Simon grinned. "Come with me."

"Toys?" Lark muttered. Shelby shrugged.

Simon took them to the back of the embassy, through a functional hallway. He stopped at a reinforced metal door with a cipher lock. Punching in the code, he twisted the handle and led them into the armory.

Trevor looked around, hands on his hips. A variety of weapons lined two walls. The third contained flak vests, handcuffs, batons, and riot shields, as well as other tactical equipment. A surgical steel table in the center supported a contraption with continuous tracked wheels and a robot arm. Lark made a beeline for it.

"It's a bomb robot, isn't it? I'm right, aren't I?"

"Yes. Don't touch it."

Trevor examined the arsenal, moving from the wall-mounted shotguns to the scoped rifles. He stopped in front of the assault rifles. Three Uzis, several Ace carbines, and a sniper rifle.

"Yours?" he asked Simon.

"Yup."

"Nice." He ran an admiring finger over the barrel, then chose one of the Uzis and slung it over a shoulder. Moving on to the neatly mounted pistols, he selected two Jericho semiautomatics. "I'll leave my assortment of crap here, if that's all right."

"Good call." Simon nodded to one corner of the room, where Trevor saw Shelby's hold-all and Lark's computer bag. "My weapons are in pristine condition."

"Knives?"

Simon intercepted Lark's hand as she reached for a shotgun, gently pulling her away from the wall. "In the case next to the bomb robot."

Trevor was pleased to see a curved folding knife. He picked it up and flicked it open.

"What's that?" asked Lark.

He slipped his index finger into the finger guard and flipped it so the blade pointed downward from the bottom of his fist and curved forward. He flipped it out and back several times to get a feel for it, then sliced it through the air in a figure eight, then a spiral. "It's called a karambit. Good slashing weapon." He looked to Simon for permission, then pocketed the knife when he nodded.

"Anything else?"

"Any chance you can get your hands on some C4?"

Simon laughed. "Just where do you think you are? Beirut? Gaza? No. No explosives."

He took one of the carbines and a semiautomatic, then unlocked a standing cabinet. Passing Trevor several boxes of ammunition, he also grabbed extra magazines for them both. Trevor opened the box and started loading the magazines.

Simon added a couple of radios, two flak jackets, and a roll of duct tape to the pile. "Can never be too careful."

He slipped the flak vest on and tightened it down, then strapped the holsters for the semiautomatics to his thighs. He and Simon looked at one another.

"We're set."

Chapter Twenty-Seven

SIMON TOOK THEM into an area of unused offices. For the rest of the afternoon, he and Trevor practiced. Assault drills, room-clearing drills, and something they called bounding overwatch, which Lark called leapfrogging. They discussed how they would team up to scale the wall, if needs be. Shelby and Lark became, by turns, hostages or bad guys.

It brought home to her just how dangerous the situation was. They might be injured or shot.

They might not come back at all.

For Trevor's sake, she put on a brave face, keeping Lark by her side as the two soldiers loaded their equipment into Simon's SUV.

Finally, it was time.

While Simon climbed into the driver's seat, Trevor came over to where they stood. He hugged Lark.

"I can't thank you enough for all your help."

Lark sniffed. "If you die, you'll suck big fat monkey farts."

That drew a laugh from him, but his gaze grew somber as he turned to Shelby. She stepped forward into his embrace, and he hugged her so hard it hurt. She didn't mind. She held him just as tightly. When his mouth found hers, she melted against him. What started as a tender kiss burst into flames as he practically inhaled her. When he pulled back finally, she was breathless and laughing.

"To be continued," he murmured. "Yes?"

"Definitely yes."

"Abso-fucking-lutely," Lark crowed. "I'm glad you two idiots finally got it together."

Simon tapped his watch. "Time to go."

Shelby stepped away from the SUV. Trevor gripped the roof as he prepared to swing his body inside. He locked eyes with her.

"Be back soon," he said.

Simon put the car into gear, and they were gone.

Shelby rubbed her arms, cold despite the mild June weather.

"I don't know about you, but I'm starving," Lark said.

She turned away from the street.

"You're always starving."

"We didn't exactly get lunch. And it's practically dinnertime. I wonder if there's a café in this place."

Their security escort took them inside and to the small café. Shelby grabbed a sandwich, unsure if she would be able to eat a bite. Lark filled her tray with schnitzel, fries, and a salad.

"You need to keep your strength up. You won't be any good to me if you pass out from hunger."

Shelby wrinkled her brows. "Good for what?"

Lark put down her fork. "Well, we're not really going to sit here and do nothing, are we?"

"Of course not," she scoffed. "But what I have in mind doesn't require strength."

"Tell me, tell me."

Shelby ticked off each priority on a different finger. "One, we get our stuff back. Two, we make sure our car's where we left it. Poor Dr. Lowenstein. We didn't return it in time for him to teach his class today. Remind me to send him a note of apology."

Lark rolled her eyes. "Apology note. Check."

"And I'm going to call the curator of the clock museum."

"But Trevor said—"

"I can pull it off," Shelby said. She hoped she could, anyway. "Trust me."

Lark gobbled her meal down. "We should escape before they lock us in for the night."

"They can't do that. Can they?"

Lark took a huge gulp of her soda, swallowed it wrong, and hacked and coughed to clear her windpipe. "I'm not taking the chance. Let's go."

Their security escort waited by the door.

"Excuse me," Shelby started.

"We're leaving," Lark interrupted. "And no one's going to stop us. Are we going to have a problem here?"

The escort looked at her quizzically. "You're a guest here, miss. You're free to leave any time you like."

"Oh. Well, good."

Shelby mentally smacked her head. "We had a couple bags with us when we came in. Simon put them in the armory. We'll need those back."

"I'll need to find the armorer, but that shouldn't be an issue," he said. He pulled the radio from his hip, keyed the mike, and spoke rapidly in Hebrew. A female voice answered him in the same language. "She's still in the building, fortunately for you. She's on her way down."

"Thank you," Shelby said. "And a bathroom? Before we go?"

She and Lark ducked into the lavatory. Lark hummed in her stall, while Shelby discovered— "Oh, hell."

"What's wrong?"

"I need a tampon."

Lark flushed and washed her hands. "I'm on it. I bet someone here can hook you up."

The proof she wasn't pregnant relieved her; of course it did. She wasn't ready for motherhood yet. But the idea of holding a tiny curly-haired infant someday didn't send her into a panic any more. A baby boy with Trevor's brown eyes.

"I'm back. Here you go."

Lark pushed the white-wrapped package under the door, and Shelby took care of her problem rapidly. "Thanks."

"Don't mention it. We ready?"

Retrieving their bags turned out to be painless. Their escort carried them to the door, handing them over as the women left. The door closed with finality behind them.

What if she was making a mistake? What if she just made things worse?

"No. No, no, no," Lark said. "You're having second thoughts, I can tell."

Shelby straightened. She'd never gone wrong trusting her gut. "Let's get this show on the road."

They crossed to the car. Lark stowed her bag in the back seat and slipped into the driver's seat before Shelby could say a word. She pulled down the visor. The keys dropped into her hand. Shelby resigned herself to a wild ride and set her gym bag behind her seat. She strapped in.

"Where to, *kemosabe*?"

"Back toward the August Museum. We have to pick something up we left a few blocks from there."

While they drove, Shelby looked up the number for the clock museum. "The curator's name is Larry Upton. Wish me luck."

She took a deep breath, and dialed.

"Intercontinental Museum of Clocks and Watches. How may I direct your call?"

"I'd like to speak to Mr. Upton, please. It's rather urgent."

"Certainly. May I tell him who's calling?"

Dropping her voice to its most soothing, she said, "My name is Jane Edison."

"One moment. I'll transfer you."

She drummed her fingers on her knee.

Lark asked, "Who's Jane Edison?"

Shelby covered the cell phone. "My tenth grade social studies teacher. First name that popped into my head."

Lark made an approving noise.

"Miss Edison? This is Larry Upton. How can I help you?"

"Oh, thank goodness I got you," she said, voice breathy. "I'm Mr. Whitcomb's personal assistant. Max Whitcomb? He told me he was heading up your way, but like a silly dolt I forgot to write anything down."

Mr. Upton's voice grew amused. "You're in luck, my dear. Mr. Whitcomb hasn't yet arrived. He's not due until six o'clock."

Shelby felt a wash of relief, and knew it reflected in her voice as she said, "Oh, yes. I do remember now that he said six o'clock. Do you . . . do you suppose we could keep this just between ourselves? I've been such a silly, forgetful thing all day."

"My lips are sealed," Mr. Upton said. "Good day, Miss Edison."

"Goodbye." Shelby sat back. "First hurdle jumped."

"Liar, liar," Lark said, admiration in her tone.

She grinned. "I deal with politicians all day. A certain amount of dissembling goes with the job."

"We're almost at the August Museum."

"Pull over up there, on that street." She pointed in the direction she and Trevor had exited the underground pipe system. "You'll have to help me with this."

The manhole cover still sat ajar, as Trevor had left it. Bending down, they tugged and pulled. The cover didn't budge.

"Try again. Put your back into it," Shelby urged. This time, they pushed with all their might. The cover shifted half an inch.

"Criminently, Nutsy! How much does this thing weigh?" Lark panted, bent over, hands on her thighs.

Too much, she could have said, if she had any air left in her lungs. She tried peering into the hole, but it was too dark.

"Okay. New plan. Stick your head in there."

Lark started laughing, but stopped abruptly as she realized Shelby was serious. "No. Hell, no."

Maybe she could reach inside, feel around . . . she couldn't find the ladder.

A man stopped beside them. "Do you ladies need help?"

"Yes," gasped Shelby, pulling her arm out and standing so fast she almost fell over. "I, uh, I . . ."

"Dropped her wallet in there," Lark said. "Silly rabbit. Can you help us move the cover off?"

The man tried. In the end, it took three volunteers to shift the lid far enough so Shelby could see in. The assault rifle was right where Trevor left it, hanging from one of the ladder rails.

"Thank you," Lark said. "We can see it now. It's all good."

Shelby saw the next problem. "How are we going to get it out without people seeing?"

"Shit—" Lark reached in and grabbed, lifting it out. "It's a Halloween prop, people," she called. Pedestrians hurried past, heads turned away. They didn't want to know whether or not it was a Halloween prop. Shelby grabbed her arm and hustled her back to the car.

"Let's go, before someone calls the police."

Once they were safely in the car, Shelby heaved a sigh of relief. She was so not cut out to be a commando. She brought her phone to her ear, hesitating. This next call would be difficult.

"Carswell."

The clipped tone threw her for a moment. He was in full warrior mode.

"It's . . . it's Shelby."

"What's wrong?" She knew from his tone she suddenly had his full attention.

She cleared her throat. "Uh, nothing. Nothing's wrong. I, um, have news."

She heard car horns honking in the background. He remained silent, waiting. His silence sounded ominous to her, as though he knew what was coming. That was her guilt talking; or, hell, maybe he had some superpower and already knew what she'd done.

She forced herself to continue. "Max has an appointment with the curator, Larry Upton, at six o'clock this evening. Uh, I guess Dr. Berkowicz was convincing."

When he finally spoke, her heart sank. "And just how in the bloody hell did you get that information, Shelby?"

"You're angry," she said quickly. "I get that. I know you said not to call, but, well, now you know exactly when he's going to arrive. That's a good thing, right?"

"You called the museum."

"Yes, but I was very convinc—"

"You. Called. The. Museum."

Shelby tightened her grip on the cell phone.

His sigh traveled down the connection. "Did you tell them to evacuate?"

"No! Nothing like that. I pretended to be Max's assistant and forgot the appointment time. That's all."

He didn't speak.

"Trevor, this is what I do. It's my job. I convince people of things. To do things and think things. I didn't put you or Simon in any danger. I swear."

"It's a moot point. We're committed now. Whatever the fallout is, we'll deal with it." He blew out a breath. "At least tell me you're still at the embassy. What's that I hear in the background?"

"Yes," she lied. "We're both safe. That noise is just a vacuum cleaner."

"That's a relief, anyway. We're stuck on the M4. A lorry rolled over, blocking all lanes. We're at a bloody standstill."

"Well, that explains the honking I'm hearing."

She heard Simon curse. "This is taking too long. We're going to have to backtrack and find an alternate route."

Trevor said, "We don't have to get there before him. We just have to get there before he leaves."

She didn't know what to say. If they missed this chance, they wouldn't get another. It just made her all the more determined.

"Hey, Shel?" This time his voice was softer.

"Yeah?"

"We make a good team."

She resumed breathing. "Then I'm forgiven? You're not mad?"

"You made a judgment call. I'm not mad at you. But—"

But don't do it again. But listen to me next time. But. . .

"But I am mad about you."

It took her several moments to process what he'd said. To realize what the words meant. He was mad about her.

"Shel?"

"I . . . I'm here." She gave a rueful half-laugh. "Buddy, your timing needs serious work. You can't say something like that without being able to kiss me senseless after."

His laugh rumbled warmly in her ear. "I'll do better next time."

If there was a next time.

"Make sure you do," she said in a rush. "So I can tell you that I'm . . . I'm mad about you, too. Now go save the day."

She disconnected. "Lark, find us the nearest Radio Shack. Now."

"Maplin's," Lark corrected absently, already thumbing through a browser window. "Here Maplin is the electronics store. You see I'm ignoring your very private conversation. Not eavesdropping at all. What are we looking for?"

As Shelby explained, a slow smile spread across Lark's face.

"Fuck, yeah!"

Chapter Twenty-Eight

Despite some very aggressive driving on Simon's part, it still took them two and a half hours to backtrack through the snarled traffic and wind their way up the A316 to the M3. Every other driver heading west seemed to have had the same idea.

"Three hours to make an ninety kilometer trip," Simon groused. "After this, I think I'll go back to the West Bank so I can take it easy for a while."

Trevor grinned, but it was mostly a warm glow from the conversation with Shelby settling into his heart. "I'll take camels and sand any day over pissed-off drivers."

Simon chuckled unexpectedly. "I'm glad you and the boxer got things sorted. Equally relieved those two stayed behind. They are quite the pair."

"You have no idea."

"The biter—Lark—brings chaos wherever she goes, I'm betting."

Trevor chuckled. "You'd be right about that, too. But she's cracking at research."

"My daughter's gone Goth. Black makeup, clunky boots, those, what do you call them, corsets? I actually think I prefer the purple hair."

Simon turned onto the long dirt road up to the Burwell Estate. The dash clock showed that it was perilously close to six o'clock.

"I hope he's punctual. Not one of those people who shows up fifteen minutes early."

"Hey, I'm one of those people," Trevor shot back.

Simon flashed a smile. "Then let's catch this son of a bitch with his pants down."

He drove slowly, each of them scanning ahead. As they eased around an overgrown, sprawling yew tree, the manor house came into view.

The building was a square, grayish-brown brick, saved from ugliness by turrets at the front two corners and multiple faux Ionic columns set into the walls. A makeshift car park of dirt and weeds had been set up to the right of the road. The only car was a dark green Mini Cooper.

"A late guest? No way that's your guy."

"No. He'll occupy by force," Trevor agreed.

Simon drove around to the back of the museum, parking next to a BMW. "Curator's still here."

That was both good and bad. It meant Max still intended to make the appointment, but it put the curator at risk. The two operators climbed down and opened the back of the SUV, distributing the equipment and weapons like they'd partnered a hundred times before. Trevor pulled out the stripped-down, bare-bones floor plan of the house, printed on plain white copy paper. He set it on the bonnet, holding it flat.

"I'm betting the curator's office will be on the ground floor, somewhere close to this door and his car." Trevor nodded toward the BMW.

"This room's a good candidate." Simon pointed to a small room blocked off from a larger, open area.

"Agreed. I'll start there." Trevor looped the strap of the Uzi across his body, settling the submachine gun so it hung from his right shoulder toward his left hip. Both twisted the radio receivers into their ears and did a comms check.

Trevor peeked in the window as they positioned themselves on either side of the door. He turned the knob. It was unlocked. He held up three fingers of his other hand, counting down. On one, he pulled the door open. He went in fast and low to the left, Simon mirroring him on the right.

They were in what looked like a mudroom. Considering the terrain outside, that wasn't too surprising. An anorak hung on a peg, with galoshes below it. Beyond the archway, a long corridor stretched ahead of them. A plain wooden door stood ajar on his left.

"Hold your position inside the door until I get the curator out."

"Understood."

Simon placed himself to the front right of the mudroom, where he could cover Trevor but not be seen by anyone in the corridor. Trevor took a quick peek into the left door. The area ahead seemed dimly lit. He pushed it open slowly and stepped inside the gift shop. Tables and display cases lined the small space; he ignored the myriad objects crowding every surface. He checked the front of the shop; the security gate had been pulled most of the way across, but had not yet been locked. He hugged the back wall as he moved across the room, heading for the second door, and, hopefully, the curator's office.

It, too, was ajar. A tall, spare man with thinning gray hair sat in the glow of the single lamp on the rosewood desk, leaning on one elbow and chewing the end of a pencil as he flipped the pages of a ledger. The soft strains of classical music drifted in the air.

"Found him. Going in," he murmured.

"Standing by."

Trevor burst through the door and was on the man before he'd even registered the intrusion. He slapped a hand over the man's mouth and put a single finger up to his own lips. The man's eyes bugged out as he saw Trevor's weapons.

"I'm not here to hurt you," he said. "You are in danger, and I need to get you to safety. Nod if you understand me."

The man—presumable Larry Upton—began to nod frantically. Trevor didn't lift his hand. Not yet.

"You're meeting a man named Max Whitcomb tonight, yes?"

More nodding.

Trevor pulled a sheet of paper and placed it in front of Upton, showing him the photo of the grandmother clock as he released his mouth. "Is this what he's here to see?"

The curator rolled his eyes up toward Trevor, unsure if he was now permitted to speak. "Go ahead, Mr. Upton."

"Yes, yes," the man said. "That's the one. The 1926 Venetian-style Kieninger moon-phase floor clock, one point eight five meters by—"

"Uh, yeah. Don't need to know the dimensions. I do, however, need to know—"

The telephone trilled faintly. Upton jerked at the small noise.

"Is it Max?"

The curator shook his head. "It's Arnall, one of the docents.

He's waiting to let Mr. Whitcomb in before he leaves for the evening. Just who are you? And what sort of danger—?"

"Later." Trevor grabbed the phone and pulled it close to Upton, sitting on the corner of the desk. "This is what you're going to do. Answer the phone. Tell Arnall you want to speak to Max. When he gets on, apologize profusely. Tell him there's some sort of . . . clock emergency. Ask him to wait five minutes. Then get on with Arnall again. Got that?"

Upton looked as though he were regaining some composure; and with it, his courage. But he nodded agreement and reached for the receiver. Trevor placed his hand over it first.

"Say exactly what I told you to," he warned. He didn't move his hand until Upton nodded again.

Upton picked up the receiver. He was breathing a little too fast, but he seemed to be hanging on. "Yes, Arnall? Oh, yes? Very good. He what? How many people? Hmm. That's rather irregular. May I speak with him?" He glanced nervously at Trevor to make sure he was following instructions. Trevor gestured for him to continue.

"Mr. Whitcomb. Good evening, sir. I am so terribly sorry I wasn't able to meet you personally when you came in. You see, one of my . . . oh, of course you don't want to hear . . . yes, I am indeed eager to discuss an endowment to the museum. Very eager indeed. And afterward, I'll happily show you the Kieninger grandm . . . er, no. These are very delicately engineered works of art. You won't be able to open it . . . why would you want to open it?"

His voice rose. Trevor held up his hand. *Five minutes*, he mouthed.

"Yes, yes, we can discuss all that in person. If you will simply give me five minutes, I can close off this issue and be down to meet you straightaway. May I speak with Arnall?" He let out some air, wiping his fingers along his trouser leg, then put a hand over the mouthpiece. "What should I tell him?"

"Tell him to go out the door, lock it behind him, and drive home. Get him out of the building, Mr. Upton."

"Is he in danger also— *Yes,* Arnall. Thank you for staying past closing. You may go home now. No!" he said sharply, with a sidelong glance at Trevor. "I do not need you to stay. Go home. Straightaway."

He took two tries to settle the receiver in its cradle. "All right. I did what you asked. Will you please explain to me just what is happening?"

Trevor placed a hand on his shoulder. "That was very well done. I know I'm asking you to do strange and confusing things with no explanation. You're disoriented and alarmed. I understand that. But now, sir, I need to get you out of this building and to safety."

Upton tried to straighten his tie, but only managed to further skew it. "How can Mr. Whitcomb possibly mean me harm? He's a patron of the arts. He intends to make a rather hefty donation to the museum foundation. And though it's a bit irregular, we do from time to time have patrons come in after normal hours."

What could he say to move this along? The longer the curator stayed away, the more suspicious Max would become.

"He brought men with him, didn't he? How many?"

Upton's eyes bugged out again. "Arnall wasn't specific. A lot, he said."

"Okay." Trevor took his arm, urging him out of the chair. "By the way, what room is the clock in? The one Max wants to see?"

The question seemed to confuse the curator. "Erm, uh, it's upstairs. Yes, second floor, far left corner. Black Forest Region, 1920 to 1954."

"That's . . . extremely specific. You know your clocks, I'll give you that. Please come with me now."

He got Upton up and moving. At the door he paused, checking the gift shop before leading him back into the mudroom.

"Coming in."

"Roger."

Upton stopped abruptly when he saw Simon. "I still don't understand what is happening. Are you robbers?"

Simon lowered the muzzle of his rifle, trying, Trevor thought, to look less lethal. It didn't seem to work, because Upton refused to take another step.

"Sir, we're a special unit of the police," Trevor lied. "Units are standing by. The museum and grounds are surrounded, but you won't see any of them. They're, uh, in hiding until my partner and I get all civilians out of the building. Once you're safely away, they'll move in and arrest all the men Max brought with him. They're charged with . . . uh . . ."

". . . misappropriation of funds," Simon inserted smoothly. "Specifically, embezzling funds from pension trusts. Stealing from widows and orphans. It's all very unsavory."

"Gawd, blimey. In my museum?" he said. Then, "I'm responsible for the art here."

"And I will safeguard every piece to the utmost of my ability," Trevor assured him. "The arrests should go easily."

He cracked the outer door, first listening, then risking quick looks. Everything seemed quiet. "Sir, your car is ready. Are you?"

"I'll leave straightaway," Upton said, sounding certain for the first time.

Simon shared an amused look with him as Trevor shut the back door and bolted it.

"We need a peek down that corridor."

"We might be too late."

Trevor anchored the rifle butt into the curve of his shoulder, aiming along the barrel, finger at the trigger guard. They stepped into the hall as one, knees bent, weapons up, weight shifted forward as they advanced down the corridor. Both paused at an open archway to the right. Trevor signaled, and Simon whipped around the corner, sweeping his rifle from left to right. Trevor lowered his weapon as Simon passed in front of him, then came in to the left.

"Stairwell's clear."

The blueprints had shown a room to the left of the stairwell. He checked the door.

"Locked. Let's move on."

They moved past it. Simon heard the voices first, lifting a closed fist in a signal to halt. Both froze in place. Trevor lowered his hand and patted the air next to him. Simon took five steps, planting himself against the wall beside him. Trevor slid forward a step at a time. At the column, he risked a look, pulling back almost at once.

"Shit. They've moved."

He entered the great hall, a space easily forty feet wide and even longer, with a double set of staircases to his left. Rifle first, he swung left, right, then left up the staircase. He could hear several sets of boots tromping up the steps. Turning, he gestured back the way they'd come. They moved back and ducked into the stairwell.

"They don't know where the clock is," he said. "They'll have spread out to find it."

"How many?"

"Couldn't tell. And they're no doubt down here as well. All right. We split up. Clear up to down, out to in, like we talked about." He pulled out the floor plan again. "You head up these stairs. Clear the rooms starting with this one, right above the mudroom. If I understood the curator right, that's where the clock is. I'll cross the great hall and start catty-corner at the other end."

Simon hesitated. "Are you sure we should split up? If Max is smart, he'll have sent his men in teams of two."

"We double our chances if we split up. Remember, silence is key. We take them out one by one."

"All right. Let's get this show on the road."

They bumped fists and headed in opposite directions.

Chapter Twenty-Nine

Even breaking every speed limit, it took forty-five minutes to get to the museum at the Burwell Estates. Shelby's knees were shaking by the time they turned onto the dirt lane. She'd let Lark drive, because time was of the essence. She'd spent most of the drive with her eyes screwed shut.

"There it is," Lark said. "Oh, shit. Look at all those cars."

Three SUVs sat at odd angles in front of the manor, as though the drivers had simply braked wherever was convenient.

"Max is definitely here. Pull over," Shelby said. "We need to go in on foot."

Lark pulled the car as far as she could to the side of the lane. Shelby got out, eyes darting around as she opened the rear passenger door.

"Holy shit, Shel, are we actually going to do this? This is, um, kind of scary."

"You can stay in the car, if you want. Just give me the stuff."

Lark straightened her shoulders, chin lifting. "You don't know how to do it. Besides, it only works with both of us. Okay. Okay. Let's do this, before I pee my pants."

Shelby slung the assault rifle over her shoulder and took her Beretta out of the gym bag.

"Here," she said, handing it to Lark. "Just in case."

Lark seemed to be having trouble breathing as she took the handgun. "Just pull the trigger, right?"

Shelby took hold of the barrel, angling it away from herself. "Here, see this little lever? You have to push it down until you see the red dot. Then you pull the trigger."

"Okay."

Her voice was as low and subdued as Shelby had ever heard it. She took the younger girl by the shoulders, leaning down until they were face-to-face. "You'll be outside the whole time, Lark. You'll be safe."

"But you'll be—"

"Shh. I'll be fine." Shelby hugged her friend hard. "We need to hurry, though."

Lark pulled out her bag and opened it while Shelby slipped into a windbreaker. All too soon, they were ready.

"Wait," Lark said. She rummaged in the bag. "Here."

Shelby looked at the can of Pledge. "Uh . . ."

"Homemade flamethrower. Here, take the lighter."

She tapped the assault rifle. "You know I have a gun, right?"

"Just take it. In case."

She didn't ask "in case what" as she pocketed both items. It seemed to make Lark feel better.

They tiptoed their way to the front door. A thick archway surrounded it, with a balcony at the top. The door itself was a solid piece of dark brown wood.

"It's locked." Momentarily bewildered, Shelby looked around. No way would she be stymied by something as simple as a locked door. Maybe she could climb to the balcony?

Maybe not.

"I'm going around back. The blueprint said there's a door back there. Like a service entrance."

Lark followed her to the edge of the building and around what looked like a turret inset with windows, but without the pointed roof. There was no place to sit.

"This feels really exposed."

Shelby put her hands on her hips as she looked around. "You'll have to sit on the ground, I guess."

Lark sat and crossed her legs. "Exposed and uncomfortable. Got it."

"Are you set?"

"Yeah. Be careful, Shel."

"You, too."

Shelby found the back door easily enough, and the SUV Trevor and Simon had driven away in. She gulped in air, relieved. She wouldn't be alone in the museum with Max and however many of his thugs had ridden in those three SUVs.

The back door, too, had been locked.

Pressing her face to the glass with both hands shielding her from the setting sun, she verified no one stood on the other side of the door to conveniently let her in.

She couldn't give up now. Trevor needed her, whether he knew it or not.

He was going to be livid.

Wait a minute. She bent at the waist, looking around for a rock. A brick. Something she could use to break the window, as Trevor had done in Lark's car when they'd been attacked. The rifle swung forward and bumped her shoulder. She mentally smacked her head. *Come on, Shelby Gibson. You're smarter than this.*

She wished there was a way to muffle the sound of glass breaking, but she had no idea how to do it. Unslinging the rifle, she reversed it, holding the stock up to the window. She pulled it back as far as she could, then slammed it into the glass. It cracked. She hit it again, and this time it broke. It made far less noise than she'd feared.

Huge shards stuck in all directions along the frame. She used the butt of the rifle again to clear the area above the door lock, then cautiously reached inside. Her fumbling fingers found a bolt. Pulling it free, she reached in farther and popped the lock in the doorknob.

She pushed it open by degrees, listening hard. Her heart pounded. No one came running to catch her, so she eased inside.

First hurdle passed.

She tiptoed to the long hallway. If anyone turned the corner, they would spot her instantly. Safer to go through the left door.

If she were a sociopathic egomaniac, where would she be?

Chapter Thirty

TREVOR TURNED THE corner into the great hall and scissor-stepped sideways to get behind the nearest curving staircase. The enormous area rose through all three levels to the roof. Load-bearing walls placed every ten feet broke up the inner space, and gave him plenty of places to duck behind should the need arise. Framed photographs of Big Ben and the Grand Central Station clock in New York decorated them. Beyond the staircase, nestled against a bearing wall on the right, he saw an enormous grandfather clock.

Thing must be twelve feet tall, he thought.

At the far end, an information desk sat near the front vestibule, maps and brochures ready and waiting for patrons to walk through the door. The simple round wall clock told him it neared—

The grandfather clock ticked once, then began to chime. *Ding-dung ding-dong. Dong ding-ding-dung.*

The sound echoed through the room, duplicated on the other side by a second, smaller grandfather clock. Six-thirty. His planned route to the stairwell in the far back corner should have taken him behind the double-curved staircases and along the left row of rooms. Instead, he headed straight for the vestibule, and, without hesitation, unlocked the solid wooden door and swung it open.

"I see three SUVs. That makes a maximum of fifteen people."

"Roger. Entering clock room now," Simon said.

"Understood."

He clicked the door closed, hurrying into the open corridor that wrapped the outside of the great hall. He could hear faint voices, but they, too, echoed through the space, leaving him unable to tell from which direction they came. Entering the far corner stairwell, he took the stairs two at a time.

A sudden grunt through his radio receiver and the thump of something heavy hitting the ground told him Simon had made first contact.

"Target down."

"Roger that. Entering whatever the hell this back room is."

It was long, but narrower than the hallway he'd just left. A velvet rope separated the middle area from the dizzying array of cuckoo clocks mounted on the walls. One decorated with carved leaves and birds, another with a deer head and antlers. He looked at the black one lined with crosses above a pointed roof, and ducked under the velvet rope. Pushing the clock hands anticlockwise, he reset the time on five of them before he heard footsteps and voices outside the door arch.

"How many goddamned clocks can there be in the world?"

He darted into the corner next to the opening, dropping the Uzi. The strap held it in place across his body. The cuckoo clocks began to chime, some playing music and some jingling.

"Fucking noisy shits. I'm taking an axe to every last— Hey!"

The first man through the door carrying an MP5 casually in the crook of his arm startled when he saw Trevor. He tried to swing the submachine gun toward him. Trevor grabbed the barrel with both hands and yanked. The man stumbled forward and past him, losing his grip and dropping the weapon.

"Oh, shit," the second man gasped, drawing his Browning 1911. Before he could raise it high enough to shoot, Trevor grabbed the barrel with his left hand, simultaneously slamming his forearm into the bend of the man's elbow. Up, under, and into a figure four, he grabbed his own wrist, yanking down ruthlessly as he twisted the man's arm sideways and to the floor. The man screamed as the tendons in his shoulder separated and dislocated.

Trevor leapt over his legs to the first man, who had scrabbled to the MP5. He grabbed the man by the collar and belt, and slammed him headfirst into the wall. Dizzy and disoriented, the man tried to get up, but stumbled to all fours. Trevor kicked him in the face. He went down and stayed there.

He took the time to grab the roll of duct tape and secure their hands and feet, putting a strip over each man's mouth for good measure.

"Targets down in the northwest room. Moving south."

"Roger. I'm in the hourglass and water clock room. What the hell is a water clock?"

Trevor grinned. "Water. In a clock?"

"Ha-ha. Funny man. Room's clear. Moving on."

He gripped the Uzi and left the cuckoo clocks behind. The hallway here opened into empty space, a balcony rail to his left and two rooms to his right. He cleared the first room—a quick peek told him it was empty—and headed to the second.

Footsteps on the stairs to his front left had him scrambling back the way he'd come, before the wearer of the squeaky shoe could climb high enough to see him. He ducked into the room he'd just cleared. The squeaky shoe turned left and headed away from him.

"Be advised tango is heading to the southwest room in the far back. I'm in pursuit," he murmured.

"Understood. Keep your neck on a swivel."

"Ditto."

He heard voices ahead of him. Squeaky Shoe had linked up with someone else.

"There's nothing downstairs. Mr. Smith says to keep looking."

"Do you see me looking?" He recognized Nathan's voice. "I'm looking. There's nothing here."

Trevor put his back against the wall and drew the karambit, flipping it open and settling it into his palm. The voices got louder as Nathan and Squeaky Shoe exited. As soon as he saw the flash of clothing, Trevor spun around the corner, clocking Squeaky Shoe in the temple with the hilt of his knife and shoving the slumping body toward Nathan. Who gave a shout of alarm, jumping back and firing a shotgun blindly. Trevor ducked, hands elevated around his head as he scrambled back into the hallway. The shooting stopped.

"Hey, there, Trevor, old buddy. How you doing?" Nathan called after a moment.

"Doing great. I'd be doing better if you came out with your hands up." Trevor flipped the karambit up and gripped the Uzi as extra adrenaline spiked his system.

Nathan laughed. "Eric said you had a great sense of humor. Why don't you come on in here, and we can talk about it?"

"Yeah, I don't think so."

Something metal pinged off the balcony rail. Several other projectiles passed so closely he felt the air move. He dove to the floor, rolled into the wall, and found the shooter on the other side of the open air, firing from the opposite balcony. He returned fire blindly and leapt to his feet, knees bent, Uzi up and searching for a target.

Nathan ducked out of the room, racking a pump-action shotgun almost in his face.

All the lights went out.

Chapter Thirty-One

SHELBY CREPT THROUGH the gift shop, looking in wonder at the assortment of clocks. Mantel, wall, and floor clocks. Radio, alarm, and cuckoo, as well as wristwatches and pocket watches. Digital, analog, and some with no hands at all. Sun clocks, hourglasses, pendulum clocks, quartz clocks. A photo-frame clock and a braille clock. Books on the history of time and timepieces. Clock puzzles. Kits for building a Roman-style, or a water clock. Even a binary clock kit.

Only a few of the clocks ticked, but the noise felt ominous.

She forced herself past the rows and tables, tiptoeing to an open office door. Was somebody still here? A single lamp burned on the desk, and Brahms played in the background as though someone had simply gotten up and walked away.

She backed out and returned to the gift shop.

Now what?

As she got closer to the front of the shop, she heard voices, but they faded and grew stronger, echoing through the cavernous area beyond the shop so she couldn't tell who or where it was coming from. She pushed back the security gate, wincing at the screeching noise. Holding her breath, she strained to hear. Were those footsteps coming closer?

Her heart, already thumping, knocked harder. Or maybe that was her knees. Where could she hide?

She saw the public restrooms ahead of her. Men to the left and women . . . she darted right, pushing open the door and forcing the springs shut again. Pressing her ear to the faint crack, she held her breath and prayed.

"See? There's nothing here. Losing your nerve, are we?" A woman's voice; probably Fay.

A man replied. "How can you tell anything in this place with all the noise?"

"Just tune it out, you twat. Anyway, I need to pee. Bugger off."

Hand at her throat, Shelby backed away from the door, looking frantically around at the three stalls. Which one would Fay use? She darted into the last stall.

Leaving the door ajar, she climbed onto the toilet and perched there so her feet wouldn't give her away. The bathroom door opened. Shelby bit her lip, breathing as shallowly as possible. One of the stall doors banged shut, something hard and metallic hit the floor, then the sound of water splashing.

She'd set down her assault rifle. If Shelby could sneak out of her stall, she might be able to catch Fay unaware.

And then what? She had only Trevor's brief instruction on how to hit. And kneeing Fay in the groin would not stop her.

The toilet flushed. Fay picked up her weapon and stepped out of the stall. The bathroom door opened and shut. Shelby let out the breath she'd been holding. She climbed off the toilet and went to the door, listening for several long minutes before cracking it open. No one seemed to be there. She snuck out, ducking back into the gift shop.

She saw another door in the gift shop, just to her left. Maybe a storage room? She tried the handle. It turned easily, so she pushed her way in.

For a moment, the bank of computer screens threw her. Then she understood.

She'd found the security room.

Closing and locking the door behind her, she looked around. Fire extinguisher, breaker box, wastebasket. And, of course, a wall clock above the monitors. She sat in the chair behind a curved table and two rows of monitors. Sixteen cameras. The labels didn't help much. Room Two East? Room Six South?

Movement on the monitors had her catching her breath. Men walking along the corridors. Max and three men inside a room, dismantling the grandmother clock she recognized from the photo. She felt a rush of relief as she saw Trevor enter one of the empty rooms.

What should she do now? She speared both hands into her hair, dropping her head into her palms. The plan that had seemed plausible in her head now seemed crazy and stupid. She could stay here, or sneak back out and rejoin Lark.

Movement on the monitors caught her eye. She saw one of the Bedlamites, Nathan, with a second man near the exit of Room Four Southwest. In another, West Hallway Two, Trevor flipped open his curved knife. He disappeared from camera view, only to appear seconds later in the room with Nathan and the other man. Hands gripping the desk so tightly her knuckles whitened, Shelby watched as Trevor hit the man in the head.

In horror, she saw Nathan start firing and Trevor crouching as he jumped back into the hallway. And in East Hallway Two, another man opened fire, spraying bullets from his assault weapon. Trevor hit the floor.

"No!"

Had he been shot? Her hand pressed to her chest, she watched anxiously for Trevor to get up. There! He fired his rifle and got to his feet. With Nathan on one side and the guy on the balcony pinning him down, Shelby didn't see how he could break free.

She needed to help somehow. He was a sitting duck out there in the open. In plain view. She rocketed out of the chair and ran to the breaker box. Wrenching it open, she grabbed the main circuit breaker bar and yanked it down.

Chapter Thirty-Two

WITH A ROAR, Trevor bent at the knees, pushing up and catching the barrel of the shotgun between his crossed wrists as it blasted over his head and into the ceiling. The hot metal seared his skin and the thunder nearly deafened him. He dropped his right hand, stabbing the karambit into the inside of Nathan's thigh and slicing upward at an angle. Nathan screamed, grabbing at his leg with both hands. Blood gushed from the wound.

Trevor tossed the shotgun away. Nathan's eyes were wide and frightened as he tried to apply pressure, but Trevor had severed his femoral artery. He would bleed out in minutes.

He turned back to the balcony, pocketing the karambit. He needed to find the other shooter. Firing two shots over the rail, he immediately ducked and moved to a new position. The shooter, predictably, returned fire to where Trevor had just been. Trevor saw the muzzle flash, fired a controlled burst from the Uzi, and heard a body fall.

Another tango down.

The pounding of feet from the other balcony had him ducking

back. He heard cursing and recognized Eric's voice. Any minute, the emergency lights would come on, exposing him.

A noise from behind him had him spinning and aiming, finger on the trigger. Simon appeared beside him. Trevor blew out a breath, dropping the muzzle away from him.

"A little warning next time."

"Who turned out the lights?"

Both spoke at the same time.

"Radio got busted in a fight," Simon said. "I got five. You?"

"Five as well."

As one, they turned and headed back toward the room housing the grandmother clock. When they got there, the room was empty. The clock had been smashed apart and lay in pieces.

"Someone had a temper tantrum," Simon said.

"Which means they're downstairs. Let's go."

They took the side stairwell, which brought them out into the corridor they'd first come through. When they hit the great hall, they saw Max and Eric coming down the last few steps.

"Freeze!" Trevor shouted. "Weapons on the ground. Now!"

Instead of stopping, Eric fired a Browning Hi-Power, and kept pulling the trigger. Trevor and Simon ducked back behind a bearing wall. Chunks of plaster exploded as the rounds hit the wall. Simon stepped out to return fire. A bullet caught him just above his elbow. Cursing, he dodged back.

"That came from the left," he said. "At least one more target."

Trevor tore open Simon's sleeve to check the wound. "Bullet's in there. We need to stop the bleeding. Do you have your wallet?"

Simon winced in pain. "Right rear."

Trevor fished out the leather billfold and took out the first card he saw.

"I don't accept Visa," Simon grunted, lips white. "Only American Express."

"Put it on my tab, then," Trevor said as he slapped the card over the wound. "Hold this."

Simon obediently held the card in place while Trevor grabbed the roll of duct tape. He wrapped the heavy-duty tape around Simon's upper arm, pressing the credit card on top of the wound. Simon clenched his jaw.

"Fast, expedient field dressing," Trevor said.

"Don't move a muscle," Fay said from behind them.

Both of them froze.

"Put your weapons down and move out into the hall."

Inwardly cursing himself for being every kind of fool, Trevor set the Uzi on the ground. Simon did the same with his weapon.

"The handguns, too. Do you think I'm stupid?"

"I think you're a dog licking Eric's boots." But he obeyed the order.

"Now move." She shoved the muzzle of her rifle between his shoulder blades, prodding him forward. "Get your hands where I can see them."

Hands raised, the two operators moved into the great hall.

"Well, well, well," Max said. "Hello, Trevor. So good of you to come. Chasing you was becoming tiresome."

"Funny, I was having such a good time."

Max chuckled. "But all good things must come to an end."

Fay cracked him on the shoulder with the rifle. "Keep moving."

Trevor and Simon crossed the polished teak floor to the twelve-foot grandfather clock. Its face glowed golden, with Roman numerals instead of numbers. Inlays of cherubs climbed its reddish wood to the swirled, ornately carved crest. The huge base ended in clawed feet.

Max stood before it, arms hanging comfortably at his sides. A glaring Eric placed himself slightly behind his boss, the Browning Hi-Power steady.

The gold-plated pendulum made a guttural clang with each swing.

"He fucking betrayed me. Let me kill him," Eric said.

"In a minute. First things first." Max's gaze slid to Simon. "Aren't you going to introduce me to your friend?"

"No."

Max clicked his tongue in mock disappointment. "So rude. Then I'll ask him directly. Who are you?"

"Just a concerned citizen."

"Israeli Defense Force." Max looked over Simon's uniform. "You're here about the janitor who got killed? Sorry about that."

Simon's hands tightened into fists, but his face remained expressionless.

"When did you get here, gentlemen?"

The question threw Trevor. "What difference does that make?"

Max's pleasant façade slipped for a moment. His eyes became slits of rage, mouth contorting. "Did you get to the fucking clock before I did? Did you search it?"

Trevor forced a laugh. "Why should I tell you that?"

Eric's fingertip brushed the trigger. "I can shoot you now and search your corpses."

"Answer the goddamned question," Max barked.

Goading Max would only cause him to order them killed. Trevor needed to stall him until his task force arrived. He lowered his hands and made a placating gesture. "I never got to that room."

"I saw it," Simon volunteered. "Both before and after you turned it into kindling."

Max narrowed his eyes. "And?"

Simon shrugged. "Nada."

Frustration and fury warred on Max's face, and a desperation that caused a knot in Trevor's gut. The man was coming unhinged. If he'd been dangerous before, he now approached lethal.

SHELBY PRESSED SHAKING fingers against her mouth, breath coming in panicked spurts. Trevor and Simon stood in the open, covered by Fay's rifle and Eric's handgun. Max would order them killed. Fay or Eric, or both, would shoot.

She had to do something. None of them knew she was here. She could take them by surprise, and . . . and . . .

She had to help. They would die if she didn't go out there.

And she might die if she did.

She picked up the rifle Trevor had left in the sewer a lifetime ago. It seemed to have buttons and levers everywhere. She pushed a couple. No red dot appeared, but the long, curved magazine fell out and hit the floor with a clang.

Muttering curses, she picked it up and wrestled it back in.

Now or never.

It took more nerve than she knew she had to step back into the gift shop. As much as she wanted to stop, to listen, she instead walked steadily past the restrooms and into the shadow of the staircase. Before she could think too much about it, she jumped out into the main room, pointing the assault gun at Max.

"Anyone moves a hair, and you're the first to die," she shouted.

Five faces turned toward her with incredulity. She forced herself to keep her eyes on Max, when what she really wanted to do was run to Trevor.

Max snorted with laughter. "Saved by a girl. That's fitting, eh, Trevor?"

Trevor sounded strangled. "Shel, what in the hell are you doing here?"

"Well . . . helping."

Fay took a step toward her, and she swung the muzzle around, taking the step to press it into Fay's chest.

"Do you think I can miss at this range?" she said in her best Clint Eastwood voice. "Drop it!"

Fay let the rifle clatter to the floor. "Bitch."

Trevor moved forward fast, scooping up Fay's rifle and tossing it to Simon, who caught it one-handed. When he turned back to Max, several things happened at once.

Fay drew a sap from her pocket and swung it at Trevor as hard as she could. He moved his head a fraction, and the blow landed harmlessly on his shoulder.

Eric, face a mask of hostility, ran at him, knife in his hand.

Crawley appeared at Shelby's shoulder, reaching around and plucking the rifle from her hands. She grabbed for it, then felt cold metal against her throat. The madman had his fingers in the holes of his enormous blade as he stroked it gently under her jaw.

"Let's watch the fun," Crawley murmured into her ear, slipping an arm around her waist and snugging her into the curve of his body.

Trevor jumped back to avoid Eric's knife thrust. Eric came at him from the side. Trevor parried his arm away, coming up with the karambit in his hand and slashing at Eric, forcing him back. He flipped it several times. Eric flickered a glance in that direction as Trevor eased one leg back and brought both hands up into a fighting position. Eric raised the knife over his head and struck at Trevor, who faded back and slapped his arm away. Eric whirled, swinging backhand. Trevor caught his arm, slicing his triceps and chopping at his elbow. Eric twined his arm free and slugged Trevor in the ribs. After that, all Shelby saw was a flurry of arms and legs. Right hand to right hand, crossed hands, lightning-fast attacks and counterattacks. Strikes, thrusts, slashes, and parries. A blur of motion so fast she could barely tell what was happening.

Eric came in low, slicing up diagonally. Trevor staggered back, the left side of his shirt torn and soaking up blood. Shelby cried out, instinctively trying to go to him, but Crawley pulled her back.

"Uh-uh," he said, giggling. "No fairsies."

The two combatants closed. Trevor looped his left arm under Eric's blade hand and brought his right on top of it, pushing his whole body into Eric's and forcing the knifepoint into his chest. For a moment, the two strained together, using brute force. Eric slammed his forearm down, breaking the hold and pushing Trevor off to the right. A circle of blood seeped through his shirt. Trevor came back with a right cross, then used his arm to sweep Eric's knife away from him. Quick as a snake, he reversed the direction of his arm sweep, twisting Eric's wrist with both of his hands. Eric tried pulling away from him, but Trevor threw his arm across both of Eric's and tried to trap his knife. For a moment, both held each other's hands, fighting to disarm the other.

"You've got to stop this," Shelby cried. "Max, please."

"Why?" Max shrugged. "No matter who wins, one of my problems is taken care of."

Trevor reversed directions, lifting Eric's knife hand up and over his head. Eric swung low, kicking Trevor's knee. Trevor spun, rolling his back along Eric's arm until he was behind him. Slapping a palm across his knife hand for extra leverage, he brought the karambit up, and buried it to the hilt in the base of Eric's skull.

Chapter Thirty-Three

Trevor straightened up, breathing heavily, and let Eric slide to the floor. His knee felt on fire where Eric had kicked him, and the stings from multiple defensive wounds on his arms annoyed him. He flexed his chest, trying to gauge how deep the slash was. Everything seemed to work fine. His gaze shot to Shelby, needing to make sure she was all right. His jaws snapped together and a growl started low in his throat when he saw Crawley cradling her body to his.

Max clapped his hands together lazily. "Well done," he said mockingly. "Very impressive."

"Let her go, Crawley," he gritted out. A red haze clouded his sight, but Trevor didn't try to stem the homicidal rage roaring through him.

Simon locked his gun sights on Crawley.

"Now we have a standoff," Max said. "If either of you gallant saviors try anything heroic, Crawley will cut her up, a piece at a time. Now, none of us wants that."

"I know I don't want that," Shelby said, sounding remarkably calm. "I am curious, though. Did you find what you were looking for in the grandmother clock?"

Max's face boiled with rage. "None of your business."

Shelby angled herself more fully toward him. "Kinda is, considering your psychopath here has a knife to my throat. You're pissed, which means you didn't find anything. Do any of your Bedlamites know what you're really up to with these museum bombings? Or what you're doing here tonight?"

Crawley stroked the thirteen-inch trench knife down to Shelby's breastbone. "I could shove this into your heart right now."

"You could do that. Or you can ask your boss what he plans to do with you once he finds the account number and password to the Swiss bank."

Fay's eyes narrowed. "What's she talking about?"

"Nothing," Max snapped.

"Oh, it's something," Shelby said, voice amused.

Trevor wanted to shout at her to stop talking. She was deliberately antagonizing Max. Didn't she realize if she pushed him to far, he would let Crawley stab her, as he had Floyd?

"Twelve wealthy British families sent valuables to Switzerland during the latter stages of World War Two," she said, "in the form of gold and works of art. Max's grandfather organized the whole thing. Coordinated shipping the items out of England. Arranged for the cargo to be delivered at the other end."

Who was she talking to? Fay? Because Max already knew all this. Trevor fought the urge to shut her up. Her training as a political officer, she'd told him, taught her to convince people of things. Right now, he needed to trust she knew what she was doing, even if he didn't understand what she hoped to accomplish.

"I did some rough calculations, Max. If the families sent only a hundred thousand pounds each, that gold bullion is worth close to sixteen billion at today's exchange rate. More than enough to put your company back in the black, and set you up for life."

"What the fuck?" Fay said. "You said we'd bring down the corrupt government. That we could make our own decisions, free from laws that keep us prisoner. No more price fixing, no more greedy oil corporations and big pharma. Putting the power into the hands of the people, where it belongs. And now it turns out this is all about money? You lying sack of shit!"

Trevor almost felt sorry for her. Of all of the Bedlamites, she seemed to be the only one who truly believed their anarchist philosophy.

Max started walking toward the front door. "Unless one of you intends to shoot me in the back, I'm leaving. You can have this lot, though. They're of no more use to me."

"You fucking son of a bitch," Fay spat. "No way you leave us to take the fall."

Max shrugged and kept walking.

Crawley spun Shelby and punched her in the face. As she staggered, dazed, an unholy gleam lit his eyes. He slid his hand to the small of her back as he tucked his pelvis to hers. "Goody. Now we can have some fun."

Trevor started toward him.

"Uh-uh-uh," Crawley said, knifepoint at Shelby's jugular. "One more step, and you can kissy-kissy her goodbye."

Shelby gulped in some air, hands on his chest, trying to push him away.

"Squirming makes me happy." He gave a high, giggly laugh.

She stilled. Trevor wasn't sure she even breathed.

Sweat popped out of Trevor's pores. Maybe he could rush the

man before he . . . no. No way would he risk Shelby. But nor could he stand here and watch Crawly cut her. Simon maneuvered away from him to get a better angle. Crawley backed up, dragging Shelby with him, keeping both operators in sight.

Trevor glanced at Simon, who gave a single shake of the head. He didn't have the shot.

"You don't really want to hurt me," Shelby said. "If you do, you'll die. I'm not worth it. Just let me go."

Trevor wasn't the only one who heard the pleading in her voice. He gripped the karambit so tightly the bottom of the blade cut his palm. He barely noticed.

Crawley sneered down at her. "Women always beg. You're weak. Only good for fucking."

Fury tightened her body. She struck at his face, fingers hooked into claws as she tried to gouge out his eyes. Crawley yanked his head away. Blood began to leak from the deep furrows.

"You fucking cunt!" he howled. He grabbed her by the throat and began to squeeze. Shelby gripped his wrists, trying to pull his hands away, the whites of her eyes showing as air eluded her. Crawley's eyes were bright. The man was getting off on this. He eased up the pressure, thumbs stroking along the pulse thundering in her neck.

"You're deranged," she whispered, clearly shaken.

Crawley bent his head and inhaled mightily just below Shelby's ear. "I smell your fear. I want to taste it."

Simon eased left, rifle trained on him.

"Drop it," Crawley said.

"Let her go." Trevor's strong voice belied the terror coursing through him. He slid to the right, trying to keep Crawley's eyes on him. As soon as Simon had a clear shot, he knew the other man would take it.

"Or I gut her like a trout."

Primal rage swept through him. "You hurt a hair on her head, and I swear to God I'll make you bleed."

"I want to see *her* bleed." Crawley pressed the point of the knife against her collarbone, slicing down to the swell of her breast. Blood welled up and coated her skin. Shelby cried out. He bent his head and licked the blood. "Mmm."

"You sick son of a bitch!"

Shelby dropped her hand to her jacket pocket, fumbling and twisting to pull something free. "You got your taste of blood, Crawley. Fun's over."

She spat in his face. As he raised a hand to punch her, she depressed the button on the canister in her hand and flicked the spark wheel on the lighter. Flame shot from the canister straight into Crawley's stomach.

He howled, backing away, slapping at the fire licking its way up his body as she mashed the button down with both hands. His hands blackened as his skin seared and his shirt ignited. Howls turned to shrieks when his hair caught fire and his scorched clothing started to melt onto his skin. The flames engulfed him as he tried to run. He made it only a few steps before he stumbled and thudded to his hands and knees. The screaming stopped. He toppled over and lay still.

Shelby scuttled back, pushing frantically with hands and feet to put distance between herself and Crawley. Trevor saw embers on her jacket and shirt start to ignite. She rolled onto her stomach. Trevor threw himself to the floor beside her and tore the jacket from her arms. Simon helped him turn her over. She flailed, gasping and sobbing, hands battling the air.

"Shel. Shelby, it's okay. I've got you." Trevor pulled her roughly into his arms, muscles shaking. "It's over."

She made frantic noises, twisting away from him and bending over to vomit onto the floor. Head hanging, she stayed on her hands and knees as she spasmed and puked. Trevor held her hair and murmured nonsense, lungs constricted, so damned glad she was alive it physically hurt.

She sat back, wiping her mouth on her sleeve. "We need to go outside."

He made soothing motions with his hands. "Take your time."

She tried to get up, but her limbs were shaking so badly Trevor had to help her. The blood from the knife wound stained her shirt. A pained noise burst from him.

"It's fine," Shelby murmured. "But I did good, right?"

"You did great," he told her, heart in his throat. Examining the wound carefully, he was relieved to see the cut was long but shallow. She would need stitches, but she was in no danger. "Except for ignoring me and coming here. What on earth could you possibly have been thinking?"

"We need to go outside," she repeated. "I need to know if it worked."

On unsteady legs, she bent and picked up her jacket. A tiny black box fell to the floor. She scooped it up.

"If what worked?" Had she hit her head when she fell? "What's that?"

"Come on." Her sly smile flummoxed him.

Right now, she could ask him to swim to the bottom of the ocean and find her a unicorn, and he would do it. He wrapped an arm around her waist, both to support her and because he wasn't prepared to let her get two feet from his side. Simon prodded Fay in the right direction with her own weapon. Shelby turned to him.

"Leave it here."

Eyes curious, Simon flicked a look at Trevor, who shrugged. Whatever was happening, Shelby seemed to know what she was doing. Simon set the rifle against the wall, keeping Fay in front of him as the four of them walked through the vestibule and out the front door.

Chapter Thirty-Four

THE FRONT LAWN was chaos. A military Humvee hunkered near the door, six or seven soldiers penning Max in nearby. News vans and police cars crammed the car park and the grass. The crush of reporters made movement almost impossible. Microphones and cameras thrust as close as the police allowed. Questions flew at Max from every direction.

"Have you been funding Bedlamite terrorists?"

"Are you responsible for the museum bombings?"

"What were you looking for in this museum?"

"How do explain your presence here today?"

The soldiers opened ranks to allow the police inside their perimeter. Max stared straight ahead while the cops cuffed him. "I have no comment."

"You do not have to say anything," a police officer barked, trying to be heard above the clamor. "However, it may harm your defense if you do not mention when questioned—" The rest of it was lost as the reporters noticed Shelby and the others surged forward.

"Officer," Simon called, "please take this woman into custody. She's a member of the Philosophy of Bedlam."

Fay glowered as she was handcuffed.

"Clear a path," someone roared. The police pushed the reporters back far enough to let them wrestle Max and Fay through to a patrol car. Shelby darted behind them, trying to find a head of purple hair in the crowd.

"Shelby!"

Lark stood near the turret, holding her laptop up with one hand and waving with the other. Half a dozen cameras had trained their lenses on her computer screen. Shelby started in that direction. Trevor and Simon eased ahead of her, somehow clearing a path simply with their presence. When she reached Lark, she threw her arms around the younger woman and hugged her hard.

"Hey, watch the laptop," Lark squeaked, hugging her back. "These guys didn't get the chance to see the footage."

"We did it," Shelby said in wonder, looking around at the activity.

Trevor cleared his throat pointedly. "Would one of you care to explain all this?" He waved a hand around him. Simon propped his hands on his hips, eyeing Lark like she was some sort of dangerous wildebeest.

Shelby and Lark grinned like a couple of truant teenagers.

"What did you do?" he asked again.

"Body-worn spy camera," Shelby said, showing him the inch-long black box she still held. "Two hundred seventy-nine pounds at Maplin's."

"Hooked into my laptop through Wi-Fi. I recorded the feed

onto my hard drive. Got every word. God, Shel, I was so scared for you. That man . . . he burned . . ."

Shelby shut her eyes, but it didn't help. She was going to be haunted by that image for a long time to come.

"We called a bunch of television and radio stations on the drive up here," she explained, since Trevor and Simon still looked confused. "High-profile philanthropist secretly an anarchist. Story of the century, blah-blah-blah. I'm not sure they believed me, but I guess they didn't want to chance missing out."

She looked at the chaos, then looked at Lark. They high-fived.

"Extremely well done, ladies."

Trevor sounded sincere, but Shelby knew him too well. "But we were stupid to put ourselves in danger?"

"Well," he started, but then just shook his head. "Never scare me like that again."

"I won't," she promised.

A tall, spare figure in an Army uniform pushed his way to Trevor, who snapped to attention. The man's receding hairline did nothing to soften his authority. Shelby dealt with enough senior military officers to recognize the three diamonds topped by a crown as a brigadier general.

"Trev, my good man," he said. "I'm pleased you were able to resolve things here satisfactorily."

The magnitude of the understatement astonished her.

Trevor gave a sharp nod. "Brigadier, may I present Shelby Gibson and Hadley Larkspur, both of whom were critical in bringing Max Whitcomb and the Philosophy of Bedlam to justice. Ladies, Brigadier Lord Patrick Danby."

The brigadier inclined his head as he offered his hand. Shelby liked the strength of his grip, but this man hadn't helped Trevor when he needed it.

"Pleased to meet you," she said coolly. Lark also looked less than enthusiastic.

"I regret you got caught up in all this," the brigadier said. "But I must say that MI-5 is grateful for your assistance."

"We were happy to help Trevor," Shelby said.

The brigadier turned to him. "We executed the warrants to search Whitcomb's business and home, as you requested. We can discuss what we found on Monday, and you can back-brief me on this evening's activities."

"Very good, sir."

"Meanwhile, you have injuries that need tending." The brigadier looked around, found what he wanted, and snapped his fingers.

One of the cops approached. "Yes, sir?"

"We need medical care. An ambulance, right away."

"Yes, sir." The cop grabbed his shoulder mike and spoke into it. "Right down this way, sir, if you please."

The brigadier lifted a casual hand, already turning away to help restore order. "First thing Monday morning, then, Trev."

Trevor kept his arm around her all the way to the ambulance, and hovered by her side as the paramedic cleaned her knife wound and put a bandage over it.

"You'll need transport to the hospital for stitches," the paramedic said. "But it should heal up nice and clean. Now you, young man." She pointed to the space next to Shelby on the tailgate of the ambulance. "Hop up. Let me take a look at those cuts."

Trevor looked like he was about to give his "I'm indestructible" speech, so Shelby patted the empty spot next to her. "I'd feel better if I could see that you're okay," she said.

He came at once to sit next to her, twining their fingers together. He didn't seem to notice the paramedic treating his chest wound or the many cuts. He simply held her hand, looking out at nothing.

"Hey," she finally said, bumping him with her shoulder. "What is it?"

He finally met her eyes. "I've never been so scared in my life," he said, voice so low she had to strain to hear it. "The magistrate issued the search warrants. Why did you feel you had to do all this?"

He gestured around them. The excitement had died down when the police had driven Max away. Now only a few reporters and police mop-up crews remained. An ambulance pulled up directly in front of the manor house. Two paramedics wheeled a stretcher out, its occupant covered by a tarp. She shivered, her hand tightening in his.

"Because of who Max is. He's fooled the public for years. He supports charities and builds schools. People use words like humanitarian and philanthropist around him."

"All right. Go on." Trevor squeezed her fingers encouragingly. She took a breath, thinking how she could explain it.

"I work with both American and foreign politicians like him sometimes. You know they have an agenda you're not privy to. You walk a razor-wire trying to puzzle out the real plan," she said. "Sometimes they get caught doing something unethical, or even illegal. In my experience, they're either reelected because word never reaches the people, or they simply find a new home in a special interest group or PAC or government think tank."

"And they're never held accountable," Trevor said.

She nodded. "Because the public doesn't know. I wanted the

public to know this time. I wanted justice for all the people he's hurt."

They sat quietly for a few minutes. The paramedic finished with his cuts and abrasions, and looked at his knee.

"It's swollen," she said. "I'll have to cut your trousers."

Trevor waved her off. "It's fine."

Shelby laughed at him. "Big strong he-man scared of scissors?"

He pretended to glare, but stretched out his leg so the paramedic could cut the material open. Shelby sucked in a breath when she saw it.

"My God, Trevor, it's the size of a grapefruit!"

"Eh. Maybe a baseball." A grin tugged at his mouth.

The paramedic put an icepack on the knee. "You'll be off to hospital as well, young man, to get that knee X-rayed. You two lovebirds will want to ride together, I'm guessing?" Her eyes twinkled.

"Yes," Trevor said firmly. "Together."

Her heart in her eyes, Shelby reached up, turning his face to her. He grinned, running a thumb over her cheek. "Trevor."

"Mm-hmm?" He was looking at her lips now.

"Do you know that I'm mad about you?"

Light flared in his eyes, a delight and possessiveness that thrilled her. "I said I'd do better next time."

"Well, get going, mister," she whispered.

His eyes brightened. "I'm completely mad about you," he said. And then kissed her senseless.

Did you enjoy Leslie's alpha heroes and strong heroines? Don't miss her other thrilling Duty & Honor novels

NIGHT HUSH

and

BAIT

Available now in print and e-book!

About the Author

LESLIE JONES was an Army Intelligence officer for many years and she brings her firsthand experience to the pages of her work. She resides in Scottsdale, Arizona, and is currently hard at work on her next book.